The Price of Freedom

Part 2: Velasia

By

Gene Rowe

Gene Rowe

Copyright @ 2024 Gene Rowe

All rights Reserved. No part of this book may be reproduced or used in any manner without the prior permission of the copyright owner, except for the use of brief quotations in a book review.

To request permissions, contact the publisher at
ministryofliespublishing@gmail.com

ISBN: 9798230161899

First paperback edition May 2024
Cover design by Getcovers
Map design by Leire Rowe-Perez

Ministry of Lies
12 Wellington Road
Norwich
NR2 3HT
UK

ministryoflies.co.uk

Acknowledgements

I'd like to thank my daughter, Leire, for producing the map of Velasia, as well as the members of my 'Orbiter' writing group (as before), whose careful readings and wise advice improved the book. In alphabetical order, the Orbiter 8 posse are/were Paul Beacon, Adam Carpenter, Adrian Deasley, Alexander Mo and Luke Nicklin. Cheers, guys!

Gene Rowe

Velasia

Gene Rowe

The Price of Freedom Part II: Velasia

Chapter 1

The party of off-worlders remained in Verano for a week after com Durrel's flight. After that, they returned to Arakkan following a request for Omdanan's repatriation from Gregor of the Jade Guild, which Archaen approved as long as he accepted the rest of the group too. Meanwhile, com Durrel remained stubbornly alive in Velasia.

Four months later, the party received a call to return to Verano. Enabeth Archaen met the off-worlders as they exited their shuttle. Irvan Sentain, still wearing Miko's burgundy, was the first to disembark.

"Enabeth—you're here!"

The Leaguer woman smiled. She wore the skin of the Black Lightning guild, with her dark, fine hair swept over her right shoulder. She also wore a thin scarf wrapped around her forehead like a bandana, which tailed down past her right ear. "Where else would I be, Irvan?"

Sentain attempted to slow his pace and disguise his eagerness—but his enthusiasm was obvious to those following, and more than one grinned at it.

"Uh, well, another stupid question, eh? Sorry. But I haven't seen you for some time."

Archaen looked past the anthropologist and gave a half-smile and nod to the others. "Welcome all!" Then she took Sentain's arm, leading him and the others slowly from the landing pad, this time towards the Gamma tower. "Actually, as it turns out, that is not such a stupid question. I have been to various places, including Omicra and Philidor. I have had to explain certain actions. I am afraid I am not the most popular person in the League at the moment."

Sentain felt light-headed at the woman's touch. He pulled in his arm to ensure her hand could not escape. "But you are well? You look… good."

"Physically, I feel fine, though mentally somewhat chastened." They reached the walkway that connected the floating platform to the top of the tower and continued over this, two-abreast. "Fortunately, we are a forgiving race. Those who have erred are not incarcerated, like in your Ghuraj, but given a chance to demonstrate worthwhile qualities, and to thereby atone. I have now received my sentence, and I am eager to serve it."

Sentain grimaced. "I know com Durrel still lives. He is a star of the entertainment networks. Most nights in Arakkan, there is some venue that reruns his exploits of the day in all their gory detail. In fact, there seems to be a general enthusiasm to get to Velasia now. Three of Gregor's best have managed to transfer to the Silver Swan high guild, and I know his loss is not unique. Everyone wants to go. The betting is there's going to be a real war. I'm guessing your forfeit connects to this."

"Naturally. Com Durrel is a problem I created, and so I have been tasked to solve it."

"With Reddas and Miko?"

"Yes. Amongst others, as you will hear. Now—here we are. Let me instruct the rest. We can talk later."

***

The party sat around a conference table on the tenth floor of Gamma—a floor that held various offices and refreshment facilities. On arrival, they found two others already present: Ryven Miko, sitting with his legs up on the table and chair tilted back, and Reddas Archaen, standing by the window, looking at the sea below. Reddas no longer wore a prosthetic, his foot having been medically regenerated over the last four months.

Archaen stood, like her son, but at the head of the table. She scanned the newcomers. Aside from Sentain, three others wore burgundy: Sarok, Vuller and Mandelson. Brutus wore the black of her guild, courtesy of his original time with

Reddas, while Omdanan wore green—and indeed, now sported three badges along his left bicep, attained for various significant feats, from climbing to free diving.

"Welcome back to Verano. It has been a while. But now it is time to bring your stay with us to an end, one way or another."

Sarok looked relaxed. Over the last four months, he had acquired a tan, his hair had grown long, and his beard had filled out. "I thought you had forgotten us. Still, the last few months have not been unpleasant, but I guess we must return to reality."

Archaen's severe expression twisted into a wry grin. "Reality? In one way, yes, but perhaps not in another."

"Ah, do I sense that you will soon have us visit Velasia? That is not a contingency I ever foresaw."

"Nor I. But you present us with something of a dilemma. In truth, we are not sure what to do with you. There have been various arguments from those in the Senate, as well as from others on Philidor, our nominal capital. I am pleased to say that only once did a dishonourable suggestion arise—as a tentative hypothesis only, I hope—" the woman glanced quickly at Miko, then away again, "and that was firmly vetoed."

Sarok coughed out a laugh. "So, we'll not be quietly put down? Thank you. I just hope you do not come to regret your decision." Beside him, Mandelson gently leant in and quietly muttered "weak", which made him smile. No one else around the table caught her words.

"Me too. But you and com Durrel are seen as part of one problem. Either you serve him and are therefore party to what he is doing, and deserve to risk his fate, or you are against him and must clearly disown him. And for this, words will not suffice. You must act. You must rise against him. You must play some part in his downfall. Not only will that convince the Senate that you are *bona fide*, but it will also provide us with some leverage against you—as active participants in the elimination of an important figure from the Confederation."

"Makes sense," nodded Sarok. "And if com Durrel dies, I assume you will allow me to take his ship? We can either frame this as payment for services rendered or as a legitimate prize from an act of war. Or piracy. Frankly, I don't give a fuck."

"That seems a reasonable request. I do not think it will be denied."

"Do I have you word on it? Your word of honour?"

"We have discussed options—and allowing you to leave and take the ship if you are successful was raised as one. So, yes, you can take the ship... if that is what you truly want."

Sarok's brow furrowed. "There is an alternative?"

"If you prove your worth, there may be."

Sarok caught Mandelson's sharp glance. He ignored her. "I think I understand what you are saying, and that is also... unexpected. And perhaps something to think about." Then he gently shook his head and his expression firmed. "In any case, given these terms, I accept. I am in. But..." Sarok looked around the table, "I cannot speak for Sentain. And maybe... maybe I should not for the others. We live in strange times. Our future—beyond these immediate events—is uncertain."

Archaen appeared surprised. "Has democracy taken root in your organisation?"

"No. Once on the ship, and in the Confederation, *no*. But here?"

"Very well." Archaen scanned the table. "I cannot say what will happen if you refuse. You won't be... *put down*... but you are unlikely to be released any time soon. We don't have prisons, but in your case, we may have to make one. But if you succeed, then the offer remains the same for most of you." The woman's eyes flicked to Sentain and away again. "That is, you may leave as passengers on com Durrel's ship and return to the Confederation."

"I am in." Omdanan spoke more sharply than perhaps he intended, and then covered his mouth with one hand, embarrassed by his outburst.

"Of course you are, Cousin Elian."

"Me too," said Vuller. "I'm used to saving the boss's life. It's my job. I reckon this is no different."

"Yeah, count me in too," growled Brutus. "There's no way I'm gonna wimp out of a fight."

"And me," said Mandelson, quietly. "Anything to get off this fucking planet and get home." Her eyes again darted to Sarok.

Before Sentain could speak, Archaen announced. "And Dr Sentain is in, too. Irvan…" she turned to address the anthropologist, "we will talk later, but I am afraid this must be so."

Miko had been looking around the table and counting. "And that makes nine—a suitable number for a questing fellowship."

Archaen couldn't restrain a smile at this. "Well said, Cousin Ryven." She looked at Sarok, the senior figure among the off-worlders. "You see, you will not be going after com Durrel alone. For our various sins, Reddas, Ryven and I will be with you, attempting to demonstrate our own worth." She had been leaning on the table; she now pushed back to stand straight, and looked across to her son, still by the window, then at each of those seated in turn. "So, it is decided. Our fellowship is formed. Go now to Alpha and find some rooms. Try the fourth floor. Gamma in unaccountably full. And later, I would advise you to go to the Hall of Weapons. Take whatever you want. Then return here at ten o'clock tomorrow morning for a briefing. We will leave the day after tomorrow."

***

Narovy Sarok led his group—bar Sentain—into the Hall of Weapons on the top floor of the Gamma tower.

"So we just take anything?" asked Brutus.

"No, not just anything," answered Sarok. "Let's start in the Velasia section. You know how they like to stay in character. Let's not piss them off."

"Then where's Mandelson going?"

The woman had already wandered off from the four men. Sarok opened his mouth to call her back, but then thought better of it. "She knows the brief. I guess as long as she chooses things that stab and cut, she'll be all right. Come on."

They entered the Velasia section at the far end of the vast room, eschewing the racks of pistols and rifles, as well as the various halberds, sabres, daggers, and other weapons from Earth's past. Within the separated section, the weapons seemed more fanciful and stylised, but they were also of notably different quality.

"Light!" exclaimed Vuller, hefting a two-handed sword. "But it looks of good quality. The blade is sharp, too. I could swing this all day."

"Looks like it's made for a woman," grunted Brutus. "So just up your street, Vuller. Try a man's weapon. Catch…" He tossed a huge axe towards his comrade, who was forced to drop his sword to intercept. He caught the weapon with the flat of the blade against his chest and stumbled backwards as he tried to absorb the momentum.

"Fuck me, Brutus! You're not going to take this, are you?"

"I reckon it'll come in useful, so, yeah. For starters."

Sarok wandered away from the pair, with just Omdanan in tow. He turned to look up at the young man, who was a head taller than him, and who seemed fascinated by everything around. "So, Omdanan, what do you reckon? You've been gaming non-stop since we got back to Arakkan. If anyone knows about these sorts of weapons, it's you."

Omdanan's eyes sparkled. He had moved on from sharpened shovels and zombies and had sliced up hundreds of automatons in a score of different incarnations over the last few months. And more, he had spent many hours in formal training, which had added skill and technique to his natural abilities. "Nothing two-handed. You'll overreach and lose balance too easily. But you need range, so not a short sword. Something with a point and an edge…" They stopped by the case where the Staff of Power had been. There were several other staffs next to it, held vertically in clasps, as well as the case containing the black sword they had seen previously. "That looks about right, but… I think it is off-limits."

Sarok nodded. "I expect you're right. So something similar? What about…" Sarok had spotted another display, and he paced over to it. "What about this?" He pulled a sword from a rack. It was about a metre long, with a hilt of about one hand length, a flat cross guard, a grip of wound brown leather, and a crescent-shaped pommel. He gave it an experimental swing and received a gratifying hiss as it sliced through the air.

"Yes. That looks about right. I would also take a long dagger. Let me…"

Sarok followed the young man as he moved from display to display, taking up swords and daggers, feeling their weight and balance, and then experimenting with maces and spears. Sarok stood back, observing. He had never really talked to the Meridian. He'd not had much chance before their first trip to Verano, and on their return to Arakkan they had found themselves in different scenes: Omdanan had spent most of the time with his official guild mates, training or taking part in games, or climbing peaks in a nearby range, or perfecting the art of free diving from the top of Arakkan mountain, while Sarok had spent most of his time on an air bike, testing himself against every circuit in the area and camping out at night when too far away to return to the lodge in good time. Indeed, Sarok had spent most of the last few months alone. In contrast, Vuller and Brutus had spent most of the period together—drinking. But in the end, they too had been convinced to do some training in the Jade guild arenas and even to try out a few games. As for Mandelson—no one knew what she got up to, although she appeared to have gained a number of admirers and didn't want for nighttime company. Sarok looked again at the young man and smiled: he now wore *two* green scarves looped around his neck: to Sorana's had been added one from a fair-haired Leaguer called Gretel. And the young man looked different, too: whereas he had once been lithe, he had bulked out over the last few months, and although he did not match the physique of Gregor or Miko, he was not far shy of this.

"I think this will do, sir." Omdanan held a spear in each hand: they were two metres long and had leaf-shaped blades. At his feet was a pile of other weapons he had chosen for the pair of them.

"Okay. So what do we have?"

"We have a sword and long dagger each, and these spears. And I have a bow, too. They take some skill to use so I thought it best to just get one for me… if that is okay."

"Sure." Sarok leant on his own chosen sword, in its black leather scabbard. "So, how are we going to carry this lot out of here?"

"Don't worry, sir. I'll deal with it." Omdanan then buckled on the belt and scabbard of his sword, followed by the two long knives across the opposite thigh. He looped a quiver of arrows diagonally from left shoulder to right hip, and slung the bow over the top of this, with the drawstring across his chest. Then he picked up the spears, using them almost like walking sticks. "Ready."

"Let's collect the others."

They found Vuller and Brutus in the furthest part of the Velasia section. Vuller was leaning against a wall, watching Brutus practice swinging a monstrous mace.

"If you hit someone with that," announced Sarok, as they drew up, "they will likely just disintegrate."

Brutus grinned. "That's the plan, Boss."

Vuller grinned. "I'm not sure why we're needed at all. We could just send Brutus. There's no way anyone watching him swing that fucker is going to go anywhere near. I can see a whole army parting like the Red Sea as soon as he comes into view."

"Maybe they'll just shoot him full of arrows."

"Well, there is that," allowed Vuller. "I just hope they've got some armour or shields for us somewhere, 'cos there's nothing around here."

"I, er, saw some old pieces of armour in another area," ventured Omdanan. "But not here, no."

"In any case, we don't have the arms to carry any more," noted Sarok. "Perhaps they have some speciality pieces in Velasia? They like their symbols. If they can't wear skins, I expect they have their own shields instead. Anyway, we can ask Archaen later. Now, who's up for a beer?"

Brutus hefted the giant mace over one shoulder. "You always have the best suggestions, Boss."

Brutus and Vuller gathered up their selections as best they could and struggled after Sarok and Omdanan with arms full.

As the party made their way from the section, heading for the exit from the Hall, they caught sight of Mandelson bearing towards then, at an angle, so as to intercept them close to the exit. They merged at a point four metres from the doors.

Sarok appraised the woman: "Mandelson—what have you got?"

The woman grinned mirthlessly as she showed her acquisitions in turn. "This is a *kris*." She held up a long knife with a wavy blade, turning it to allow the room lights to glisten off the curved edge and emphasise the shape. She then buried this into a tapering wooden sheath on a belt at her waist. "And this is a kris sword." She unsheathed a longer weapon from her other hip that was of similar style to the knife, with a blade that looked like a crawling serpent. She re-sheathed this. "And this is a *kerambit*." She produced, as if from nowhere, a small, curved blade, with a ring of metal at the bottom of the hilt. She held the weapon with her little finger through the ring and the curved blade pointing downwards. She gave a couple of experimental slashes—decapitating a pair of invisible enemies—and then the blade was gone as if by magic.

Brutus muttered "Why is it I always feel like shitting myself whenever that woman has metal in her hands?"

Vuller patted him on one giant shoulder in sympathy.

Mandelson saw the spears that Omdanan held. "Spears? Okay. Wait!" She about-turned and stalked back the way she had come.

Sarok frowned after the woman's retreating form. "I suppose we had better wait."

"Yeah, Boss," said Brutus. "I reckon that would be safest."

Five minutes later Mandelson returned. She now carried a spear. Like her knife and sword, this had a wavy blade, though the metal was set on a long wooden haft and there was an evil spike on its butt. She nodded at the waiting party and headed through the door.

The men looked at each other; Sarok shrugged, and they followed her.

***

"You could have let me answer!" Irvan Sentain approached Enabeth Archaen where she waited for him outside the topiary archway to the park, not far from the foot of the Alpha tower. His tone was mildly accusatory.

"I'm sorry, Irvan. I did not want to get into an argument. I'm afraid the Senate was more concerned about you than anyone else, especially after Ryven spoke to them. I cannot say how this will turn out if we succeed in ending com Durrel's threat. But by going on this quest and proving yourself, there is a chance you will be allowed to leave. But they… *we*… need to be absolutely certain you will not reveal our secrets. It is hoped that by taking part in the quest, the game, and seeing the yeltoi and ganeroi first hand, this might affect your judgment and persuade you over to our way of thinking."

"Am I really that different to the others? That much of a threat?"

"Maybe. The others have no incentive to talk to the authorities in the Confederation. They have nothing to gain. And perhaps they still harbour a fear that our wealth means we can reach out into the Confederation to harm them. But you… not only would you be likely to speak to the authorities, but you might actually be believed. And we do not think threats will work so well to deter you."

"I don't know how to take that." Sentain was both disgruntled and flattered at the same time. "Am I thought to be so much braver than the others?"

Archaen smiled. "Perhaps not braver, but more stubborn."

"Well, okay. Still, it would at least have been nice to have been asked."

"And if I had asked, how would you have answered?"

"I would have said 'yes', of course. I knew you were going, so someone needs to be around to protect you."

Archaen tensed momentarily, then caught the gentle smile on his face. "That is... very funny."

Sentain held up his hands and laughed. "I'm sorry. That was a cheap response. I know I am far more likely to need your protection than the opposite. In fact," and now he turned gloomy, "I am not entirely sure what help I will be able to provide. Perhaps I could throw myself in front of an arrow heading your way?" And then he looked down. "I would, you know."

The woman smiled. "That is a kind offer. But I think you can be useful in other ways."

"How? I cannot fight like the others. I wouldn't know which end of a sword to hold. And in any case, my inclination is to study intelligent creatures from another culture... not cut their heads off."

"I realise this, though I think you do yourself down unnecessarily. You are fit and strong. You just lack training, and maybe a touch of aggression. But I do have another suggestion for you. Let's go to the Hall of Weapons."

The pair walked over to the Gamma tower and took an elevator to the top floor. They arrived just as Sarok and his party were leaving, dancing around each other in the antechamber to the Hall. Brutus smirked at the young anthropologist as he passed, carrying a huge axe among other ironmongery. "I wouldn't bother, mate. There's nothing left."

Archaen led the way to the Velasia section. She stopped before the display where the Staff of Power had once rested.

"There you go. Choose one."

"What... of the other staffs? Are they *magic* too?"

"Yes, though nowhere near as powerful. They are effectively prototypes, but they do similar things and are activated in a similar way. If com Durrel is a black wizard, you will be our white wizard."

"Uh, wow. I mean—why me? Why not you, or Miko, or anyone else?"

Archaen considered the young man, her expression inscrutable. "For one thing, we can all fight. And for us Leaguers, using such a weapon would seem somehow ignoble. An unfair advantage. Like carrying a machine gun into Velasia."

"I see. But I lack nobility so I can wield it, right?"

Archaen's expression softened. "You have a different type of nobility, Irvan. Do not be insulted. I know your qualities. And I am sure bravery is amongst them. So please, choose."

"Okay. But they all look the same to me, so I'll just take this…" As he grasped the nearest staff, made of a mahogany wood with a single embedded golden runic symbol, he felt something throb under his hand and an electricity course along his arm. He pulled the staff fully away from the wall clasp and held it somewhat awkwardly away from him, as though it might burn if he brought it too close. "Uh, what now?"

"Now it is yours. It will only respond to your voice and your touch. Do you remember the word of release? Don't say it! And now you must return to your room to do some homework. After this, I will instruct the infonet to send the operational instructions to your room, where you can access and study them. You will have a lot to learn and remember. Oh, and please be very careful not to hold the staff while practicing the incantations, or you'll cause all sorts of destruction."

"Er, right. Note to self: be very careful. What about you? Now we're here, will you take something?"

"Good point. I will reclaim my sword." She reached for the black weapon with the silvered edges from the adjacent case… and smiled.

The Price of Freedom Part II: Velasia

Chapter 2

The fellowship had gathered.

In the tenth floor room in Gamma tower, *the nine* were joined by Yasmina, who threw a cube into the middle of the conference table and spoke a word of command. From the cube sprang a hologram that initially overspilled the table and cast projections of mountains and forests onto those around it. With several more commands, the three-dimensional image shrank and reorientated until it neatly fit on the long, oval conference table. Velasia was like a frilled circle with a single off-centred horn to the right; it had one bottom quadrant diagonally sliced away so that it stretched and tapered off to the north east. The image showed a mountain chain splitting the large island, starting in the west and then running roughly east across the land until it hit the opposite coast, where it met a second chain that formed a steep-slanting coastal edge running all the way from the far south to the north-east. A third mountain chain curved off from the horizontal one to the north-west, essentially splitting the landmass into three segments. Several major rivers crossed the land, running from mountain sources to coastal outlets. Much of the land was forested.

"This is your stage," announced Yasmina. "I will show you the main landmarks and point out the location of your target. It will then be up to you to decide how to proceed. First: *show ports.*"

On the hologram, a dozen points flashed around the coastline, three of which were coloured, the rest being in black. Above the three, small banners floated.

"These are the Elven Ports—so-called by the yeltoi. You will have seen them on your last visit, several months ago. To the north-west, and north of the Sundering Mountains, is Narvik, which lies in the Northlands. This is held by the High Guild of the Silver Swan, as you see by the banner. On the coast to the south-west, and south of the mountain divide—in the Southlands—are Ranvik and then Sorvik, held by the High Guilds of the Black Lightning and the Golden Sword, respectively. The other ports scattered around and between are small fishing ports of yeltoi. Next: *show yeltoi settlements over five hundred.*"

On the map, around twenty new black dots appeared. These mostly lay next to rivers and clustered mainly in the Southlands, though there were some in the Northlands, and four in the tapering north-east sector, called Bratha, which was separated from the others by the Sundering Mountains to their south and by the chain that ran to their west.

"Now: *permanent roads and passes.*"

Several lines appeared on the map, running between the larger settlements. These cut through the two mountain chains that crossed the island at four different places.

"And now: *all ganeroi settlements over five hundred.*"

The map came alive and began pulsing with dots along the three mountain chains.

"Fuck!" exclaimed Vuller, who stood between Sarok and Brutus. "That's not fair."

Archaen looked across the hologram towards the man; she stood between Sentain and her son, Reddas. "Indeed not. I think I told you on your last visit that the ganeroi are fecund. Here you see it."

Sarok mused: "There may be many more ganeroi than yeltoi, but they are concentrated in the mountains, especially here… there… and *there*…" he waved at the map towards three small areas, one in each mountain chain.

Yasmina nodded. "That's right. In the Sundering Mountains, they have a capital, of sorts, where the chain first hits the east coast. They call it Ullah-Bor. In the Skythrust Mountains, about fifty kilometres from the north coast, they have another, called Krajja-Min. I say capitals, but they are really just the settlements of the most powerful tribes centred around early towers we constructed for gameplay before the creatures were imported. The tribes around these pay flesh tribute to their kings—one child per fertile female per year."

"Flesh tribute?" asked Sentain. "That doesn't sound good. Does that mean what I think it means?"

Yasmina smirked. "I can't read your mind, but I suspect so. The flesh tribute ends up on the dinner plates of the kings and their champions."

Miko snorted. "Still want to save these poor souls, Sentain, and bring them into your Confederation? Hah!"

Sarok ignored the exchange between the two men, still focused on the map. This was a strategic problem and therefore his realm. "And what about this third concentration, further up the coast from Ullah-Bor? *There*. It's smaller, but still significant."

Yasmina approved. "Yes. Well spotted. And that is where your target lies. Tartax-Kul in the northern arm of the Shield Mountains. We began to build a great tower there for our gameplay some thirty years ago. But then the ganeroi spread too quickly and we had to desist to prevent our automated builders from being discovered. It was ninety percent done. You'll love it. We took inspiration from all the very best—or perhaps I should say *worst*—nightmare fortresses from past human imagination."

"It sounds formidable," noted Sarok. "So why isn't it as well populated as the others?"

"To start, the ganeroi came to it late, after becoming established elsewhere. They are territorial creatures. In any case, there is less wildlife there to feed a population. But around fifteen years ago, they discovered fishing—dangling very long lines from the cliff face, accessed by tunnels beneath the roots of the tower. That allowed the population to surge, and it has gotten even bigger recently: it's at least double what it was three months ago and increases every week. You see, the ganeroi of Velasia now have a *third* king and his success has attracted many new adherents."

"Com Durrel?" mused Sarok. "So quickly?"

"Yes," said Yasmina. "He is clearly a remarkable man. We thought he would die quickly but instead, thanks to the Staff and his drive, he has exceeded all our expectations. The ganeroi worship power and cruelty and he has shown that he has both in abundance. Plus, he has fed them well."

"Okay," continued Sarok. "So, he is here, in this castle. Does he ever leave?"

"In the past, but not much now. He clearly knew about the tower before he arrived, as he headed straight for it, although it took him a couple of weeks to complete the journey from his landing zone, and he had to demonstrate his power on several occasions before his arrival. Rumours of him and his destination spread. Then he reached Tartax-Kul and…"

"Yeah, we saw," interrupted Vuller. "It was replayed in Arakkan. We saw the fight at the gates. He froze the king and all his champions."

Yasmina nodded. "Yes. That's true. But you won't be aware of what happened next. One of our own scouts picked up a stray ganeroi last week, far from home—apparently itself a scout for com Durrel. Of course, we have no direct communication with our people there, as advanced technology is not allowed, but we were able to listen in to the subsequent conversation via a satellite combined with lip-reading technology. It seems the old king wasn't dead, so com Durell left him conscious, partly unfroze him, and invited his new subjects to feast upon him while he still lived. Apparently, they really appreciated that gesture."

Sarok again waved away this subsidiary matter. "You were talking about whether he left…"

"As I said, he does, but not much now. In the two months after his arrival, he had to sally out to cow other tribes, and he also led an assault on one yeltoi settlement. There used to be four large settlements in Bratha—the land here, to the north-east—but now there are three. Ultis had good walls, but com Durrel destroyed them and… let's just say, his army ate very well that evening. But he has not left for at least nine days. We think he has been finishing the tower. We also fear he is preparing his next assault."

"Where? The other three yeltoi settlements to his north?"

"Possibly. Probably."

Sarok looked up from the map at this. "You're not sure?"

Archaen stepped in. "There is some disagreement between us. Most think he will strike at Haradan, the next nearest yeltoi settlement, but Yasmina has another opinion."

Yasmina scrunched her face. "I have grown to appreciate com Durrel to some degree. He was clever in where he chose to land and how he got rid of the shuttle. He showed us that he knew our concerns and demonstrated that he didn't plan to ruin the game, which might have caused us to attack him directly. Now, he has chosen the strongest fortress on the island. Why? In part because he knows we will try to come for him, but we will do so fairly. This is the most secure place in Velasia. He knows that every time he leaves, he becomes vulnerable, or perhaps I should say, slightly less invulnerable. Presently, to conquer, he needs to lead his army, which relies on his staff's power, but if he gains a big enough army, then he might not need to lead in person. The ganeroi could—if they band together—destroy the yeltoi and even drive us from Velasia. But they haven't had a leader with the power to unite the various tribes into a large enough force… until now. So…"

"Ullah-Bor." Sarok nodded in approval. "You think his next move will be down the coast instead, to conquer Ullah-Bor and unite most of the ganeroi of the Sundering Mountains. Then he can send his army against the yeltoi—and you—and stay behind his tower walls."

"Yes, that's what I believe. This move would also exposes him less to observation. There are subterranean routes through the mountains that the ganeroi have built, and which our satellites cannot pick up. So we might not even see him move until it's too late."

"I fear Yasmina might be right—yet hope not," said Archaen. "If this is the option he chooses, then it seems we must we either try to face him down in Tartax-Kul, or near Ullah-Bor. And the latter is not much better as an option and might even prove more dangerous."

"So where does that leave us now?" asked Sarok. "What is the next move? Where do we go tomorrow?"

"One of our ports," said Archaen. "All entry into Velasia is through these. It is one of the rules of the game. Otherwise, we could just pop up anywhere at any time. So the question really is, which one?"

"You are the expert," declared Sarok. "What are the pros and cons of each?"

Archaen considered the map, but before she could respond, Miko volunteered: "Not Narvik. Although the three ports are approximately the same distance from Tartax-Kul, the travel time would be considerably longer from there. The easiest passage would probably be by water, and the rivers north of the Sundering Mountains are less navigable than those to the south, while the land is rockier and pathless in places, and swamp-like in others."

"Horseback would be quicker," noted Reddas Archaen.

"For experienced riders, true, but…" Miko gave a lop-sided grin and indicated the other members of the party, "I doubt whether many of these have seen a horse, let alone ridden one. And I am also not sure we have any that would bear Brutus easily, so we'd have to take a wagon and then walk when the roads run out."

Enabeth Archaen nodded in agreement. "Yes, I had already dismissed Narvik in my head, leaving the other two. My heart says we should go to Ranvik, which is the home of my guild in Velasia, but my head says Sorvik, as this lies on the Tessellac River, which is navigable most of the way to the Copper Gates, which I suspect we will have to take."

Sarok had been studying the hologram intently. "The Copper Gates? I take it these are one of the two routes through the Sundering Mountains. *There…*" he pointed.

"That's right," said Yasmina. "There are four passes through the mountains: two through the Sundering Mountains connecting the Southlands to the Northlands, and two through the Skythrust Mountains connecting the Northlands to Bratha. From Ranvik or Sorvik you need to take either the Stone Gates or the Copper Gates to get into the Northlands. If you leave from Narvik, you don't have to risk these passes, but it is further and longer to get to the Cobalt and Iron Gates that cut through to Bratha, which is your ultimate destination. If you leave from

Sorvik, the Tessellac and its tributaries lead most of the way to the Copper Gates, which are further east along the chain than the Stone Gates, and once you are through, the distance to the Iron Gates is not great and avoids most of the difficult terrain in the northern shadows of the Sundering Mountains."

Sarok traced the route with his eyes. "To Sorvik… then the river to the Copper Gates… then turn east and march to the Iron Gates… then into Bratha… and then… we are perhaps two hundred kilometres, maybe three, to Tartax. And what then? Play it by ear? Will you—Yasmina—then let us know where com Durrel is, and when he leaves his fortress?"

Yasmina frowned and shook her head. "No. Let me be clear. Once you are in Velasia, you will receive no further information or aid. Though we can track com Durrel and his forces' movements, we will not pass this intel on to you. That would be cheating."

"But com Durrel is already cheating," interjected Sentain.

"Maybe, maybe not. He cheated in taking in the shuttle, and we are unhappy that he and Yadzen still wear their skins, but he hasn't really cheated in taking the Great Staff. In any case, there is an old expression: two wrongs do not make a right. We are who we are. We will not debase ourselves because others have. If we play against unfair odds, and lose, then that is the way of things. But if we win, in spite of this, then greater is the glory." Yasmina smiled. "In the Confederation, from what I have heard, you would mewl against the injustice and stamp your feet until 'fairness' was returned. Here we almost embrace the imbalance."

Miko was nodding. "That is well said. The odds excite me."

"*Us*, Ryven," growled Reddas Archaen. "*Us*."

Sentain looked across at Enabeth Archaen and saw her smile—as broad a smile as he had yet seen from her. "Enabeth… you too?"

"Irvan—do you not see my honours? They cover my skin. Do you think I gained these for administration? I am of my people, no more nor less. So, yes, like Ryven and Reddas, I am excited. Don't you feel it too?"

"I certainly feel something. Let's generously call it concern. Or perhaps *anticipation*?"

"Good choice of words. Excitement... anticipation... fear... in many ways they are one and the same. I hope to show you another way to experience the universe and help you rename your emotional response to it."

Sarok refused to be sidetracked. "I am glad we are all getting in touch with our feelings," he scowled. "But can we focus on the problem? If you cannot help us from here, what about your people in Velasia? I assume you also keep the true situation from them?"

"We do," said Yasmina. "The only intel they have is what they gather themselves. But I am aware that—over the last month—the various guilds have been sending scouting parties into the mountains and even into Bratha, which is not yet entirely closed. Though the passage through the Iron Gates is risky, it is still possible to access that land through the Cobalt Gates to their north. Possible, but not easy. Com Durrel's presence has somehow energised the yeltoi around Krajja-Min, which lies just three days' rapid march from the Cobalt Gates. So, yes, they will have more relevant and up-to-date intelligence and you will need to consult with them."

"Don't they update you with what they find?"

"Again—how?" asked Yasmina. "They do not have communications equipment. We do learn more when someone leaves Velasia to return to one of their other guild bases, but no one has wanted to come out for months. Instead, we are having to control those arriving for fear of unbalancing the game. We have a frustrated queue, including many now moping about on Verano, hoping to be able to fill dead-men's shoes. Of course, *you* get a special pass because of the nature of your quest and its origins."

"I am overjoyed at our great luck," mocked Sarok. "At least, our route is now becoming clearer. So what else can you tell us before we land in this information black hole? What do you know about the risks on the route being proposed?"

Yasmina exchanged sharp glances with Enabeth Archaen. "Well, there are several. Obviously, we did not contrive this world to be easy. Far from it. There are various perils, but I think Cousin Enabeth is aware of these and can say more when appropriate. The route you are planning has some difficulties and dangers that the other routes do not have—although those others have unique dangers too. The key thing here, though, is *time*, and so I agree with your choice of going via Sorvik. Com Durrel is moving at pace. By the time you manage to confront him, his plans will be more advanced. Even now, I fear for the yeltoi in Bratha. And if you fail, our very presence in Velasia will be threatened, as will the yeltoi's."

"The yeltoi population can be restocked if needs be," muttered Miko. "And should our ports fall, then at least there is the prospect of a crusade to retake the land, and that is... mouth-watering."

"Even if you are not alive to take part in it, Cousin?" wondered Archaen. "No. I do not think we should be so glib about this prospect." She looked askance at Sentain, who seemed appalled at Miko's callousness. "In any case, as Yasmina says, the other perils are broadly known to us and our kin already there. For now, our rough strategy is in place: to get to com Durrel as quickly as we can."

"So we are all set," concluded Sarok.

"Not quite," said Archaen. "Yesterday you chose your weapons. This afternoon, you will need to select the rest of your gear. Clothing. Equipment. Your *skin* must stay here, along with any modern devices, like data pads. These will be stored in lockers for your return. Let us eat first, and after I will take you to the storerooms."

"Eat?" muttered Brutus. "I'd rather have a drink. The prospect of no more free beer is the worst part of this thing."

Archaen couldn't stop the twitch of a smile. "Oh, don't worry, Brutus. You are not alone in having this thirst. All of the Elven ports have breweries, and the one at Sorvik is run by a particularly conscientious kinsman."

"Hallelujah! I am much cheered! Then lead on..."

Gene Rowe

***

Elian Omdanan had separated from the others in the storeroom. This was a vast chamber that held items made by programmed manufacturing automatons according to certain stringent criteria in order to match the Velasian ecosystem. It was divided into sections, the largest of which held clothing that was made of natural fibres and materials that it was theoretically possible to produce on that island continent, given the resources and technology available there.

He had left the Leaguers to choose appropriate camping gear and utensils for their packs—items that might be got in Sorvik, though probably not, given the limited and imperfect production facilities there. Enabeth Archaen had been the first to admit that, although the Leaguers liked to take on hobbies—such as beer or leather making—they weren't so enthusiastic as to produce a surplus of gear, and often had to trade with the yeltoi for more mundane products.

Omdanan ran a hand along a line of woollen smocks, that then turned into a line of leather surcoats. The latter were strange to him. On Meridian, the people would have been appalled by these—using animal products for human benefit. The thought made him smile, and suddenly he felt an urge to try something on. The items were of various sizes, though a better fit could be got by choosing a style and going to one of the printers in a side room and instructing it to replicate the item bespoke. But that would emphasise the artificiality of the thing, whereas he felt a need at that moment to choose and wear something that was or seemed real; something that had actually once been part of an animal—not because of any particular malice to the creature itself, but rather because of the horror it might induce in his distant kin.

He selected one long coat that narrowed at the waist and then fanned out beneath as it dropped to the back of the knees. This was made of black and brown leather, somehow interwoven. He whirled it onto his shoulders and let it hang, not bothering to put his arms into the sleeves. For some reason, a picture came to his mind of his mother, with her disapproving frown, standing amid Enbargo's elders. That made him smile: "*Fuck you!*" he muttered.

He would be sad to leave behind the dark-green skin he wore, even temporarily. It was an important part of his identity now, and he understood why the Leaguers prized the clothing so highly. It was something he had earned—alone of those from his party—and he had already embellished it with various badges of achievement. It represented the new Elian Omdanan. He was no longer an outsider, a difficult youth who thought and did things others abhorred, but rather someone of substance, who people respected and spoke to as an equal and treated as an adult, and more… He thought of Sorana. And Gretel. Strong, attractive women who had somehow, in some way, been drawn to him. And then he remembered Mira Lowes and frowned. She was a kind girl, and attractive, but in a *softer* way. He wished he could have taken her from Meridian and shown her this place with its different perspective on living. But although she was fond of him, she truly was one of her people, and would have been scarce less shocked than the others at the item he now had draped over his shoulders—although she would have perhaps responded differently, with a pained smile and a sigh. Yet aside from Mira, there was nothing for him on Meridian. Or in the Confederation. This was his home now, and yesterday, Enabeth Archaen—she of the Black Sword, the Nemesis Blade—had called him *Cousin*! Him!

Omdanan wiped a sudden tear from his eye, smiled broadly, and then threw back his head and gave a shout of joy. What the others must have thought, back in the depths of the storeroom, he did not know or care.

The coat fit. He would take it. It was a second skin, and scarcely less than his other, and in some ways even better.

Tomorrow, he would join his new family and set out to earn himself further plaudits, further badges of merit, and further distance himself from a past and a place to which he knew he would never return.

Chapter 3

The shuttle came in low, almost skimming the waves of the Encircling Ocean. Through the largely transparent fuselage, the party could see the smudge of Velasia on the horizon, steadily growing, with higher topography to the left where the Sundering Mountains' western-most peaks were visible. Then the shuttle slowed, and they were able to make out—following Miko's shouted instructions—something on the water, like a piece of flotsam. The shuttle slowed further, and the flotsam began to take on detail: there were masts, a flagpole, a large banner rippling in the sea breeze, a platform. Closer still, and the emblem on the banner became clear: a golden sword, vertical upon a field of red. And the masts were now revealed to belong to two vessels, moored on opposite sides of a large, wooden platform that had a small, sheltering hut in its centre by the flagpole.

The shuttle came to a complete halt, hovering in the air some ten metres above the waves. The pilot held up one hand as a sign for those in the passenger seats to wait while he consulted various scanners on his console.

"What's he doing?" asked Sarok.

"Just being sure," said Miko. "On the flight in, he will have been checking to make certain there are no yeltoi fishing craft in range to observe us. Now he is checking for anomalies in the water. We don't want to come within range of a black flenser or a kraken. Okay. He seems happy…"

The pilot dropped his arm, then swung the shuttle around and gently lowered the craft, edging towards the nearer end of the platform, perpendicular to the sides against which the two ships were moored. A two-metre wide ramp dropped from the aft of the shuttle, gently nudging the surface. Though the aircraft automatically locked in vertical space, the movement of waves meant the ramp rose and fell slightly.

"Let's move," said Enabeth Archaen. "Careful. Make sure you take your gear. Ryven and Reddas will bring the group equipment."

The Price of Freedom Part II: Velasia

The party descended onto the platform—Mandelson first, followed by Vuller, Omdanan, Sentain, and then Brutus—with a huge axe resting on one shoulder and a similarly preposterous mace on the other. Sarok and Archaen walked down the ramp together. Finally, Reddas Archaen and Miko descended, carrying one crate between them. The latter pair returned to the shuttle for two more trips, until the entirety of the party's gear was offloaded. Miko then turned to shout towards the pilot and give a thumbs up. As soon as the Leaguer stepped off the ramp, this began to retract, and almost immediately the shuttle rose to about fifty metres and streaked away towards Verano.

The party members followed the shuttle with their eyes, until Archaen called them to attention. "Load the gear onto the ship…" she pointed to the smaller of the two craft, which was about ten-metres long and had a single mast with a currently furled sail. "As the breeze is light and none of you are skilled sailors, we'll have to row. Find a partner of similar size and strength and sit opposite. Forgive me if I take the tiller."

With the stores loaded, Reddas and Miko went to the front of the boat, then turned to sit with their backs to land. Vuller slapped Omdanan on the shoulder, and the two took the next row. While Archaen busied untying the craft from the platform and seeing to the tiller in the stern of the boat, the remaining four looked at each other.

"I don't think this is going to work," said Sarok. "We'll all be needed to balance Brutus."

Mandelson scowled. "You sit with him," she gestured at Sentain. "I'll take Brutus." She settled onto a bench and started to haul an oar from where it lay on the bottom of the boat.

Sarok leant in to the giant. "Though I admire her self-belief… take it easy, big man, or we'll be going round in circles for the rest of the day."

Those sitting nearest the platform followed Archaen's instructions, using their oars to push off from it, and then the group quickly settled into a rhythm, taking cue from the steerswoman's shouted commands. Once Archaen was sure that the rowers were in time, she attempted to pick up the pace: "There are things in the sea we do not want to encounter, so the sooner we are on dry land the better. Pull!"

***

It took the party the best part of an hour to cross the sea from the platform to land. Though not unfit, Sentain soon struggled, and by the end he was sure their forwards progress owed very little to his laboured strokes. Matters weren't helped by his uncertainty as to the duration of the row: with his back to shore, he couldn't tell how close they were to their destination, and he stopped twisting to find out after he got a touch of cramp that ran from his neck through his shoulder and into his upper back. But on the plus side, from this position, he was able to admire Archaen as she directed their efforts—dressed in a black leather outfit, her hair in a ponytail set upon her right shoulder and secured by a leather chord, her sword at her waist in a black scabbard that hung to the ankle of her boot.

And then Sentain could sense they were close. The call of squabbling gulls increased in volume and frequency, and Archaen's stroke-calling slowed, while her movements on the tiller became more precise. The colour of the waters also seemed to change slightly and lighten. And then he heard a shout of greeting, which Archaen answered with a raised hand of acknowledgement.

"Steady now," said the woman. "Near oars… *up*! One more pull. All oars, *up*!"

And suddenly there was a stone quay off to one side of the boat. They coasted towards this and a line of floats that bobbed on the water along it, protecting the quay and the sides of approaching craft. Archaen threw a rope up to the unseen figure—for them to tie onto an iron ring in the quay wall—then she tipped an anchor over the opposite side. As the boat groaned to a halt, Sentain was able to stretch his neck and return his oar to the bottom of the boat—narrowly avoiding braining Brutus in front of him—and then turned to get a proper look at where they were.

On the quay, about two metres above their heads, looking down, was a large man, dressed in red leathers with long blond hair. Stone steps were cut in the quay nearby. "Cousin En! This is a glorious surprise!"

"Cousin Bastian! Permission to come ashore?"

"Permission granted. All kin are welcome, whether from the guild or not, though it is rare we receive visitors. Are you sure you haven't erred? Ranvik is further up the coast."

Archaen had by now stepped through the boat to a position where she could access the steps, close to Vuller's station. She lightly stepped across, skipped up the steps, and embraced the grinning man. Then she took a pace back: "Though navigation is not my strongest suit, it would have taken a real brainstorm to end up so far off course. No, our visit is intentional."

The man rested a hand on the woman's shoulder and considered the rest of the party as they wobbled to their feet. "And is that your son, back with us? Reddas? Last I heard, you were on Procession, and there were rumours of trouble."

Reddas laughed. "Trouble? You have missed much. I will tell you all I can, when I can, subject to the rules. I am sure Mother will keep me on course there."

"I understand. And Ryven—you also? This is quite a gathering. But I don't know your colleagues, and in fact… you seem to be in very strange company."

Archaen tugged the man's attention back to her. "Bastian—I will explain what I can, but perhaps first we should unload. Have you a place for us to stay? And can you help us unload?"

"Of course. We always have place at the inn. I will take you there. Leave your gear: I will get a couple of the lads to bring it across."

The party left the boat in single file. Three carried spears, using them as props, while Brutus again hefted his weapons onto his shoulders and then had to walk sideways, being too broad for the path. Bastian—whose muscularity even exceeded that of Miko and Reddas—shook his head in astonishment at the size of the man.

On top of the quay, Sentain was able to get a clearer view of Sorvik. The port was small, with a second quay a hundred metres away and a stone waterfront in between the two. There were no more than half-a-dozen other boats present, bobbing in the small, enclosed bay or tied up against one of the quays. Handsome, two-storey stone houses sat back from the waterfront, with cobbled roads cutting gaps between these. Further to his right, he could see the broad outflow of a river—the Tesselac—which emerged through low woodlands. A thirty-metre-high stone watchtower was also evident in that direction, while there were a couple of similar towers in the mid-distance beyond the houses, and one more just beyond the quay to his left, which seemed to mark out the boundary of the settlement.

Taking just his personal pack and staff—and armed with only a long knife at his waist—Sentain was less encumbered than most of the party. He was therefore able to manoeuvre himself to the front of the group, behind Archaen and the blond-haired man, settling in beside Miko as they moved off. He tried to listen to what was being said by the front pair, but when it became clear that they were exchanging personal news about friends and family, he gave them space and concentrated on the view. They walked in shadow down a small road lined by stone houses that ran straight for perhaps four hundred metres before ending in a fortified gate, over which a flag flew—identical to that on the platform, showing a gold sword upon a field of red.

Sentain saw the flag and turned to Miko: "I just realised. This place belongs to the High Guild of the Golden Sword. But your guild is the Golden Spear. Is there any relationship between the two?"

Miko slowly shook his head. "The high guilds are selective, though they do have alliances with other guilds. Bastian is the Grand Master of this guild, a position I once held in the Golden Spear, and that's how we know each other."

"Once?"

"The position is not hereditary or permanent. As you know, we like to have representation in the Confederation. Your society amuses me. So some years ago, I passed on the role and took my turn as a point of contact for our Processionals, giving me the opportunity to further explore your worlds. But I do not think I will go back after this, even if I survive."

Sentain decided to ignore the ominous hint. "But I understood only those belonging to the high guilds are permitted here. Does that mean you are…?"

Miko gave a curt laugh. "Yes, Dr Sentain, it does. I am as much a virgin here as you. As is Reddas. He wears his mother's colours and was accepted into the Black Lightning on probation before leaving on Procession, but he lodged at their other base on the mainland. Only Enabeth has been here before, but not for some time."

"So, strictly speaking, only Enabeth and Reddas should be here, as the Black Lightning is one of the three high guilds?"

"Strictly speaking, yes. But exceptions are often made, for one reason or another. Our reason is a good one. Don't worry, we are not likely to be challenged, though we might invite questions from the curious."

Sentain looked about; they were most of the way down the street, and the town gate was nearing. To one side of the gate was a larger building, three storeys high, made of stone and timber, with a slate roof and a sign depicting a tree in full leaf swaying above the portal. He guessed it was their destination. "Talking about the curious, where is everybody? I saw a few people along the waterfront, but there's no one else around."

Miko shrugged. "The population isn't high. Maybe three hundred? Four at most? I guess some will be at sea. Others training or practising a craft. Many will be exploring or scouting, or perhaps gone to a yeltoi settlement to trade. I am sure come evening, they will return, and it will be busier."

The pair in front came to a halt and turned as one. Bastian declared: "Welcome to the Noble Oak Inn. Enter and make yourselves comfortable. I will organise some rooms and then you can eat and drink. But be careful talking with the landlord. His name is Omadai and he brews his own beer, of which he is proud. Be certain to complement him on it, and you will make a quick friend."

The interior was empty of people. Small wooden tables and chairs were scattered across the stone-flagged floor between the bar and a large stone hearth. The fireplace was clearly well used, but currently unlit, as were the fat candles placed on metal plates in the centre of the tables. Light spilled in through the windows along one side of the building, casting odd shadows throughout the space. The party members seated themselves at several of the tables near the fireplace, while Bastian went in search of the innkeeper. They heard their host call out, and a muffled voice responded. Bastian then disappeared through a side door in the direction of the voice.

"Well, Brutus," exclaimed Vuller. "It looks like we'll drink after all."

"Perhaps. We have no coin, but I guess it will still be free… eh, Ms Archaen?"

The woman's expression was placid. "You need not fear about that. Omadai undoubtedly runs this place as a hobby and makes beer for the artistry of it. I suspect he is more likely to pay you to try his concoctions than vice versa."

"This place gets better and better," laughed Brutus.

Bastian returned through the door he had taken. "It is sorted. Omadai will be with us soon, and he will force beer on you until you can drink no more. Hopefully, at some point, he will break away to at least check your rooms have bedding."

They heard clattering in the direction of the bar and a large man appeared: he had a dark complexion and a black beard that was unusual among Leaguers. He beamed at the party, then set about pouring beer from one barrel into a collection of leather tankards. Once finished, he came over, carrying three mugs in each hand, which he distributed among the group; he then returned to collect and relay four more.

"This is a session ale," he declared on return, wiping a damp hand on a white woollen shirt that burst open across his muscular chest. "A good starter. Please enjoy… oh, and greetings Cousin Enabeth. Long time no see."

Archaen smiled and nodded to the man, who then scurried off to consider his stock and no doubt contemplate further liquid courses for them.

With all settled and supplied, Bastian seated himself besides Enabeth Archaen. "So… now we can relax. Cousin, please elaborate—who are these people you find yourself amongst? A couple look other-worldly." He glanced towards Brutus, and then his eyes lingered over Sarok and Sentain.

"Yes. This is so. I must be careful in what I say, but I think the tale of their origins will not breach any rules of disclosure or bias the game in any way. The rumours about Reddas are true. He was incarcerated in the Confederation, and we needed local help to free him, which came at a price. The man who bankrolled the scheme now sits in Tartax-Kul."

Bastian nodded grimly. "I wondered about this dark wizard. His possession of the Staff of Power is known, yet we don't understand the nature of he who brought it and wields it, or why this was allowed. I take it his actions were not sanctioned?"

"They were not."

"Then who are these others? Also members of the off-world team that aided Reddas?"

"Yes."

"So, why are they here now, with you? Only members of the three high guilds are permitted in Velasia… though we occasionally allow white skins to the ports to learn trades, or esteemed visitors…" He nodded at Miko. "But the way your party is armed suggests you don't plan to remain here; that you plan to *game*; and so their indulgences exceed all others of our kind."

Archaen toyed with her ponytail as she composed her thoughts. "The other off-worlders in our party were mostly paid to enact the rescue. When their paymaster eloped, they found themselves betrayed and stranded, although the Senate has also deemed them—fairly or not—at least partly at fault for this problem. Ryven, Reddas and I also share this guilt by association. And so the Senate decreed that we should… *must*… right the wrong we have involuntarily caused."

Bastian raised his mug of beer and took a drink. He then lowered it, but didn't speak immediately. He cast a critical eye over the party ranged among the tables around him, all of whom returned his gaze, save for the woman with red-streaked hair, who looked into some other distance. At last he ventured: "And you think you can achieve this thing? Destroy this wizard? Reclaim the staff? With just this small group? En—your skills are renowned. And in Ryven and Reddas you have two stout warriors. But I doubt these others—"

"Do not dismiss them so readily, Bastian. They all have significant abilities."

Bastain's gaze settled on the giant Brutus and his face twitched into a smile. "Perhaps. But still, this dark wizard has a powerful weapon, and he already has more orcs at his command than any previous king of their kind."

"I am not suggesting it will be easy. In any case, we have our own wizard too…" Archaen indicated Sentain, whose staff rested against one wall.

Bastian looked at Sentain uncertainly. "I saw the staff, but dismissed it as merely a club or prop. Is it truly one of the other staffs? If so, it's power is surely much less than the Great Staff, though I suppose it might be of use."

"Yes. That is our hope. We plan to take the Tesselac from here to the Copper Gates, then cross to the Iron Gates to Bratha and then… the rest is still unclear. Is there any way you can aid us?"

"You shall certainly have a boat and supplies. What else do you need?"

"Mostly information. What is the situation between here and Tartax-Kul? What do you know?"

Bastian took another drink, then gently placed his tankard on the table and sat back and folded his arms. "In truth, I can tell you little of events beyond the Southlands. Matters have progressed apace, and it is a couple of weeks on the fastest horse between here and the Copper Gates—and the same back again. Nevertheless, if I could use one word to describe the situation here, it is… *infested*. Over the last few weeks, the land has been flooded with roving bands of orcs. Small groups mostly. Six. A dozen. But lots of them. The wizard is gathering information, creating terror, and worse."

"What do you mean?"

"The orcs seem to be trying to ensnare our kin. I have had scouting parties out—as has your nephew from Ranvik—and several have had lucky escapes. Just two days ago, a party of three were ambushed by a group of a dozen orcs. While they kept two of mine busy and at a distance, they managed to stun the third and carry them off. But the others rallied and retrieved their kin, largely unhurt. Even so, the orcs did not give up, and seemed particularly determined to capture their initial target, almost ignoring the others. They eventually broke off after half their number were killed. Still, I dread to think what they might have done with any captives."

At this, Sentain coughed into his beer.

Bastian and Archaen looked at him.

"Irvan, are you okay?"

"Er… sorry… beer went down the wrong way… but…" he looked over at the man. "Bastian. This third person, they were *female*, right? And her colleagues were male?"

"Yes. That is correct. How did you know?"

Sentain gave a grim smile. "It's com Durrel. The dark wizard. He has probably not had, er, *congress*, for some time. I suspect he is trying to catch a mate. Or knowing him, a lot of mates. A harem. He probably sees that as his right."

"In that case," noted Bastian, "you should be particularly careful, En. There are indeed things that are worse than death…"

***

They continued to talk into the evening. Candles were lit inside, and other Leaguers arrived from whatever labours or quests they had been about during the day. These looked at the newcomers suspiciously on entering, but on seeing their Grand Master among them, they gave the group space. At one point, Bastian went off to talk to one of the new arrivals.

On his return, Bastian sat. "It is arranged. I know you are keen to be off, and time is of the essence, so I will meet you at the riverside dock, mid-morning tomorrow. Two riverboats will be waiting there. You'll also have provisions of dried food for several weeks, and some wine skins to provide cheer. Wait for me. I will come with maps and the latest intelligence. Is there anything else?"

"No, thank you, Bastian," replied Archaen. "Short of an escort, I could have wished for no more."

"And I would provide you with that, too, if I could," noted the man, sombrely. "But our resources are thin, and we have few other riverboats available… though you won't be entirely alone. Over the next few days, I plan to send scouting parties along both banks of the Tesselac. They will clear any infestations they find and update you if they learn anything of note. Look out for them."

"Thank you again. But what of Sorvik and the Southlands generally? Do you have any other plans for when the gan… the *orcs*… arrive in force?"

The blond-haired man smiled. "Oh yes, I do indeed." He leant forwards, almost conspiratorially. "I have decreed a muster for two weeks' time. Your cousin, Patryc, has done the same for Ranvik. I hope to be able to field maybe two-hundred horsemen under the Golden Sword banner, and perhaps we'll see the same number under the Black Lightning flag. Then we will move in parallel towards the mountains and the Stone Gates, an *elven* host assembled to defend the *men* of this land. That will be some sight, I promise you!"

"I can see the excitement in your eyes, Bastian."

The man sat back, and cast his gaze around the attentive group. "Excitement? Yes. No doubt. We all feel it. This is something new and grand. And you—all of you—have unwittingly brought this storyline to our great game. Perhaps I should be thanking you instead?"

"I'll drink to that," declared Brutus, who raised his tankard and did just that.

Chapter 4

"Heel, Wormtongue, *heel*!"

Rostus Dettler approached the throne, walking gingerly across the cold stone flags of the audience chamber. He was unshod, dressed in a black tunic of the sort worn by the orcs—com Durrel having insisted he burn his tattered Confederation clothing once he had alternative attire. "Yes, sir. I am here."

Anda com Durrel sat on a nightmarish throne of carved stone: the armrests were worked into the shape of tormented, human-like faces, while a great winged beast with outstretched wings rose up from behind his head to glare down upon—and cow—all who approached. Com Durrel still wore his burgundy skin, but he hid this beneath a black leather outfit and a black cloak with a silver clasp at the neck; he gripped the Staff of Power in his right hand. Yadzen stood by his side, wearing black chainmail over his own burgundy skin, with a great sword hanging from a belt at his waist. And to either side of the throne was a giant orc, each two metres in height. These were dressed in mail surcoats and held long halberds topped with spiked cleavers.

"Hurry hurry! Now drop to your knees. You know the form by now."

Three metres from the throne, Dettler sank to his knees, bowing his head, in no little part to hide his embarrassment and shame… and rage.

"I have inspected it."

"You took your time. Anything decent?"

Dettler looked up, having managed to compose his features. "Apart from some slightly mouldy bread, no. The caravan was carrying haunches of mutton and pork, but this went off during the time it took to get here."

"I don't need bread—we pillaged plenty of grain from that *mannish* settlement, and even the orcs know how to make bread. I need protein, not more *fucking* fish. This isn't how royalty should dine, let alone gods!"

The supplies they'd brought with them from Verano had run out five weeks ago. Conscious not to leave any evidence of the outside world in Velasia, com Durrel had used his staff to incinerate the last of the packaging. Ever since, they had lived on fish caught by the orcs on long-lines from the entrances to the tunnels beneath the great tower that opened out above the Encircling Ocean... that, and a few apples gathered from a small orchard in a nearby valley. And one time, they had eaten venison—but once only, for there was little game in the spindly forests that furred the foothills of the Shield Mountains near Tartax-Kul.

"Perhaps... perhaps we need to move from here," ventured Dettler. "To somewhere with better food sources. The only other alternative is... what they eat." The thought of what he had seen made Dettler suddenly feel queasy, and he looked askance at one of the giant orcs. It was human-like in almost every detail and could, with plenty of make-up, be disguised as an ugly human. It was pale-faced, almost albino, with two large ears, a slightly drooping nose, and a somewhat tapered head. Its teeth—currently hidden behind purplish lips—were sharp and long, at least in the upper jaw, and well-suited to tearing flesh. He knew the latter well, having seen the creatures' feeding in action. *Feeding frenzy*. When the orcs got a sense of blood, whether of their own vulnerable kind or of the yeltoi, which they called *men*, they tended to break off from whatever they were doing and descend on the injured creature to literally tear it apart. Dettler supposed it was an evolutionary adaptation to a low-food environment, in which the quickest and most desperate ate and survived, and the less-quick starved and died. The first time he had seen them eat, he had retched. And the second. And the third.

"Ha! It's too soon for that. I am not safe yet."

"But if we took one of the other settlements of... *men*... and we stopped the orcs from killing them all, we could have them farm for us. And then you could feast like a king. Every day. Surely we will be safe in the plains of Bratha? Who would dare attack you?"

"I said *not yet*, Wormtongue. I'll not let your lies sway me again. Until the orcs are united under me, and the *elves* are thrown into the sea, I won't be secure. They are coming, you know. I have to be ready. So you must try harder. I think I have been too kind to you. You perhaps need a little more motivation. So…" com Durrel's smile was malign, "I now make this decree: if you don't get me some decent food by tomorrow, *you* will have to eat what *they* eat. The sight of that is bound to suppress my appetite and give me some entertainment at the same time. So go to Ganna. Tell him you have my authority. From now on, he and his men are to dedicate themselves purely to filling my plate. And tell him, if I have nothing by tomorrow, *you* will be feasting on *his* flesh in front of me. So… *fuck off!*"

Dettler felt himself pale to the colour of the nearby orcs.

***

The first sight of the tower of Tartax-Kul had left Dettler chilled: it rose like a thick, black needle, three-hundred metres high, set within a bowl of land near the ridgeline of a mountain chain, the eastern edge of which dropped sharply into the ocean. A shadowed courtyard separated the tower from a gatehouse opposite, which sat in the middle of a thick stone wall that ran between the sheer rock faces forming the natural edges to the bowl. The gatehouse was topped with crenelations and a parapet walk, with a bastion snug against the rock wall at each end and a gate beneath each rounded tower. Beyond the wall, the land plunged between two mountain spurs into a deep crevasse. Access to the two gates was gained along broad paths that hugged the edges of the crevasse to either side.

Dettler took the eastern gate, opened for him by the guards there. Once through, he kept as far left as he could to avoid the dizzying view into the thousand-metre drop to the side. He would have kept a hand trailing against the wall continuously, but after a short distance, open stone windows and wooden doors began to appear in the wall, as well as wickedly-steep stone stairs that led to second and third level dwellings above. These rough-carved steps were open-sided, lacking handholds, and were treacherous when slick with rain. Of course, Ganna, as a Champion, lived in a top-level dwelling that was relatively safe from opportunistic child snatchers.

At the third stairway along the wall, Dettler stopped. He focused on the steps, refusing to look behind, and immediately began to climb, one sweaty palm held against the rockface, leaning into this, concentrating on each successive tread of his dirty feet. Three metres up, there was a ledge, which led to the second-level dwellings, but he had to turn and take another flight. By the time he ascended to the third level, he was six metres above the pathway and the view was vertiginous. He couldn't help but look: the sight over the edge of the path into the chasm made his knees buckle, and he had to throw his chest against the cold, cracked rockface. He closed his eyes and began to chant a calming mantra. It took a full minute for him to regain control of his breathing and clear his mind of the precariousness of his situation, and only then did he straighten and complete the last few steps along the ledge to Ganna's home. As soon as he reached a stone window, he sensed eyes on him. The orc was in his front chamber.

"Ganna, it's Wormtongue." He used the name com Durrel had given him, and with which he had been introduced to the orcs. It shamed him.

"Show hands," came a voice, slow and deliberate.

He carefully raised his arms, the traditional way of confirming he held no weapons and had not come to kill and eat.

From the shadow within, Dettler felt the orc's eyes forensically examining him. After some seconds, he heard the scrape of wood on rock floor and saw the indistinct figure rise and disappear from view; he heard a bolt being thrown. He waited for Ganna to retake his seat, before lowering his arms, taking three paces to the door and creaking it open.

The anteroom was sparsely furnished. In the middle, there was a rough wooden table around which were a number of seats: only Ganna had a proper wooden chair; the other seats were blocks of stone hewn from the mountain. Some woven rugs were heaped on the uneven floor by one wall… but there was nothing else. Nothing of value that could be stolen. Dettler knew there would be a larger space behind a wooden door in the back wall—perhaps two rooms, or maybe even three—which would comprise a larder of festering meat and rotting fruit, plus space for the orc's family. As a successful champion, Ganna might have a dozen or more children back there, and his 'wife' would undoubtedly be pregnant with a litter of several more. In times of famine, with which the orcs were familiar, the fate of the weakest children was something hideous to contemplate…

"I have been sent by the God-Sorcerer." Com Durrel had thought about how he wished to be addressed on the trek of devastation from their landing site to Tartax-Kul: Dettler had heard him muttering about it to himself. By the time they'd reached the external gates of the settlement at the foot of one of the tower's mountain paths, he had settled on *God-Sorcerer* for himself, *Terminator* for Yadzen, and *Wormtongue* for Dettler. After he'd annihilated a number of the ever-increasing forces sent against them—by fire, radiation and frost—com Durrel had loudly announced their identities while standing on the semi-frozen body of the orcs' king.

"That is obvious," said Ganna. His voice was actually quite pleasant—rich and low. "I have been waiting for his commands. Tell me what he wants."

"What do we all want? Food."

Ganna growled and waved one muscular arm. "He is surrounded by food. This is a time of plenty. I still have the corpses of two salted men in my larder; take him one of these."

On the last words, the orc leant forwards menacingly, baring his sharp teeth, attempting to intimidate him. But Dettler had learnt many roles as a negotiator; he could be meek, but he could also be strong. In spite of the other's fearsome aspect, he managed not to flinch and firmed his expression. "You know he eats other things. He protects his children, rather than eating them. He wants animal flesh. He *demands* animal flesh. And he will have it by tomorrow, or he will host a banquet where *you and yours* will be his dinner gift to the other champions."

Ganna shuffled on his seat and frowned. A low growl came from the back of his throat. "How am I to achieve this? Where is this food?"

"The Splinter Forest. It is your only chance. You must take your whole company and lay traps. Take every piece of game you can. Leave the company there. They must hunt at night, too. Go immediately."

"Even so, it will take me until late afternoon to get there. How can I go there, hunt, and return food by tomorrow?"

Dettler had been giving the matter some thought. "You must form a relay squad. At intervals on the way, leave teams of strong runners. When you make a kill, send this along the line. This way, you will be able to return food as if your fastest runner were able to travel the whole way himself." Dettler pursed his lips. "Of course, it would be easier if you kept horses at each station—but you have none. Perhaps it would be best to refrain from eating the next ones you capture?"

Ganna assessed him with a calculating eye. "That is one way. It might work. I will do it. But maybe I need a reserve strategy in case I fail." There was a long knife resting on the table; Ganna reached a hand to it and started stroking its naked blade. "Your flesh is soft, Wormtongue. You smell bad to me, but different. Would he notice, I wonder, if your carved flesh were served up in a basket?"

Dettler knew the orc was not joking; his heart suddenly beat faster. "He might not notice the difference. But he would notice my absence. I think the old king's torturers would soon have the truth from you."

Ganna's hand stopped caressing the knife, and another growl escaped through his clenched teeth. His deep eyes sought and held Dettler's and seemed to communicate an unspoken promise. "Very well."

As the orc stood, Dettler hastily turned and headed back through the front door.

***

"I have brought you some boots. I hope they fit."

"Ah, Yadzen, thank you!"

"It is nothing. I needed to keep busy."

Dettler and Yadzen were in a side chamber to the throne room, one level up from the entrance hall of the tower. A broad balcony faced in the direction of the lowering afternoon sun, providing some illumination to the dimly-lit room. Although he would have had more light on the balcony, Dettler kept well back from that balustraded opening, and lounged on a thick bear pelt on the floor instead. He took the proffered boots, swept the dirt from a blackened foot, and tried one on.

"Yadzen, this is excellent! It fits and is comfortable."

He eagerly repeated this process with the second boot, then placed one hand on the pelt and pushed himself upright. Then he strolled about experimentally. He couldn't keep a smile from his face. "Really, Yadzen, I don't know what to say. I knew you have many skills, but I never realised this was one, or that you were doing this for me."

As ever, Yadzen's expression was neutral. "I could see you were suffering. And I am at something of a loss in this place. Mr com Durrel is using you for tasks he would normally give me."

Dettler paced some more, testing the suppleness of the leather. "That does seem to be the case. I guess he needs you as a bodyguard more than anything else now." He stopped and looked up. "I just realised, we've never really spoken, have we? When did we first meet? On Maloratious?"

"Yes. Mr com Durrel asked me to look after you."

"And I rather shamefully looked on you as nothing more than the hired help, although I did suspect you were something of a spy." Was that the hint of a smile on the other man's broad face? "And then we were on the *Fantasia* together," he continued, "though you always seemed to be on duty. And in Arakkan, it was the same. And Verano. And… ever since we landed in Velasia. Always on duty."

"That is my way. That is my purpose."

Dettler ceased pacing, settling on a bench at the sole table in the room, his legs crossed, leaning back against the table top. "Maybe it is time we talked more. After all, we are the only real humans for many miles, apart from Mr com Durrel, and I often wonder whether that term actually applies to him."

Yadzen stood in the centre of the room, in his chainmail, with a hand resting on his sword. Now his expression definitely did twitch—downwards, not upwards. "I… think it is important that you do not disrespect our master."

"Ah, right." Dettler raised his hands in a *mea culpa*. "I am aware of your loyalty, which is admirable. But I do wonder where this loyalty comes from. It seems somewhat unnatural. I hope you don't think I am being too nosy, and if so, please accept my apologies. But do you mind if I ask why? He can't pay you *that* much, surely?"

This time Yadzen shuffled his feet, uncertainly. To Dettler, it looked as though he were suffering some inner conflict. The man's mouth actually contorted in different ways, as though words were trying to come out, being suppressed, and trying again. At last, Yadzen muttered: "It is a complicated story."

"If by *complicated* you mean *long*, then that is no matter. What else have we to do here to pass the time?"

"No. Not long. Complicated. It is perhaps best if it were left alone."

Yadzen started to turn to leave, but Dettler sought to delay him. "Wait! I'm sorry. Please don't go. I will refrain from prying if you wish. But it is usual when getting to know someone that you exchange information on your pasts. Come and sit down. I am more than happy to go first. *Please.*"

Com Durrel's bodyguard hesitated. He looked through the door back to the throne room, but com Durrel was not there; they both knew he had retired to his chamber to rest. So he turned back and stalked over the table at which Dettler sat, and lowered himself onto the same bench, sitting side-on so he could face the other…

***

"… and that is me, up-to-date. You know the rest." Dettler gave a smile meant to soothe. "The tale of a small man with high ambition and modest talent. And I wonder which of these three characteristics is most responsible for my current straitened circumstances?"

"In my experience, it is ambition. That is always the seed of self-destruction."

"I suspect you are right. But where did this ambition come from? Short man syndrome? A need to compensate for my, ah, physical inadequacies? The sort of inadequacies that seem to have acted as a red rag to your master? Or perhaps it has primarily been because of my talent: any less, and I would never have been involved in this affair; any more, and I would have been able to negotiate my way out of these troubles."

"It is clearly a complicated matter."

"For me, perhaps." Dettler tried to affect an air of unconcern. "But what of you? Has ambition been the seed of your own downfall? Or perhaps you don't see this as a downfall. Our… master… seems to see this as literally an apotheosis."

Yadzen ran one hand over his close-cropped grey hair, a gesture Dettler had never seen before. "I… do not see this as negative or positive. I am merely doing my duty."

"Sure. But in the same way I wonder about the source of my ambition, I wonder about your sense of duty. Where does that come from? I have always thought you have a military bearing. A soldier? A very good soldier, I am sure."

"Yes, I was once a soldier."

"A Confederation marine!" Dettler snapped his fingers and smiled. "The best of the best. I'd put my money on it."

"Yes. But…" Yadzen's voice trailed off.

Dettler reached across to pat the other man on the knee in a familiar way. "I see you are struggling. Never mind. Although… I am not sure why this history is such a difficult one for you to relate." He leant back, pouted and shrugged. "Maybe in your past you had to do some bad things. It happens. Soldiers follow orders. Sometimes orders are bad. Sometimes maybe they should be disobeyed?"

"No. It's not that."

"Then you are home free. A noble and long-serving marine! As I said before, *admirable*."

"Am I, though?" Yadzen looked away, and his voice dropped low. "What if that loyalty is not freely given? What if the duty doesn't come from noble intentions?"

"Well, that would be a different story. That would make things more complicated. Our *mot du jour*? But I don't believe it. Your reactions are so natural, so instinctive. I think if our master had some hold over you—financial? blackmail?—then you would pause before acting. Anyone would. It would be natural to consider acting just a little bit too slowly and suddenly your problem goes away. But I have never seen you pause—not once."

"Maybe I cannot."

Dettler's brow furrowed. "Cannot? You mean, your responses are automatic? Conditioned? *Programmed?*"

Yadzen looked back at him, his expression almost sad. He opened his mouth to speak, then closed it. Looked away and then looked back. "I… There was… There was a military research program, many years ago. The aim was to create a super soldier. They sought volunteers from elite units and my pride pushed me forwards."

Dettler spoke softly. "I am sure these schemes are common, no?"

"Not like this one. Others have focused on weaponry, or physical enhancements. But in the elite units, we are already strong, and fast, and our kit is the best. So this program focused on the psychological. The problem is not about having a weapon, but about using it. The main problem with soldiers isn't that they aren't tough enough, but that they often won't use all that they have. They think. They hesitate. They fear. They instinctively look after themselves first."

"I think I see. And I think I can guess: the program didn't work out so well?"

Yadzen smiled, but grimly. "It worked out far too well. In a live-fire exercise four of my five comrades threw themselves recklessly in front of heavy shells. They died, but it gave my friend and I a chance to reach our target and… neutralise it. Neutralise them. *All* of them."

"Oh, I see. And the program?"

"The program was cut. It was buried. They attempted to de-condition my friend and me. I don't know about Mikel, but it wasn't wholly successful. Then we were discharged."

Dettler nodded, thoughtfully. "And somehow, Mr com Durrel found out and… picked up your tab?"

"He is now my general and will be for as long as he lives. So, I urge you, Mr Dettler, be very careful around him. If you misstep and he tells me to kill you, please be aware that I will try my very best to do this. But I assure you, it won't be personal."

Dettler gave a wry smile. "Don't worry. In the split second before you snuff out my life, I'll try not to think badly of you."

***

Anda com Durrel was cold and bored and tense.

Night was falling outside—a time he dreaded. It was at this time that he really questioned who he was, what he was doing, and why he was here. In Maloratious, he would be drinking, eating fine food, perhaps watching a show. And after that, there would be girls—as many as he wanted. But he'd not had a girl for so long now. And even though he'd been celibate since leaving his home world, at least he'd been entertained on the *Fantasia*, and at Arakkan and Verano.

He looked around his chamber. He had a large bed, covered in sheets and pelts, mostly pillaged from the yeltoi town he had attacked. But otherwise, the room was empty save for a few bits of furniture scattered about, a woven green-and-black yeltoi rug on the floor, and a large map inked on canvas that covered another part of the floor. Drapes hung over archways to balconies on either side of the room, though these didn't fully keep out the cold. And the only light within the room came from oil-filled lamps in sconces on the wall and several thick white candles on one table. It was all somewhat depressing.

Com Durrel grasped his staff tightly and walked over to the map. He'd had this hastily drawn up by his new minions to show Velasia as they knew it. And he'd had his chief scribes add to this with further detail gained from returning scouts. A much larger version was now being drawn up in a chamber on the floor below, which he had named the Map Room. Contemplating this, and the extent of his conquests already, was almost his sole pleasure, a reminder of what he had achieved and what he still had to achieve. Once the world was his, he'd be able to move to more salubrious surrounds—maybe one of the yeltoi settlements, or even one of the elven ports?

He stood on the map, his feet to either side of Tartax-Kul. He had two plans in contention—one to strike south and claim the orc's greatest citadel, at Ullah-Bor, a second to strike at Haradan, Jinna and Faltis, the three remaining yeltoi towns in Bratha. He knew he should move against the other orcs first, but the second option offered more plunder, including slaves—if he could stop the orcs from eating them. He frowned at the thought of the orcs. They were terrifying, disgusting creatures. Though they feared him, they also revered him for the *food* he brought. But did they fear him enough, revere him enough? Would he ever be able to trust them, or must he always be wary of a knife in the back?

And thinking of fear, com Durrel nodded to himself. It was time for a reminder…

He left the map and stalked over to one of the curtained archways. He pulled aside the thick, black drapes and walked onto the balcony. This looked directly over the wall and gatehouse and to the crevasse beyond, with the orcs' homes dug into the rock faces on either side of the great cleft. He then turned to look up. Evenly spaced around this arc of the tower, perhaps ten metres up and twenty metre's below the tower's peak and the observation platform at the apex, hung half-a-dozen orcs, secured by iron bands. Some of these had looked at him the wrong way during the day; others he'd simply chosen at random.

"Now begins the next lesson," he said aloud to no one but the wind. He raised his staff and pointed at the orc furthest to one side. "*Arak-Karaka-Polotia!*"

The tip of the staff lit up, and then a fireball shot from it to engulf the wriggling, fearful creature. The orc screamed and burned. Then com Durrel turned, repeating the words of power, until all six of the creatures were aflame. They burned so hot that for a time it took the chill off the air, and com Durrel basked in their terminal warmth.

Chapter 5

The party found the single-masted riverboats waiting at a small quay by the mouth of the Tesselac river, close by the town walls, over-looked by a tower from which fluttered the red-and-gold flag of the high guild. Moments after they arrived, a horse-drawn cart pulled up to the stone-flagged area, driven by a pair of tall, blond-haired Leaguers dressed in leather tunics and trousers. Miko shouted a greeting and went to talk to the new arrivals. Soon after, the men leapt down and moved to the back of the cart, from which they wrestled various sacks and small wooden cases that, under Miko's direction, they distributed into storage spaces at the aft and bow of the two boats.

The rest of the party assembled around Enabeth Archaen, out of the way of the activities of the loaders.

"So how are we going to do this?" asked Sarok. "I have no experience with such boats, and nor do most here, I guess."

"I'll take the helm of one," said the woman, "and Ryven will take the other. We know how to sail, though the sails will only be of use some of the time. Here, by the coast, we will be able to take advantage of sea breezes for much of the day, until we are perhaps thirty or forty kilometres inland. Beyond that, the wind will be more temperamental, and we will need to resort to muscle power more often. But I do not want to delay, so we will row as well."

"Fine," said Sarok. "But there are nine of us and two boats. How will we split?"

Archaen looked about the party, frowning in thought. "I propose Reddas and Brutus join me, as they will be well-matched at the oars. You join Miko with the rest of your team."

"And Sentain?"

"He can come with me."

Sarok grinned and glanced aside at the anthropologist. "I suspect that is a distribution with which none here will disagree. You will take the lead boat, Ms Archaen, no?"

"I will. And I see our provisions have been loaded, and our crates are now here too. As we don't have room for the crates aboard, everyone needs to recover their equipment and stow it in the appropriate boat. Distribute the weight as evenly as you can, and keep your chainmail surcoats to hand, though we shouldn't need these for some time. Here's Bastian—excuse me while I go talk to him."

Archaen nodded to Sarok, then turned towards the cobbled road—leading towards the centre of the small town—up which Bastian was striding, holding rolled parchments in one hand.

***

They were ready for the off. The sails had been raised in the two boats, with Enabeth Archaen and Miko sat at the sterns at the tillers, holding thin guide ropes attached to the sails. As the breeze caught the sails, the untethered boats began to pull away from the quay.

"Good luck, all!" cried Bastian. "Look out for my scouts. And maybe we will meet again."

The three Leaguers shouted back their own over-lapping farewells, and then a gust caught the sail of the lead boat, and it surged forwards against the river current.

In the front boat, Reddas and Brutus sat forwards of the sail, out of the way of the controlling ropes. To order, they took up an oar each and began to dig into the water in synchronicity. Seeing this, those in the following boat did the same, though with two pairs at the oars instead of one.

Irvan Sentain sat towards the aft of the wide, shallow-bottomed boat, close to the steerswoman, holding his staff to his chest. He remained silent to begin with, allowing Archaen to focus on sailing. Occasionally, he glanced behind to keep track of the second boat, which varied its position constantly—sometimes coming to within five metres of them, sometimes dropping back to twenty or thirty metres distance, and sometimes directly behind—though usually to landwards of them. Across the broad river, Sentain saw that the bank was lined with trees, though the land on the near side was initially clear of tall vegetation, and occasionally horses could be seen roaming the grassland. After several kilometres, however, the near bank also succumbed to encroaching forest.

By the time an hour had passed, the river had narrowed to a width of two-to-three-hundred metres. Reddas and Brutus were taking a break from rowing, talking low and occasionally laughing. Sentain looked up at Archaen, who was focused on the watery path before them, manoeuvring the tiller and sheets to ensure the sail made best use of the wind.

"So, what are the immediate plans?" he said at last. "Did Bastian have any suggestions?"

Archaen glanced at the speaker and then quickly returned her attention to the way ahead. "He did. We are heading for one of the yeltoi towns along the river, called Hustem. Bastian is spreading the message to his scouting parties to send any intelligence there."

"Is it far?"

The woman twitched the tiller to adjust their course slightly. "Perhaps two weeks, maybe three if we're unlucky with the wind or otherwise delayed."

"*Oh*. I'd hoped to see some yeltoi before then."

Archaen briefly looked down and bestowed a quick smile. "Don't worry, Irvan. You will see some before then. There are a number of nearer yeltoi settlements on the left bank. I have a mind to pull into one in a few days' time, as long as we don't arrive too early in the morning and risk losing the best part of a day's travel."

"That's better! I admit, I'm excited at the prospect of meeting members of a new race—especially one that's been taught English, so I'll even be able to understand them." Then Sentain's face creased into a frown. "Though that's *also* a shame. I mean, an alien language would reveal so much more about them as a people than an imposed language. The yeltoi might have developed words for concepts completely different to us. Untranslatable. Do they still speak their own language here?"

"Not so much in Velasia. On Omicra, they have various dialects and often struggle to communicate with others of their kind living more than a few kilometres distant. English was taught to the first generation before they were brought here—sedated, of course, so they never experienced the journey on the starship. It gave them the unifying language they needed to understand each other. But don't worry, on their home world they have been left to their own devices, so nothing has been lost. And here, I suspect they are already changing our language to fit into their way of seeing the world, inventing new words and expressions. These aren't matters of great interest to us…" she looked askance again and smiled, "but perhaps they are to you?"

"Absolutely! I would sell my soul to… er… well…"

Archaen laughed lightly. "It's amazing the price we are willing to pay to follow our heart's desires, Irvan. *Our* souls have already been sold. It is easy to do. But don't you already have enough material for a new book without being distracted by the yeltoi?"

Sentain grinned. "You mean, a book on you Leaguers? What have you been told?"

"Ryven tells me you have spent the last few months interrogating absolutely everyone in Arakkan who will talk with you, and he suspects you have been recording the conversations. He also says you've been caught filming with your datapad while lurking in shadows and other hidden places. He thinks your latest thesis is already well advanced."

"Ha! And I thought I was being careful! But it's been too much of a temptation, like a child in a sweetshop. And now I find myself in a confectionary factory. My colleagues on Ustaria would be green with envy." Then Sentain turned sober. "Although… although I do wonder whether I will ever have an audience for my work, and whether anyone in the Confederation will ever see it."

Archaen looked him, longer this time. "I don't know what will transpire after we have dealt with com Durrel if we are successful. But hold onto your dreams, Irvan. Keep recording your observations and writing down your insights. If the worst comes to the worst, your chronicles of a people, and of new alien races, will not go unread—even if your readership might prove more restricted than you hope."

Sentain nodded. "Yes. You're right. This is important work. I shouldn't be doing it for the vanity of it, but for posterity. Thank you, Enabeth. Thank you for *everything*."

***

Aboard the second boat, Sarok ceased rowing when Mandelson—in the adjacent seat—declared herself bored and shipped her oar. Rather than issuing commands he wasn't sure would be obeyed, he accepted the inevitable, called on Vuller and Omdanan to keep it up, and moved to the back of the boat to sit near Miko, perching on the gunwale to be out of the path of his manoeuvring.

For a moment he observed their surroundings in silence. The water was dark, almost black. The banks on both sides of the still-wide river were lined with trees, which often bowed over the water, so that the area close to the banks seemed forever in shadow. Above the nearer left bank, birds glided and swooped in high numbers, but over the right bank there was noticeably less activity.

"We are sticking quite close to the left bank," noted Sarok. "Is there any particular reason for this?"

The breeze had slackened from that in the morning; it was now early afternoon. Miko rested an elbow on the tiller and only lightly held the sheets to the sail in one hand. He looked over at his new companion. "For a start, the river flows fastest in the middle, so it makes no sense to venture far out and increase resistance to our progress, but yes, as I suspect you sense, it is safer to this side."

The Price of Freedom Part II: Velasia

"I don't recall the geography of this land well from the maps I've seen, but… doesn't the forest cover much of the land to the south east?"

"It does. In fact, the forest stretches from here all the way to east coast and the southern extension of the Shield Mountains. The forest is many thousands of square kilometres of barely explored wilderness."

"So no one lives there? The yeltoi? The ganeroi?"

"No, no one. Although I promise you it is far from empty of life. It was seeded in the early days with all sorts of interesting creatures. And some of these have adapted well and thrived. A number of challenges were also sprinkled through the land by the great game designers of the past—the forerunners of Yasmina. Old stones and totems. Ruined temples. There is even rumoured to be a buried geode of rare gems. But the imported life has rather gotten away from us."

Sarok laughed. "What, it's got too tough for you? Seriously?"

Miko gave a wry smile. "I wouldn't say *too* tough. But from what I hear, talking to members of the high guilds, there are places deep in the forest that have not been accessed for decades, and those who have tried to reach them have been lost. Before com Durrel came on the scene, I expected that Reddas and I might be charged with some quest into the deep forest. And I'm still not sure which of the two tasks is the one to be most feared."

"But there is forest on the left bank, too."

"Sure, but it is far less extensive and fades to grasslands and moorlands to the west. And the yeltoi—or *men*, as we should get used to calling them while we are here—have built a number of small towns along the left bank, usually where other tributaries run into the Tesselac. The river itself acts as a natural barrier to the denizens from over there," he shrugged his head to indicate the eastern forest, "and whatever gets across tends to be dealt with by hunters."

"And don't the *men* ever venture into that forest to hunt?"

Miko shook his head slowly. "No, never. They call it the Forest of Shifting Shadows, or more commonly now the Forest of Ghosts."

"And the ganeroi… or should I say, *orcs*? What about them?"

"We can't say for certain, but we suspect not."

Sarok turned away from Miko and focused on the treeline across the water. He was silent for some minutes, just watching, attempting to catch movement, to sight anything emerging through the trees to drink, but he saw nothing save the green, brown and grey of trees, fully in leaf.

At last he turned back. "So, you say *creatures*. What sort of creatures? The wolf-like beasts we saw in Verano?"

"Not them, no. There might be some in the northern reaches, where the forest meets the Sundering Mountains, but we are more likely to encounter them in the Gap of Gelion—the narrow piece of land between the Copper and Iron Gates. Rather, there are some semi-aquatic creatures that live around the tributaries that run from the mountains through the Ghost Forest and join the Tesselac from the east, and these sometimes venture into the main river. We call them *sashai*, and they can be nasty. And there are several other species that live in the trees. Oh, and there are also things related to the orang-utan hybrid you saw in the animal pens."

"Holy shit!" Sarok remembered the chameleonic creature that was a breath away from taking out Sentain's eye, and particularly its calm, malevolent, amused expression. He wouldn't want to ever face one of those again, let alone a group of them. And what else was in there?

Miko saw Sarok's startled expression and nodded sagely. "But I think it best if we refrain from talking about these things. We are unlikely to meet these creatures, and I wouldn't want to give you nightmares."

"You're too bloody late for that."

***

As light began to fade, Archaen hauled down the sail and steered the boat—moving under the stroke power of Reddas and Brutus—to the riverbank. She had spotted a break in the trees and a cleft in the bank between two large boulders.

The Price of Freedom Part II: Velasia

In the second boat, Elian Omdanan realised something was afoot when Miko came forwards to drop their sail before clambering back to his position facing the four rowers. He banked the tiller one way and the boat began to sweep the other. The Leaguer then called for the rowers to slow their strokes and—after a few more pulls—cease altogether. Omdanan brought his oar aboard and set it in the floor of the boat, then turned in time to see them slide neatly in beside the first boat. Reddas was waiting on the bank to catch the prow, and then a rope thrown by Miko, who was suddenly by Omdanan's side. Reddas took the rope and tied it off against the nearest tree.

Miko leapt onto the bank, paused to stretch his back and shoulders, then turned to address his crew. "Out, all. We'll camp here tonight. Take what you need and pull the oilskin over everything else."

"And what will we need?" wondered Sarok.

"Your sleeping cloaks and perhaps a long knife. I see Cousin En has already offloaded some supplies for our meal; we'll take from our stash tomorrow. Leave the mail and heavier weapons. We won't be attacked here."

Omdanan was first out, excited to step onto land and see a new place. He found a small clearing just back from the riverbank cleft, where perhaps half-a-dozen trees had been felled, and the trunks of these lay about in a rough circle. Sentain had already discovered that these made for useful seating. Even so, the other trees, with thick oval leaves, hunched in on them, leaving little space through which the darkening sky could be seen.

"Who made this place?" wondered Omdanan, to no one in particular.

Enabeth Archaen looked up from the centre of the clearing, where she was crouched, arranging kindling for a fire. "Yes, it is artificial. Probably scouts from Sorvik. We are still two or three days away from the area fished by the men of these parts."

Omdanan nodded at this, then continued his exploration. In the trunk of one tree he found the carving of a sword, which seemed to support Archaen's hypothesis. While the others settled themselves on the fallen logs, or looked among leather sacks for food, or helped gather wood for the fire that the Leaguer woman soon had going, Omdanan wandered off a way into the forest. The trees were dense, and by the time he had gone a hundred metres or so, the clearing was lost from view, with only a slight orange glow in one direction indicating its presence. Although he was confident of his sense of direction and woodcraft, he decided to go no further: this was in any case liable to be the furthest point from which they might be detected by others. After a moment's thought, he brought out his long knife and cut out a small piece of bark from the nearest tree, at eye level, to the side facing the camp. Then he slowly followed the circumference of a circle around their resting place, pausing at every third or fourth tree to make a similar guide mark.

He practised moving as quietly as he could, watching where he put his leather-booted feet, avoiding small twigs or old leaves that might crackle, instead treading on moss or softer ground. The light began to fade quickly now, so that he began to direct himself as much by feel as sight, and then he closed his eyes altogether to sharpen his other senses. He heard noise from the camp—muffled by the intervening trees, but ever-increasing as he tilted his head and really listened. And then he caught other sounds—softer, some closer, others further away. A gentle wind rippled through the canopy; insects thrummed and chirruped; a bird called from some distance away and was answered by another slightly closer-by. He heard scampering across leaves, and then a slight creaking of something moving in the branches of a nearby tree. Before long, Omdanan had a mental image of his immediate surroundings, almost as though he had a photograph in his head.

And then he sensed the scurrying creature getting closer. He dropped into a crouch and slowly slid his knife from its scabbard. The creature didn't know he was near. From the volume of sound and the way it rose and fell, Omdanan drew a picture in his mind of the size of the creature, and how it moved; he could *see* it, scuttling, pausing, raising up its head to see or smell, bowing to examine the tree litter, moving again. It was tempting, too tempting, and then easy, so very easy.

Several minutes later, Omdanan returned to the camp. He didn't try to mask his movements as he didn't want to startle anyone, and in fact, he made a point of being clumsy in how he moved. When he emerged into firelight, he found half the party alert and looking up in his direction.

Across the fire, Brutus smiled broadly at him: "There you are, mate. That must have been quite a shit."

Omdanan smiled gently back and waited for the others to notice what he now held, by long ears, dangling at his side.

Miko saw it first and laughed. "Cousin Elian, is that fresh game you have? Welcome, then! Come sit next to me. It's been one day, and already I tire of salted meat. Let me help you skin that beast."

As others called out praise, the young man felt his heart swell with pride.

Chapter 6

The next three days followed a similar pattern to the first since the party's departure from Sorvik. They progressed upriver by oar and sail (when the winds were agreeable), took lunch on their boats anchored by the left bank of the river, then late in the day pulled in to camp at a place where the trees were less thick and allowed better access to the interior of the forest. Each time, Omdanan disappeared into the trees, and twice he returned bearing game: on the first occasion, he delivered a couple of squirrel-like creatures, and on the second, a plump brown-and-gold bird. The young man had been apologetic and clearly annoyed with himself the one time he'd not been successful at supplementing their salt-and-smoke-preserved rations.

Just after lunch on the fifth day since leaving Sorvik, Enabeth Archaen spotted the first sign of intelligent life and drew Sentain's attention to it: "Look! A boat. Come this side."

Sentain was seated on the gunwale next to the steerswoman—a position he had taken for most of the journey. He felt somewhat embarrassed at being the only member of the party who never contributed to their progress, though the ever-competitive Reddas and Brutus assured him that they did not need substituting at the oars, and nor did Archaen at the tiller, while the woman also reassured him that his constant stream of questions was in no way annoying or distracting.

"Where? Oh, wait…" The young anthropologist stepped over the sheets to the sail and took position on Archaen's left hand side, closer to the riverbank. "I see. A small boat. There are two yelt… *men*. What are they doing?"

"Fishing. They use handlines, as their kin do on Omicra. They haven't developed fishing rods, and we have tried not to influence them too much, though we've obviously failed. Several of their towns are located among stone ruins laid down previously by our game designers, and they have picked up architectural hints from these. And we also introduced them to more efficient weaponry after their first encounter with orcs led to disaster."

Sentain was leaning forwards, trying to make out more details during their slow approach. "Why? What happened?"

"The orcs have developed all sorts of vicious tools for dispatching each other, and they are larger, stronger and much more bellicose than men. The result was slaughter. The men only had short throwing spears, knives, and no appreciable armour. We elves gifted them pikes, hardened leather armour and the concept of the phalanx. Now, when they have time to properly organise, they can compete with—and even beat—a significant force of orcs, as the orcs tend to rush on and fight as individuals."

"Like Roman Legions against barbarian hordes?"

"Just so."

Archaen steered them out towards the middle of the river, leaving the fishermen the channel nearest the bank. She peered back to the boat behind and raised a hand to gesture to Miko.

As they approached, Sentain hunched forwards, barely able to contain his excitement. He was able to make out two figures in the boat, which had no sail and was propelled by oars only. One of the figures leant over the bow, intent on the line looped around his hand, which he bobbed in the dark water, while the second sat up and observed them calmly. As they got closer, the seated figure raised a hand in acknowledgement, a gesture Archaen returned.

"They… they're human! My god, they're human!" Sentain could now clearly see the seated man. His skin was an olive-brown colour, and his head was remarkably human, with a long nose and ears and two eyes, while his upraised arm was topped by a hand with five digits.

Archaen was somewhat amused. "Yes, Irvan, but you know this. You've seen them before in the control room in Verano, and probably in infotainment broadcasts in Arakkan."

"Yes, but it's not the same as seeing them up close." Their boat passed the other craft, just ten-metres away. As they did so, the fishing man looked up and saw them too, his eyebrows (eyebrows!) arching in surprise, his mouth forming an 'O' of astonishment. "I mean, how is this possible?"

"Parallel evolution, I guess," answered Archaen. "Nature has found a solution to a particular problem that works, and she repeats it. After all, you have not shown the same amount of surprise at the trees around you, which are not trees that evolved on Earth, or the other creatures, from fish to birds, that are also highly similar to those on Terra."

"Still," Sentain switched position so he could look back at the curious fishermen, "the degree of similarity is astonishing. I mean, why not three eyes, or seven fingers on each hand, or a snout like a dog, or… or…?"

"I know, Irvan. Nature is often hard to comprehend. Do we all come from some common stock? Are we all part of some greater cosmic game being played by other beings—or gods—above and beyond us? I will say, though, that internally men and orcs are more different to us than externally. But I am not an anatomist, so I will leave that lecture to others."

"And their behaviour? What of that? They fish. Build towns. Farm. Trade? Do they play games? Are they monogamous? Do they have religion? What are their origin stories? What do they think of us—?"

"Stop, Irvan, stop!" Archaen laughed. "I fear you will have a meltdown!"

"But… but… there is so much to learn, to record. I need to… *blast*! I don't have my datapad. Do we have writing material? Can I get some?"

"Okay, enough now!" But the woman was still smiling. "I will tell you what I know. But you will be able to find out more soon enough. They don't travel far in their boats, so we must be close to one of their towns. In fact, I think the nearest is called Lissom, and it was a target in my mind as a stopover when we set off. We can't be more than an hour or two away. Can you restrain your enthusiasm that long?"

Sentain grinned. "Not really, but I guess I will have to."

The Price of Freedom Part II: Velasia

***

Over the next hour, the party passed several more fishing boats, each new one scrutinised fervently by the anthropologist. He had mentally already taken enough notes for a whole chapter in his newly planned work on the yeltoi of Omicra. The first hint of the approaching town, however, was unexpected, causing Enabeth Archaen to rise up from her seated position, crane her neck and frown. Sentain caught this: "What is it, Enabeth? A problem?" He turned to look in the direction of the woman's gaze.

"I thought I saw some smoke. Yes. Clearly. *There!*" Archaen pointed ahead and off to her left.

"I see it. Is that where the town is? A fire?"

"Let's find out." The woman tugged on the ropes she had in one hand and shifted the tiller, searching for the right angle to make best use of the wind. Then she called forwards to Reddas and Brutus: "Double time on the oars. Pull! Pull!"

Sentain looked behind, where he saw Sarok and Mandelson scrabbling for their oars. Miko had clearly seen the smoke too and was making best use of his resources.

A bend in the river lay between the lead boat and the column of smoke that rose into the pale blue afternoon sky. As they rounded this bend, Lissom came into view, appearing beyond the out-jutting trees from the left bank, and growing with each surge forwards caused by the strenuous efforts of the two giant men at the oars. The town was low, enclosed within walls, with no building more than two-stories high, and a pale brown colour from its wood construction—reminding Sentain of medieval settlements he'd seen drawn in old books from Earth. As they completed the bend, he noticed a further gap in the treeline to the left of the town, where a smaller tributary swept in to join the Tessellac. Half-a-dozen wooden piers jutted out into the tributary. Archaen moved the tiller to aim for these.

Sentain spotted the source of the smoke, near the righthand edge of the town. He saw a lick of orange flames in that direction, then noticed scurrying figures on a wharf along the Tessellac itself. As they got closer, the figures became clearer.

"It looks like they're forming a relay team," called Sentain. "They're passing buckets of water along the line to the fire… whoa!" Suddenly, a second spasm of flame shot up into the sky from a little left of the first. "There's another! What's going on?"

Archaen stepped into the heart of the boat. The wind had shifted as they'd passed the bend and was now against them. She grabbed the downhaul sheet and with a few swift pulls, lowered the sail. They were now entirely reliant on the oarsmen. Sentain looked behind and saw that Miko had already brought down his own sail. In spite of having four rowers instead of two, the other boat had gained only a few metres on their own.

The woman regained the tiller but continued to stand. With the sail gone, she was better able to appraise the scene in front of them.

"Two fires?" she muttered. Then she glanced at Sentain. "Irvan—do you remember your incantations?"

"What, oh, yeah, I guess. Oh!" And suddenly it occurred to him that he might be of use after all. Did he truly recall? He'd not had any chance to practise using the staff until now, and frankly he'd felt no inclination to try. It all seemed somehow absurd and even embarrassing—muttering spells! But he should have practised, not least because certain phrases were used to moderate whatever force he called forth, and so he'd have to be careful.

The second boat surged forwards and was suddenly beside them, the four at the oars putting every effort into their strokes. Archaen shouted across to Miko: "There are two fires."

"I see. It's unlikely to be a coincidence. I suggest we head for the newest fire. If there is any mischief, it will be nearer to there."

They were bearing down upon the piers at the mouth of the tributary. These were deserted, with the townsfolk's attention elsewhere.

"Oars up!" shouted Archaen, and then she tugged hard on the tiller, bringing the small boat about to the further side of the nearest pier. Sentain heard Miko shout his own instructions, aiming his boat for the near side of the same pier. Such was the momentum from Reddas and Brutus that, in spite of the countering river flow, their boat jerked and thudded into the pier, and then rode up onto the cleared sandy bank, grounded.

"Out now!" shouted Archaen. "Take up arms. Leave your mail—there is no time." She leapt onto the pier and lightly raced along it. Sentain watched dumbly for a couple of seconds, then roused himself, following after Reddas and Brutus—the latter grasping his huge mace in one hand. As he attained the pier, he was nearly jostled off of it by Sarok's party, sprinting past from their own boat. He then heard Miko call out:

"I'll secure the boats! Go on!"

Sentain hefted his staff onto his shoulder and followed Vuller, who was at the rear of the group ahead. He kept up easily, for he wasn't unfit. They cleared the cobbled harbourside and headed down one narrow street between rough wooden buildings. He caught sight of a woman holding a young child, standing in a doorway, looking towards the flames that could be glimpsed over the roofline of houses further down the street. She shrieked in surprise as the party passed and fell back into the darkened interior of her home.

Then they were out of the street and in a small square. Around a dozen of the locals rushed about, with a small clot of pike-bearing men in the centre, milling around one man who had a sword on a belt at his waist and a light studded helmet on his head. At the sight of the newcomers, several of the men shouted, and a couple began to lower their pikes. The leader looked around and gaped in surprise, raising both hands before him.

Enabeth Archaen drew to a halt several metres from this group, and the rest of the party formed up beside and behind her. Sentain arrived just after the first exchange of greetings.

"...started at the northern wall," the leader said, ashen-faced and appearing confused. Though he was the tallest of the party, he was still shorter than the Leaguer woman, and seemed like a child compared to Reddas and Brutus. "Now this one!" He gestured behind. "And screams were heard. I don't know... I don't understand... and now you are here... elves in Lissom!"

"We will help," said Archaen, speaking softly. "But first, tell me, have you seen any orcs around town in recent times?"

"Orcs! No! Never! We are too far away... aren't we?" he suddenly hunched and looked about nervously.

"Yet you are here, armed," growled Reddas. "Why aren't you helping to put out the flames?"

"Oh... the screams. Yes. Someone heard screams. We..." he waved a hand behind him and then ran out of energy to speak.

"They can't be this far south, can they, Mother?" asked Reddas. "But what else?"

"Let's go see, shall we?" Archaen turned from her son to address the leader of the men. "Continue your muster here and send others to put out the first fire. We will investigate the second."

"Yes... yes... thank you! Yamaga must have sent you. We are blessed." As he turned back to his pikemen, Archaen stalked off towards the second column of smoke.

They had not gone more than fifty metres down another cobbled street—flame ahead of them, with a crackling sound accompanying an acrid smell of burning wood—when they heard a shriek, and then a second of slightly lower pitch.

"There!" shouted Omdanan. Suddenly the young Meridian was in front, moving like a cat. He had his bow with him and an arrow already notched.

"Careful," cried Archaen. "Spread out. Keep close to the walls. If they are orcs, they don't use bows, but they do like spears."

The party did as instructed. Sentain found himself on the opposite side of the street to Archaen, behind Mandelson and Brutus, with Omdanan at their head.

Then the Meridian brought up his bow and let loose an arrow. Two figures had tried to cross the road, forty metres ahead, running in front of a burning house. The first was a small woman with long brown hair wearing a green dress; the second was a tall albino creature, dressed in black, with a hooked spear in one hand. Omdanan's arrow took the chasing creature in the shoulder and forced it to stumble and crash into the wooden building beside it.

The orc screamed in rage, and turned to face the party, bearing its long front teeth. Without waiting for instruction, Omdanan plucked a second arrow from his quiver, notched it, and shot the creature through its open mouth, pinning it to a door jamb of the building.

Reddas was already on the move and reached the impaled orc first. The heat was now significant, coming from a building two doors along the perpendicular street that capped off the one they were on. Seeing the creature was dead, he looked left and right. The woman had disappeared inside another house. There was nothing but flames to his right. To his left, Reddas ducked and raised his sword arm. The incoming spear deflected upwards and skipped off down the street. Reddas gave a roar and started to move in that direction, but while he had paused and crouched it gave the others a chance to catch him up. Archaen was there, and so was Mandelson. Sentain was the last to the T-junction: all he saw was his comrades' backs, and then a black sword with a silvered edge rise up, fall, rise, and fall. The second time it rose it was smeared red with blood.

Sentain stood back as the others moved forwards. There was little he could do with his magical staff at close quarters, and it was clear his help wasn't needed. There were more shrieks, and then, after a minute or so, silence. He could see the others down the street, some way ahead, ducking into houses, emerging, moving further. There were four corpses on the cobbled ground. Then Sentain noticed Mandelson strolling towards him, swirling her wickedly curved spear like the baton of a cheerleader from the past. She gave him a mirthless smile, and quietly declared: "Looks like we missed this one…"

The woman reversed her spear and thrust the spiked butt over Sentain's shoulder, missing his ear by a whisker. Something wet splashed onto the side of his face and over his shoulder, and then the spear was withdrawn and he heard something thump onto the cobbles. Reaching a hand to the goo on his ear, he turned around and then jumped backwards, startled: behind him, another of the albino creatures was sprawled, spitted through one eye. "Oh... *fuck*!"

***

"Now, Irvan!" cried Enabeth Archaen. "Show us your power!"

Sentain stood at the intersection of cobbled streets, directly across from the second fire, which had rapidly grown in the few minutes since the party's encounter with the group of orcs. Seven or eight of the wooden houses were aflame, including the one opposite—to which the first orc was affixed by an arrow. The heat was a fierce, invisible barrier that prevented him from getting any closer. Nevertheless, they had drawn a crowd: he was aware of a growing presence in the street behind them, but he could also see people filling the street away to his left, even hanging from second floor windows to have a look. But to his right—in the direction of the first fire—the street was empty, and black ash swirled in the air and floated to the ground.

He raised his staff, somewhat self-consciously. Which spell did he need? Perhaps he could blow the fire out? Wind!

He raised his staff and ensured the end was pointed towards the inferno: "*Bellasor-medazum-farax!*"

The staff vibrated as hidden technology excited the immediate molecules of air in just the right way, invisibly, seemingly miraculously. From the staff head, a wind began to emanate, which steadily grew, sweeping outwards in a growing cone of effect. The flames opposite were caught and forced away and back, from the vertical to a less acute angle, but they did not diminish and even seemed to intensify.

The Price of Freedom Part II: Velasia

Sentain repeated the phrase, more strongly this time: *"Bellasor-medazum-farax!"*

The wind grew slightly, and the flames flattened further, and now seemed more uncertain. Was it working? Did he need more? An image came to his mind of a birthday party when he was young, his family following the ancient tradition of putting candles on his cake for him to blow out. A vigorous huff would extinguish the flame, whereas a modest one would not—and indeed, would feed oxygen to the flame and cause it to spread. He changed up the incantation, as he had been instructed in the infocast in Verano: *"Bellazor-tritarium-farax!"*

And now the wind really blew, whistling and pounding. Tiles began to whip away from roof tops; a wooden sign hanging on an iron bracket flapped manically and then tore off and shot into the air and over the roofline. But the flames could not catch enough air to breathe. In the nearest two houses, the flames simply blew away, leaving trails of smoke. With the heat before him lessened, Sentain walked forwards and turned to his right, holding the staff before him. Once more he cried: *"Bellazor-tritarium-farax!"*

He continued down the street…

***

In the small square, the people of Lissom were hard at work, setting out tables and benches, and hoisting cauldrons over makeshift pits. Those not working stood around the edges, staring at the party of strangers, whispering and pointing excitedly.

Archaen stood next to a flushed Sentain, resting a hand upon his shoulder, facing the helmet-wearing man they had talked to previously, who had introduced himself as Rogrix, Mayor of Lissom. The man had already thanked them profusely and explained that he had ordered a communal feast in their honour, for which the woman had given thanks. However, Archaen was not yet satisfied that all was well: "… but are you sure we have them all? How did they get into town? Where did they come from?"

Light from a fire beneath the nearest cauldron, in which some form of stew was being readied, revealed beads of sweat on the man's dark face and wide pupils. "I have my men searching every house, and every cellar. If any have escaped your wrath, they will soon be uncovered."

"And how did they get through your defences in the first place?" wondered Miko, who had secured both boats before joining his colleagues just in time to see Sentain extinguish the last of the flames. "Or did you have none? We were not challenged when we arrived."

Rogrix looked at the man, who stood next to Archaen on the other side to the wizard. "No. No defences. Why should we post defences? This has never happened before. Orcs in Lissom? Never!"

At that moment, another man pushed through the crowd behind the mayor and came up to his ear, frantically whispering and all the time glancing wide-eyed at the party of elves opposite.

"Ah, is that so?" said Rogrix. Then he turned to face the newcomer: "Then you must check this. Follow the trail."

"What have you discovered?" asked Archaen.

"The town walls are made of timber. They are not high or thick or deep. The loam is soft. A hole has been found under the wall near to the first fire."

"Can I see?" Omdanan was suddenly at the shoulder of Miko. "I might be able to help trace their movements."

Miko grinned at this. He put an arm behind the young man's back and propelled him forwards. "I would take up this offer," said the Leaguer. "This is an elf of great skill and perception."

Rogrix nodded enthusiastically. "Yes! Thank you! Sir, please follow my man. He will lead you to the breach and take instruction from you. Kalla…" he turned back to the newcomer, "make this so."

The conversation paused, as the party watched Omdanan, with his bow looped over his shoulder, follow the shorter man away through the crowd. Archaen used the pause as a chance to address Miko: "I do not like this, Ryven. We are less than a week from Sorvik, and already we have come across orcs. Should we warn Bastian? How?"

"I think Bastian has many scouts and will know soon enough." Miko turned to address Rogrix: "Mayor, have you seen any other elves recently?"

"Not for two months, maybe three. The last were a pair from Sorvik. We have never had such a party as yours before… an ageless from Narvik…" he nodded towards Sarok, "a giant…" he indicated Brutus, "and… and… I don't know what is more astonishing, an actual wizard, or she who wields the Black Sword, for, yes, I recognise the blade from legend."

Archaen smiled gently and nodded in acknowledgement. "Yes, we are an unusual party. And these are unusual times. Can I therefore make a request? Could you send a boat downriver to Sorvik, to warn my kin of what has happened here?"

"For you—anything. Please, find a bench. Sit! We will celebrate our salvation and pay tribute to our dead, and I will arrange for your accommodation. The evening draws in, but I will have a boat made ready to leave downriver tomorrow morning at break of day."

The Mayor turned and scurried off.

***

The party ate well that night, and slept far better than they had the previous few nights, when they'd only had their sleeping cloaks for warmth.

Chapter 7

"How is the head of our *ageless from Narvik*?" Miko smirked at Narovy Sarok as the latter entered the common room of the inn, striding from the stairs that led to the upstairs sleeping chambers. "You seemed to like their homebrew well enough last night—as did your colleagues." The Leaguer gestured at Vuller and Brutus who sat at the table to either side of him, staring dolefully at breakfasts of old bread and sour yoghurt. Similar food was set on the table before the chair that the newcomer now took.

"My head is fine. I only pretended to drink out of politeness. These two," Sarok indicated his men, "would drink the contents of an old internal combustion engine, if that was all that was available." Then Sarok frowned. "But… what did you call me? Ageless…?"

"*Ageless from Narvik*. Do you not remember how you were referred to by their mayor yesterday?"

"Ah, that, yes. I wasn't sure who he was talking about. What did he mean? Why me?"

Miko gave a lop-sided grin and rasped his chin. "Something you have that we don't."

"The beard?"

"You must have noticed that facial hair isn't common amongst us. In Arakkan. In Verano. But the men of the High Guild of the Silver Swan currently follow this fad."

"Right. Hence *Narvik*. And *ageless*?"

"You know the quality of our regenerative biotech, which far exceeds yours in the Confederation. While the men of this land show signs of ageing, we, the elves, do not. Indeed, Enabeth, Bastian and I, and many others in the ports, are considerably older than even the most decrepit ancient of their race. They also refer to us as *the childless*, usually behind our backs, as they have never yet seen one of our children and they wonder whether these exist. I hear one myth they have about us is that we emerge from the sea fully formed and mature, which come to think of it, is not far from the truth. How is the breakfast?" He nodded at the food set before Sarok's place.

Sarok spooned a mouthful of the yoghurt, his nose wrinkled, then he shrugged. "Tolerable. I've had worse. I'm surprised you can stomach it, or the dried rations we've been eating, given your upbringing in luxury."

Miko laughed. "Yes, we eat well when we can, but we eat bad when that is *right*. If you understand what I mean. To complain would be indecent, effete, un-stoic." He tore off a piece of bread from a central platter and watched as a small insect fell to the table. Winking at his comrades, he stunned the creature with a brisk slap on the table, then plucked it up and tossed it into his mouth. "Extra protein. Delicious!"

"And speaking of rations… where is our source of fresh game? Now I think on it, did anyone see him at the feast?"

"You mean Elian?" croaked Vuller. "Nope. I haven't seen him since he left with that guard yesterday."

"Me neither," growled Brutus. "But knowing him, he probably copped off with one of the locals."

Miko laughed again. "He is a man of many talents. Perhaps he'll soon walk down the stairs, with a maiden on each arm. And talking of maidens," he lowered his voice and leant in conspiratorially, "here comes Mandelson, looking as cheerful as ever."

"She's as much a maiden as Vuller," observed Brutus, also quietly.

"You don't find her attractive?" mused Miko.

"Oh, yeah. Attractive like a hungry tigress. Or a female praying mantis. You know—the bug that eats its mate's head after they've shagged. I suspect she does the same."

Sarok nudged his giant companion a warning, and spoke more loudly: "Morning, Mandelson. Grab a chair. Our hosts have laid out a breakfast of sorts, though it's poor fare compared to what they fed us last night."

The woman considered the party of men wordlessly, nodded, then sauntered over to another table some distance away, on which a jug of milk was set out, with a platter of bread and cheese.

Sentain was last down the stairs, five minutes later. He took a table between the men and the sole woman. When Enabeth Archaen and her son arrived they came through the front door.

"Cousin En," called Miko. "I was certain you wouldn't be the last to rise. What news?"

Archaen sauntered over, Reddas tall at her shoulder. "We have been speaking with the mayor. The hole under the fence has now been filled and the walls are manned. It seems the orcs were only intent on causing mischief and using the disruption to scavenge some… *food*. We stopped them carrying off any of the townsfolk, though two died in the flames and two more were cut down when they got in the way of the orcs." The woman looked about the room. "Are we almost ready to be off? I'm concerned the orcs have come so far south. We'd better not tarry."

Sarok pushed his chair back from the table. "That is all very well, but we are one short. Omdanan isn't here."

As though on cue, the front door opened once more and Omdanan strolled in. His hair was tousled and his leathers were dirty, as was his face. His bow was looped across his chest and over his back. He faltered as all eyes turned towards him. "Ah, I saw… one of the people said… she said you were here… and I…"

Brutus roared with laughter. "*She?* You've been at it again! Come, tell us what the local flavour tastes like. I assume the women have the same apparatus down below as us elves?"

Omdanan smiled and looked away. "Ah, no. I have not been *there*. I just got back from beyond the walls."

"Take a seat, lad," said Sarok. "You missed the feast. You've not slept?"

The Archaens were suddenly at the young man's side, guiding him to the table where Sentain sat, and all three pulled out chairs.

Enabeth Archaen was concerned. "Elian, where did you go? What did you find?"

Reddas poured the man a tankard of milk and pushed it towards him. Omdanan smiled a thanks and took a long drink. When he set the tankard down, he again found all eyes on him, watching expectantly.

"Oh. I, er, went with their guard to see the breach. Then I went through to the other side. The guard didn't fancy joining me, but I thought it would be best to see how the orcs got there, so I followed their trail as best I could."

"All this time?" said Sarok. "You must have followed it far."

"I did. There is an area of open grassland between the wall where they entered town and the edge of the forest. They took the shortest route. Not a problem with no guards on the walls. Their path in the forest was easy to follow at first. They are clumsy creatures, hacking everything in their path. But then the light began to fade, and under the trees it was dark. I had to move more slowly, and let my eyes acclimatise. I would have lost their trail, but then I noticed there was a faint bioluminescence, here and there, where they had bruised certain plants, so I was able to keep going."

"The forest is hard going," noted Archaen. "Surely they did not take this path for long?"

Omdanan gave a brief shake of the head. "No, not long. Four or five kilometres. Their trail came out to the river. I found the place where they landed. Their campsite was a mess. And one of their boats was still there."

"One?" Archaen clearly understood the implication. "*Still* there? You mean, they came by more than one?"

"Yes. They had two small boats. There was clear sign in the mud of two boats hauled onto land, and one was missing."

"So only part of their group stayed and conducted the raid," said Sarok. "The rest are still at large?"

"No. I don't think that's what happened. I checked the margins of the camp and found a second trail. A much fainter one. Probably made by one or two orcs rather than half-a-dozen. Well, I couldn't follow the boat, as that had gone, but I was able to follow the second trail, though it was difficult, and I went wrong a few times." Omdanan looked slightly embarrassed at this admission.

Archaen looked severe. "And it came back to the town?"

"Yes. I followed it to a place by the wall a little further along from the second fire and the place where we fought them."

"So one or two escaped," nodded Sarok, "and made it over the wall and back to their boat, then sailed or rowed away."

Archaen glanced over to Sentain, who had been quiet throughout. "And that might mean that news of our intervention is making its way to com Durrel as we speak, and in particular, news of the feats of our very own wizard."

"Can we catch up with the orcs?" asked Sarok. "They can't have more than twelve hours start on us."

"Also, there are other towns en route," noted Miko. "They won't be able to boldly sail past them. So… did they travel all the way by boat, or did they join the Tessellac between Lissom and… Tolvac? Or Hustem?"

"Whether we can catch them or not," said Archaen, "this confirms our need for speed. If they pass their news back to com Durrel, he will know that we have come for him at last, as he knows there are several staffs, and only one of these can have been responsible for the magic used here in Lissom."

Sarok was the first to rise. "Well, I have eaten. Omdanan—you'll have to eat on the boat. Let's grab our gear and move."

The rest of the party began to rise. As they did so, Reddas slapped Omdanan on the back in acknowledgement of his efforts, while Enabeth Archaen smiled and nodded her own gratitude to the young man.

The Price of Freedom Part II: Velasia

***

They were back on the river, with Lissom three hours behind them. During this time, they made only limited progress: the winds were contrary and the weather, which had been largely fine for their journey, now seemed as though it was about to turn. The clouds above were blacker and seemed more ominous to Sentain than any that had previously overborne them.

In exasperation, Archaen at last gave in to the inevitable. She hauled down the sail and returned to the tiller. As usual, Sentain was perched on a gunwale to one side, cradling his staff. "I'm sorry, Irvan," said the woman, "but I think I'm going to need you to exert yourself. Come take an oar opposite me. We have been lazy too long."

Sentain smiled. "You mean, I have been lazy—you have been working the sail. But I don't mind some exercise—just don't expect me to match the efforts of Reddas and Brutus!" After his labours in Lissom, Sarok had wondered why Sentain couldn't use his magic to help propel the boats, but it was soon apparent that the staff was a bludgeon not a fine instrument, and his first attempt had nearly blown the boat over… and so muscle power it now had to be.

The pair settled into place on the near side of the mast, putting their oars into rowlocks. Reddas and Brutus paused until the new rowers managed to synchronise their strokes—with the second boat catching them up and momentarily pulling alongside them—then the two large men matched their tempo to those whose backs were facing them. Their boat pulled in front of the other once more.

No one spoke for some minutes, as the four rowers concentrated on their work. Then Archaen, still facing the second boat, broke the silence. "So, Irvan. Now you have met both alien races. What do you think?"

Sentain didn't respond immediately as he was caught mid-stroke. He finished, exhaled, and raised the oar to dip into the water once more. "The yeltoi are… astonishingly human." He pulled again, panted, and missed the chance to speak on his next cycle.

Archaen laughed lightly. She timed her words perfectly between bouts of exertion: "Never mind Irvan… We'll pause to eat in an hour… we can talk then…"

By the time Archaen did call a halt, Sentain was breathing heavily, and his arms and thighs ached. He fell backwards into the boat and waved a hand to signal to the woman that he was fine and just needed to recover.

A couple of minutes later, Archaen regained her seat, having retrieved some salted meat and bread from a sack at the aft of the boat. She handed some to Sentain.

"Better now?"

"I should have made more effort to exercise at Arakkan. My rugby teammates on Ustaria would be laughing their asses off if they could see me now."

"It'll be hard today. You'll ache tonight. But you'll gradually get used to it."

"What about you? It's the first time you have rowed for some time too."

The woman gave a gentle smile. "True. But I have not been remiss in exercising since we parted in Verano. And in any case, my muscles have certain gene-engineered advantages. Twitch response. Lactic acid build up and recovery. Other things. It's not really fair."

"Well it certainly wasn't fair on the orcs in Lissom. I didn't really see what happened, but I saw your sword was red." Sentain frowned. "Does it… does it not bother you? What you did… what you had to do… to the orcs?"

Archaen suddenly looked severe, reminding Sentain of the business-like and humourless Jessica Warsteiner he had first met. "You got a first glimpse of them, Irvan, but you have really seen nothing. An ugly creature with a fierce expression. Elian shot the one chasing the woman. Had we been a few seconds later, you would have been shocked at what would have transpired. And even that is nothing compared to what would have happened if it had caught the woman and managed to smuggle her back to its camp."

"What would have happened? Back in Lissom you mentioned food. They eat the yeltoi?"

"Mother Nature has not been kind to them. They evolved in a harsh environment with scarce food, yet they breed rapidly, in a kind of arms race, attempting to flood the gene pool with their own offspring at the cost of the offspring of the rest of their kind. And when times are hard and there is no other food, they eat their own children."

"Their own children!"

Archaen nodded. "So to them, the yeltoi are simply food. It doesn't matter that they are thinking, feeling beings. Just food. And us too. And they cannot be reasoned with: this is a lust that is deep within them. Instinctively so."

"But surely, the ones you brought from Omicra are now in a better, richer environment? Surely they will quickly adapt? Change?"

"Perhaps in time, but so far there is no sign of it. All that has happened is that more of their young now survive, which means there are more mouths to feed, which means… you can work it out. It is only really natural barriers that have stopped them from completely flooding the land. But population pressures keep pushing and pushing, and the men here are hard-pressed to fight them off. Com Durrel's magic is liable to prove a tipping point."

"But you are here. Leaguers. Elves. You can stop them, surely?"

"It's become more and more difficult. I know you disapprove of this particular game we play, here, in Velasia. But what else would you have us do? Send an army with guns to annihilate them? Catch them and return them to Omicra, where they will tear each other apart?"

"I don't know. I just feel there ought to be another way. A better way."

Archaen leant forwards to pat him on the thigh. "And when you think of what that is, you can let us know. In the meantime, the yeltoi are here, and have made a good home—a better one than they had on Omicra. They rely on us, and we will not let them down." She gave an ironic smile. "So you see, Irvan, we are not all bad. Eat up. It'll soon be time to exercise some more."

***

Three more days passed. It rained intermittently, and occasionally heavily. The wind was inconstant, so the party rarely had the assistance of their sails. To give the rowers a break, pairs staggered their rest periods—even Reddas and Brutus—while in the second boat, Miko spelled individuals, so that one occasionally got a longer break. The second boat also had the advantage of having its extra person able to keep them on course via its tiller, whereas those in the lead boat had to rely on well-synchronised strokes to keep them travelling in a straight line, with occasional adjustments made through those on one side pausing so that those on the other might put in an extra stroke to tug them over to port or starboard.

In the second boat, Sarok had his turn at the tiller, giving him the advantage of being the only one able to clearly see where they were going and what was happening around them. By this time, the narrowing river was no more than eighty metres across, and the furthest bank began to seem ominously close. Sarok found himself spending more and more time watching the right bank, where the line of trees seemed somehow darker and more forbidding than on the nearer left bank. Occasionally—between or over the *splash* of oars into water—unnerving sounds carried from the forest: a sudden crash among the trees, or a shriek from some unknown creature. Once, when they wandered further over into the centre of the flow at a bend in the river, Sarok thought he saw a dark figure on the far bank, a shadow between two trees, which slowly extended a long arm and human-like hand to seemingly beckon them over. Then the vision was gone, and Sarok was unsure whether it had been an arm or simply a twisted branch.

But Sarok *was* sure of what he saw a short time later. He called out to his crew, loud enough so that those in the lead craft might also hear: "Boat ahead! Fifty metres. Near bank." The call unsettled the rowers, who ceased their endeavours in a disorganised manner, turning to look behind and to their right. "Do you want to check it out?" continued Sarok.

Enabeth Archaen shouted back: "Yes. Moor up to either side. Be alert."

They were soon positioned a few metres off the bank, one boat forwards of the beached boat, one aft, both held in the shallows by their anchors.

"Elian," called Archaen, "is it the orc boat?"

"Yes. It's the same size and style as the other."

"We are a half-day at most from Tolvac," cried Miko. "I don't know where they got the boats from, or how they got them here, but they are not likely to have travelled all the way down the Tesselac past the river towns."

"Another tributary joins the Tesselac at Tolvac," mused Archaen. "The *Spiris*. That has its origins in the mountains to the north. Perhaps they rowed down that and passed the town at night?"

"Perhaps. But why not return the same way now?"

The woman stood tall, scrutinising the area around the beached boat—set in a muddy clearing of perhaps twenty square metres, surrounded by forest—looking for movement. Seeing nothing, she turned to look up river, calculating. At last, she ventured: "Maybe they worked out that if they continued they would pass Tolvac in daylight, so they pulled up here instead?"

"To wait or decamp?" asked Miko. "Are they lurking in the trees, ready to reclaim their boat later, or have they abandoned it and taken to foot?"

"There's only one way to find out," Sarok intervened. "We need to look."

"Carefully then," called the woman. "And only some. The rest stay in the boats." She quickly appraised the two crews. "Reddas, Elian, Sarok... and me. Come then."

The four identified members of the party slid into the water, which was no more than waist deep, all armed with spears taken from the floors of their boats. Shortly after, they cautiously began to wade ashore, Mandelson retrieved her own curve-bladed spear and—ignoring Miko's hiss of disapproval—followed.

Elian was first ashore. He stalked past the boat, scanning the trees, then the ground, then the trees again. He crouched and waited for the others. Sarok was soon at his shoulder, though Enabeth Archaen and Reddas deliberately spread to the furthest edges of the small clearing, also moving in a crouch. Mandelson, however, ignored the rest and walked upright through the clearing to beneath the first fringe of trees. Daylight speckled the forest floor, pushing through gaps in the trees' foliage, giving a reasonable field of view.

"Come out, you fuckers!" Mandelson called. "Come out, come out! I have a gift for you!" She laughed and twirled her spear—but there was no response.

The others slowly moved forwards. Sarok was closest and soon at the woman's shoulder. "What the fuck do you think you're doing, Mandelson? This isn't a game."

"Isn't it?" The woman glanced at the man, coolly. "I thought it was." Then she spoke more loudly, addressing the forest again. "Come on! I'm bored! Time to play!"

"Enough!" Enabeth Archaen arrived. She put a firm hand on the other woman's shoulder.

"Take your hand away," said Mandelson, icily, "or I'll cut it off."

At that, Archaen suddenly *moved*. She slid the offending hand back onto her spear's shaft, then swept this at the other's legs. Mandelson was surprised and unbalanced. Archaen's spear haft then took her in the side of the knee, at which she crumpled facedown into the forest litter. As Mandelson tried to rise, Archaen used the haft again to thump her in the back between the shoulder blades, forcing her down once more and causing her own spear to fly from her hand.

"I said *enough*!"

For a moment, no one moved. On the ground, Mandelson tensed… and then slowly relaxed. She waited for the other to step away. Then she slowly got to her feet, still looking forwards into the forest. Without a word she took two steps and casually picked up her fallen weapon. Then she slowly turned to view her attacker and the rest of the team—who all stared at her warily. And she smiled. "You are no fun." She sauntered back towards the boats, passing between Sarok and Archaen, who half-turned and stepped away instinctively, ready for any response… though there was none. Mandelson reached the water and waded back to her own boat, where Miko looked on in fury.

At last, Sarok noted: "Well, if they are here somewhere, they certainly now know we are here too."

"They're not here," said Archaen, her mouth set firm. "At least Mandelson has fast-forwarded this play. But you need to control her better."

"Me? Control her?" Sarok laughed, then turned and followed Mandelson back to the boat.

Omdanan quickly confirmed that there were no recent signs of activity, then Reddas took delight in smashing a hole in the bottom of the lounging craft, rendering it useless.

Archaen was the last to clamber aboard her boat where Sentain, seeing her expression, decided it was best not to speak to her for some time.

***

They were closer to Tolvac than Miko had estimated, the town coming into view three hours later—and only half an hour after the party had paused for a rapidly taken lunch. They had seen no fishing boats during that time, although they now noticed a clutch of these in the tributary—the Siris—that flowed into the Tessellac from the left.

Sentain paused when Vuller—at the tiller of the other boat—called out his sighting. He turned to look, then turned back to Archaen, who had barely said a word since the incident at the orc boat. "Are we going to stop? Perhaps we could have a rest, and maybe check for information?"

"No. We will go on. It is too early to stop, and I still worry about how far south the orcs are roving." However, she also shipped her oar, then stood up and bellowed to the other boat: "Ryven—we go on."

The other man didn't turn around but raised one arm in acknowledgement.

"Back to the oars, Irvan. Brutus and Reddas too."

Sentain groaned but did as he was told. He shortly saw more, once they drew parallel to the town. This seemed to be smaller than Lissom, with just two jetties protruding into the main river. Turning right he saw a group of children, jumping up and down, pointing and waving. He lifted a hand to wave back, but then his oar snagged in the water and he had to quickly grasp it again.

Archaen looked aside at him and smiled for the first time in hours. "Never mind, Irvan…" Stroke. "There is nothing of particular interest here…" Stroke. "Except for a temple to Yamaga, their god…"

Sentain groaned again. "Now you are… teasing me." Stroke. "You know how interested I am…" Stroke. "In primitive peoples' religions…"

"After what you did in Lissom… they might soon have a new god… and then you will have to study… yourself."

"What a thought!"

***

That evening, they pulled into the left riverbank some kilometres north of Tolvac. As the light was waning and they'd seen no ready spot to land, they chose a less-than-ideal place where the trees seemed slightly thinner, and then they set Brutus loose with his huge axe. The giant man waded to the shore and started hewing at the trees, which split apart under his onslaught. From the boats, Vuller and Reddas yelled out encouragement. After some minutes, Brutus paused and swept away the resultant kindling, having created a six metre wide space through which the party could access the slightly less dense forest beyond the riverside barrier. The two boats were then tied to still-surviving trunks to either side of the new clearing, and the rest of the party came ashore.

Miko made a fire, and they ate rations as the last of the light faded, seated on the ground or on felled trees. Not long after, Omdanan rose, checked the knife at his belt, and then tested the drawstring of his bow.

"Off to hunt, Elian?" asked Miko.

The young man smiled shyly. "I get nervous staying in a confined space. I need to know what lies beyond the boundaries. And if I spot some game, I will try to take it."

Mandelson rose from her spot at the edge of the circle of firelight. "In that case, I will join you. I want to see your technique."

"Ah… okay." Omdanan was clearly at a loss. He looked around at the others, whose faces showed surprise or amusement or, in the case of Enabeth Archaen, concern. "But… you must tread softly."

"I think you'll be surprised at how quietly I can move. Do not worry about me."

Omdanan smiled uncertainly, nodded, and then headed off into the forest without another word. Mandelson stalked after him.

After a judicious wait to ensure the duo had truly left, Sarok re-adjusted his posture and looked at Enabeth Archaen, who sat on a tree stump to his right. Softly, he noted: "Mandelson seems to be taking her earlier besting remarkably well. I am surprised. But I would watch my back if I were you, Ms Archaen. She has a vengeful personality."

"I have sensed this," replied Archaen, cautiously. "But how did you acquire such a follower?"

"In truth, I don't know. Vuller and Brutus know more about her than I do."

"Not me, Boss," said Vuller. "The first time I ever saw her was at the spaceport, on our return to Corvus."

"And I only met her when we took ship from Corvus," said Brutus.

Sarok frowned. "I thought you two knew her better. Then she must have been recruited by Cape. He was with her and Martinus at the spaceport. He never mentioned her—but then I suppose he had no need to. I once had many followers and I didn't know them all. Perhaps I should have made a greater effort to evaluate those I've been paying."

"But what do you know of her now?" asked Archaen. "You must have learnt something over the past few months. She's been with you since before Ghuraj."

Sarok's frown deepened. "I still know little. She is not one for conversation. Violence, *yes*, talking, *no*. All I know, is that she claims she was orphaned young and is genetically enhanced."

"That makes sense," said Archaen. "The way she moves. Her strength at the oars. The speed and skill she showed at Lissom. She is more like one of us than someone from the Confederation."

"Aside from that," Sarok continued, "I get a sense she wants to be gone from here and to return to Corvus. I don't understand why: she seems to have nothing to go back to."

"Nothing that we know of," hinted Vuller, darkly. "But yeah, Boss, I get that sense too. She wants out of here as soon as possible."

Sarok looked at the flames of the fire, and suddenly smiled. He looked back at Archaen. "Perhaps I now understand her restraint. Harming you, Ms Archaen, is not likely to expedite our return home. I suspect you are safe—at least for now."

When Omdanan and Mandelson returned an hour or two later, it was to find Sarok, Miko and Archaen clustered around a parchment map that Bastian had provided in Sorvik, while Brutus, Vuller and Reddas sat a short distance away, quietly talking and laughing. Sentain was already wrapped in his cloak, fast asleep. The others ceased their various conversations and looked up at the returnees. Omdanan held four dead rabbit-like creatures by the ears.

"More success!" cried Miko. "Your best haul yet."

"Ah, yes, well, I only got one of them. Ms Mandelson got the rest."

The woman passed an inscrutable gaze over the others, pausing when she got to Enabeth Archaen. Then she gave a sly smile, hefted her spear onto her shoulder and—reversing it so that the sharpened butt was facing forwards—she threw it into the felled tree trunk where she had already laid out her sleeping cloak. The spear thudded into the wood and quivered. Without a word, she stalked over to her pitch.

Chapter 8

Two more days had passed. During this time, the wind had picked up and was occasionally useful, even though it also brought rain. In the distance, the Sundering Mountains became more than just a smudge on the horizon—the chain's increasing height and definition providing a tangible sign of their progress. Meanwhile, the Tessellac continued to narrow and was now only fifty to sixty metres wide.

Enabeth Archaen was at the tiller with Irvan Sentain sat off to her side, spared from having to row by the steady south-westerly breeze that had diverted his partner to sailing duties.

"Is Hustem where Bastian said he would direct his scouts?" asked Sentain.

"It is."

"And we're close, right?"

"Yes. With luck, we'll reach it well before dark. But we may see life before then. There should be a small fishing community between us and there."

"I don't remember that from Bastian's map."

Archaen gave a small shrug. "It is there, but not named. I understand it's a temporary station for a few boats that lies opposite to where the Blackflood joins the Tessellac. The Blackflood originates in the mountains and passes through the Shadow Forest: it seems to bring lots of nutrients with it and so the fishing is better than around Hustem—which itself lies on the confluence of the Everbright River and the Tessellac."

"So, this camp isn't counted as one of the Rivertowns?"

"No. Officially, only Hustem, Tolvac and Lissom are now counted as these."

"*Now?* There's nothing on the river beyond Hustem?"

The woman gently shook her head. "There was a fourth Rivertown further north—a small settlement called Trastere—but that was abandoned twenty,

twenty-five years ago, when the orcs became too numerous and posed a significant threat to the people there."

"So Hustem is the edge of the universe, so to speak. The closest to the mountains and the Copper Gates?"

Archaen was momentarily distracted by a sudden gust and had to tug on a rope to keep the sail taut. "Closest? No. Barak-on-Wold is nearer, but it's still some distance to the north-west and sits by a small lake on a hill. It might have been abandoned too, but the Masters of Ranvik and Sorvik encouraged the people to stay, and there is a small detachment of our people there—lending tactical, material, and moral support."

"And at the gate itself?"

"No. It is just a path through the mountains—quite barren, with little around to sustain a population. And it's now somewhat precarious, although the orcs don't actually guard it for the same reason that men don't: there's nothing around to eat."

Satisfied for now, Sentain settled back and watched the landscape slowly move by. The forest on the right crowded the bank, like too many people in too small a space, holding onto each other and trying to prevent those on the outside from toppling over. He tried not to look that way, as there was an eerie, malignant feel to the trees, and in fact he had moved to sit to Archaen's right-hand side a day earlier to avoid this perspective. To the left, though the trees also crowded the bank, these seemed less-tightly packed and somehow cheerier—although Sentain suspected it was just his mind playing tricks and reinforcing what he had been told: left bank good, right bank bad.

A short time later, it was Sentain who was the first to notice the change in features—a difference in the forest's texture ahead and to the left. Peering intently, he thought he could make out an arc of brown and black, bereft of the green-grey of tree leaves. Buildings? And then he spotted something bobbing on the water several hundred metres ahead.

"Boat in the water, Enabeth. And I think I see the camp."

The sail must have obscured the woman's view, sitting as she was high at the middle of the stern. She stood up and tried to look left and right, then tilted the tiller to change their angle of advance one way then the other. "Yes, the mouth of the Blackflood is ahead to the right, and the camp is to the left. But I don't see the boat."

Sentain was able to crouch down to look under the sail, although the rising and falling oar of Reddas, who sat on that side, made viewing difficult. "Yes, it is there. And there's a second. They're small, but I can't see anyone onboard."

Archaen frowned, but said nothing at first. Then she called: "Slow on the oars. Half-time."

Reddas and Brutus obeyed, and shortly the second boat came close, Miko steering it to their right, further out into the current. Archaen looked back and waited until the other boat was almost level and she could easily speak to Miko.

"Problem?" called the other steersman.

"Maybe. Boats dead in the water." She began to haul down the sail. Miko took the hint and did the same. Soon, those at the back of the boats had much better views over the slow-acting rowers, who seemed to be getting nervous about what was ahead and therefore at their backs.

Then the lead boat groaned and twisted.

"Fuck!" cursed Brutus, whose oar had struck something submerged. The effect was to jag the boat to the right and cause Archaen to stagger. "I hit something," said the giant man. "A snag?"

"Dead slow!" called Archaen.

Brutus and Reddas raised their oars. In the second boat, the others faltered, seemingly unsure whether the instruction was meant for them too.

The first of the two small boats was perhaps sixty metres ahead, seemingly static in the flow, anchored in position. Overhead, the clouds were dirty grey and bulbous, with spots of moisture in the air, but no rain at the moment. The world was silent, save for the occasional creak and mutter of the stressed timbers of the party's own boats.

"I don't see anyone at all," muttered Sentain. "No one in the boats, and no one ashore."

The camp to their left was slowly becoming clear: it seemed to comprise a single longhouse, two stories high, with a wooden pier along the river front and a couple of jetties. Sentain noticed that there were three more boats tied up at the wooden dock, of similar size and design to those in the river.

"We'll dock," announced Archaen. "But let's check the nearer boat first. Slow on the oars."

The rowers followed instruction. To the complaining of wood in the craft was now added the soft splashing of oars as these gently dipped into the water. Then Sentain heard another splash ahead. He glanced at Archaen and saw that she had also noticed the disturbance and was looking at the same spot. Then she looked down at him, frowned, and gave a single abrupt shake of the head. Sentain returned his gaze ahead but saw nothing more and the sound didn't repeat.

They approached the boat from both sides, coasting the last few metres. Miko's boat swept around from the right, advantaged by an extra stroke, with Sarok standing to get a better look. Sentain watched the crime boss take up his oar so he could use the head to snare the small vessel and pull it closer.

"Got it! Hold still." Sarok manipulated the boat nearer until he could look within. "Yep, empty, except… fuck!"

"What is it?" asked Archaen.

"The bottom of the boat… it's full of blood. Let me…" Sarok leant over and used his oar's head as a crude dipstick, withdrawing it for consideration. Then he gave a whistle. "About two centimetres deep. Whoever was here lost a lot of blood. And the gunwale is smeared with the stuff."

"Okay. Leave it," commanded Archaen. "Let's dock. Everyone keep an eye out and beware the water."

It was but a few strokes from here to the wooden jetty. As they got close, Archaen was first to leap onto the platform, holding a rope that she used to secure the boat in place, avoiding the other craft already moored. A few metres along,

Miko followed her lead. Then the rest of the party cautiously rose and stepped ashore.

By now, Enabeth Archaen had drawn her black sword. Others took this as a cue to find and heft their own weapons; Sentain held his staff tight to his chest. The woman looked back at the group. "Elian—come with me. Ryven—watch the water."

The other Leaguer nodded, knowingly. As Archaen and Omdanan approached the long covered porch that ran along the front of the house, Miko addressed the others: "Everyone—step back from the water and watch carefully. I suspect the risk is there and not behind us."

Sentain waited nervously with the others. From here, he could see the two local boats just forty metres from the bank: the one Sarok had inspected, and the other a little way upriver of it. Directly across from him, the opposite bank opened up to reveal the outflow of the Blackflood, perhaps thirty metres wide, with trees crowding either bank. The Tesselac was a brownish colour above the confluence, but where the Blackflood merged with it, the water's colour changed and darkened, almost to black, and then, downriver past the join, it gradually lightened again. As he scanned the waters, a spear of sunlight made it through the thick clouds and appeared to glint off something in the midst of the black pool. But then the cloud again covered the sun, and the reflection disappeared. Sentain strained his eyes but could make out nothing more.

Archaen and Omdanan were soon back. Sentain heard footsteps on the boards and the swish of a sword being sheathed. He looked around.

Miko had already closed the gap to the returnees. "Anything?"

"No. Deserted. The top floor is a dormitory, but there is little evidence of activity. There are some messy sleeping pallets at one end, and in the kitchen area there is an unwashed cauldron and fish bones in the litter. I don't think there were many here—perhaps just those on the two boats."

Miko nodded. "That is fortunate."

"Or unfortunate. It might be that the low numbers encouraged the attack."

"Attack?" Sarok, as ever, had moved close to the party leaders. "By what? Not orcs, no?"

Archaen assented. "Orcs would have attacked from the land side. Something dragged the fishermen into the water."

"Something? You're being very cagy. Say more."

Archaen shook her head. "Not here. Not now. Let's just say that sometimes creatures come down the Blackflood from the forest. They could be out there, in the depths, watching us. They are not likely to leave their hiding place, and I suspect we are too large a party to accost. Hustem is not far. We can talk more there and alert the townsfolk as to the likely fate of their fishermen. To the boats, quick. And don't lean over the sides."

***

Two hours later, the party arrived at Hustem. The town was the biggest of the three Rivertowns, possessing a sizeable dock. Here, they found space to moor just along from a couple of grain barges that had come down the Everbright from the fertile hinterlands beyond the forest. Further along the dock, a third ship of similar size was currently the main focus of the denizens' attention as it was in the midst of being loaded up with barrels of fish.

Nevertheless, the group's arrival didn't go unnoticed, and as they disembarked they were approached by a trio of nervous-looking men, two of whom held spears. The leader of this party—who had a shock of spiky black hair and a particularly long nose—had a sword sheathed at his waist, on which he rested one hand.

"Greetings to you all! Greetings!" The leader bustled up to Miko, who was nearest. "I am the master of the docks. You are of course welcome to tie-up, though for the records, I am required to note your names and status. I have worked here many years and have seen none of you before, so forgive my impertinence."

"There is nothing to forgive." Miko smiled and bowed his head respectfully. He towered over the three men, who were typical of their race, being slightly shorter than Narovy Sarok, who was the shortest of their own party. "We are from Sorvik, travelling upriver to gather information for the master of that place. We are led by Enabeth Archaen of the High Guild of Black Lightning. Cousin En?"

The woman moved to the front of the party to stand beside her kin. "Greetings to you, master of the docks. Is there anything more you need from us?"

"Ah, my lady!" The man bowed, and as he did so, he caught sight of the blade at the woman's waist, its handle bound in black leather with a silvered rune set into it. He straightened and frowned. "That is quite some blade. It is somehow familiar…"

Archaen laughed lightly. "There are many elven blades with history and renown. I got this old thing from my father. But on a more serious matter, if you require nothing more from us now, I need to speak to your mayor. We have urgent news."

"Ah, okay. I suppose the one name will do. You may leave your gear aboard your boats—there are no thieves here. I will take you to our town master."

"Thank you. And might we have accommodation for the night? We hope to be away tomorrow. We can pay for our keep."

"Of course!" The man turned to give instruction to his colleagues—one to remain to patrol the dock, another to lead the party to a nearby inn.

Archaen spoke to her colleagues quietly. "There is no need for all of us to go see the mayor. Perhaps Elian can accompany me, as his eyes seem sharper than mine and he might be better at confirming what we saw at the camp. Ryven, you lead the rest. We can both ask about the presence of other elves, although I suspect we'll already have been spotted, and Bastian's scouts will come to us soon enough."

With instructions provided, the party split into two.

***

Elian Omdanan walked boldly alongside Enabeth Archaen, resting a hand on the hilt of his covered blade. He felt like a lord. He'd sometimes felt this way back on

Meridian, when out in the wilds with a party of peers—ostensibly to study and survey, although he'd invariably try to divert the group to riskier activities to enable him to demonstrate his prowess. But there were important differences between then and now. On Meridian, everything had seemed trivial and contrived, yet here, every action was serious and consequential. And on his home world, he had felt little but scorn for his undeserving, deluded, entitled peers, whereas here he felt protective towards a people that seemed honest, weak and child-like. On Meridian, he'd been driven by selfishness and vanity, yet here he felt an odd sense of duty: to the incredible woman beside him, to his heroic fellowship, to the guild that honoured him in a way he'd never been honoured on his home world, and to the people who now scurried around him, casting nervous glances, or holding longer stares and surreptitious conversations as he strode past. Several months ago, he had been uncertain and almost timid—first finding himself among the deadly competent Corvans, and then the immaculate Leaguers—but his confidence had grown: now he was prepared to walk with shoulders back and head raised high, staring any and all in the eye as an equal... *at least*.

Their guide led them along a cobbled street. The style of buildings was similar to that of Lissom: two storey, timber and white plaster, with rough doors and small windows open to the elements or curtained off from within. They soon came to a main square, in which a market was set up, with traders selling fruit, vegetables, fish, meat, baskets, woven mats, jewellery and other decorations. To one side was a taller building with a back-sloping roof with an open frontage, from which fluttered many blue and green pennants, and beside this was a wider wooden building that had two grand wooden doors that were currently open, outside of which stood spear-bearing guards wearing lamellar cuirasses of blue-stained leather.

Their guide led them between the unflinching guards into an open area with a wood floor leading to a wide set of ascending stairs to an upper mezzanine floor, with wooden railings protecting over-lookers from a fall. A man with white hair, dressed in a blue robe, waited at the top of the stairs. Beyond him, they could see a room with a tall ceiling and windows, to the rear of which was a throne of sorts raised to look over a large feasting table with many chairs. Tall, dark-blue curtains closed off alcoves to either side of the room.

The master of the docks whispered to the white-haired man, then turned to Archaen and Omdanan: "Ah, it seems you have been beaten to it. The mayor is already meeting with other ageless. I will leave you with the chamberlain now and return to my duties." His eyes flicked down to Archaen's sword, and then he closed his eyes and affected a bow: "And it has been an honour to meet you, your ladyship. I hope your return will bring better times."

Archaen inclined her head, and the man scurried off down the stairs.

The chamberlain also gave a small bow. "My lady, my lord, please follow me. I am certain the mayor will wish to speak to you at once." He led them to the curtained area to their left. As they neared, Omdanan caught the sound of voices from the hidden alcove. They paused at the curtain, allowing the chamberlain to slip around the other side. There were more voices, then the chamberlain returned, smiled, and beckoned them to pass through the gap he held open for them. He then pulled the thick curtain closed, remaining on the outside.

Inside the annex, three people turned to view them: two were tall and fair-haired, wearing bright chainmail over red tunics, with swords sheathed at their waists; the third was much shorter, in a rich blue robe with green trim and a thick brown leather belt around his considerable waist. Though there was a table with a rich table cloth and six chairs, the trio stood to one side. It was the short man—with white hair, like the chamberlain—who spoke: "More of our guardian-protectors. Welcome. Come join your kin."

Omdanan followed a step behind Archaen, who strode confidently towards the small group. She placed one hand on her heart and inclined her head once more. "Mayor of Hustem, I am Enabeth Archaen of the High Guild of Black Lightning, and with me is Elian Omdanan, a kinsman from a sister guild. Thank you for seeing us."

The man smiled serenely, but his eyes were wide. "No, I should thank you for the honour of your presence. She who wields the Nemesis Blade—here, in Hustem! I can scarcely believe it!"

Archaen frowned. "I had hoped my nature would not be so easily discerned, but I suppose it matters little. It means nothing to the one we hunt."

The smile faded from the face of the mayor too. "I know the one to whom you refer. The chaos of his coming has been a source of great concern. But how can I help you, lady? Ask anything, and I will give it."

"Thank you, Mayor. I see two of my kin here—and speaking to them is the purpose of our visit. But first, I bring some disturbing news. On our way upriver, we passed your fishing camp not three hours ago. I am sorry to say that it is now deserted, and I fear your fishermen have gone to sit at the feet of Yamaga to relate the stories of their lives."

"Dead? Orcs?" The man tensed. "They truly are everywhere!"

Archaen held up one hand. "No, not orcs. I suspect it is something come down the Blackflood. Most likely sashai. Have you encountered any of the creatures recently?"

"Assailed from every angle!" The man clasped his arms about himself. "Yes, they have been seen more and more this last year. But only singly. And none have attacked. I do not know who was... how many were there...?"

"Three of your people, maybe four. No more." Omdanan surprised himself, wondering at his own temerity. But then he smiled inwardly and straightened his shoulders. "They were in small boats. They must have been taken simultaneously. There was no sign of anchors being raised or any attempt to flee."

"Ah, thank you, my lord. That is... good news and bad. Good that there were so few. Many fishermen remained here because of the weather and to help with the latest delivery from the Everbright. But also bad. To take even two boats would have required several of the creatures acting together."

Archaen nodded. "Four at least, but probably twice that many. Acting... *intelligently*."

The Price of Freedom Part II: Velasia

At last, one of the two elves spoke. "Cousin Enabeth—I am Grisen Lacklan, and my colleague is Heffred Peneza. We have been waiting for you, with intel to impart. But first… you say 'intelligently'. That is a worrying conclusion, and one voiced by some of us for months now. Do you think really think it so?"

Archaen considered the man, then pointedly directed a glance to the mayor and back. "We always knew the sashai were clever, as though Yamaga *designed* them that way." Again the eye-flick. "Perhaps they have now passed some threshold, and this is certainly a mystery that should be considered… but not now."

"I understand."

"Perhaps, Mayor," Archaen turned, "once you have dealt with the latest cargo, you should send some force down to the camp to investigate. And maybe consider leaving a permanent detachment of lookouts and guards?"

"That is something I will need to think about. Guards? I only had a dozen until last month. We are training many more to watch for orcs, and now this?"

Lacklan spoke to the mayor. "You will have our support, should you wish it. The Grand Master is already assembling a force. We may be able to lend you some arms soon, and perhaps later send an expedition down the Blackflood. You will not be deserted."

"I am ever grateful for your aid, but unless the lady and her party remain, we shall soon be just that: deserted."

"Cousin Grisen?"

"Alas, Enabeth, we cannot be in two places at once. And this is perhaps the time for me to update you on affairs. The lands about are swarming with orcs. Here, and in all of the Southlands. The grain barges were attacked on their voyage downriver, and so Heffred and I will join the return trip with them and the town's own cargo ship. Our bows are more than a match for the spear-throwers on the banks. But that leaves us without a presence in Hustem, and I know you cannot remain."

"I am sorry, but that is so. We must continue up the Tessellac tomorrow. What else can you tell us?"

"Only this: the orcs are moving in small groups, but there are many of them. They are not yet working as an army, but rather as a mischievous swarm—pillaging and killing wherever and whatever they can. They are moving in squads of six—their holy number—rather than companies of thirty-six. And until a week ago, every orc we encountered bore the emblem of the White Skull regiment from Tartax-Kul. So, we supposed their total complement to be just over two hundred, or six companies of thirty-six. But then last week, we encountered a squad just north of here with a different insignia—the Black Tree—so we suspect a second regiment may have been sent into the Southlands, doubling their numbers. I do not know if the Tessellac is safe to travel from here on."

"That's why we've tried to move with haste. I'm not sure what we can do if the door is shut. We have to risk the Tessellac. We have no choice."

Lacklan nodded severely. "If you must, you must. But how is your armour? If you are to continue, you must increase your precautions."

"We all have mail and helms. We will don them when we move on."

"And shields?"

"No. We wanted to travel light, and already haul too much."

Lacklan turned to the mayor, who'd been following the conversation keenly. "Sir, if you have spare shields, I ask you to lend them to my kin. I fear they will need them."

The mayor nodded enthusiastically. "Of course! They shall have whatever they wish."

Omdanan felt a shiver of excitement at the upcoming phase of their journey.

Chapter 9

Rostus Dettler stood below his master on a rocky crest, looking down a steep and scrubby hillside. Anda com Durrel, God-Sorcerer of Tartax-Kul, had assembled the best force he could at short notice—and it paled in comparison to the one opposing it at the foot of the long slope.

The day after Yadzen had presented Dettler with a new pair of handmade boots, com Durrel announced his intention to move against Ullah-Bor. But with much of his force already spread across Barra and the Southlands, allied to the hurried timetable for departure in two days' time, all he had managed to muster was six regiments—totalling fewer than fifteen hundred orcs.

"It is enough," he had declared, on surveying his army hunched together at the foot of his mountain, in the wide fringe before the Splinter Forest. "They only need to ensure my foes do not get too close, and then occupy key positions afterwards."

And so here they were, after two weeks of forced marching beneath spindly trees, over rugged mountain foothills, and through hidden gorges—the main fortress of Ullah-Bor now a black smudge half-way up a mountain in the mid-distance—facing the roused forces of the enemy citadel.

"How many do you reckon, Wormtongue? Five thousand?"

"I don't have an eye for this," said Dettler. "But I can see they well outnumber us."

"Yadzen?"

From the opposite side of the two-metre-high boulder on which com Durrel stood, the grey-haired man had been using his martial experience to assess the scene. "I count around thirty banners. Given the orcs' superstition about the number six, we can be confident their regiments each hold about six-cubed men, which gives around six thousand in total. I thought they'd field more. Perhaps they do not believe our assault is serious."

Com Durrel nodded, seemingly pleased that his estimate had been close. "It makes no difference to the outcome. But where is their king? I'd rather not slaughter all these fine and rapacious fellows—I need them to serve me. A surgical strike should do, with just a token lesson of obliteration."

Dettler looked up at his master, who'd chosen his platform to dominate the scene well. Com Durrel wore a black cloak with silver stitching—once belonging to the previous master of Tartax-Kul—over black leather clothing that hid the burgundy skin he'd been given in Arakkan. A silver circlet rested on his brow, and he held his black staff in one hand. With his two-week-old white beard—trimmed by Dettler as yet another of his menial duties—and the wind swirling his cloak, com Durrel looked suitably and deliberately messianic. The man's eyes were wide, and his smile was broad and perilous. Dettler knew it was at times like this that com Durrel came alive, revelling in his power, and in utter contrast to the dire evenings, when doubt and depression seemed to settle over him as he sat in a cold hall, contemplating an unappetising meal before retiring alone to a rough bed.

Dettler turned his attention to those around the boulder on which com Durrel stood—beyond an exclusion zone of three-metres radius, intended to keep all out of range of a tempting spear thrust. The orcs formed six distinct bodies, each comprised of a different regiment with its own set of banners: The Black Sun, The Devil Fish, Mangu's Reapers, The Tormentors, The Rock-hammers and The Flesh-Renders. The host was largely dressed in toughened leather armour of brown or black, though the Reapers' armour was stained a dark red and the Tormentors wore white. Most of the orcs held shields, decorated with the emblem of their regiment, and held cruel-looking spears, usually with two barbed prongs at the end, though some had additional hooks or slashing razors set into the haft. The regiments' leaders—invariably the tallest and cruellest of the orcs—stood at the edge of the semi-circle, close enough to their new god to hear his commands.

Yadzen called out: "There! To your left, sir. The army parts for their king and his champions. They are making their way to the front line."

"I see him," exclaimed com Durrel, excitedly. "The fool has come to embrace death. Excellent!"

They watched patiently, as a clutch of huge orcs pushed its way to the front of the opposition force, four hundred metres down the slope. One orc held a royal banner—a blood-red flag, topped by a skull, rumoured to be that of the previous king. From this distance, they could see no fine details beyond a single figure, now with space cleared around it, turning to exhort its host. After a moment, the army replied with a roar, which started low and then ascended in volume. Spears were waved and shields were struck with spear hafts; the late afternoon sun glinted off metal.

"What are your plans, sir?" asked Yadzen.

"We wait. I will let the first of them get close, to raise their hopes. Then... we shall see." He turned to look at his own army and spoke more loudly. "They will soon come. When they do, hold your ground. Do not be concerned. When I have dealt with the first wave, I will go meet their king. Spread into a line and follow me down. You may feast upon those we pass—except the Reapers, who must remain close by me, ignoring the available flesh. But do not worry, Mangu..." he addressed the largest orc, dressed in red leather armour, "you and yours will soon have a richer meal!"

The orc called Mangu—whose albino face was a patchwork of scars and who lacked an ear—raised his spear and roared in approval.

"Sir!" said Yadzen. "They are about to charge!"

Com Durrel turned back just as the first of the orcs began their advance; a wedge of regiments surged past the king and his champions, screaming and shouting as they started up the slope.

Dettler watched the scene nervously, occasionally glancing up at com Durrel, who seemed unperturbed. Ten seconds passed, then twenty... and at last the man on the rock reacted. Com Durrel raised his staff in one hand and slowly brought it around in front of him, grasping it with his second. He started to speak loudly, drawing out each syllable: *"Fermious... Tertious... Ballatax..."*

Then Dettler staggered. Something... *happened.* The air changed subtlety, as though a heavy blanket had been thrown over the world. All sound fled, and then gradually returned. Dettler's buckled knees straightened; he passed a hand over teary eyes; and when he looked downhill he saw... confusion. The first orcs had gotten to within a hundred metres before being struck by some unknown force. Most of the closest were prostrate, but further back the orcs sat on their bottoms, swaying uncertainty, or were on their hands and knees, trembling and retching. And further back still, at the foot of the slope, many were upright, but staggering, weaving, blundering. Dettler could see the king—visible over the prone creatures—being propped up by a couple of his champions.

Com Durrel climbed off the boulder and took position between his two human companions. Then he straightened himself and shouted a reminder of his orders: "Reapers around me—wait until I move! Others *advance.* Clear a path for me!"

The orcs in the five now-unleashed regiments howled and laughed. They started down the slope and within seconds were at the front line. Dettler watched those nearest reach their enemy... prey... *food...* and drop their spears to take up short, butchering tools sheaved at their waists, which they used to start slicing flesh off the still-living, ravenous from their two weeks of marching without supplies, now taking advantage of this time of plenty. He looked away.

Com Durrel began to move, jolting Dettler into motion. The red-armoured orcs moved with them, though still leaving ample space around the God-Sorcerer. Ahead, orcs were pulling insensible foes out of their path, and below Dettler could see the bulk of Ullah-Bor's forces attempting to re-form. But com Durrel did not give them the chance. On reaching the new front line, he raised his staff and repeated: "*Fermious Tertious Ballatax!*"

The wave of pressure rippled down the slope, felling the next tranche of orcs, including the king and his champions. This proved too much for the rear echelons of the army, which turned to flee the invisible force and the terrible sorcerer. Com Durrel continued, and now members of the Reapers—following Mangu's commands—dashed in front, roughly grabbing concussed enemies and casting them to the side and out of his path. And then they were at the foot of the slope, and the king and his bodyguard was vulnerable before them.

Com Durrel drew up three metres from the royal company. One of the bodyguards made it to his knees, but Mangu strode out from the line and thrust his spear into its head. Flicking his weapon free, the great orc then took two more steps to the king and pointed his spear at his face in readiness. The king was also clearly of great size and would have been over two metres standing, but he now lolled on his back, trying to rise with floppy arms that refused to work.

"I do not know your name," said com Durrel to the king, loud enough to be heard over the screams of those being slaughtered by his other regiments. "And I do not wish to know it. In fact, from now on it is death to say it. You end here. Your line ends here, soon to fill the bellies of my warriors."

The king managed a grunt, saliva running from his non-functioning mouth.

Com Durrel momentarily cast his gaze at the other felled champions lying about. "I am the God-Sorcerer of Tartax-Kul. If you serve me, you will be spared his fate. Decide, and decide quick."

There were around a dozen bodyguards and champions in the immediate area, distinguishable in that they wore black leather gloves and had silver pendants at their necks. At this offer, these redoubled their efforts to roll around until, one by one, all were lying prostrate, face down, their arms out-stretched towards com Durrel, indicating subservience.

At last, com Durrel nodded. "Do not worry, my Reapers. Though these are denied you, by the close of this day, a lottery will be held. One regiment of Ullah-Bor and all its brood will be yours instead." The orcs in red growled and cheered. "And for you, Mangu, a royal dish. You will be my regent here. All that was this king's will be yours." He smiled and gave a gesture of encouragement. "Please begin!"

Mangu snarled and grinned at his new god. Then he turned to the fallen monarch, dropped his spear, and pulled a blade from beneath his leather cuirass. "You have two ears, lord, and I have one. That is unfair." He leant down and sliced off an ear, which he popped whole into his mouth. The king screamed and managed to jerkily move one weakened hand to the side of his head. But Mangu had only just started. He swallowed his first course. "But now we are equal, yet I am your superior." He moved his blade to slice off the king's other ear.

Dettler turned away and caught sight of Yadzen, frowning. Their eyes met, and Yadzen gave a slow shake of the head.

To hoots of encouragement from his regiment, and under com Durrel's amused eye, Mangu slowly dissected the king of all of his extremities. At last com Durrel got bored and left his new regent to his play, taking a company of the Reapers with him—to carry the now-compliant champions of the old order—as he strolled towards the capital of his new domain.

***

"Is he sane?" wondered Dettler. "Is any of this sane?"

"Perhaps not." Yadzen was clearly uncomfortable at this line of conversation. "But he doesn't see them as sentient beings, merely animals."

"Do you think he would behave any differently if they were human?" Dettler felt nauseous and exhausted to the point where he almost didn't care what he said or who heard it. "Really? And... and... even if they are just beasts, how sick is his behaviour? He's effectively torturing animals!"

"You are defending the orcs?"

"God, no! They disgust me! They are an abomination! But that makes what he is doing worse. You know he plans to set these creatures onto the yeltoi. It's like he's just hosted a barbaric dog fight and has decided to let the winning beast loose upon a nursery of infants. And you condone this?"

"I do not condone this." Yadzen was plainly troubled in spite of his measured response. They were in a side chamber to the throne room in Ullah-Bor, having left com Durrel to rest in another chamber on the floor above, all access to which was guarded by his new favourites in red armour. "But you know I must serve. I cannot help it. It is a compulsion."

"There must be a way to break your programming. You must have looked into it?"

"I told you, Mr Dettler, that the military tried and failed, as though a key used to open a box had broken in the lock. When Mr com Durrel employed me, and had me swear an oath, that sealed my allegiance. Even... even the words you use about him... even though I know at one level that they are true and you are right... even so they... *concern* me. I do not like your tone."

Dettler saw Yadzen's two hands slowly clenching and unclenching, with one moving almost involuntarily towards the hilt of his sword. He looked from the hands to Yadzen's strained face and back again. Then he slowly stepped back, increasing the distance between them, and raised his hands. "I am sorry, Yadzen. I know how constrained you are. I will... I will be silent."

"That is for the best. Perhaps you should change subject."

Dettler nodded. He attempted a smile. "Yes, well, okay. Ah—did you notice the orchards below the outer wall? Apples, nuts, and other fruits. I think we will eat better here..." and then the thought of eating brought back to him a vision of the battlefield: he turned around and was violently sick.

***

The news arrived four days later, as com Durrel, his human servants, the champions of his regiments, and the regent, Mangu, stood about a large map drawn in charcoal on the floor of the new map chamber of Ullah-Bor.

"Come. Approach. Tell me!"

The pale-faced orc scuttled over to com Durrel from the broad doorway to the room, where guards had divested it of its weapons. At two metres distance, it fell prostate upon the ground. "God-Sorcerer! I was told that you had taken Ullah-Bor and was re-directed here."

"You are one of my scouts from the White Skull regiment?"

"Yes, Lord. I am the end runner in one of the message chains set up by Lord Wormtongue. I bring news from Lissom."

"Lord Wormtongue?" com Durrel turned to face Dettler in amusement. "It seems you have been promoted—but I wouldn't let it go to your head." He turned back to the orc. "Well, what is this news? Get on your knees—you'll find it easier to speak."

The orc did as instructed, but still baulked at meeting his master's eyes. "My lord, a squad of raiders were at the mannish settlement of Lissom, causing mayhem as instructed. Then some elves arrived and killed them all—except one. He escaped, and passed his news along the chain. I have been on the run for two days: I am the ninth carrier."

"So there are elves in Lissom?" com Durrel shrugged. He had received other reports over the last few weeks of elves popping up here and there, but nothing that warranted any concern or special attention. Nevertheless, he strode across the map, careful not to scuff any of the drawn lines, and placed himself at the mark for the Rivertown on the Tessellac. "This is not a surprise. Still… give your report. What can you tell me about them?"

The orc looked down, clearly thinking how best to relate its message. "They were… just elves. But one was huge. The survivor said he had never seen his like before. He was twice the breadth of most…"

Dettler leant over and whispered to Yadzen: "Brutus?" The other frowned but did not respond.

"… but the matter most odd was, they had a sorcerer among them."

"What! A sorcerer? Explain!"

"One of them held a staff like yours, my lord. He is said to have chanted words of power, causing a great wind to arise, extinguishing the fires that had been set."

"Another staff?" Com Durrel looked keenly across to his human comrades. "This is also not unexpected. I have been waiting for a challenger. What else can you tell me?"

"Nothing, my lord. That is all the survivor reported."

Com Durrel frowned at first, but his mouth quickly transformed into a smile, and he laughed. "They have taken their time about it—but they are too late. I am too strong now." He turned back to the map. "If this party of elves is heading here, taking the elven gates, they could in theory arrive soon. But that is not likely, is it?"

"No, lord. They might gain time through the gates, but we travelled day and night without rest—and even the elves cannot do this. And their most direct routes would force them to fight through our regiments between Lissom and here."

Com Durrel paced the outline of the Tessellac until he stood above the legend that indicated the Copper Gate. Then he traced the path to the Iron Gate, along the area of the Northlands in the lee of the Sundering Mountains known as the Gap of Gelion. And then he thumped his staff onto the mark indicating the Iron Gate—the pass through the Skythrust Mountains into Bratha. "Here!"

All those in the room remained silent, waiting for their master to speak. At last com Durrel looked up, first to the messenger. "You have done well. Engorge yourself. Guard—take him to the pantry, and let him choose whatever he wishes, alive or dead."

"Thank you, lord!" The orc got to its feet, and then, while still crouched, rapidly scuttled back towards the door.

"Mangu—unleash your regiments! Send more to the Gap of Gelion to guard the approaches to the Iron Gate. Leave a force to guard its entrance and exit and string some companies throughout the Gap. I want nothing and nobody to get through that gate, or if they do, beyond the shadow of Ullah-Bor."

"As you command, lord!"

"My other champions—prepare the rest of our regiments to return to Tartax-Kul. We will leave tomorrow. And we will take thirty more regiments from Ullah-Bor to help raise the rest of Bratha."

The various champions shouted their understanding and assent.

"Return here in two hours, after you have set things in motion, and we will discuss our strategy further. In the meantime—Wormtongue, Terminator, come with me. There are other matters we must discuss."

***

They were alone in the throne room. Com Durrel had dismissed his orc bodyguards and then had the great doors to the room closed and sealed, with the royal guard left outside.

"So, here they come," noted com Durrel, wryly, as he splayed across the uncomfortable iron throne, with one leg swung over a grotesquely carved armrest. "And they are still largely playing by the rules—as you predicted."

Dettler gave a nod of acknowledgement. "It's in their DNA. They were never going to come at you from out of the ocean in STEALTH copters armed with machine guns. I suspect many are secretly pleased with your intervention. They will never have had such an adversary. They will see it as a chance to perform heroic feats."

"Well, I am happy to play along with their game. I just hope they aren't poor losers. What do you think, Yadzen?"

The grey-haired man stood erect to com Durrel's left, while Dettler sat on the floor in front of the throne in the absence of any nearby chair. "I agree with Mr Dettler, sir. They will play fair, and should you win, they will accept it. But then they will try again. And again."

"And with each defeat they suffer, I will grow stronger and their chances of beating me and evicting me from Velasia will recede further. But what of this other staff? I did not expect them to bring it, given that mine is deemed *unsporting*. It changes the odds slightly."

"I suspect that once you used the staff you made magic an acceptable tool of gameplay," said Dettler. "I understand there are three other staffs aside from yours?"

"Yes. They made four. Mine has an extra level of power, and a few more modes of action. But the others are not insignificant weapons. Do you think they have just the one, or have they brought them all?"

Dettler shrugged. "Who can say? I suspect they only brought the one, to maintain balance and fairness." Although he suspected this was so, he sincerely hoped that their adversaries had forgotten their scruples and come armed to the teeth...

"And who do you think wields it?"

Dettler looked down, giving the matter a moment's thought. "I don't think the Leaguers will touch it—as you say, it is not sporting. That would probably leave Mr Sarok as the wielder."

"Why?"

Dettler smiled without humour. "He is a leader. I cannot see him allowing one of his party to have such a powerful weapon instead of him. And would the others be trusted with it? Brutus would be a natural with traditional arms, and the orc implied by omission that it was not him. The woman? I am not sure she is fully trusted. The bodyguard, Vuller? His role is more like Yadzen's."

Com Durrel swung his leg off the armrest and suddenly stood. "We still lack information. All we know is that Brutus is with the party, which implies Sarok will be there as well as the rest of his team. But we don't know which of the Leaguers are with them. Miko? The woman? Her son? Any more? I need to give further instruction to Mangu and my generals. Come."

The God-Sorcerer strode towards the throne room door.

Chapter 10

On the jetty of Hustem, the company of the Black Lady—as the party had become known in the chain of whispered conversations about town—prepared itself. Watched by Grisen Lacklan and Heffred Peneza of the High Guild of the Golden Sword, the Mayor of Hustem, and the master of the docks, the members of the party hauled their surcoats of mail from the storage areas fore and aft of their boats and proceeded to don them.

"How do you expect us to row wearing this?" muttered Brutus, whose giant coat had been especially extended from the biggest set in the stores of Verano prior to their departure for Velasia.

"Is it too heavy for you?" smirked Mandelson, who had easily slid into her own armour and stood watching. "Perhaps you should take the tiller like the other shirkers."

From his position beyond Brutus, Miko caught the insult and simply scowled.

"Heavy—no," responded Brutus, choosing not to rise to the bait. "In fact, it's fucking light, but it hinders the free movement of my arms." To emphasise the point, he windmilled his shoulders, setting the interlinked rings of iron rippling.

"I would let you have some of our lamellar armour instead," volunteered the mayor, "but we have none your size, or so effective against orc spears."

Lacklan gave a quick shake of the head. "Your armour would do well against weapons flung from the banks of the river, sir, but perhaps less well at preventing scratches and minor punctures, and it is the poisoned blade that they must fear the most."

"Poison, Grisen?" mused Enabeth Archaen. "Is this a common tactic of the orcs now? I have… been abroad for some time."

"Common, no, but on occasion if they have had time to set up an ambush, then yes."

The mayor had caught Archaen's slip. "Abroad, lady? In the homeland of the elves beyond the sea?"

Archaen smiled down on the town's leader, who this morning wore his best outfit and a small gold circlet on his head. "Indeed, Mayor. In the lands of my kin—about which we do not speak. Forgive me for mentioning it."

"Ah—you elves and your secrets! I can't help but wonder, though, if you might not have more that could come to our aid in these troubling times."

"I am afraid not. But you should know that you are not forgotten, and even though we are few, we will do our best to protect you."

"Speaking of which," interjected Lacklan, "our own convoy appears ready for the off. I see the sails being unfurled on the barges. The wind is easterly, Cousin En, which will aid us, but perhaps not you. I fear you will have much rowing to do today. At least, I am happier about your state of protection now that you have adorned your rides with our host's spare shields." He waved at the boats, where circular wooden shields—that were white, with the black symbol of Yamaga, the yeltoi god, painted across for protection—were lashed along the gunwales. "Still… watch the trees and try to keep as far from the left bank as possible."

"Thank you, Cousin Grisen. Good luck to you and Heffred."

The two tall men gave small bows to Archaen and the mayor, then sauntered off towards their craft—clasping hands with Miko and Reddas Archaen as they passed.

"And now we seem to be ready," continued Archaen. "Once more, thank you, Mayor, for your hospitality and gifts." She turned to leap aboard the boat that nuzzled against the jetty.

***

A couple of hours of hard rowing passed under a constant drizzle. During a short break for one of the pair of rowers, Irvan Sentain took off his helmet and wiped the rain from his face. Across from him, Enabeth Archaen wore a similar helm—

leather, with an iron crosspiece and iron cheek and nose guards—though on her it appeared natural and un-burdensome.

"I thought I was getting used to the rowing," said Sentain. "But Brutus was right: it's more awkward and tiring dressed like this. Is the armour and helmet really necessary?"

Archaen had been using the break to scan the surroundings forwards of the boat, over the heads of the toiling oarsmen who faced her. She briefly looked at Sentain and then away again, continuing her survey. "Necessary? No. Prudent? Yes. It's likely the river is under surveillance and we are being watched, even now."

"Now?" Sentain quickly placed the helmet back upon his head and shifted to look forwards too. "Really? But... where from? The trees are still thick to the waterline on both sides of the river, and you say they are unlikely to be on the right bank."

"I said that, yes, but now I wonder."

"What has made you change your mind?"

Archaen didn't answer. Something appeared to have caught her attention over to the right. Sentain noticed her shoulders stiffen and watched the woman's head slowly rotate as their boat moved towards a particular wedge of trees that poked out into the river. She then turned to look behind, raising herself slightly so that Miko—at the tiller of the second boat—could see her. She raised one hand to gesture towards the trees, then returned her attention to the knot of foliage.

"What have you seen?" Sentain tried to follow the woman's gaze, speaking low.

After a moment, Archaen responded, also speaking softly: "There is something in those trees. It could just be a creature. If it is an orc, then there is just the one. It has stepped back now."

The right bank was less than thirty metres away as they had edged over to the middle of the flow, following Lacklan's earlier advice. Archaen kept an intense watch on the area of concern as they gradually pulled opposite to it and then slowly carried on past.

"Is it... are you...?"

"Yes. There is something there, hiding. And where there is one…" the woman continued to scan the bank, switching her attention forwards again, still focusing on the right bank.

"How vulnerable are we? You said the orcs don't use bows. Is that true? That seems a bit odd."

A quick smile crossed the woman's face, and she again passed a rapid glance at him. "Use your intellect, Irvan. What is the driving force of the orcs and their culture?"

"Uh, well, I suppose it's their need to feed. Their low-food, high-energy environment means they're always looking for a meal. Is that what you mean?"

"Good. Now go on. What is the advantage of a bow, or perhaps, *disadvantage* if you are an orc travelling in a group?"

Sentain momentarily looked away from the banks, down at the deck of the boat, as if the reduction in stimuli would help his thinking. "It is… *range*. You use a bow to kill from a distance. So, if an orc uses a bow and shoots some prey then its kill will be some distance away. And its party…" He looked up, realisation dawning. "The other orcs in its group! They might be quicker, and nearer. First to the food!"

Archaen nodded, without looking at him. "Yes. They like to get up close for their kills. So they don't use bows—but they do use spears, mostly for close quarters fighting. But because they have them, they *do* have something that can be thrown and they will use them in this way if they have to."

The second boat had closed to within three metres, moving over to the port side of its twin. Vuller and Omdanan continued rowing there, but Sarok and Mandelson had also taken a spell, having been directed to do so by Miko, who'd been watching the front boat and synchronising with it.

Miko called across, his voice just loud enough to carry the short distance over the gentle splashing of water from oars: "The terrain draws in, Cousin."

"It does."

For most of their journey, the land to both sides of the river had been largely flat, but since Hustem there had been a gradual increase in gradient, with the terrain higher and more undulating in the mid-distance. Tree-covered hills were now apparent on both sides of the river, and as they continued, more sizeable hummocks rose up close to the water. Several hundred metres ahead, the riverbanks protruded inwards as the underlying geology changed, making it tougher for the river to carve its course. A sizeable hill, furred with trees, rose to the left, while to the right the riverbank momentarily lifted up into a steep rock face, three or four metres above the river's surface, with tree roots jutting through its upper area.

Sentain wasn't sure where to look—forwards, left, right, back. "Enabeth, what…"

"*Shhhhhhh*! Reddas… Brutus… ease up. Half-time."

The two big men had been watching the woman the whole time, saying nothing, saving their energy for their exertions. They lifted their oars, quickly looked at each other, and dropped them again, keeping a sedate stroke that barely did more than neutralise the current of the river. Behind, Sentain heard Miko mutter similar instructions to his crew.

The second boat nudged further to the left until the craft were almost abreast, and Miko was able to address Archaen from close by. "I am wary. I suggest we hold position until—"

And then there was movement from the left bank. Sentain happened to be looking in that direction. He saw the trees in front part slightly, and suddenly there was an object in flight.

"Look out!" cried Sarok, who'd also seen the motion. "Spear!"

The weapon didn't have far to travel and it was thrown with some strength. Miko's boat was nearest, and Miko was the most exposed at the tiller. But he had heard the warning, glanced to his left, and suddenly jerked back, causing the spear to pass in front of him, clean over the boat and into the water.

No sooner had the first spear flown, than a second came from the same direction, and then a third from the right bank—accompanied by a warning shout from Archaen. The spear from the left thudded into a shield along the port side of Miko's boat, while the other clipped a shield rim in Archaen's boat, splintering it and deflecting into the deck just behind Sentain.

Suddenly there was chaos, as the rowers in the two boats stuttered, while those resting looked about frantically, checking for the next source of danger…

"We're sitting ducks!" shouted Miko.

"To the oars everyone," shouted Archaen. "Row hard!"

As all set about the oars, two more spears arced through the sky to bury themselves into shields on the gunwales. Then Miko, who had their sole forwards-looking eyes, cried out again: "Halt! The river ahead is blocked! Take cover! Let the flow take us!"

Sentain nearly lost his oar in the ruckus: as he raised it up he managed to inadvertently deflect another incoming missile. "Shit! What…?"

Archaen was quicker and pushed the man down to keep him low. She peered ahead. "*Cunning.*"

Sentain managed to slide his oar onto the deck and also turn. Ahead, he noticed the narrowing of the river, where a rope—which must have been resting unseen on the water's surface—had been hauled up to form a clothesline barrier. If the prow of their boat didn't catch on this, then their masts definitely would.

"Vuller!"

The cry came from the other boat. Sentain jerked his head in that direction, where he saw that a spear had passed between two shields and struck Sarok's bodyguard in the shoulder. He also noticed Omdanan scrabbling in the store area at the prow—then straighten, bow in hand.

The current had them, and was taking the two boats back downstream, but only slowly.

More spears came, but these were sporadic. Sentain saw Sarok pulling Vuller forwards, flat onto the deck, then he returned his gaze to his own boat, his attention drawn by Enabeth Archaen, who had slithered to the storage area at the aft of their craft. She also emerged with a bow and notched arrow—the only skilled archer in the party beside the precocious Meridian.

There was little Sentain could do but grasp his staff and crouch low. He tried to ignore the happenings on the other boat—the right bank proving enough of a distraction. But he could see little beyond the occasional shake of trees, darker shadows, and then a new launch…

"Shot, Elian!" came Miko's cry, from the other boat, though Sentain did not dare turn to look. He twitched as another spear came from the grey-brown foliage until he realised it was directed towards the aft of his boat, which was suddenly the fore as they backed down the river. Archaen had seen it too; she ignored the wayward dart and leased one arrow, then a rapid second, and then an even-more rapid third. There came a scream, and something large tumbled off the bank and into the water.

Then something ahead caught Sentain's eye. He turned to see the out-jutting knob on the right bank that they'd passed a short time ago: from behind this a small boat emerged, followed by a second.

Archaen cursed. "There were more behind the watcher. Fool!"

The spears from the bank had ceased. By Sentain's reckoning, there could have been no more than twenty in total. The peril now lay ahead from the two boats… and then he noticed two more emerge from a hidden recess in the other bank. The boats each held two or three figures.

Across from them, Miko stood tall at the abandoned tiller of his boat, helm on head, mail sparkling in a stray ray of sun through the dismal clouds, a shield on one arm that he'd torn from the gunwale. He laughed and shouted: "Is this all? Come, you sons of whores, come on! Elian, leave some for me!"

But Omdanan did not.

The archer moved up to Miko's side and unleashed arrow after arrow with deadly aim. A huge orc with an albino face took an arrow in the eye, and even as it tottered in the boat, a second arrow pierced its other eye. Two more arrows emptied that boat, then the orcs in the second to that side appeared to appreciate their peril and started paddling at the water with their hands.

Sentain quickly shifted his attention to the two boats from the right bank, in time to see Enabeth Archaen calmly shoot the final orc in the neck.

The party's two boats gently swept past the four orc boats and their slain crews, back the way they had come, but at least out of the trap.

***

Archaen and Miko returned to their tillers, turning their boats to face downriver. Mandelson and Omdanan rowed in one, Reddas and Brutus in the other. When she judged that they were clear of danger, Archaen steered her boat to the left bank and cast their anchor into the shallows so that they bobbed a few metres from the tree-thick shore. Miko anchored next to the first boat.

Narovy Sarok felt a slight bump as his craft came to settle next to the other, though his attention was elsewhere.

"Vuller, you gave me a fucking shock!"

The target of the man's wrath was sitting up: blood covered one cheek and had splattered down across the shoulder and chest of his mail coat.

"Sorry, Boss. Just winded."

Miko stood behind the seated Sarok, peering at the injured man. "You bleed," he noted, with concern.

"Ah, this is nothing." Vuller held a hand to his bloodied face, then looked at this, smiling wryly. "The mail did its job, but the spear punched the air out of me. I guess it caught me on the cheek as it rebounded."

"Don't give me a scare like that again, you fucker," fumed Sarok. "You're meant to be protecting me, not the other way round." He reached towards Vuller's cut face, then paused his questing hand and turned to look up at Miko. "You mentioned poison. Is he at risk? What should we do?"

"I would say clean it quick," muttered Miko, "but it's been several minutes already. If that dart was poisoned, we will know soon enough."

Sarok pulled off his helmet and leant over to scoop out some river water. Then he leant forwards, ignoring Vuller's half-formed protests, and began to splash his cheek and use his bare hand to wash the wound. At some point, Miko found a square of cloth from somewhere, which Sarok received from over his shoulder, using it to tamp the cut.

"Well, you're not going to bleed to death. It's not as bad as Brutus' shaving cut the other day. How are you feeling?"

"Really, Boss, I feel fine. It's nothing. Thanks for your concern."

"Concern?" muttered Sarok. "Ha! Just don't fucking die."

"I suspect he will be fine," noted Archaen. In her hand, she held the broken-off top of the orc spear that had thudded into her boat during the attack. "The tip is dry. Although Grisen mentioned poison, I admit this was news to me. I doubt it is common."

Sarok gave his bodyguard one last critical look, then half-turned to better consider Archaen across from him and Miko behind. "Right. So where does this leave us now? Our way ahead is blocked, though the rope shouldn't hinder us for long. I guess it's just a question of how many lurk on the banks at either end of it. What are their numbers?"

"Much fewer now than at the start of the ambush," noted Miko, smiling. "There were ten or eleven in the boats, and Elian took one on the banks."

"And Enabeth got another on the right bank," volunteered Sentain, standing to the side of the woman.

Archaen nodded severely. "We killed a dozen or so. That means they were more than a typical squad of six. I guess they must be in company strength here. Thirty-six. So there are perhaps two dozen more at the top of the ambush by the narrows."

"What if there are even more?" wondered Miko. "A couple of companies?"

"I don't think so, given the number at this end of the ambush and the number of spears they threw—"

"About twenty," interjected Sentain. "I was counting."

"Okay," said Miko. "Assuming you are right, their numbers are not great, and with your bow, En, and that of marksman Elian, they should not pose much of a problem."

Archaen lapsed into silence for a moment. Sarok watched her, then volunteered what he guessed she was thinking: "But they now know more about us—that we have skilled archers. It is not wise to assume an enemy will fail to learn from a defeat. But what I want to know is: why are they here in the first place? Who are they hoping to trap? Not us, surely?"

"The town of Trastere lies further upriver," replied Miko, "though it was abandoned some years ago. The ruins lie at the junction of the Tessellac and the Wilding river—which flows north west towards Barak-on-Wold. The trade route is still used. I guess they were hoping to snare vessels between Hustem and Barak, but they did not anticipate trapping a party of elves. We do not roll over so easily!"

"Okay. But if their plan was as you suggest, doesn't that imply they might have another group waiting even further upriver, ready to close the trap on any craft coming downriver from Barak? In other words, perhaps they can reinforce their force at the narrows."

Archaen looked at Sarok sharply. "That… is a good point. I am still not sure they number more than a company in total, but I worry about how we might assault them, if they are ready and dug in."

Sarok looked grim. "An amphibious assault in these boats would be difficult to say the least. Could we disembark here, take the forest to the ambush site on this side, clear the ambushers, untie the rope across the river, then return to collect our gear? Or perhaps we could just push ahead on the water and cut the rope or otherwise negotiate it when we reach it? Will they be keen to show themselves and throw things at us, given what just happened?"

"We would have less of an advantage going by land in these thick woods," said Miko. "It could get messy."

Archaen seemed to have made up her mind. "Whatever we do, we will not be able to kill them all in this terrain. Some will escape and warn their colleagues—and perhaps our foe, too. We could soon find the upper reaches of the Tessellac swarming with interceptors, with ambushes every few kilometres. They only wounded one of us this time—next time could be worse."

"I regretfully concur," said Miko.

"Which brings us back to my initial question," said Sarok. "Where does that leave us now? You seem to be suggesting it would be unwise to carry on up the Tessellac. What other options do we have? To abandon our boats and go by land—perhaps to cut across to Barak-on-Wold? Or back to Hustem, and take the route of Lacklan and the barges?"

Miko shook his head. "No. The Everbright flows west and is no good to us. And Barak also takes us away from the Copper Gate."

"Then where?"

At this, Archaen and Miko looked at each other. Archaen nodded and Miko closed his eyes.

Sarok saw this exchange and knew the answer. He continued: "I remember something of Bastian's map. You mean for us to go back and take the Blackflood, which rises in the mountains east of the Copper Gate, rather than west. That's your plan, isn't it?"

Archaen looked down at the deck, then up again at the Corvan. "That way will almost certainly avoid any further orcs and any chance of detection." Then she gave a tight smile: "And at least it should prove *interesting*."

"Why do I get the impression that we have different interpretations of that word?" Sarok slapped his thigh and returned his gaze to Vuller. "Still alive, I see? Excellent. I feel you'll soon be hard pressed to earn your wages at your primary job, which is keeping me alive."

Chapter 11

The party returned to Hustem, arriving some five to six hours after having left. Enabeth Archaen insisted on a short stop only—to quickly update the mayor on the new problem upriver—and then they were on their way again, back downriver to the camp opposite the Blackflood. It was late afternoon when they arrived. After a brief discussion, Archaen and Miko decided that they would spend the night there, allowing a full day's travel up the Blackflood and into the heart of the Shadow Forest the next day.

As the two boats were tied up alongside each other at the jetty beside the longhouse, Omdanan leapt ashore, his bow looped across his chest. He felt Mandelson's eyes on his back but didn't turn to explain his plans. Instead, he walked along the full length of the jetty, past the boats still moored there from their previous visit, checking for signs of activity. He wasn't sure what he expected to find, but at the far end he spotted an anomaly and squatted down for a closer look.

***

Sarok found himself standing next to Archaen, watching the young Meridian, as those around noisily hauled equipment and supplies onto the dock, with Miko having already headed into the longhouse to investigate.

"Omdanan is proving valuable, no?" he said.

Archaen briefly glanced at him then returned to observing the crouching man. "Very. He is coming into his own."

"It seems I may have found an able replacement for Vuller when the time comes."

"Do you expect to replace your bodyguard?"

"Not now. And hopefully not ever. Vuller has been at my side for many years. I owe him much. But earlier today, that was a shock. It has got me thinking about succession."

Archaen frowned. "But you have others. Brutus. Mandelson. Do you really need Elian?"

"Brutus and Mandelson each have their own strengths and weaknesses. I see qualities in Omdanan they don't possess." Sarok gave a wry grin. "Though I know you would like to claim him, too, no?"

"He has become one of us. One guild has already welcomed him. Others may come to envy them. Even my own. It would be a shame if he were taken from us. But he must honour his commitments."

"Honour? Yes, he must. And here he comes."

Omdanan approached. He came to a halt and looked between the two, uncertain who to address. Sarok gave him no choice: "So, what did you find? Anything interesting?"

"Uh… sir… there are marks along the jetty. They look like claw marks. From their spacing and depth I think they are from one creature. It hauled itself onto land."

"Are the marks fresh?"

"I don't think so. There is already some debris in the scratches."

"Perhaps you should continue your investigation. See if you can find where this thing went."

"Yes, sir." Omdanan nodded to the man, then the woman, and hurried back to the spot he'd been examining.

Sarok turned to fully face the woman. "And maybe, Ms Archaen, it is time for you to tell us what exactly happened here, and what we may be facing from tomorrow?"

Archaen slowly nodded assent. "But let us get settled first. Fire and food. And then I will tell you all about my suspicions…"

The Price of Freedom Part II: Velasia

***

"We call them *sashai*…"

The party was spread about the top floor of the longhouse at one end, where a hearth allowed a fire to be lit to cook and provide warmth. They lounged on their sleeping cloaks, light from the fire casting strange shadows throughout the space. Enabeth Archaen sat next to the hearth, with Miko opposite. After they had eaten, she began her tale.

"They were created in our labs decades ago. Their base form is of a creature from Regulon, which dominates the waterways of that world. They are black in colour, and appear hairless, though their skin is covered in fine cilia through which they detect movement in water and air. Added to their two large, black eyes, they are extremely sensitive to their surroundings and any prey that enters it, particularly in the water, where they spend their days. At night they emerge to sleep in hollows under leaf litter or in burrows by the roots of trees. They always were clever, and off-world biologists have suggested they at least match dolphins in intelligence. But that was before *we* got at them."

Sentain's eyes widened. "You're kidding me. Enabeth, are you saying we are now going to be faced with yet another intelligent species?"

The woman maintained her severe expression. "No. Or… maybe." She glanced quickly across the hearth at Miko, whose expression was unreadable in the half-light. "When they were amended, this was part of a project by a group of teenagers. And teenagers here are like teenagers everywhere, except that they are far cleverer than those in the Confederation, as I think you saw on your tour."

"Children playing with matches?" chortled Sarok.

"Just so. The creatures have a remarkably similar biology to us at the molecular level. And so the students decided it might be interesting to splice in some DNA, suitably adjusted of course, from… humans."

No one spoke. Sentain stared at the woman, a deep frown on his face, his head gently shaking. Archaen continued. "Of course, when we found out, the students were sanctioned and their project was terminated, but the creatures themselves—of which there were a significant number of young—were not destroyed. You see, we are not fond of euthanasia: as Ryven would say, it is unsporting."

"In my business, people as sporting as you rarely survive for long," noted Sarok. "When you have your foe at a disadvantage, it is best to finish them. My nemesis, Brundt, knows this well. You might learn something from her."

"But these creatures aren't *foes*, Mr Sarok."

"I suspect they soon will be. But I disrupt your story. Please go on."

The interruption seemed a relief for the woman, who had been given an excuse to look away from the disapproving anthropologist. She continued to focus on Sarok as she spoke. "The students had set up their breeding centre on an island in the stream near Verano. But the creatures matured quickly, and without predators, their large brood sizes meant they soon overran the island, stripping it of life. So it was decided to move them en masse here, to the Shadow Forest and its riverways. We suspected the other creatures here would provide them more of a challenge."

"But what doesn't kill you makes you stronger, eh?" said Sarok, wryly. "This seems to be the code you live by. So, you shouldn't be surprised they have endured and perhaps even thrived."

"You are right. We have had little to do with them for many years, as their potential range in the depth of the forest is huge. But they have been encountered a few times these last five years, and there have been several suspicious deaths along the Tessellac we guessed might be due to them."

"Intelligent?" Sentain's voice was strained. As he spoke, the others looked at him. "What exactly do you mean by *intelligent*, Enabeth?"

"They look after their young and teach them. They communicate with each other, though we do not understand their language. And we suspect they have learnt to use tools, to dig, to construct. But you, Irvan, should know more than any that the term *intelligence* is a subtle and unsatisfactory one. On Earth, dolphins and whales and chimpanzees have been declared 'intelligent', but they are not like us. The mongoose teaches its young to deal with scorpions. Various birds have been shown to use tools to break open nuts. Bats have been shown to have complex communication systems. And the same is true of creatures on other planets we have settled. We—humans—are still different. And the yeltoi and ganeroi are clearly like us. But the sashai? We truly do not know where they lie along the scale of intelligent things."

Miko stirred. He spoke slowly and carefully. "Yes, Cousin En. That is true. But some of us have wondered about whether the sashai have become something more. Bastian for one. In Sorvik, he privately urged me to be cautious."

"But what does this mean for us?" asked Sarok. "What threat do they pose? I still do not know whether they are the size of mice or giants!"

Archaen returned her attention to Sarok once more. "They are slightly smaller than us. Streamlined in water, but clumsier on land. They have four upper limbs, which they fold into themselves when swimming. Two of these have claws of sorts, which they use to fix and hold things, and the other two have rasps, which are used to grate prey so that the mush can be lapped up with a long tongue, which itself is like sandpaper and can cause burns and flesh loss if it touches you. And they have short, powerful legs on which they have flipper-like feet. You would not wish to be kicked by them, but they are used for propulsion, not attack."

"And one of these was nosing around up here? Omdanan?"

"Yes, sir. There are marks throughout the longhouse."

"And are you sure it's gone, Elian?" asked Vuller, from his place near Sarok. "I would hate to think there is one of these things lurking in the shadows."

"Yes, it is gone. The marks are old."

"But surely an equally important question," mused Sarok, "is whether it will come back? And whether its friends will too? Someone suggested the fisherman must have been taken by several of these things. Ms Archaen—what are your thoughts? Are we safe here? And even if we are, how do we stay safe from tomorrow when we head up the Blackflood?"

"I cannot say for sure, but I suspect we are safe here. They are most likely to attack in the water as they are clumsy away from it, and we would hear them move about if they were here. Also, their numbers this far down the river are likely to be low. From tomorrow, I don't know. We need to have caution while on the river anyway. But I'd suggest camping some distance from the water's edge at night."

"But you said they sleep on land," noted Sarok, "which suggests we could end up sharing the water margins with them."

"True, but on land we will have the advantage and they may leave us alone even if they know where we are. I'm not sure they would tangle with a party of our size just to get something to eat. They are not ravenous, like the orcs."

"But you're assuming their reason for attacking us would be for food," noted Sentain, who still looked deeply unhappy. "Maybe they are highly territorial? Maybe as we push up the river, we will come to breeding grounds, or nests of young, which they'll try to defend?"

"Maybe. But unlike the orcs they have no special reason to harm us, and nor will the sashai have contact with our enemy. So this still seems to me the best option open to us."

"There is little merit worrying about these ghosts at the moment," mused Miko, "though it may now be prudent to leave a watch at night." He slowly stood. "And I will take first one. In two hours, I will wake another. Elian?"

Archaen looked up at her kin. "Yes, this is a sensible plan. But Ryven, please keep to this floor. Your bravery is beyond question, but I sometimes worry about your lack of sense of self-preservation."

Miko laughed. "Cousin En, I will stay here, away from the water. I am not that careless of life!"

***

It was the afternoon of the second day after leaving the fishing camp on the Tessellac. On the first, they had made good progress on the black waters—taking advantage of a change in wind direction to hoist sails—and then they'd camped a couple of hundred metres from the river in a natural dell, returning to their tied-up boats in the morning.

Although there had been no sign of danger since setting off, Omdanan had nevertheless found the last day-and-a-half unnerving: the forest was preternaturally quiet, both on the water and off. And his sense of disquiet had grown throughout the day. They rowed against a subtly increasing river flow, with the only noise coming from the sound of oars dipping into water: there was no bird song or insect chirrup. Indeed, the leaden atmosphere had infused the party: talking was rare, and when conducted, done quietly, as if those speaking were fearful of breaking a spell.

Omdanan currently sat at the aft of his boat, nursing the tiller: he had the best view of the entire party, being the only one looking forwards. Miko had recognised his visual and sensory acuity, and ceded this position to him more and more—in preference to the others in the boat. The Leaguer had also admitted to feeling more comfortable knowing that they were being watched over by one of their only two archers. At the thought of this, Omdanan quickly flicked his gaze towards the bow at his feet and the quiver of arrows next to it, which now held just twenty-three darts after previous expenditures. He knew Enabeth Archaen had a similar number, as he has queried her on the matter in the morning while fretting about his own limited supplies.

And then he caught a glimpse in his peripheral vision of a shape in the water off the starboard side of the boat—but when he turned to look, it was gone. A shape? The black water had risen up in a hummock that might have been confused for a wind-blown wave—but the contours had seemed unnatural to him. After his heart initially jumped, it quickly settled, and he almost felt relief: he'd sensed that they were being watched, and now the invisible had just become, momentarily, visible. Now he knew he was right.

He quickly glanced at his crew: Miko and Vuller were rowing at the very front of the boat, with Sarok and Mandelson sitting nearer to him. None had noticed his sudden concern—which was probably for the best. He chose to say nothing for the moment to avoid alarm and wait until he was absolutely certain of the nature of the threat.

Now that he knew what he was looking for—the subtle uplift of water—the watcher became more obvious to him. For the next hour or so, the thing in the water periodically rose near the surface, sometimes to port, sometimes to starboard, sometimes closer to the lead boat and sometimes closer to Omdanan's rear boat. The river was now barely twenty metres wide, and at times felt more like a tunnel than a road, with trees on both banks rising to heights of five to ten metres, and the landscape now hilly, such that one forested hill or another frequently interceded between the party and the lowering sun as the river curved, casting them into a succession of twilights. It was as they passed from light into shadow that Omdanan noticed upticks in activity from the watcher, as though it was aware of its increased advantage caused by the above-water conditions.

And then there were two.

He caught sight of a careless splash—so soft, none of the rowers noticed it—some metres from the rising hump of the watcher. A spooked fish, or another sashai? He instinctively knew the answer to this question.

It wasn't until he noticed a third distortion of the water, a mere four metres from his boat, too distant from the other couple to be one of them, that he started to become concerned. These three all lay within the patch of river he could cover in one glance—but focusing on them meant he couldn't watch the rest of the river. There could be more. *Many* more. Omdanan slowly reached down to pick up his bow...

"Elian?" Miko had seen the young man's movements. He spoke softly, his voice just carrying from the front of the boat, startling the others and raising their attention levels until they too were fixed upon their steersman. "Is there a problem?"

"Uh... *yes*." With bow in hand, Omdanan plucked an arrow from his quiver and set it to the string. Raising his eyes to look at Miko, he caught yet another shape off the port side beyond the man, close to the bank, and then yet another shape closer-to. "We are surrounded."

"Steer to the bank," said Sarok, also speaking low. "We need to cover our backs."

"Yes—but wait," commanded Miko. "We must synchronise with En. Elian—signal her. Give her a countdown. Left bank."

Omdanan stood up in the aft of the boat. The other craft was five metres ahead; already his activity had been seen by the rowers there. He managed to catch Enabeth's eye, then raised one hand—leaving bow and cocked arrow held in his left hand by the stave—and pointed over to the left bank, and then opened his hand to show five fingers. He hoped the woman understood his gesture. She half-turned and he could see her mouth moving. When she stopped speaking and looked back, he held up his hand once more. "Five seconds," he said quietly, but loud enough for his crew to hear. Then he slowly peeled his fingers into his palm, one at a time.

As his final finger dropped, Omdanan sat back onto the gunwale and pushed the tiller with his free hand hard right, swinging the boat to the left.

"Pull!" shouted Miko, and the rowers dug violently into the water. They were no more than ten metres from the river's edge and it took mere seconds for the boat to surge across the water and thump into a muddy bank between the roots of a couple of large old trees. Omdanan had already released the tiller, and plucked up the anchor, which he tossed overboard. Looking up, he saw the other boat struggling, taking the bank at a more oblique angle a couple of second later, with its power coming from the port oarsmen alone—Reddas and Sentain—as their lack of a steersman meant they could only turn by the unequal application of force. He saw Archaen scrambling to the aft of the boat, having shipped her oar, grabbing for their anchor.

The sudden move appeared to confuse the creatures. A number had been between the boats and the left bank, and these disappeared below the water in a medley of splashes as they attempted to get out of the way.

While Miko and Reddas jumped ashore with ropes to secure their respective craft to riverside trees, the other members of the party seized weapons and readied themselves to ward off any amphibious attack, and Omdanan and Archaen held their notched bows at the ready.

But no attack came.

The shapes in the water had gone.

"What… what just happened?" Sentain's tremulous voice was loud enough to carry across to Omdanan in his boat. "I don't see anything."

"I did," said Mandelson, loudly, challenging the shroud of silence. "Something in the water. It dived out of the way. But it can't have gone far."

"What did you see, Elian?" called Archaen.

"Black shapes in the water. Following us for over an hour. There was one at first; now there are many."

"Well, they've shown us no aggression yet," noted Miko. "If they're just curious, that's fine. But will they stay just curious?"

"So what do we do now?" asked Sarok, clutching a spear. "The light is starting to fade, and they must still be out there. Should we stop and camp—or will that give these things time to think and maybe gather in greater strength?"

"If we carry on, we will not be able to out-run or evade them," replied Miko. "And perhaps all we will do is travel closer to their home. If they do plan to attack, it might be best to prepare for it here and now."

"That makes sense," concurred Sarok. "Ms Archaen?"

"Agreed. Let's camp. Same form as yesterday."

"But what about the boats?" asked Sentain. "Won't it be a risk leaving them here, now that we know the sashai are out there?"

"They didn't attack or take the boats at the fishing camp," said Sarok. "So why would they do any different to ours? But perhaps you are right. Maybe they will feel emboldened closer to home and in greater numbers?"

"We have no choice," said Archaen. "We cannot take the boats with us through the trees. But take whatever supplies you need and… *Elian?*"

Omdanan had raised one hand, which he slowly lowered to indicate a spot in the water, close to the further bank. All turned to follow the line of his arm. There was a small upwelling, a darker patch in the black water, one that might easily be taken by the unpractised eye to be a glassy river-smoothed stone jutting from the flow. The shape remained still for some moments, before slowly lowering beneath the surface. But the party continued to stare, in silence. A moment later, another patch of water near to the first changed in texture, and this rose slightly higher.

"Eyes!" whispered Mandelson, harshly, as she changed her grip on her spear. "Two large, lidless eyes."

"Yes," said Miko, next to the woman. "Like orbs of black onyx. And… now another pair."

The first upwelling was joined by a second, and then others, until more than a score of disturbances marred the river surface, forming an arc from a spot just upriver from the first boat, to downriver from the second.

"I wish I had a throwing spear," muttered Mandelson.

"And I am glad you do not," countered Miko, still speaking softly. Then he spoke more loudly so that they could also hear him in the other boat. "I suggest we do not antagonise them. Elian—careful on your bow."

"What now?" hissed Sentain, holding his staff out before him.

"Wait!" said Archaen. "It is their move."

The party and the sub-surface watchers faced off for some seconds… and then, slowly, the shapes submerged almost as one. More seconds passed.

"Are they gone?" asked Sentain, nervously. "Have they… *fuck*!"

The first boat rocked violently as something struck it below the surface. The crew members still aboard swayed to retain their balance, with Sentain having to clasp onto the rim of one of the white-black shields that lined the gunwales.

"To shore, quick!" commanded Archaen.

But as the party moved to join Miko and Reddas on the bank, the first boat was struck once more, and then so was the other, causing Omdanan at its front to stagger. As he attempted to steady himself, the arrow slipped from between the fingers of his left hand and dropped into the water. Sarok reached forwards to grasp him by his mail shirt and pull him back. As he did so, a dark claw appeared over the edge of the aft, by the tiller. The men backed away along the boat towards the shoreline and their colleagues, who had already clambered over tree roots and onto firm land beneath the trees. But the intruder did not stop. The black head with two bulbous eyes rose further up, and beneath the two clawed limbs two more came into view, these flattened and tipped with rasps, which steadied the creature as it flopped forwards on top of Omdanan's abandoned quiver of arrows. By now, the two men had reached the other end of the boat. Omdanan's face burned red in embarrassment; he drew a long knife at his belt.

Sarok whispered: "*No*, Elian. Let it be."

Omdanan and the creature stared at each other—watched by the others, who'd made it safely ashore. The creature nudged further forwards, pulling its short, powerful legs onto the boat, then pushing up with its four front limbs until it was in a crouch. It continued to observe in silence, with its fellows bobbing in the shallows, making no move to join it or make landfall. Then the sashai unfurled a clawed limb and waved it back and forth in front of its torso, as though attempting to communicate.

From behind, Omdanan heard: "Fuck this…"

Past his right-hand side, a projectile flew. The spear was clumsy in flight, not intended for throwing, but at close range and propelled with strength it had sufficient aerodynamics to fly true: the spiked butt of Mandelson's spear, with its curved blade now at the tail, struck the creature low in the abdomen. There was a piercing shriek and a fountain of black-red blood spewed over the deck. The sashai scrabbled at the spear with its four limbs, managing to tear it from its body with claws and rasps, and then it swayed and pitched backwards into the water.

The river came alive, becoming a frothing fury that was accompanied by a wave of shrill cries that made the members of the party wince and recoil. As Omdanan turned and was pulled to shore by Sarok, the boat rose up from the water, battered from beneath, pummelled this way and that. The second boat received similar treatment, rising up and then almost flying, its port side crashing into the shoreline roots, with a splintering of the protective shields lining that gunwale.

"Away now!" cried Archaen. "Into the forest!"

Without a backwards glance, Omdanan and the rest of the company turned and fled under the trees, leaping over undergrowth and swinging around trunks, the two parties following converging lines into the shadows of the forest.

Chapter 12

"That was fucking stupid, Mandelson," Sarok wheezed, almost doubled over from the exertion of their flight. "What the *fuck* were you playing at?"

The company had come to a halt in a small clearing of the forest caused by a fallen tree, sparsely lit by the descending afternoon sun. Archaen had passed an arrow to Omdanan from her small supply, and both crouched with drawn bows at the edge of the clearing nearest to the river—perhaps four hundred metres away behind intervening trees. The shrill cries of the sashai had ceased; the only sound now was that of Brutus and Sarok panting.

"Stupid?" sneered Mandelson. "This whole affair is stupid. They..." she waved one arm towards Miko, who stood opposite her, "...should have just bombed com Durrel from the air. But as we're here, it's time to stop fucking about. A couple of days ago you lectured our hosts about what Brundt would have done with the sashai. Well, *Sarok*, what would she have done *here*?"

"You tell me." Sarok glowered at the woman.

"She would have let the creatures gather together, and then burnt them out. And then she would have killed the survivors as they fled."

"Burnt them out? In the water? How, exactly? We're a little short of napalm!"

"Yeah, but we have a wizard with us. A fucking useless one, but I'm sure he could have done something."

Sentain looked at the woman in shock. "What do you mean? I couldn't... I wouldn't murder all those..."

"*Murder*?" the woman's voice dripped with scorn. "I don't know who is worse here—the boy with his scruples or this lot..." she waved towards Miko again, "who still think they are playing games. If we fail in this... *quest*... it won't be as a result of *my* strength but of *your* weakness."

Sarok had been fuming; he reached for the short blade at his waist. But Vuller was ready and quickly stepped across, acting as a barrier between the arguing pair.

Brutus was also nearby and took a half-step, raising his hands. "Whoa, Mandelson, take it easy, man!"

Sarok spoke around Vuller. "Your value to me is waning, Mandelson. Take care—"

"Or what?" The woman smiled, but without an iota of humour. Then she spat on the ground and turned and walked away, further into the forest.

**

They decided to camp in the clearing, rather than risk returning to the boats in the fading light. Omdanan took it upon himself to patrol the boundary, a little way back towards the river, while the others slouched around a small fire, which Archaen judged to be the lesser of two evils, more likely to deter than attract the creatures of the forest. But their supplies were on the boats and they had nothing to eat except scraps in some of their personal packs, which were shared around.

Mandelson returned some twenty minutes after she had stalked off, emerging from the gloom carrying a long, roughly straight branch. She didn't say a word but perched at one end of the fallen tree that had created the cleared space, where she started to whittle the branch into the haft of a new spear.

Sarok tensed when he saw the woman but managed to calm his heart rate. He turned his back on her and looked at the others scattered around the campfire, sitting on their cloaks, some still wearing their mail overshirts, others having taken these off for comfort. He fixed his attention on Enabeth Archaen.

"We should discuss our options, Ms Archaen. How fucked are we?"

The woman had been gazing into the fire. She looked up at her interrogator. "Matters are not good, but perhaps not terrible. At first light, we need to return to the boats to see what we can salvage."

"And if the boats aren't there?"

"Then we will have to continue on foot."

Sarok grimaced and shook his head. "You mean, through this deadly forest, that even scares your own people? With no supplies? Great. And would you have us continue to follow the river and risk the attentions of the sashai, whom we've royally pissed off, or go some other way?"

"From my estimations, we are still west of the Copper Gate, but not by much. Our original plan was to take the Blackflood all the way out of the forest, emerging east of the gate, then backtrack west. In distance, this would be longer than necessary, but quicker and less dangerous... barring the wrath of the sashai. But the option has always been there to leave the river and cut north through the forest. Still, it is a shame: one more day on the river, and I think we would be almost due south of the gate and the shortest distance from it as the crow flies."

"There is still hope the boats are whole," noted Miko, who sat at the woman's side. "Again I would remind you, they did not damage the fishermen's boats. These are of no use to them."

"They might not take them for their own," said Sarok, "but they might not leave them intact, either. They were doing a good job of taking out their anger on them as we fled."

Miko shrugged. "True. But as we cannot affect the matter now, it is best we sleep and see what morning brings. Someone needs to remain awake to replace Elian as sentry when he returns."

***

But Elian Omdanan didn't return—at least, not until the black, star-infused sky began to grey and the early sun washed out the light of the other stars. When he did, he found all in the camp asleep. Although he felt tired, he was surprised at how alive he felt. The Shadow Forest was a place of hints and subtle signs, ever demanding attention. Although he'd seen no creature above the size of a rabbit, he had heard plenty more: snuffles and grunts from some, a tick-tick-ticking sound from another, a distant shriek that seemed to tell of the pain of captured prey, and… something else.

It had first manifest as a soft whisper, which might have been taken for a gentle stirring of wind, but which Omdanan knew was something else, a creature of caution, a hunter supreme. He had sensed this early in the night, between the clearing and the river, but then it had moved away, as if aware it had been heard. He had sensed it again a couple of hours later, as he had been circling back to his companions and about to hand over watch duties, now off to the west of the camp and closer. Again, the creature had grown wary and faded back into the deep shadows. But Omdanan's concern had grown, along with the thought: did any of his companions have the woodcraft to follow the creature? And so he had paused at the edge of the firelight, observing all asleep bar Brutus, whose head was already nodding on his giant neck as he attempted to keep awake, and he'd decided to stay out a little bit longer.

For the rest of the night he had circled the camp, unconcerned about the sashai, clumsy on land and never venturing far into the forest, but vigilant for *the stalker*, as he had named the unseen creature. He'd detected it twice more, and once almost thought he saw it, a blacker black than the night-shrouded trees themselves, almost a void in vision. And he was sure that whatever the creature was, it had seen him, considered him, and then dissolved into the background. Somehow, Omdanan did not feel that it was fear that had caused the thing to pause.

Reddas Archaen was first to stir at Omdanan's deliberately noisy entrance. The large man rolled onto one arm and looked about.

"Elian? What time? Is it morning? Brutus never woke me…" And then the man came fully alert. "Ah, our poor giant could not stave off sleep. You have been up all night?"

"I have. But it is nothing. I couldn't sleep."

Others began to wake at the sound of the voices. Brutus came awake with a start, one leg kicking out involuntarily. He scrambled to his feet and looked about, slightly bewildered. Then he saw the young Meridian. "Ahhhhhh... *fuck*. Sorry, mate, but you should have woken me."

"A supernova wouldn't have woken you," laughed Reddas. "At least you didn't snore like the previous night, or else none of us would have gotten any sleep and we'd all look as bleary eyed as Elian... or as bleary eyed as he should look. By God, Elian, are you a machine?"

Omdanan smiled gently and looked away.

***

Soon all were up, dressed in their mail, and armed. They crept back towards the river, then paused to allow Omdanan to go ahead alone. The young man returned ten minutes later.

"There are no sashai, but there is only one boat."

"Fuck!" hissed Sarok. "Well, one is better than none—so lead on."

At the river, overhung by trees, they found Miko's boat, bobbing in the flow a couple of metres from the bank, held in place by its anchor, but the other boat was gone.

Enabeth Archaen observed the situation grimly. "There go half our supplies, a couple of spears, and your axe, Brutus." She smiled wanly at the giant, who'd managed to take his huge mace with him the previous night, but he'd not had the time or hands to take his other weapon. "But Elian may have got his arrows back."

"And my spear is there, too," observed Mandelson. The woman was nearest and used her new weapon—a makeshift spear with a sharpened wooden point—to snare the boat and tug it towards them. After a second's thought, Reddas slid into the shallow water to reach out and grasp the gunwale—in a gap between two shields, where another had been shattered—and complete the task of pulling the craft to the bank.

"Hold fast!" said Miko. "Quiet! Elian—anything?"

The Meridian scoured the river for any disturbances. The rest of the company did the same, though all knew that the young man was the most likely to spot anything that was there. After some moments, he rose from his crouch and shook his head.

"Good," continued Miko. "And better still, I see our archer's toys are still in the bottom of the boat." The Leaguer stepped across onto the craft, steadied by Mandelson and Reddas at the bank. He scrabbled around, fore and aft, then announced: "Nothing seems to have been taken. We still have half our supplies, both sets of oars, and the weapons that were abandoned. What now, En?"

"The boat will take us all, at a push. But we do not know how far off the sashai are, nor how they will react when they see us. It may be safer to abandon it and take to the land."

"Uh, sorry, but that might not be wise."

The company turned as one to look at Omdanan.

"What do you mean, Elian?" asked Archaen. "What have you seen?"

"Last night, there was something around the camp. It was watching us. Sizing us up. It knew I sensed it, otherwise…" he shrugged.

Sentain whitened. "It wasn't one of those chameleonic orang-utan hybrids, was it, Elian?"

"I couldn't tell. I never actually *saw* it."

Sentain turned to Archaen, who stood next to him: "Enabeth—could it have been?"

"There are many creatures in the forest. But it's not impossible."

Sarok swore under his breath. "Like the boy, I would not be keen to face one of those again. And we know that whatever it is will probably be nearby and may well be watching us now. Whereas—"

"Whereas the sashai may *not* be." Archaen looked down in thought, then up at her kin standing in the boat. "Last night, I asked for one more day on the river. Perhaps we have my wish. We should divvy up the supplies and keep our packs near, ready for a rapid decamp. Then I suggest Reddas, Brutus, you—Cousin

Ryven—and Vuller, take the oars. We will need your power as we will be overladen, and the wind in this close country will be of no help to us. We will at least have more eyes and two notched bows to see and deal with any threats."

Miko nodded. "I concur."

"Me too," said Sarok. "And… I hate to say this, but Mandelson did have one point last night. Sentain—you need to be ready. Think up a spell. If the creatures attack us en masse, you may prove the difference—and God help us if that is the case."

Sentain opened his mouth to protest, but must have seen the intent eyes of his companions upon him and thought better of it. He half-heartedly raised his staff and muttered: "Abracadabra!"

***

With all aboard, the boat was crowded. Omdanan perched at the prow with his bow, ahead of the four rowers, while Sarok took the tiller with Archaen beside him, also holding a bow. In the space between those at the stern and the mast sat Mandelson, now reacquainted with her exotic Indonesian spear, and a sombre Sentain, nursing his staff. All wore their packs on their backs, save Brutus, who kept his on the floor in front of him, along with his giant mace.

As they began their journey upriver, time seemed to drag. Every rustle of wind through the trees, or ripple in the water, seemed ominous to the watchers. The land now rose up about them in a series of forested hills. In places, old trees—dead or dying, often leafless—leant out over the black water, like the grasping skeletal fingers of ancient giants. And whereas the banks had until now largely been smooth, low, and root-lined, geologic changes in the land meant they were now rockier, with clusters of boulders and occasional thin, shingle beaches. Sometimes broken branches flowed past them, and got snagged in the oars, having to be shaken off.

They rowed for an hour, then rested for five minutes—with the anchor deployed to prevent the current from undoing their progress—then repeated the pattern. The morning passed, and with it some of the company's tension. They took a slightly longer break at noon, to eat cold rations from their regained supplies, and soon carried on.

An hour or so into the afternoon, Sentain was ostensibly looking off the port side—though secretly admiring Enabeth Archaen's heroic pose at the stern—when he noticed a gentle splash in the water behind them. He frowned and shook his head, uncertain of what he had seen. All the same, he scrunched forwards to rest against one of the protective shields on the gunwale to scrutinise the water more intensely. Several minutes passed, and he was about to settle back, convinced that he'd seen nothing unnatural, when he noticed a more pronounced splash around five metres off the stern. As he rose slightly to gain a better angle of sight, Archaen noticed him.

"What is it, Irvan?"

"Uh, not sure. Just fish, I think. Behind us."

Mandelson looked sharply at him, then turned to peer back from the starboard side of the boat.

"Why do you say that?" asked Archaen, also turning to look behind.

"I just… well… it just reminds me of how fish sometimes break the surface to take insects."

"That's certainly one reason why fish might breach the surface," noted Sarok at the tiller, who continued to look forwards. "Another is when they attempt to elude predators. Take that from a man who enjoys his fishing."

"Sure. But if it were anything else, Elian would have noticed."

"Not if we're being followed," continued Sarok. "Elian's a talented lad, but he doesn't have eyes in the back of his head."

Silence descended, as the three at the rear intensified their observations. Several minutes passed. Then Mandelson growled: "*Fuck*! There—by the right bank."

"I don't see…" said Archaen, twisting further around.

Sentain's view was obscured by his colleagues.

"It's gone now. I just saw the top of its head. Just like yesterday."

"Let's not panic yet," muttered Sarok. "It might be by itself. They didn't attack until they had numbers."

"So let's make sure they never get the numbers," scowled Mandelson. "When it pokes its head out again, shoot it, Archaen."

The Leaguer quickly looked back at the woman from Corvus. "I didn't agree with your actions yesterday, Ms Mandelson. But you have now determined our relationship with the sashai. Still, I will only shoot if I think I can get a kill."

"Enabeth, are you sure?" Sentain asked anxiously.

"Yes. The situation has changed. Please be ready, Irvan." Then she faced forwards and spoke more loudly to the rest of the crew: "We have contact. We are being followed. Just one at the moment. Elian—if anything approaches the boat, *kill it.*"

For perhaps another half hour, the situation remained stable. The sashai periodically rose up to observe them, always at a different place, and never closer than a couple of boat lengths. Meanwhile, the river flow increased, making the task of rowing increasingly difficult. More and more debris was also evident in the river—leaves, branches, and even the occasional animal corpse.

"River's getting more turbulent," noted Sarok. "I'm reminded of the downflow from rapids. What does Bastian's map reveal?"

"Very little," admitted Archaen. "The map only shows what has been charted by our people, and as you know, the Blackflood has not been extensively travelled. In Verano, Yasmina may very well be shaking her head at our folly."

"Well, if there are rapids, then that will be it for us. The portage of this boat overland past any rapids—through these trees—would be untenable."

"Perhaps it's no bad thing if nature makes the decision for us. We have been lucky so far today—"

"Don't speak so soon," muttered Mandelson. "Our friend is back, and now he has company."

"Yes, I saw a second, too," squealed Sentain.

And at that moment, Omdanan shouted from up front: "One in the water, and one on the shore, behind a tree."

A low sound was evident, a steadily increasing hiss. The water became distinctly choppy, and white wave crests began to speckle the black water. They were coming up to a bend in the river, around which they could not see because of low hanging branches. At the oars, Vuller cursed at the extra effort required.

"Scylla and Charybdis," murmured Sentain.

Archaen looked down at him and smiled. "Perhaps. But Ulysses never had a wizard. Ready your spell."

They reached the curve of the river, and the hissing rose in magnitude. Ahead, they could see what Sarok had feared: three hundred metres distant, the river tumbled over and around a series of boulders, and on these…

"Sashai ahead!" shouted Omdanan. "Scores of them!"

The creatures had assembled and were waiting: they clung to the rocks in the spray, or bobbed in the bubbling waters, or held onto the roots of trees on the banks on both sides, half-in and half-out of the water, raising themselves to better see their approaching prey.

"And behind!" echoed Mandelson. "It's a fucking trap!"

At that moment, the whole boat lifted as it was struck from beneath. The craft rocked and turned. Ahead, the sashai from the rapids slipped under the water, presumably heading towards them. From behind, many more also slid beneath the surface. Then black claws began to tug at the four oars, and more sashai rose out of the water, clasping the side of the boat at the row of shields or the bare gunwale where other shields had been dislodged the previous day.

"Kill the fuckers," shouted Mandelson. "Kill them all!" She slashed with the curved blade of her spear, severing the limb of a creature that was tugging at one of the shields with clawed digits.

At the front of the boat, Omdanan was a sudden whirlwind of motion, drawing and firing one arrow after another.

At the aft of the boat, Archaen did the same, but more slowly, and with greater deliberation.

"To the shore!" shouted Sarok, throwing the tiller hard right. But though the boat began to turn left, it did so slowly, pushed backwards by the current, with the oars no longer at work.

Various exclamations, shouts, and curses came from the rowers. Vuller's oar was pulled away, as was Miko's, but the other two big men kept hold of theirs and attempted to wrestle them back from the creatures tugging at them from below the black surface. With a huge roar, Brutus levered up his oar, lifting two sashai completely out of the water. Omdanan turned and fired arrows through the eyes of the creatures before they could release their grip, and they fell dead into the water. But as soon as Brutus dumped his oar back into the river to attempt to give them impetus towards the bank, it was snagged again by more creatures. Meanwhile, Reddas cursed, dropping his oar as a lower-limb rasp from one sashai slapped at his vulnerable hand and bloodily tore a strip of flesh from it.

"Sentain, wake up!" cried Sarok.

Momentarily stunned by the suddenness and ferocity of the attack, Sentain now came alive. He stood in the rocking boat, stumbled forwards, and steadied himself against the mast. He had been rehearsing the words he needed in his head ever since sighting one of the creatures: he began to chant aloud: "*Fortious... Sondaralus... Yashup!*" And as he finished pronouncing the last word, he leant over and thrust the head of the staff into the water.

A deep, low, thrumming sound reverberated through the air, and the water around the staff's head blasted upwards, showering those in the boat and throwing Sentain backwards into Mandelson, pitching the woman into one of the shields and splitting her brow. Around the staff's entry point, a wave surged outwards, tipping the boat to one side and sending black water foaming onto the opposite bank.

As the boat tipped back upright, the attack ceased... completely.

The Price of Freedom Part II: Velasia

***

Sarok had saved himself from falling overboard by reflexively grabbing at the tiller, winding himself as it dug into his belly. But Enabeth Archaen had been less fortunate, pitching into the water. Wheezing, Sarok held out a hand to the woman: "Quick, my hand…"

But Archaen was not alone, and her path to the boat was suddenly blocked by a flotsam of bodies bubbling up from beneath—of fish and sashai. Indeed, all about the boat it was the same, the river carpeted with stunned and killed creatures, either motionless or flapping about insensibly on the surface. Sarok watched as the woman's eyes cleared and she assessed the situation, then made a decision: she turned in the water and struck out for the nearest bank, not ten metres away.

Sarok quickly turned and stood: the devastation caused by whatever spell had been cast by the anthropologist was wide, but not terminal for their attackers: those furthest downstream were already splashing their limbs, showing signs of recovery, and while some of the sashai nearby seemed dead, others started to twitch…

"Follow Archaen!" Sarok shouted. "Now's our chance! Into the river! Swim!" And without waiting to see if his instructions were being obeyed, he dived into a momentary clear patch of water, following the Leaguer woman.

One by one, the others followed. Mandelson reversed her spear and threw it at the shore, where its sharpened butt sank into a tree trunk, and then she dived in. Miko, Vuller and Reddas all rolled into the water from their side of the boat. Omdanan hastily slipped his bow over his shoulder before he too abandoned ship. And that left Sentain and Brutus.

The giant, seeing the young man's trepidation, growled: "Let me give you a hand." He grabbed hold of Sentain's mail shirt and heaved him into the water, where he landed atop one of the dead creatures. With a gasp, the man rolled into the cold water and struggled to fight the current and the weight of his armour while attempting to keep a hold of his staff. Brutus ruefully looked at the giant mace he had retrieved from the foot of the boat, shook his head, gave it a good swirl, and launched it towards the bank, where it splintered one tree. Then he dived in after the anthropologist.

Enabeth Archaen had made the bank, in a spot between two boulders overhung by gnarled, grey-trunked trees. She had lost her bow, but the black sword still slapped against her thigh. With one hand she took hold of the tip of one of the boulders and leant out a hand to the floundering Sarok, helping to haul him onto the rocky bank. As he spluttered, retching out river water, the woman edged down the bank to help others intersecting land further down. Mandelson ignored the offer of help, scurrying ashore and then heading back upriver to reclaim her embedded spear, but others didn't, and soon after, Miko, Vuller, and a bloodied Reddas stood beside her.

Brutus and Sentain were the last remaining in the water, the giant ignoring the weight of his own massive mail shirt as he swam, dragging the ineffectively flapping Sentain with him. As Brutus neared the shore, he pushed Sentain forwards to where Miko and Vuller had re-entered the shallows. The two men grasped the reluctant wizard and pulled him ashore.

But before Brutus could make landfall himself, something buffeted him sideways...

"They're coming-to," shouted Archaen. "Elian!"

Omdanan now had the sole bow—but very few arrows. He jumped upon a boulder to get a better angle and fired into the water at a shape near the giant's leg. Brutus was momentarily freed, but as he made another overarm stroke, now just two metres from the shore, something else came at him from beneath.

Brutus gave a roar of pain, and thrashed about, but the water absorbed his blows and negated his great strength. The area around him paled, as red mixed with black. Then Brutus gave one last heave and appeared to have set foot on the river bottom. But as he started to straighten, something propelled itself into his side, turning him around, and something else grasped an arm. A third creature then emerged from the water onto the man's back, and brought its four limbs around his head, stabbing and tearing. A final arrow from Omdanan split the sashai between its eyes, but as it peeled off Brutus' back, this revealed the mess it had made of the man's face.

The giant pitched into the water, suddenly covered in a writhing mass of creatures…

And then he was gone.

"Brutus!" cried Vuller. He turned to look at Sentain, prone on the rocks a short distance away. "Quick, Sentain! Your spell again!" He staggered over to the gasping man, but Sarok was there also, and he intervened, placing a restraining hand on his bodyguard's arm.

"Not this time, Vuller. We're at the river's edge. Whatever he did will not have the same effect, and even so would likely kill Brutus along with the creatures. Let's get away from the water. We can do no more here."

The fellowship had lost its first member.

Chapter 13

The company left the river, following Enabeth Archaen into the forest and up the incline of a low hill. They struggled in sodden clothing, burdened by mail armour, carrying full packs and whatever weapons they had retained—mainly swords and knives scabbarded at waists, although Omdanan had kept his bow and empty quiver, while Mandelson had her spear and Sentain his staff. Most still wore their helmets, though Sentain and Reddas had lost theirs during the evacuation.

By the time Archaen drew them to a halt twenty minutes later, the Blackflood was well behind them and they were no longer able to hear the splashing of the rapids or the screams of the sashai. They stopped in a small clearing, created by two trees that had fallen towards each other, into which the mid-afternoon sun penetrated. The undergrowth was thicker here, full of shrubs and fern-like plants fighting each other for the chance to feel the sun on their leaves.

"Rest now," said Archaen. "See to your gear. We must assess our plans and options." She drew her black sword and used it to clear some space around one of the tree trunks. As she did so, several small, rodent-like creatures bolted from her harvesting blade, and something reptilian slithered away through the green-grey foliage.

Miko and Reddas moved up to the woman and drew their own swords, which they used to help her clear more space. Others followed this cue, and soon there was a bare, trampled patch between the fallen trunks into which they were able to gather and slouch. Some took the opportunity to remove their armour.

Sarok cast his mail noisily onto one of the trunks, then reached out his arms to stretch his shoulders and back. He watched Archaen search through her backpack for moment, and then he turned to consider the rest of the party: Sentain sat on the ground in mail and pack, hunched over and disconsolate; Vuller perched on a trunk, staring at his boots; Mandelson further along, examining her spear and testing its sharpness; Omdanan stood off to the side, alert, scanning the forest eaves; and Miko and Reddas sat on the second trunk, leant in to each other, talking low.

"Well, that was exciting," declared Sarok. "What else do you have planned for us today, Ms Archaen?"

The woman found what she was looking for and withdrew Bastian's map. She already held a primitive compass in the palm of one hand. She looked over to him. "That is about to be determined. Perhaps you would like to come and see." She moved her pack off the trunk and put the map in its place, smoothing it down onto the split, brown-grey bark. Sarok noticed Miko and Reddas halt their conversation and turn to look towards them, then Miko stood and made his way over.

Once Sarok and Miko reached her side, Archaen waved a hand over the map. "As you can see, the scale is small. It is not of great help."

"Perhaps Bastian should send some mapping parties in future?" noted Miko.

The woman didn't respond; instead, she used one finger to trace their route up the Tessellac and the Blackflood. "I estimate we are *here*—almost due south of the Copper Gate. Perhaps a little to the west also. And that would mean we have another forty to fifty kilometres to travel through the forest, and then another ten to twenty from the edge to the gate itself."

"No problem," declared Sarok, with a hint of sarcasm. "We should be there by nightfall."

Archaen looked up sharply. "No. But we might be through the forest in two days. The distance isn't great, but the terrain is difficult. We will have to spend tonight and tomorrow night in the forest, which I fear. I am determined not to risk a third night here. We have been fortunate so far, but we should not press our luck."

"Fortunate?" The voice was that of Sentain, who had been listening like the others. "Tell that to Brutus."

Archaen turned to look at the anthropologist, her expression initially severe, but then it softened. "I did not mean to downplay Brutus' fate, Irvan. But in truth, I'm surprised we got this far with only his loss and a couple of scrapes."

Sarok turned to face the young man also. "You seem overly emotional, Sentain. I didn't realise you two were friends."

"We weren't, but… he was part of our fellowship, and so I will miss him. Won't you?"

Sarok found the anthropologist's glare surprisingly sharp and uncomfortable. He initially matched it, but then he looked away and shrugged. "Of course. But in my business, death is an occupational hazard. I have lost a lot of men and women. More than I can count or even remember. Brutus is simply the latest."

"But he was with you a long time, wasn't he? Doesn't that count for anything?"

Did it? Sarok wondered. He glanced over at Vuller, who was also looking up at him, a tentative expression on his face. "Of course it does. Brutus was loyal. Ever since I recruited him on his release from Ghuraj some years ago, he has been one of the few not to betray me. But before you burst into tears, Sentain, you should remember that he wasn't a good man. He hastened the progress of many others into the afterlife."

"That is true," interjected Vuller. "But most of those he hurt deserved it."

"Most?" wondered Archaen.

"As the boss said, he wasn't a saint. He had a thing about people in uniform."

Miko intervened. "We have a custom amongst our people, that when we suffer a loss in our games we speak briefly about the one who has left us, *once*, and then put all further thoughts and talk about them aside until they can be properly honoured. So this discussion is apt. All who want to speak of Brutus should do so now, and then not again until we return to Sorvik or Verano."

Archaen nodded. "Well said, Cousin." She looked about the party, and her eyes alighted on Mandelson. "What about you, *Beth*. You also knew him for some time. Do you wish to say anything now?"

The Price of Freedom Part II: Velasia

The woman with red-streaked hair at last turned her attention from her spear. Her expression was inscrutable. "Me? I knew him for less than a year. All I would say is that he was not as dumb as he looked. He knew not to mess with me, so he learnt quicker than most of Sarok's lackeys."

Sarok tensed at the disrespectful tone of the woman, but his reply was pre-empted by Reddas.

"I knew him for less time. But we were together on com Durrel's ship, and he came with me when we first arrived on Arkon. For my part, I found him entertaining. He had a big appetite and was a happy drunk. For that, I will miss him."

Sarok clamped his mouth shut and glared at the woman, while Vuller cast worried glances between the two. As no one else spoke, Miko then declared: "Does no one wish to say anything more? Well, that was a brief eulogy, but it is *done*. None should now dwell on Brutus' demise until we are finished with this quest."

"Suits me," muttered Mandelson. "So are we going to sit around here all day, or what? I share Archaen's desire not to spend any longer here than we must." She stood, leaning on her spear. "Which way now?"

***

They set off, following Enabeth Archaen's lead, though their progress proved slow and stuttering. The Leaguer paused frequently to refer to her compass—a lodestone on a bronze plate—after which she would shift their direction of travel subtly.

Following directly behind the woman, Sentain noticed after a while that these course changes were invariably to their right by a few degrees, suggesting that they had a natural bias to bear off to the left, perhaps down to Archaen's stride length being slightly shorter for one leg than the other. He recalled having read that this was typical and tended to lead people in featureless terrains to travel in circles, ending up after some time back near where they started. Though the forest wasn't as bland as a desert, the tall trees—spaced out by perhaps two or three metres—were difficult to tell apart, and together prevented sight very far into the distance. He supposed Archaen was fixing on a particular tree after each compass reference and heading for this, but the land was not flat, and old roots, patches of fern, and sudden outcrops of boulders, meant target trees were not necessarily reached head-on at their mid-point—hence the need for constant checks and corrections. On top of this, the land undulated severely, so that a direct line northwards would have taken them constantly up and down over some significant hills, and clearly Archaen was making some adjustment for this, letting them drift eastwards at times if this would ease their passage and keep them on lower, flatter slopes.

At the start, Sentain trudged dolefully and unaware, enervated by their close escape from the sashai and emotionally drained by Brutus' loss. But after a while, his energy started to return and he began to take a keener interest in their surroundings. Aside from watching Archaen and her compass, he turned his attention to his comrades. He noticed that Omdanan tended to keep out to the right flank, his head up and alert, often with Mandelson close behind, while to the left flank, Miko and Reddas—the latter's left hand bandaged, following his encounter with a sashai rasp—seemed to take turns in front. By default, this meant Vuller and Sarok travelled together behind him, although Sentain could never summon the energy to turn around to confirm this.

After assessing the condition of the party, Sentain next turned to consider the forest itself. The first thing he noticed was how quiet it was. There was no sound of birds or insects, and for much of the time, all he could hear was the crashing of the company through the undergrowth and an occasional curse or pant. And then, after perhaps half-an-hour, he heard a strange, echoing hoot from somewhere off to his right, followed by a sharp crackling of snapped branches. The others heard this too, and stopped, turned, crouched. No one spoke, but after some seconds, Omdanan—who was nearest to the sound—rose up tall, turned towards the watching Archaen, and a gave a signal with one hand. The woman rose also, and continued forwards…

They did not hear the mysterious 'hooter' again that day. But once he had fully acclimatised to the sounds of the forest—or rather, the absence of sounds—Sentain began to pick up more subtle whisperings and cracklings from the branches above. At first, he thought this was due to the wind, and although he couldn't feel any air movement on his face, he supposed that weather still existed in the realm outside the forest bubble, and that the upper branches of the canopy were being jostled. Indeed, he had almost forgotten these liminal sounds when he heard a muttered exchange from behind.

"…pity Omdanan has got no arrows…"

"…take the fuckers down…"

"… before they get us…"

And then Vuller and Sarok must have been forced to separate, going in opposite directions around a tree or clump of ferns, and their voices faded out.

Sentain would have turned to look and question, but at that moment he had to scramble over a large, moss-covered tree root and push through a patch of grey fronds, and his intent dissolved. Afterwards, he attempted to listen harder to the sounds above, and peer more intensely at the canopy ten metres over his head, though his inadequate senses were unable to resolve the source of the disturbance with any greater acuity.

In fact, for most of the time, Sentain could see little at all. The denseness of the canopy gave the impression that he was walking through a vast, gloomy cathedral of grey pillars with a rubble-strewn floor, where only the occasional shaft of light made it through sporadic holes in the metaphorical roof. But when, on rare occasions, there was some bigger breach in the canopy, and a more substantial beam of light was able to spear through to the forest floor, it was like a spotlight had been turned on, and suddenly there would be an island of light and colour, a burst of green, a patch of red flowers, ferns revealed as yellow or russet instead of the assumed grey. Indeed, at one point Sentain felt a pang of resentment when Archaen stopped to look at her compass and then turned to head off several degree to their right, taking them away from a glorious island of light and colour that had been directly in their path.

After three or four hours at a constant pace, without a break, and with the gloom growing, Archaen came to a halt. She briefly glanced at her compass, shook her head, folded the device within her palm, and thrust it into a leather pouch tied onto her belt. Sentain came to a stop beside her, and wearily leant against a tree.

"Is that it, Enabeth? Are we done for the day?" It was now so dark that the woman's face was in complete shadow, and Sentain could see nothing but a slightly lighter patch of chin where a few stray photons had penetrated the deep murk.

"I fear it must be. Beyond the forest, it will still be light for another hour or two, but in here, it might as well be night."

Sarok came up to the pair. "Good call. I can barely see where I am stepping. I lost sight of our flankers some minutes ago. Ah—and here they are."

The rest of the party gathered around Archaen.

"How do we play this, Cousin En?" asked Miko. "You have experience of this land that we haven't."

"Not of the Shadow Forest, Ryven. But you are right to ask. Near the river, we kept a light guard and our focus was on the water. But Elian's detection last night of a… *stalker*… suggests we have been careless. And now we have another *dimension* to be wary of."

"You mean *up*, don't you," volunteered Sarok. "We may not all have young Omdanan's freakish senses, but even Vuller and I could tell there is something shadowing us from above. So what is it?"

Archaen frowned in the dim light. "I am not sure. They could be one of several creatures."

"*They!*" stuttered Sentain. "So there's more than one?"

"Yes, Irvan. The creatures of the canopy are smaller, lighter, and often work in family groups or hunting packs. I have heard them too, but not seen them. Elian?"

"No, I haven't… Enabeth." The Meridian still seemed to find it uncomfortable being so informal with such an important woman. "They are well suited to this environment. Good camouflage."

Sarok grunted. "That's Nature's way, eh? Fuck it! So… are these creatures now gathering over our heads getting ready to strike? Can we expect an airborne horde to descend at any moment?"

Miko laughed softly at the crime lord's sarcastic questioning, but Archaen was more serious. "They will certainly be sizing us up—"

"As food?"

Miko clapped Sarok on the shoulder. "Of course, Mr Sarok. We must appear quite appetising to the beasts of the forest. With luck, though, they'll think you look less tasty than the rest of us, and perhaps they'll be too full after their main course to bother with having you for dessert?"

Sarok smiled, though his face was completely in shadow and none could see it. "Who knows which of us they might consider the choicest delicacy, eh? So for all our sakes, what are we going to do to persuade them that we are indigestible?"

"We must build a roof of sorts over our heads," said Archaen. "So we must find a spot around here where the trees are close and we can build between them. And then we need a fire. So everyone—look about. Collect long branches, and also kindling. I have twine and fishing line in my pack, so I will fashion the roof. But first, let us find the best spot for our camp."

***

They chose a place where three trees grew close together, one of which was sickly and canted at an angle, leaning in towards the other two. Archaen fashioned a roof of branches with Miko and Reddas' help, which they secured about two metres up between the trees. Archaen then assembled and lit a fire, while the rest of the party collected more branches to create a low fence around their camp, or else worked to clear any foliage around them that might act as cover for anything attempting to creep up on them. They then ate from their reduced supplies of dried food. But few spoke, and there was tension about the camp as the members of the company strained to listen for any sound above the *pop* and *crackle* of the fire that might suggest peril.

Sentain, however, was exhausted. He had no sooner finished eating than his head drooped and he was asleep.

He woke once during the night, momentarily confused, lying on his side, staring at a humped form before him, one half a dark green colour, the other half in shadow. After a moment, he realised it was one of his companions, wrapped in their sleeping cloak, but he wasn't immediately sure who. He shuffled about on his own cloak uncomfortably, his chain mail rustling and clinking, until he was staring directly at the fire, which still burned yellow and orange. He noticed a booted foot off to one side, which shifted as he watched. Raising his head, he found that the foot belonged to Miko, who sat on the opposite side of the fire, absently toying with a dagger as he looked up towards their makeshift roof. Then Sentain slowly raised himself on one elbow, making sufficient noise to draw the attention of the other.

"Nothing to see here," murmured Miko. "Return to your dreams."

But as Sentain opened his mouth to respond, the thought occurred to him that he had managed to avoid all guard duty since they had started up the Blackflood—and in fact, in spite of the need, he had never even been asked to perform this task. Feeling suddenly shamefaced, he wriggled fully upright.

"Ah... is it late? Early? How long have I...?"

Miko gave a lop-sided grin. "Dawn is still hours away."

"Right. Have you been on watch long? Would you... would you like me to...?"

"Would I like to entrust our safety to you?" The Leaguer's smile—exaggerated by the shadows from the firelight—seemed to take on a different, unreadable quality. The man slowly shook his head. "No, Dr Sentain. Do not worry yourself. I do appreciate the offer—no matter how insincere and half-hearted—but *no*. Sleep now."

Relieved at the response, and embarrassed at the same time, Sentain lay back down. In spite of the discomfort, he was soon asleep once more.

***

Sentain was nudged awake by a booted foot belonging to Reddas Archaen.

"Up now, scholar, white wizard, and pet of my mother! Day is upon us… possibly. We have survived the night and must be away."

Sentain opened his eyes, failed to comprehend what they revealed, and closed them again. Then he felt a pain in one shoulder and stiffness in his neck. He groaned softly, flexed his neck, and opened his eyes again. This time, he noticed various boots and legs moving about near his head, faintly lit by the fire, which still burned—though with little vigour. In addition, a pale light seemed to provide a background wash, giving everything a grey tint. He closed his eyes one last time for several seconds to compose himself, and then he rolled onto his back and sat up. Now he saw that all of his companions were standing: Sarok was nearby, tearing at a strip of jerky, while most of the others were settling their packs onto their backs or appraising their weapons. Across the fire, Enabeth Archaen and Miko were in conversation.

"I'd get ready if I were you, doctor," said Sarok, through a mouthful of tough food. "We're about to leave."

"Ah, okay. Sorry. No one woke me."

Sarok appeared amused. "No one needed to wake the rest of us—only you were dead to the world. I don't know whether to envy you or not. Some additional actual sleep would have been nice—but history has forced most of us here to become light sleepers. Ah, to be innocent once more." He finished his scant breakfast, adjusted his helmet, the straps of his pack, and the position of his sword at his waist, and then strolled over to the pair of Leaguers to join their conversation.

By the time Sentain was on his feet, had rubbed life back into his legs, packed away his sleeping cloak and hoisted his pack over his mail shirt, the others were ready, facing Archaen and Miko in the gloom. He hefted his staff and moved to stand at Vuller's shoulder.

Archaen's face was barely visible, as Reddas had stamped out the fire. "We still have some way to go. I don't wish to spend any more than one further night under the trees, so we will walk hard and rest little. Whatever was tracking us yesterday from above seems to have decided that we are too many or unusual to challenge, but there are other creatures in the forest that may not be so timid. Let's remove ourselves from their potential interest as quickly as we can."

The woman gave one quick glance at the compass in her right hand, turned, and set off.

***

True to Archaen's word, the party walked for a long time, and at an increased pace to the previous day. For Sentain, the going was tough and soon his legs began to ache, adding to the pain in his neck and tightness across his shoulders. He started the morning close to their leader, but gradually fell back. As the party had adopted a similar marching order to before, when he lagged, Sarok and Vuller moved up past him, leaving him in the rear. He even began to fear that he might lose touch with the others, and it was with significant relief that—after perhaps three hours of marching and scrambling—Archaen called a halt, giving him a chance to catch up.

The woman noticed Sentain's late arrival to their resting place—in a small patch of the forest under a rare breach in the canopy, lit up like the stage in a theatre. She approached him, concern in her voice: "Irvan—are you okay?"

"Yes, thanks Enabeth. Well, when I say 'yes', I really mean 'no'. I'm ashamed to say I'm finding the going hard. But don't worry—a bit of rest now, and I'll be good to go again."

Archaen didn't look convinced. "You must keep up, Irvan. If you fall behind, we will never find you, and you do not want to be walking alone in this forest."

"Yep. I know. Understood."

They rested for no more than ten minutes then were off again, though Sentain suspected the break would have been shorter had Archaen not allowed him a little extra time to recover. And once more, he quickly found himself falling behind Sarok—though not Vuller, who seemed more watchful than before, sticking close to him and even allowing a gap to develop between them and the man's charge.

After some minutes, Sentain looked aside at Sarok's bodyguard: "Ah, Mr Vuller... can I assume that someone has had a word with you?"

The tall man glanced at him quickly, then returned his attention forwards. "She just wants to make sure you don't stray. Says we can't risk losing our wizard. But it's more than that, eh?"

Even the half-light couldn't disguise the upwards movement of the side of the man's mouth. Sentain looked away, embarrassed. "I'm not sure what you mean."

"Oh, come on, Sentain. She has been protecting you since Ghuraj. I'm only surprised she didn't take you with her when she disappeared after our first visit to Verano. What's going on between you two?" Vuller gave another quick side glance, a wry expression on his face. "You can tell me, you know. I won't rag on you like Brutus would have."

"Nothing! Really, nothing!" Sentain was sure he even *sounded* flustered. "I mean... we just, kind of, get on. Does that make sense?"

"No, it doesn't. She's *hot*, and age means nothing here. It's impossible to tell anyway. Back in Arakkan, Miko took up with this bird who was apparently one hundred and sixty. *One hundred and sixty!* I mean, fuck me, but she looked like she was in her late twenties, and acted like it too. Mind you, I don't know how old Miko is himself, so maybe she's jailbait to him. So, you're not gay, are you?"

"No!"

"But you don't find her attractive?"

"Yes, of course. She's the most stunning woman I have ever met." Sentain was glad the gloom prevented the other from seeing him blush. "But I doubt she looks at me in the same way."

Vuller glanced once more. "Don't do yourself down, man. I'd change faces with you anytime."

"Er, thanks. But, well, I am sure she can have her pick of any of her kind. And they are in much better shape than me. And they are probably braver. More noble. What am I? What do I offer?"

Vuller didn't immediately respond, and they trudged on in silence for some seconds. Then he volunteered: "Something different. She's lived among her kind for a long time. Maybe she's bored and is looking for a different flavour. She certainly finds you interesting. And although you seem like a complete wet blanket to me, I can see how she might think of you as… compassionate? That sort of shit."

"I suppose you're right." Vuller's analysis made his heart skip a beat. He knew how he felt about her, deep down, in a place he refused to access. Perhaps the situation wasn't entirely hopeless? But then he shook his head. *Absurd!*

Still, he smiled.

***

They made it through the day almost without incident. At one point, something bolted across their path into a patch of ferns, where it hid. The party gave the area a wide berth. At another, as they crossed a small stream, Sarok stumbled, reporting that something had grabbed at his ankle—although he might well have been the victim of nothing more sinister than a clump of riverweeds. And then, in the early afternoon, the 'hooter' announced itself from off to the east again, beyond Omdanan. The company paused and waited as before, but nothing else occurred, so they went on.

The second time the 'hooter' called, an hour or so later, it was towards the party's rear, and near enough to make Sentain jump.

"Fuck—that's close!"

By his side, Vuller whipped out his sword and crouched. "Too fucking right!"

Then Sentain was startled by movement off to his side… but it was only the Meridian, noiselessly sliding across the forest floor. He watched as Omdanan came to a halt ten metres beyond their line of advance, just visible around the trunk of a large and gnarly tree. Everyone in the party turned to watch, holding their breath, waiting to see what might transpire. But nothing happened. A minute passed, and then a second…

At last, Omdanan rose cautiously. He had drawn his sword, but now—to Sentain's relief—he slid this back into its scabbard. With the stealth of a cat, the young man stalked back to his position on the party's flank, ignoring those at the rear and looking towards Archaen at the front, who took his reduced concern as a sign to move off again.

Sentain looked over at Vuller—who simply shrugged, scabbarded his own weapon, and turned to follow the others.

And on they walked, for hour after hour.

Archaen allowed a short break for them to eat at around midday, and then another in the afternoon. When they came upon an area with a vertical wall of bare rock rising up to the left—too steep to bear soil or trees—the woman decided that this would be an advantageous place to spend the night. As before, they built a roof of branches to protect them from anything that might drop on them from above, lit a fire, and cleared a zone around the camp.

Sentain slept even more deeply than the previous night.

Again, no one woke him to demand that he perform guard duty.

**

They had been on the move again for a couple of hours, heading more east than north to avoid a steep hillside that rose up to form an obstacle in their path. Sarok came up to Archaen as she fretted over her compass—with Miko having already moved in beside her.

"Do we have a problem?"

Archaen looked up at him. "No… or at least, not a serious one. This morning, I estimated we had maybe a dozen kilometres to the forest's edge, but we have got no closer over the last hour. Perhaps we should have gone more directly north?"

"I don't think so," said Miko. "The terrain was getting steeper. We might have found ourselves at a cliff face or some precipice, unable to move on and having to backtrack. I trust your navigation."

"As do I," admitted Sarok. "Let's press on down the slope—it must slacken soon and then we can turn back north."

Archaen gave a slight nod, then quickly assessed the rest of the party, which had halted in formation, taking the interlude as a chance to rest. "Very well…"

As they headed off, Sarok kept close to the pair of Leaguers—at least, close enough to hear their conversations—accepting that his bodyguard had other temporary duties. He was also sufficiently near to see the direction in which the lodestone was pointing when Archaen referred to it, and so he was reassured when, after perhaps another half an hour, the woman made a clear course change, turning to traverse a noticeably less-steep slope and heading towards an area where the trees grew more closely together. Shortly after, he noticed the woman nodding to herself and caught an approving comment from Miko. It seemed as though they were back on course.

Sometime later, as Archaen paused for yet another direction check, Sarok ambled up to her. He was about to comment, when he glimpsed movement high up in the trees, slightly off to his left. His stride faltered. "Er… what… is… *that*?"

Archaen and Miko turned their attention from the compass to first glance at Sarok, then to look in the direction of his stare.

"I don't see…" began Miko, and then: "ah!"

Archaen shouted: "Everyone—stand still! Do not move!"

The thing Sarok had noticed became clearer. Perhaps eight metres ahead, a long, grey object continued to unfurl from the canopy above. It was as thick as his forearm, with a wedge-shaped head: it had no apparent eyes, but quivering finger-length tentacles furred its head and formed a frill around the upper part of its snake-like body. The creature was somehow anchored in the branches above and extended around ten metres in length from there to the tip of its head, which hovered about two metres above the ground. Its mouth slowly yawed open, and two slick tongues slithered out and twisted in the air, as though tasting it.

"There's another," whispered Miko, urgently, and Sarok saw a second creature coil down several metres from the first, still off to their left, nearer to Reddas than anyone else.

"Are these the things from the canopy that were following us two days ago?" asked Sarok, his eyes fixed on the creatures, which gently swayed this way and that, turning, coiling, uncoiling.

"I don't know," admitted Archaen, softly. "But I do know these hunt by motion. Stay as still as you can."

Omdanan called from over to the right: "Two more here."

"And one back here," cried Vuller, hoarsely.

"Ooooooh... *shit*! Archaen!" Sarok noticed yet another of the creatures slowly slide from the branches directly above, almost on top of him. He was about two metres behind the Leaguer woman, who had been looking away, but who now, ever-so-carefully, turned towards him. The reptilian beast slowly uncurled, so that its head was approximately mid-way between the pair, hovering just above head-height. Its bifurcated tongue licked the air, one part questing in the direction of Sarok, the other towards Archaen.

"What the fuck do we do now?" hissed Sarok. And as he spoke, the tongue-part nearest him stiffened and the head drew back slightly, the mouth parted wider, and an array of sharp teeth slid through the creature's gum-line...

And then a voice called out, loud and clear: "*Bellazor-tritarium-farax!*"

A sudden wind tore through the patch of forest, so strong that nothing unfixed to the ground could resist it.

Sarok was lifted and thrown through the air, missing a tree trunk and pitching into a patch of ferns, which shredded away from him with the force of the wind. He noticed Archaen go down, and Miko glance off a tree trunk. As for the creatures, these were blasted sideways and torn from their anchors above. As Sarok lifted his head, his helmet was stripped from him and whipped off into the air. But he was satisfied to see one of the creature smack bloodily into another tree.

The wind abated as suddenly as it had arisen. Sarok gasped for breath and looked about. As he did so, he noticed Archaen leap to her feet, sword in hand, scampering after one of the stunned and now-vulnerable creatures. Then he heard a pig-like squeal off to one side, and saw Mandelson slashing at something with her curve-bladed spear. He raised himself onto his hands and knees, and only then noticed that yet another of the creatures was twisting and thrashing on the forest floor not three metres from him. In a sudden rage, he drew his knife and crawled over to it: "Fucking... die... try to... fucking... lick me... up... stupid..."

Some moments later, Vuller appeared beside him: "I think that is well and truly dead, Boss. I'd save your strength."

Sarok got to his feet and observed the corpse with satisfaction. He sheathed the still-bloodied knife and turned to look at his bodyguard—and at Sentain, who'd wandered up behind him.

With a smirk, he noted: "You see, Vuller, I was right to have you protect our wizard. He's not the useless piece of shit you said he was."

"*You... me...?*"

Sarok laughed and clapped his confused bodyguard on the shoulder. Then he called past him: "Good job, Sentain. *Again.*"

***

They had escaped the hanging serpents with nothing but a few bumps and bruises. And having found some flatter terrain, they now made good progress. As the hours passed, it seemed as though they would escape the Shadow Forest with little loss.

But the forest was not to be denied.

"Why have we stopped?" asked Sentain, last to join the congregation.

Archaen had been speaking low. She paused to update him. "Elian has sensed something." She indicated the young Merdian, who was at the side of the party, his eyes fixed on some spot ahead. She continued speaking to Omdanan's back: "Are you sure?"

Without turning, Omdanan replied: "Yes. I am convinced. The howler and the stalker are the same type of creature. It's been tracking us. And it's *there*. Waiting for us. No. Not *it*. *Them*."

"Fuck, Elian," declared Vuller, "you're seriously freaking me out, man. *Them?*"

Sentain paled. "He means the chameleon ape, doesn't he? And there's more than one? How many?"

Omdanan risked a quick glance back at the party, but only spoke once he was facing away from them again. "I can't say. At least two. There are two areas ahead that aren't right. I know what to look for now, but I can't explain it. It's like two voids; deeper silences; deeper darknesses. And…" he turned, his eyes suddenly wide, his sword rapidly in hand. He took three steps, and lunged.

To the others, it appeared as though he had gone mad, pushing between Sentain and Vuller and then thrusting apparently into the trunk of a tree. But then the vision of those watching trembled and changed, and the tree trunk was no longer a tree trunk, but a pale-skinned creature, two metres high, with human-like fingers topped with long, dagger-like nails and the face of an intelligent ape with large, white eyes.

Omdanan's sword had pierced the creature through the gut. It threw back its head and gave an ear-splitting scream, then swiped at the Meridian with one long hand and arm. He tried to duck, but the creature was too fast: the hand caught his head a glancing blow, knocking off his helm, and the fingernails opened a long cut in his scalp, splashing blood over the nearest party members.

But the creature didn't get a chance for a second swipe: Archaen's black sword took off an arm, and Miko's blade cleaved its face diagonally across its wide nostrils and between its eyes.

Suddenly there was a sense of movement behind them. Sentain turned just in time to see a second blur of movement, and sharp nails resolved from the trees, sinking into the backpack of Sarok—who was still turned to face the first incident. As Sarok pitched forwards, Vuller threw himself into the rippling, grey-green anomaly…

Then there was another one, materialising beside Reddas. Sentain turned to see the man's face explode in red, raked by nails. As the Leaguer fell, he saw Mandelson's curved blade flash once, but then she flew backwards, as though swatted by a giant hand or pulled by a magnet.

Sentain stumbled backwards against a tree, holding his staff protectively before him, his eyes and mind trying to distil meaning from the chaos. The party moved around him in the area between the trees, waving weapons, shouting, falling. Miko twisted and fell; Omdanan, his face bloodied, swung his blade savagely at seemingly empty space, though the sword tip snagged on something and more blood flowed from a smudge of grey that seemed to float in mid-air. Sarok attempted to right himself. Mandelson was suddenly leaping with her spear out-thrust and rage in her eyes. And Archaen was suddenly next to the him, panting, black sword parallel to his staff, adding protection…

"Stay here, Irvan!" Then Archaen was off too, leaping over Sarok and heading towards her fallen son, whose body was being tugged at by an invisible force. But Vuller was there, and he moved his blade in an upwards arc, so that whatever was tearing at Reddas screamed—and disgorged glistening bowels out of thin air. Archaen's blade then rose and fell twice, in rapid succession, and the screaming stopped. A long leg materialised and trailed over Reddas' still form, with guts and brain matter splattered about the man like a gory halo.

Then there was a last scream off to the right, and Sentain turned in time to see Omdanan and Mandelson simultaneously admit the coup de grâce to another creature—the Meridian's sword splitting the creature's breast while the woman's curved spear sank into its neck. But as the creature fell back, the other two did not stop—striking at its body again and again in rage. Sentain was transfixed by the remorseless intent of the two. But at last they ceased, and as Mandelson spat on the corpse, Omdanan stepped back, swiping an arm across the blood that coursed into his eyes from his scalp lacerations.

Then there was a peculiar stillness. Several of the party panted; others groaned. Miko woozily tried to get to his feet. Vuller crouched beside a cursing Sarok, helping him up. And Archaen knelt at the side of her son, whose limbs twitched ineffectually.

Sentain attempted to calm his beating heart and assess the situation. Then he used his staff to lever himself up and staggered over to Archaen and her son. Once there, he dropped his staff and hurriedly pulled off his backpack. Scrabbling through this, he discarded several packs of dried food until he came out with a leather water bottle and a roll of bandaging material, which he offered to the woman.

Archaen looked back at him absently and took the offering with a nod of thanks. She began to clean Reddas' face, attempting to stop the flow of blood by pressing the bandaging tight against his mangled face. Sentain moved around to assess the man's other wounds, finding that he had been slashed on his unprotected arms and thighs, though his mail shirt had protected his torso and vital organs. And so—in spite of all the blood—nothing seemed terminal.

Aside from Reddas, Omdanan also had deep wounds to the head, which bled ferociously even though they were superficial. The cuts eventually stopped flowing after cleaning and a lot of pressure, though the bandaging prevented the Meridian from wearing his helmet—and so he passed this to Sarok, who had lost his in the forest after their encounter with the hanging snakes.

The crime lord himself had only been winded, having been protected from worse by his backpack. And the only other member of the party with visible wounds was Miko, who had been slashed across his left arm, which hung uselessly by his side.

"I fear a tendon has been severed," winced the Leaguer, "and we have not the microsurgery to correct it here."

"Hurt much?" asked Sarok, brusquely.

"As Brutus would have said—rest his soul—it stings like a fucking beast."

"At least it's not your sword arm."

"And we have no shields anyway," gasped Miko. "So there's an unexpected bonus."

Repairing Reddas took some time—as well as the rest of the bandaging the party had in its packs. Archaen then ushered the others away and spoke softly to her son before resting her head on top of his. Then she kissed his bandaged forehead, wiped one hand across her eyes, and stood to address the others.

"We are close to the forest's edge," she began. "Though my son should rest, it would be dangerous for him and all of us to spend another night here. So we must push on. We should make a litter—"

"No!" Reddas grunted in pain and struggled to push himself upright. The effort started a bleed, evident through the bandaging on his left thigh. "No one will carry me. Help me to my feet."

Miko rushed over to the man, and with some struggle—due to only having one usable arm—managed to get his right shoulder under the other's left arm. Sarok turned to look at Vuller and gave a twitch of the head, at which the latter scurried over to Reddas' right-hand side.

"Reddas... my son..." said Archaen, hesitantly. "You have nothing to prove."

"I do, Mother. I have *everything* to prove. I must show the world that I am worthy to be your son."

Archaen turned to look away. She took several steps to one side, where she leant with one arm against a tree.

Sentain looked between the two and began to move towards the woman. But then Archaen straightened, and when she turned, her look was severe and almost fierce. "Very well. We will be strong. Come then."

Though they were close to the forest's edge, it took them another three tortuous hours to complete their escape from the trees, due to the effort of supporting Reddas. By then, the sun was low on the horizon, about to dip beneath the forest's crown to their west.

In the end, they had to camp beneath the trees, but at least there was clear sky and bare foothills to their east, and that was some comfort.

Chapter 14

"Is it wise to pause here?" asked Sarok, as he approached Enabeth Archaen and Miko where they stood upon a stony mound. The pair were hunched together in conversation, the man a head taller than the woman, his head tipped downwards so that it seemed as though he were bowing.

The Leaguers turned to look at him. Behind Sarok, in an undulating dip in the rocky landscape that was dotted with thorny bushes, the rest of the party was strung out in a line. At the rear, several score metres away, Omdanan and Vuller bracketed the injured Reddas Archaen.

"No, it's not," replied Archaen. "But we have no choice. Our exact location is unclear." She waved a hand towards the mountains in the near distance, which rose dramatically in a line across the horizon. "I think we are to the west of the gate, but Ryven thinks we may be slightly to the east. If we miscalculate, we might spend a day or even longer searching in the wrong direction and then having to double back. It's time we cannot afford to lose."

Sarok noticed the woman glance over his shoulder and guessed that she was looking towards her son. "Lack of signage is a real bummer, eh? But there must be some way of telling where this gate is, surely? I thought you had been here before?"

"I have passed through the Copper Gate at least six times—but Ryven hasn't. However, he speaks from a conviction that we travelled further along the Blackflood than I estimated, and he could be right. Anyway, it was years ago that I was last this way."

"So there is no path? Then how does anyone find this place?"

"The Copper Gate lies in a sheer cliff face, perhaps two hundred metres tall. We should spot this once we are close. But the usual approach is from the west, guided by the profile of Mount Caryssan, which has a distinctive shape, like a witches' hat bent at the tip, and rises almost directly north of the gate. Small cairns are sometimes set along this route, though weathering and orcish vandalism often wreck these. The problem is, approaching from the south, I cannot tell which of these peaks ahead is Caryssan. I am hoping that I might get a better clue from one of these rises."

Sarok removed his helmet—the one donated by the incapacitated Meridian—and wiped a hand across his sweating brow. The overcast weather had been replaced by sunlight and was warm in spite of their increasing altitude. "I understand. But we're exposed on these heights. Any scout might see us, no?"

"It's a risk we have to take," noted Miko. "Ideally, we should have made this short journey at night, but—"

"But I don't want to waste a whole day of inactivity while waiting for nightfall," stated Archaen, still looking at the hobbling trio in the mid-distance. "And our navigational difficulties will be even worse then." She shook her head then looked back at Miko. "So what's it to be, Cousin? Shall we bear north-north-west?"

"To me, the peaks before us look of similar height. I just cannot tell. But let us at least continue due north and we can amend our course one way or the other if inspiration does strike."

Sarok looked at the helmet in his hand, and then a thought occurred. He looked up. "We have been on the move for three or four hours, Ms Archaen. Your son needs to rest. Perhaps while he does, you should instruct Omdanan and let him loose. If anyone can find this gate, it will be him."

The woman pursed her lips and nodded. "Yes, that is a good idea. But we cannot wait for him to go to the mountains, search, and return. Perhaps a small rest, then we will continue north and he must find us."

Sarok started to nod, then paused and developed a frown. "*Fuck*! That means someone else will have to act as a crutch for Reddas. Miko—do you know the old children's game *rock-paper-scissors*?"

***

Omdanan scrambled over rocky slopes, along shallow gulleys, and around bare hillocks. His destination was obvious: forwards and upwards, and always with an eye on his position in relation to Arkon's sun as it continued its slow descent into the west.

The Sundering Mountains towered over him, their foothills surprisingly narrow, their sides steep and sharp, being geologically recent and too young to suffer much from smoothing by weather.

Omdanan felt exposed. It was odd how abruptly the Shadow Forest had terminated, but the paucity of soil in this barren strip of land before the mountains meant that there was no purchase for tree roots, and the only vegetation was skeletal bushes or occasional grassy tufts that sprouted from cracks in the ground. The same was true of the rising mountains ahead, which were bereft of trees or other significant vegetation. Yet in the end, this lack of cover proved a boon…

He soon found evidence of sapient creatures in a small hollow. Scattered about were a few bones bearing scraps of flesh that seemed to be the remains of a meal. Examining the hollow more closely, Omdanan noticed scuffs in the rock, and a bush that appeared to have been randomly hacked. Further inspection suggested that a number of creatures had spent the night here, having entered from the west and exited to the east, where imprints in the thin, loose soil seemed slightly fresher and deeper.

Orcs? Men? Elves? And were these going towards the gate, or coming from it?

Men made no sense. According to Enabeth Archaen, the Copper Gate was locked and could only be opened by Leaguers. By *elves*. But the orcs had been swarming the land. So might it be orcs, keeping an eye on the gate even though they couldn't use it? Bastian had not mentioned sending any emissaries this way, and if the elves were communicating with their kin in the Northlands, then using the gate further west and closer to the Elven ports—the Stone Gate?—would make more sense. So… the odds seemed to suggest that any creatures in this infertile and treacherous part of the world would be orcs heading to the gate to keep watch, or perhaps returning from it to be replaced by another contingent.

He decided to follow the trail to the east, and within the hour, his suspicions were confirmed.

In spite of appreciating the need for caution, Omdanan had nowhere to hide, and in any case, his need for haste was paramount: he saw the orcs at almost the exact same time that they saw him.

One of the orcs gave an incoherent shout, alerting his fellows. These were strung out along a ledge, perhaps one-to-two-hundred metres up a steep slope.

Omdanan froze and stared at the nearest creature, which had a ghostly pale face and a broad cap on its head. It rested against a boulder, nursing a spear in its arms. As he watched, it rose to its feet, revealing that it wore brown leather clothing with a chest guard that seemed to be made of the ribs of another creature, possibly one that the orc had vanquished itself.

"Is it alone?" cried a second orc, to the left of the creature and another five metres along the ledge. Four more orcs were evident, spaced at similar intervals further along the shelf, all of which rose up for a better view.

"It seems to be," shouted the nearest orc.

For a moment, the man and the orcs simply stared at each other. They were too far apart to make a direct attack, lacking any projectile weapons: Omdanan had a bow but no arrows, and the orcs' spears were meant for close-quarter combat rather than throwing and would be easy to dodge if they were launched at him. Omdanan quickly realised that he was safe, and started to edge away from the mountain slope, assuming that the Copper Gate would be around the out-jutting mountain buttress and set into the cliff face further on.

"Where do you think you're going, elf?" shouted the first orc.

"That's not an elf," cried the second. "It's a vagabond. An injured one. Look at its head."

"But it's going for the shiny door," responded the first, which edged forwards and prodded at the slope with its spear, perhaps calculating how fast it could slip down the decline and whether it might be able to catch the intruder after all. "Only elves can use it."

"Should we pass on this message?" called a third orc, further along the shelf. "We have orders."

"Nah, not for only one," shouted back the second. "that's not what we're watching for."

"Then let's catch it," responded the third. "I'm hungry."

"Hold fast!" said the first, having finished its calculations and decided that its chances of a successful chase were low.

Omdanan decided he had no need to see more. He now knew where the gate was and needed get this information to his company before it went too far off course. He started to move away, but then had second thoughts. Turning back, and with a mischievous smile, he raised a one-fingered salute to the nearest orc.

To a responding volley of insults, he about-faced, and set off at a jog in the direction of the party.

***

Three hours later, Omdanan was back. He had intercepted the company and led it here, just short of the angle of the slope from beyond which the orcs had been visible. Or rather, he had led some of the party here: Archaen, Sarok, Mandelson and Sentain were with him, though Reddas and his two helpers were some distance away and moving very slowly. The afternoon was waning, and Archaen had been keen to get to the gate by nightfall and enter it if they could, so she had sanctioned the temporary separation.

"You counted six?" said Archaen.

"Yes."

"Well, that's manageable," said Sarok, "if they are prepared to come and fight. But are they?"

Omdanan slowly shook his head. "I don't think so. I heard one of them even mention having orders. I'm sure they're waiting for a group like ours. I guess they've been instructed to pass on news if we turn up."

"So you think they'll bolt as soon as they see us?"

"I do."

Sarok turned to Archaen. "So where does this leave us? We've been trying to avoid prying eyes, and now it seems we can't. And if we can't creep past them, and we can't kill them, what then?"

Archaen had been staring at the crumpled slope. Without turning, she replied: "Maybe it doesn't matter."

"Why not? Is the route via the gate so much quicker?"

"In normal circumstances, yes. But…" she shook her head briefly and looked back at Sarok. "But it would be best not to take the risk, although I do wonder what is already known about us."

"You are thinking about the orc that escaped at Lissom? But what could it say about us? Did it see us well and work out our nature? And even if it has outrun us with its rumours, our foe clearly hasn't had time to move his pieces to stop us *here*, and we will reduce our enemies' potential advantage further by taking this path beneath the mountains, no?"

"All true, and yet…"

As the others watched Archaen mull over options, Mandelson lost patience. "We should kill them all to be safe. That is clear. Can't we outflank them, boy?"

"Ah… no," stuttered Omdanan. "Not a chance. We would have to climb these slopes and get above them, but that would take hours and we would probably be discovered before we got too close."

"Then Sentain can blast them with his wand. What's the problem?"

Archaen stirred. She looked at the other woman and nodded. "That may be our best choice, but I worry about getting all of the orcs. If they are distant and dispersed, some may escape, and then our nature will definitely be revealed. Irvan's staff may be our one advantage, and I would rather keep knowledge of it from com Durrel until the end, when the surprise may work best."

"I agree," said Sarok, frowning. "Sentain and his staff give us an edge: we must conceal knowledge of this from com Durrel if we can. A secret weapon is no good if it is not secret. But what can we do milling about here? We have to move and force the orcs' hands, one way or the other. And perhaps I should lead out, and you, Ms Archaen, should keep that sword of yours sheathed. They seem to know it and fear it, and that is something else we should keep secret."

"Very well. Lead on then, Mr Sarok. For now, we are your party."

Sarok nodded tersely, then advanced to the rocky protrusion that crossed their path. He noticed activity, high-up, as soon as he emerged from around the out-jutting rock. The six orcs on the ridge above were already on their feet, with spears to hand, watching intently. But they did not speak immediately, apparently waiting to see the size of the newly arrived party.

Sarok strode some metres into the flatter area beneath the slope, then turned, with hands on hips, and looked up. Omdanan, Sentain, Archaen and Mandelson arrayed themselves behind him. "Who are you, skulking up there like cowards? Do you wish to play? Then come play!"

The orc on the left of the line, at the edge of the shelf on which they perched, shouted down: "The vagabond has brought some friends! There was one, and now there are five. And how many more are lurking in the gulleys behind? No. We are comfortable here. If you wish to play, come up!"

Sarok turned to Sentain and spoke low. "Do you think you could get them all? Have you other spells that might work? Streams of fire? Lightning bolts?"

"I, er, don't know. The wind spell might blow some off the mountain, but I can't guarantee it will get the furthest ones. And the other spells... I just don't know. I've not had a chance to test them."

"Then the risk is too great," said Archaen.

"But how else do we shift them?" wondered Sarok.

Behind, the woman with red-streaked hair made a sound of disgust. "I'll show you how."

Mandelson strode from the pack and approached the rising land at a less-steep part. She began to traverse the slope, using the spike in the butt of her spear as an aid to balance. Her eyes quickly picked out the route the orcs must have taken to ascend to their ledge and she followed it.

The orcs began to jeer, but faltered quickly as they saw the ease of the woman's movement, and their tone altered altogether when she was joined by the man with the bandaged head they had seen earlier. Omdanan attacked the slope with the nimbleness of a mountain goat and quickly caught up with the woman. Then he leant down to pick up a loose stone. He stood up, legs braced, and skimmed the stone with ferocious power. The projectile glanced off the rock face just below the lead orc and ricocheted into its chest, cracking the ribbed plate it wore and forcing it to fall back against the bare rock.

And then they were off.

The orcs exchanged frantic words, turned, and scampered along the ledge away from the party, heading upwards. They were well rested and had their escape route already planned, so within moments they were out of range of Omdanan's arm.

"Mandelson… Omdanan… hold!" shouted Sarok.

"I can get the fuckers," retorted Mandelson.

"Maybe, maybe not. But they have the lead, the numbers, and the advantage of terrain. You have scattered them. Well done. Now return. It will take them days more to cross the mountain than it will take us going through the tunnel—so any message they deliver to their master will come too late to make a difference."

Omdanan slid down and retook his place with the group. After a pause, and muttering, so did the woman. They then spent some minutes watching the orcs' scrambling traverse of the low mountain while giving the remaining members of their company time to catch up.

***

"So, this is the Copper Gate," said Sarok, looking upon the great stone doors set into the mountainside. The gate was barely three-hundred metres along the slope from where they had encountered the orcs. "I now see why it's so-named."

Bands of copper, tinged with verdigris, were set into the stone, marking out the pillars and lintel, as well as the edges of two giant doors, which were each three metres high and about one metre wide. There were also semi-spherical copper receptacles set into the lintel to each side at waist height, with text above these in more pristine, unoxidized lettering of the same metal. But the doors were closed, and there was no sign of a handle or keyhole.

Intrigued, Sentain approached one of the partially inset copper bowls and perused the text above it. "This part is clearly newer than the rest: it's not had time to react with the elements. And it's clearly meant to be a message or instruction of some sort… although I can't read it." He turned to face Enabeth Archaen, who had followed him. "What language is it in? What does it say?"

"It is a made-up language. When Velasia was being designed, to add to the ambience and gameplay, Yasmina's predecessors concocted a language based upon Tolkien's Elvish, and they used this to etch mysteries and instructions wherever they could. Had we spent more time in Sorvik, you would have come across it on signs and documents. It is called the Secret Tongue and it is only known to those of the three high guilds… and of course, to Yasmina and her understudies."

The rest of the party had clustered around. Sarok nudged Miko: "So, can you read it?"

"No, I cannot."

"Nor I," grunted Reddas, through a spasm of pain. "It is generally taught in the elven ports to new arrivals. I never had the chance to learn it."

"So it's a good job Ms Archaen made it this far," said Sarok, wryly. "Or else we would be fucked, no? I am assuming this tells us how to get the doors to open. And I'm assuming it's a safeguard against the yeltoi and orcs accessing the passageway."

"That's right," replied the woman. "The orcs cannot use it, and the yeltoi emigration to Barras was led through here many years ago by elvish guides who opened the doors for them. There are other routes through the mountains, of course, but these are difficult and time-consuming. Taking the passage behind this door will save us days in crossing to the Northlands, and likewise, taking the Iron Gate will save us more days when passing from the Northlands into Barras. This gives us a significant advantage. The orcs that escaped us will not be able to pass their intel on about our approach before we make Tartax-Kul—unless we are somehow delayed or forced to detour elsewhere—no matter how quickly they move."

"But you still haven't told us what the text says," said Sentain.

"Let me see." Archaen moved next to Sentain and bent to consider the message. "It says: *To gain entrance, a sacrifice is required. Sate the gate's thirst, moving three to the left.*"

"And what the fuck does that mean?" asked Sarok.

"That is what we need to work out. Yasmina ensures the riddle is changed periodically. This is not one I have encountered before."

From behind, there was a barked laugh. Archaen turned to look, and the others followed her lead. Standing a little way behind the cluster, leaning on her spear, Mandelson was shaking her head.

"Are you serious? A fucking *riddle*? Your son is bleeding to death and we've got to stop a psychopath with a god complex from murdering half the yeltoi… and yet now we've got to piss about here playing childish games? You're fucking insane." The woman looked up into the sky and bellowed: "Yasmina! I know you're watching! Open the fucking gate! Come on! We haven't got time for this! I want this over, and I want to go home!"

"Okay, Mandelson," said Sarok, with intent. "You've made your point. I sympathise. But it's their world, their game, their rules. If you're not going to help, step aside."

"Gladly!" The woman turned and stalked off, her spear resting on one shoulder.

Sarok turned to look between Archaen and Miko. "She is right, though. You *are* fucking insane. But I have learnt to accept your madness. So, let's solve this riddle and push on before the orcs cut into our lead too much."

***

The party applied itself to solving the riddle. To begin with, this involved contemplating the expression 'three steps left', with Archaen standing at various places in front of the gate, moving to her left, and examining the area around— the bare rock face, the ground, and the door. But there were no signs of hidden recesses, keyholes, or other marks or clues.

Then they moved on to contemplate the copper receptacles in the pillars, beneath the riddle.

"You mentioned *sacrifice*," said Sentain. "Sacrifices are usually performed in primitive societies in special places. On altars. In temples. If we are truly meant to perform some sort of sacrifice, I think it must be here: we must put something into this bowl."

"I agree," said Archaen. "The question is *what*, and how this relates to the 'three steps'. I need to think."

After an hour, the party still had no solution. They dispersed around the area before the gate, standing in thought, or resting on sleeping cloaks, while Mandelson glowered at them from a small rise a hundred metres away.

Reddas sat on his cloak, resting against a boulder, beathing heavily, the bandages on his face and around his arms and thighs tinged pink. At one point, he hawked and spat. "Anyone got any water? I can't get the taste of copper from my mouth."

Sentain had been drinking from his own bottle. He moved to the other man and started to hand his bottle down. As he did so, he gave a half smile and shrugged. "Copper? Our *mot du jour*. I wonder why blood tastes of copper?"

Miko was nearby, a foot resting on another boulder. "It doesn't really. People have some familiarity with the taste of copper, or at least they did—from water pipes and the like, back on old Earth, where the expression came from—so that's why the metallic taste of blood is described as such."

Sentain looked at the man. "Is that so? I didn't know that. Of course, they are really tasting…" He had a lightbulb moment and his brow furrowed. He looked down, then up at Reddas as he drank deeply from his bottle, then over again at Miko. "Ah… although I am a scientist of sorts, it's of human behaviour. I'm not a natural scientist. Your thesis was on spaceship design, wasn't it?"

Miko looked uninterested. "It was."

"So, you know physics and chemistry."

"Naturally. We all do, *Dr* Sentain. Why?"

"So, you know the periodic table? I mean, without the need to reference a database?"

Miko's interest has been piqued. "I do. And I'm guessing you are on to something."

Others saw the exchange and caught Sentain's growing excitement. They perked up and looked over, intrigued.

"So, what is copper's atomic number?"

"It's twenty-nine," replied Miko, without hesitation.

"Great. And on the same row of the table, moving left, what's next?"

"Nickle is twenty-eight."

"And next?"

"Cobalt is twenty-seven."

"And next," said Sentain, barely able to contain himself. "What is the *third step to the left*?"

"Ah! Dr Sentain, I have perhaps never given you any credit, even when it is due. Cousin En?"

Archaen was leaning against the rockface next to the left-hand pillar, smiling faintly. "Very good, Irvan. We need blood."

Reddas struggled up. "You can have some of mine—what little I have left." Miko stepped over to help his kin as best he could, with his one good arm, and the pair made their way to the gate, where Archaen waited. Vuller, Omdanan and Sarok moved closer too, and even Mandelson noticed the activity and began to wander over.

At the pillar, Reddas again hawked and spat into the copper bowl. The bloody spittle slowly trickled down the smooth, curved surface until it came up against the rock face.

"What the hell is going on?" hissed Sarok, standing next to Sentain.

The young anthropologist was smiling. "The third step to the left, Mr Sarok. Atomic number twenty-six. It's *iron*. Blood comprises haemoglobin, and when people say they taste copper in their mouth from blood, it is really iron they are tasting."

At the wall, Miko wondered: "How much is needed? Is it enough?"

And the gate answered: a sharp crack indicated that the two giant doors, which had not moved for months, if not years, had started to move. Ever-so-slowly, with the smooth scrape of stone on stone, the doors began to slide outwards.

"Quick, grab your things," cried Archaen. "I don't know how long the doors will stay open for, but we should move while we can."

"Aye," said Reddas, "and because I have so little blood left, the next sacrifice will have to come from one of you."

Chapter 15

Beyond the doors of the Copper Gate was blackness—a tunnel of indefinite length that could have been kilometres long or merely metres.

The great stone portal began to close almost as soon as Reddas was ferried through it by Miko and Vuller.

"Quick, Irvan," commanded Enabeth Archaen, "a spell of light."

"Uh, right. Let's try: *Lumosus-Mendarial-Perbellum!*"

As the copper bands that edged the stone doors squeezed together and extinguished the last rays of the late afternoon sun, the tip of Sentain's staff flared bright—so bright, that several of the party gave sharp exclamations and turned away.

"*Fuck*, Sentain, give us some warning!" scowled Sarok. "You could have burned out my retinas!"

"Uh, sorry," stuttered the anthropologist, blinking and looking away himself. "Let's try: *Lumosus-Tinabular-Perbella!*"

The sharp glare subsided, leaving a white glow that was sufficient to illuminate perhaps the nearest twenty metres' length of the four-metre-wide tunnel.

"That's better," said Archaen. "Thank you, Irvan."

Sarok considered their immediate environs. By the doors, which were outlined in copper bands as on the exterior, was a copper bowl, a stone step, and more of the elvish script, which he assumed told another riddle that needed to be solved to get the doors to open from this side. Otherwise there was nothing: the floor was perfectly flat and smooth, as was the curve of the tunnel. "Clearly man-made," he muttered.

Archaen heard him. "Yes, that's right. A laser was used to bore out this tunnel, and those at the other gates, using technology similar to that used for the Interplanetary roads."

"Tunnels… but no lights. *Nice*. How are people meant to navigate through this? Don't tell me you Leaguers have engineered yourselves to see in the dark?"

"No, Mr Sarok. But not far from here there is a side chamber that leads to a grotto in which lives a bioluminescent moss. This will live happily on the edge of a stave for days, as long as it is periodically watered. And the grotto holds a pool, where we can refill our water bottles."

"Once more, I am left concerned that these are important facts you have not freely volunteered. I wonder how we would have fared had you been killed?" Sarok noticed Miko, who had let Reddas slip to the floor and now stood to one side, stretching his neck. "Did you know?"

"Me? From experience, no, but Cousin En spoke of this some days ago. You must have been asleep."

There was a short bark of laughter from behind him, which Sarok ignored, well-aware of its source. "Fine. But I don't like this drip-feed of information. Before we go a step further, Ms Archaen, I want to know what we face here. Knowledge is power, and you need to share."

The woman gave a small bow. "You are right, and I apologise if it seems I have been withholding information. I have not. Perhaps I have been too focused on immediate concerns and have not wished to tempt fate or confuse thinking with extraneous details. Very well." She paused a moment to gather her thoughts, then turned from Sarok to look into the tunnel and the edge of the light cone created by Sentain's staff. "The distance to the other gate is perhaps three or four days' march, straight and true, cutting through the mountains at this level. Much of it is a tunnel, as you see here. There are various side chambers containing pools, fed by subterranean streams, and these are inhabited by the mosses and other small creatures that live off them. Some of these creatures can be persistent, so we should not camp in any of the grottos. There are also three places where the tunnel emerges for a time into the mountains, two of which are short, but one is longer, and will require us to scramble along a steep river valley before re-joining the tunnel. We may have to be careful there: orcs travelling through the mountains have occasionally stumbled on the valley and explored it, and even gotten into the tunnels to either side, but not for any distance as there is nothing for them to eat and they could not get out either end even if they made it that far."

"You're sure of this?"

"Yes. Once, the remains of a party of orcs was found at the other end of the passage by the northern gate, and remains have been found in one or two of the grottos and along the river valley too—where they have fallen from height, or starved, having dropped down and not had the strength or skill to climb back out again."

Sarok nodded and quickly glanced at the closed doorway, with the bowl and stone plinth. "So, there will be another riddle in Elvish at the other door, for us to get out, no?"

"That's correct."

"And that will have also been changed since you were last here? Ms Archaen, have you ever fucked yourselves over in this game? You know, created a riddle so complex that your people have not been able to solve it, and perished?"

Archaen shrugged. "There have been a couple of occasions where parties have taken some time to solve a riddle, yes. But none have failed yet."

"And if they did, I suppose Yasmina wouldn't take pity and open up?"

"Of course not. *Once in, all in.*"

Sarok nodded. "In which case, Ms Archaen, please do not die. And maybe you can spend some of the time over the next few days teaching us this Elvish script, so that we can at least work out the exit riddle should something happen to you."

"That makes sense, but… I cannot teach *you*."

"A damned outsider, eh? Okay. Teach your kin."

"Nor me, Mr Sarok," noted Miko, wryly. "I am not of a high guild. She cannot teach me. But Reddas is of her guild. And in the circumstance, that may be a wise thing to do. Fortunately, we are extremely fast learners."

Sarok detected something in Miko's voice. He glanced at Archaen, and saw that she had caught it too, looking at Miko questioningly under furrowed brows.

"This… makes sense. I will teach some basics to my son when we stop. But we should carry on now. The first grotto is perhaps half a kilometre away. We can replenish our water and collect some of the moss in case it is needed later. And then we should push on for another hour or two, and camp a safe way from the grotto."

"We have a plan," declared Sarok. "So, let's go. Miko—why are you smirking?"

"I was wondering whether now might be the right time for another game of *rock-paper-scissors…*"

***

"Any better?" Irvan Sentain spoke softly to Enabeth Archaen, as she settled at his side in the eerie half-light. They didn't have the material for a fire, but most of the party had collected some of the bioluminescent moss from the walls of the tiny grotto they'd found off the right-hand wall, and patches of this had been set about their uncomfortable camp. Archaen had spent the hour since their stop checking Reddas' bandages and then providing him a very brief lesson in Elvish.

"Not really. His face will be badly scarred and his nose is almost gone, but these things can be easily rectified back in Verano, although knowing my son, he would probably wish to retain some evidence of his encounter with the ape. He was lucky not to lose an eye. The problem is his arms and legs. He needs to rest to let them heal. The constant movement keeps opening up his cuts."

"What about the risk of infection?"

Archaen shook her head absently. "That is not an issue. Genetic engineering has given us particularly vigorous immune systems. Elian's scalp wound is much more likely to become infected than any of my son's."

"Ah, okay." Sentain was uncertain how far to probe the matter. "Do you think he'll be better by morning? It's a shame we can't fashion a sled or trolley of some sort. The floor here is so smooth we could push or pull him."

Archaen gave a tired smile. "That is a nice idea, but we don't have the material. We must carry him if he lets us."

"If?"

"Our pace is slow now, and Reddas knows this. I hope he is significantly better after a night's sleep, but… we will see. A decision will be made tomorrow."

"Decision… what…?"

"Good night, Irvan." Archaen turned on her side on her sleeping cloak, facing away from him.

***

"I will not delay you any further." Reddas Archaen had struggled upright against a wall of the tunnel by himself. This act had over-stretched the wounds on his legs, caused by the chameleon ape's sharp nails, and a damp patch on one thigh was evident in the pale light of the moss. "I will stay here and rest. Maybe in a day or two, I will be fit enough to proceed. I will then catch you up."

Miko was closest to the man and first to respond. "That is a noble call. We will leave you with sufficient food and water."

Enabeth Archaen closed her eyes and looked down for a moment. Then, without speaking, she approached her son, embraced him carefully, and whispered something into his ear.

Sentain watched the scene with growing unease, looking between the Archaens and Miko. "Is this wise? Will Reddas be safe? Shouldn't we stick together?"

Reddas put his hands on his mother's arms and gently pushed her away from him. He redirected his gaze from her to Sentain, looking over the top of the woman's head. "I will be fine. There is little immediate danger here, and none I cannot handle. Do not worry, white wizard. We heal quickly. A couple of days and I will be fit enough to proceed—and move much quicker and longer than we have been moving so far, without having to temper my pace to that of you outsiders."

Miko barked a laugh. "Your confidence hasn't left you, Cousin! And I don't doubt you are right."

"But what if it takes longer to heal or catch us than you anticipate?" continued Sentain. "What if you don't catch us by the end of the passage? Will you be able to get through the gate?"

Enabeth Archaen looked back at him, sharply. "You have a point, Irvan." She turned to her son. "You don't yet know enough to translate the riddle that will be there."

Reddas' face was unreadable, still being completely swathed in a tight bandage, once white but now stained pink and brown. "Then I will have to move quickly. If the worst comes to the worst, I can climb out of the valley at the long break. If that occurs, I will likely have to abandon the quest and return to Sorvik, which I admit, is not something I wish to do."

Archaen nodded to herself. "Then we should increase your odds of staying the course. I will stay back awhile and torment you with one last lesson." She turned to look to her kinsman at her side. "Ryven—you lead the others on. There's no chance of going wrong: forwards, forwards, and then forwards again. I will tutor my son some more, then catch you up."

Sarok pre-empted Sentain. "Dividing our forces yet more? I don't like this at any level."

"Do not worry, Mr Sarok. I will leave here by midday at the latest and should catch you up by nightfall. We cannot afford to delay any further. This scheme will save my son from pain and save us a couple of days that would be lost if we waited here for Reddas to heal or moved on at the best pace he can now manage. If I do not catch you by the time you weary, just remember, do not camp within a grotto, nor in the open if you reach one of the breaks in the tunnel."

Miko pushed himself away from the wall with his one good arm. "The plan is the best we have. Come all. You too, Dr Sentain. No need to pine for my cousin—she will not be away from us for long."

The Price of Freedom Part II: Velasia

***

The passage under the mountains was monotonous. The party walked on and on, dead straight, through the featureless tunnel, surrounded by shifting shadows cast by the conflicting light from Sentain's staff and the make-shift torches carried by Mandelson and Vuller—the only two who had retained their spears, around the tips of which they'd wrapped bioluminescent moss-covered fabric. A third spear was possessed by Reddas, but that had been left with the man and his tutor.

Hours passed, though the absence of sunlight—or any other indicator of the passage of time—left most of the party members somewhat confused and even disoriented.

"Is it time for a break?" asked Sentain at one point.

"Are you serious, Dr Sentain?" asked Miko, who walked at his side. "We have only been travelling for a couple of hours."

"How can you tell? It feels like we have been walking all day."

Slightly ahead of them, Omdanan—who stalked out in front—turned to look back. "About two hours and twenty minutes, I think."

"And how can you be so precise, Elian?" asked Miko.

"Counting footsteps," he replied. Then he faced forwards and continued to keep pace with the moving edge of light.

After four hours—accepting Omdanan's reckoning—they rested for a short while. Then they repeated the exercise, walking for another three, then taking a short break. Their third stint was even shorter, as a malaise settled over the party.

"I hate to say this, but I think I am starting to miss the Shadow Forest," muttered Sentain, as the party sat about on the flat stone floor, arrayed about his still-bright staff.

"While I understand where you are coming from," said Miko, "I can't share your sentiments. I have no wish to walk under those trees ever again."

"So, the great Leaguer suffers fear after all," scoffed Mandelson.

"Fear? Of course! I have often wondered at that strange expression 'brave *and* fearless'. That is an oxymoron. Without fear there can be no bravery. Am I afraid of that forest? Of course. Would I travel under its eaves again? The answer is *yes*. Always and ever. But what of you, who mock so readily?"

The woman pouted. "I do not understand fear. It is something for weak people. Emotions never direct my efforts, only calculation. I would not swim in a tank of razor-sharks, not because of fear, but because it would be stupid to do so."

Miko gave a short laugh and looked over at Sarok, who sat next to Vuller on the opposite side of the tunnel to the woman. "You have a formidable servant, Mr Sarok, though I don't know whether to envy you for it or not."

Sarok gave a forced smile but didn't answer, the atmosphere weighing heavily upon him.

When it was clear that Sarok wouldn't rise to the bait, Miko sighed. "Well, let's continue. One more session, so let's make it a significant one."

They soon came to another side chamber, which was larger than the one near the gate entrance and turned out to be a water-filled cave, with further exits to two smaller caves that were only accessible by swimming—which they had no desire or need to attempt. They filled their water bottles at the chance and wasted little time before moving on.

They continued for another three hours, then a fourth, and then even longer, with Miko determined to get the journey done. Then at last Sentain pulled up. He made a show of stretching his shoulders and back.

"A problem, Doctor?" asked Miko.

"Stiff. Tired. Bored. You name it. But I also wonder, are we outpacing Enabeth? If we walk all day and all night, will she, and then Reddas, really have a chance to catch up?"

Miko nodded. "Very well. We'll stop here for the night. We must have covered many kilometres."

So they set up camp, and Sentain waited at the rear of the group, ever glancing back the way they had come. He was the last to fall asleep.

The Price of Freedom Part II: Velasia

***

"Up, Dr Sentain!" cried Miko. "It is morning, I think, though in truth I cannot tell and I am guided by Elian's estimations."

Sentain rolled off of his cloak onto cold, hard stone. He suffered a moment of panic at the darkness, thinking he had gone blind, until he recalled that he had cancelled the light spell as the party had settled to sleep, and so the only light now came from a few greenish exudations from moss left at the boundaries of their campsite. He sat up and wiped at his eyes, then looked up to see Miko standing over him.

"Ah, morning? I guess I'd better…" And then a thought occurred, and Sentain looked at the activity behind Miko, where the rest of the party was standing or sitting, addressing their rucksacks, drinking water, or tugging at strips of dried meat from their rations. He noticed Sarok, Mandelson and Vuller… but no one else. "Where is Enabeth? Did she… is she…?"

"She has not yet arrived. Though before you panic, I must say I am not surprised. Though Reddas is intelligent and educated—perhaps even beyond you—learning the essentials of a new language in a morning seems to me an ambitious undertaking. I suspect my cousins' plans have changed."

"What do you mean? Ah, yes, that makes sense."

Miko frowned, perhaps uncertain as to whether Sentain had come to the same conclusion as he had, and so he decided to elaborate. "Yes, I suspect she will wait with him to heal up. Maybe they will set off today, or they are on the move even as we speak."

"So, should we wait? I mean, we can't be sure. Maybe we should go back and check and—"

"And undermine our plans? No, Dr Sentain. We proceed as before. Nothing has changed."

Then Omdanan appeared from out of the gloom. "Are we ready to go?"

"Look, Sentain. Our sharp-eyed friend is eager to be off, with or without your magic light. You can eat on the move. Cast your magic and take your place. Hup hup!"

***

Omdanan was the first to notice something different, around three hours into their march. As before, he strode at the front, at the limits of the light cone from the staff—or at least, at the limit as far as the others could see, though Omdanan seemed to have unnatural sight and was able to see further and sense more.

"Light ahead!" And then he disappeared.

The others' sight was affected by the glare of the staff, so it took them another half-a-minute before they began to notice a grey smudge in front. Sentain spoke three words to extinguish the light spell, and then the anomaly became clear to all: several hundred metres ahead, the tunnel came to an end, and an indistinct figure could be seen standing there, with hands on hips, waiting. It was Omdanan.

"The first breach," muttered Miko.

"Thank fuck!" swore Sarok, from behind.

The party soon came up to Omdanan, who had moved into full daylight and was staring ahead.

Sentain approached, with a hand up, shielding his eyes from a modest light that seemed all the greater because of their time in the dark. "What is… bloody hell!" He stepped back quickly, realising that the four metre wide path was now nothing of the sort: the path disappeared into a vertiginous drop, surrounded all about by grey-brown mountains. Then Sentain realised that a narrow ledge ran along the face of a steep slope off to their immediate right. In the mid-distance, the tunnel could be seen to continue at the end of the ledge, into the face of the opposite mountain.

"Well, Ms Archaen cannot be accused of exaggeration," said Sarok. "This is indeed a very brief break in the tunnel. I had hoped for something more. Still—Miko—let us stop for a short while. I at least want to recalibrate with nature."

Miko did not object, so the party paused for an hour or thereabouts, lounging about on the small area between the tunnel and the drop, enjoying the cool mountain breeze and the occasional jab of sunshine through thick clouds as the sun ascended from the east. At last, Miko chafed at any further delay, and they roused themselves. By this time, Omdanan had already crossed to the further side of the ledge and done some preliminary exploration of the tunnel on the other side.

"It is much the same as on this side," said the Meridian.

"As I feared," responded Sarok, sourly. "So we have hours more of shuffling in the gloom to look forwards to. *Great*. How's the ledge?"

"It is firm all the way, and about a metre-and-a-half wide."

"Do any of you fear heights?" asked Miko. "And of course, my question here is directed to all except Mandelson, who has already admitted to fearing nothing in this universe."

Mandelson scowled, while the others muttered negatives.

"We're okay," noted Sarok, before wryly adding, "although I suppose Mr Dettler might have struggled to cope were he here, and we would have had to stun him and carry him across on a stretcher. Speaking of which, I wonder what the little man is up to now?"

"Probably sitting on a throne of gold, feasting in his fortress with com Durrel," suggested Vuller.

Sentain frowned and shook his head. "I still struggle to imagine he would have gone with com Durrel willingly. He may not be having as good a time of it as you think."

"Given what he has put us through," scowled Sarok, "I can only hope you are right."

They crossed the ledge without difficulty and re-entered the tunnel through the mountains. Then they trudged on in a similar order to before—with the occasional break—for the rest of the day.

They spent a second night in the barren and stifling tunnel.

***

"She's still not here," fretted Sentain.

"Clearly not," said Miko. "This perhaps confirms that she and Reddas will come together, which is preferable to them travelling alone, is it not? Onwards!"

And the third day passed much as the second, although this time it was early afternoon before they reached a short break in the tunnel. This proved similar to the first, although the gap between the ends of the tunnel was longer and the path this time was complete, following a ridgeline between two separate mountain shoulders that was wide enough that even Dettler with his vertigo wouldn't have been fazed.

***

It was early on the fourth day that they came to the third and longest interruption to the tunnel. The party emerged behind Omdanan into the open air, onto a step in the mountainside about twenty metres above a sharp valley through which tumbled a vigorous river that was perhaps four metres wide. Though the slopes were barren—save for the occasional thorny bush—the small valley was full of clumps of tall, pine-like trees interspersed with rockier ground that could bear no vegetation.

"This looks like a pleasant spot," said Sarok, after a moment's reflection. "In fact, after that blasted tunnel, it's almost like paradise."

"It would be a nice spot for a bar, Boss," concurred Vuller. "Or a restaurant."

"True. And speaking of food, surely there is wildlife here to hunt? We could do with enriching our meagre rations—eh, Miko?"

The Leaguer shrugged. "I cannot tell from experience. I guess you are right, but we haven't the time to hunt, and in any case, I suspect the game hereabouts will be small." He indicated the ledge that ran from their current position across one steep hill face, keeping above the valley. "Also, the going below is clearly tougher than that above. We should stick to the path. Cousin En told me it is two to three kilometres to the last stretch of tunnel, which we cannot see from here."

"Us—*no*. Eagle-eyed Omdanan, *perhaps*." Sarok turned to the Meridian, and only then caught the tension in his posture. "Boy—what's up?"

"I don't know. Something doesn't feel right." Omdanan ran his gaze along the steep valley sides, then peered hard at the strip of trees and water. And then he looked down at his feet and took a pace back, examining the hard-packed soil. Then he muttered: "I should have checked…"

"Everyone on guard," barked Sarok. "Vuller, Mandelson, ready your spears—but preserve the moss." He touched a hand to the hilt of his own sword, then took the helmet from his head, wiped his brow, and settled it back in place.

Omdanan crouched to inspect the soil, then moved several metres along the ledge, looking at the ground closely.

"Anything?" asked Miko.

"Yes. But not recent. I mean, not very recent. Maybe a few days."

"Your people, Miko?" asked Sarok.

The Leaguer shook his head slowly. "I think not. Bastian didn't mention sending scouts through the gate, though we are an independent people and I suppose some could have taken it upon their own initiative to come through. But if not from Sorvik, they could be from Ranvik. As you have seen, communication is difficult in this realm, so Bastian wasn't likely to be fully aware of the intentions of our kin from further north."

"In other words, we should assume the worst and be ready for danger," said Sarok. "I recall Ms Archaen talking of orcs occasionally getting down into this valley. They may not have had any need to visit in normal times, but today? If I were com Durrel, I'd post a contingent here on a more permanent basis."

"Agreed," said Miko. He looked up into the sky. The sun had just made it above the easternmost mountain peak but was hidden behind grey clouds. "The orcs have no better eyesight than us. In fact, it's less good than that of my people. If we were to make the crossing at night, we might slip past any sentries without being seen, especially with Elian as a guide. But we cannot waste a full day."

"Why not?" asked Sentain. "It might give Enabeth the chance to catch up. We might need her sword and Reddas' spear. And in any case, we should warn them."

Miko was uncertain. "That is worth considering, but… no. We will press on. Still—scratch a warning in the earth at the tunnel exit for them to see."

Sentain immediately stepped back and started to dig with his staff into the ground, to little effect. Then Mandelson emitted a curse and pushed him aside. With the sharpened butt of her spear she soon marked out: *Beware—orcs?*

"And now let us proceed with caution," continued Miko. "I suggest Elian in front, Mandelson at the rear, and Dr Sentain in the centre somewhere. And Sentain—be careful with your magic here. We are not well arranged and I would hate for any spell of yours to bring the mountain down upon us, blow us off this slope, or collaterally incinerate someone."

"Understood."

The party moved forwards in single file.

"We are exposed up here," hissed Sarok from behind Miko. They were twenty metres behind Omdanan. "Anyone above or below will see us easily."

"True. But if above, we will see them too, so any watchers will be below among the trees. And remember, they are not fans of the bow. It would take a good spear throw to catch us from down there. And more, if they wish to chase after us, they will find the going tough, whether matching us below, or climbing up to our level."

Omdanan crouched, looked back, and then waved a hand at the slope on their right, across the valley. The rest of the party closed up to him.

"What have you seen?" asked Sarok.

"There! Don't you see?"

"See what? I just see rocks and shadows and a few bushes."

"Ah… your eyes truly are keen, Elian." Miko looked back at Sarok. "Do you not see those lines against the rock face? There are two—"

"*Three*," interjected Omdanan.

"Really? I stand corrected. There are three faint lines, like striations on the slope. I believe they are ropes, strung down from the crest of the opposite peak. They are tricky to spot as they are a similar colour to the terrain. I guess that is how they descended into the hidden valley."

"I still don't see," grumbled Sarok. "I don't have your x-ray vision, or whatever it is you Leaguers have endowed yourselves with through genetic manipulation. But I'll take your word for it. Three ropes? That suggests a significant party hauling significant supplies. If there was just one squad of six, why would it need more than one rope?"

"Good point."

Sarok was in his element. "And so there will probably be some orcs at the top, too, perhaps as lookouts, or maybe just acting as a link between those below and a foraging party or supply chain."

"Again, a sound observation." Miko looked around their environs, then focused on the spot in the valley directly below the lowest drop of the ropes. "But would any necessarily remain up top? It would be more mouths to feed. And how big a force might there be below? Perhaps a company, with more up top relaying supplies when they arrive to keep them healthy?"

"A company would be thirty-six, yes?"

Miko nodded. "Six squads of six. They have their superstitions. More would be overkill and difficult to maintain, but fewer might not suffice to overwhelm and capture a scouting party. Yes. I suspect a full company lurks in the valley below."

"Well, while we are forced to guess their numbers and disposition, I guarantee they know ours, and are even now waiting for us to move into a position for them to attack. The question is, where will that be?"

Omdanan had continued to listen to the debate behind him, while scouring the valley for signs of orcs. Behind Sarok, the rest of the party crowded close in an attempt to hear the discussion.

Miko pointed out the key features as he saw them. "The ropes are some distance away. There is a thick knot of trees on both sides of the river directly below them, which seems ideal terrain in which to hide. The tunnel entrance is on this side of the river, at the end of this ledge. I can't see the entrance from here…"

"I think I can," said Omdanan, softly. "It is perhaps three-hundred metres beyond the copse of trees, over the river, and up the slope."

"Ah. *Good.* And so… this is our battleground. If we assume they are company strength, then they have the numbers, but we have the slope and perhaps the skill at arms. What are their plans? To simply rush us when we get close?"

"Could there be some waiting in the tunnel to receive us?" wondered Sarok. "They know how to set a trap. We saw it on the Tesselac."

"Yes. We should assume some are waiting in the tunnel and that they will attempt to drive us from the valley towards those within. They might have a thicket of spearmen waiting—good terrain for them. It would be like rushing onto a cactus. I would not fancy our chances—except for the fact that we have a wizard."

Sarok nodded grimly. "As we cannot avoid them, we will have to go *through* them. There is little to be gained by waiting. But they will expect confusion and that we will throw down our arms. Yet the only way to survive an ambush is to respond with speed and aggression. To shock them and turn the tables. There is no choice. We must prepare ourselves now: a quick drink, some food. Tighten our packs. Ready our weapons. Approach the tunnel boldly, and when they appear, *run*. Sentain must move to the front, with a spell prepared. At the entrance, he must cast quickly. We should then continue to run until we have space, and then we can turn and face any chasers, on our terms, further inside."

***

The party walked rapidly along the ledge, with a nervous Sentain just behind the long-striding Omdanan. They were followed in turn by Miko, Sarok, and Vuller, with Mandelson at the rear. Their path curved around a spur of the mountain, above the winding river. After some minutes, the entrance to the tunnel became apparent.

As they drew closer, Omdanan said loudly over his shoulder: "Movement in the trees below. They are getting ready."

"And they're not being particularly subtle about it," noted Sarok. "Even I can see them crashing about."

The tunnel entrance was five hundred metres away, then four hundred…

The orcs made their move. They peeled out from the edge of the trees with a volley of shouts and insults and began to clamber up the twenty-metre incline to the ledge. Rather than attacking the party from the front or side, they seemed content to close in behind and usher it along. The first orcs attained the slope some fifty metres behind Mandelson.

"Run now!" shouted Sarok.

They broke into a lope, moving as fast as they could while encumbered in their chain mail and limited by Sentain's pace, who none would pass.

The hole in the mountainside came closer and closer, and then Sentain was next to Omdanan, raising his staff. He chanted a three-word spell and a percussive blast tore from the tip of the staff into the confined space of the tunnel ahead. Then all instinctively slowed for fear of stumbling in the dark over corpses.

"Sentain!" shouted Sarok. "Light!"

The anthropologist stuttered, causing Miko to run into his back with a curse. But he recovered rapidly and shouted out the requisite spell. As he did so, light flared from the staff.

"What the…" said Sarok.

"Fuck…" said Mandelson.

Omdanan skidded to a halt just in time to avoid the obstruction in front of him, but momentum caused Sentain and Miko to carry on past him and into the thick ropes that were secured across the width of the tunnel in a criss-cross pattern, from which they rebounded and staggered. But those behind had time to pull up. Mandelson quickly about-faced to meet the oncoming threat, with Vuller—also armed with a spear—just a split-second later.

"Turn!" shouted Sarok. And then he gave a roar of anger and frustration, drawing his sword. "Kill the fuckers—kill them all!"

Even Mandelson was caught by surprise at the man's sudden violence, although she recovered almost instantly and was at his shoulder as he piled into the nearest orcs before they could completely lower their spears, while Vuller materialised at his boss's other shoulder. Even though many of the orcs were larger than the elves, they were stunned by the ferocity of the assault, falling back into their on-rushing comrades. Then Omdanan was at them too, flailing his sword, as was Miko, the strongest of their party and still potent, even though one of his arms was all but useless.

Sentain stood with his back to the web of ropes, breathing heavily, his staff raised to illuminate the confused and confined battle. With his company in front, he had no opportunity to cast any other spell. He could only watch as his five colleagues, side-by-side, slashed and stabbed, forcing the screaming orcs backwards, at first with alacrity, but then more slowly as some fell and became stumbling blocks on the tunnel floor, with the mass of their colleagues squeezed together at their backs, forming a wedged cork in the neck of the tunnel. And then, slowly, the party was forced back.

"On... on!" roared Sarok, but to no avail. A spear thrust caught him in his mailed chest, punching the air from him. Another spear aimed at Miko's head forced the man to duck, and then he stumbled as the orc directly in front pushed him across the midriff with the spear it held across its own chest, forced there by the press.

And then, above the shouts and grunts, a surprisingly light voice shrieked: "Drop your weapons! Drop or die!"

The five were being forced back into a smaller and smaller space, a few scant metres in front of Sentain, soon to be penned against both him and the ropes.

The voice came again: "Drop your weapons! Surrender or…*aaiiiiiiiiii*!"

The scream cut off, and then there was a second scream, and a third. And above these voices, from somewhere behind the scrum of orcs, a great roar came: "*I bring the lightning!*"

The orcs in front now tried to turn, sensing something awry. Then one of the group cried out: "The black sword! The black sword!"

"On again!" cried Sarok.

"Eat this you fucker!" cried Mandelson, finding the room once more to swing her curved blade into an albino face.

Assailed from the front and behind, the orcs were slaughtered.

***

Seven members of the company from Sorvik stood amid a pile of corpses, splashed with blood, bent over gasping, leaning on spears or swords. The eighth held his staff high to illuminate the scene.

"Enabeth!"

The woman looked up, blood splattered across her pale face, a distant look in her grey eyes. She blinked and refocused on Sentain, who started to pick his way towards her through the corpses on the ground. Near her, something moved. She carefully placed her sword on the twitching body, leant on it, and the movement stopped. Then she gave a small and weary smile at the man.

"Irvan."

"You arrived in the nick of time. I can honestly say, I have never been so happy to see anyone in my life… ugh!" Sentain's booted foot found a pool of blood, resulting in a noisy *squelch*. "Let's get into the daylight."

The woman found a rag tucked into her belt, which she used this to wipe the blood from her black sword. Then she turned and led the way to the outside of the tunnel, with Sentain close by. After using his spear to dispatch another wounded orc, her son—still wearing a bandage over much of his face—trailed after the pair. The others cautiously followed the retreating illumination of their wizard's staff, Mandelson at the back, systematically using the spiked butt of her spear to ensure that none of their foe would ever rise again.

Under the clouds, and with sounds of splashing water carrying up from the river, Enabeth Archaen's legs suddenly buckled, but Sentain was close enough to catch her elbow and keep her upright.

"Are you all right, uh, I mean, what a stupid question." Sentain gave a shy smile. "After all that, how could you be?"

The woman straightened and drew her arm in to her side, trapping the other's hand. "Yes, Irvan. I'm fine. Just tired. We have been on the move for many hours."

"So you waited with Reddas until he was well enough to travel? We guessed that's what you would do."

"Yes. Sorry. I am not a tutor, it seems, though my son has at least picked up some basics."

"You need to rest. And I… sorry…" Sentain spoke some words to end the spell causing his staff to glow. "I think we all need to rest a bit. Let's get down to the river. I assume it's now free of orcs."

"Rest?" the woman still seemed somewhat dazed. "Yes. But not for long…" She allowed Sentain to guide her down the slope to the knot of trees directly beneath them and the river from which it drew sustenance.

***

Archaen did not allow the party to stay long in the hidden valley, fearful that other orcs might observe them from up high. They cleaned themselves and their kit, then returned to the tunnel, where the web of ropes strung across the passage between iron brackets was cut, and the fallen orcs were examined further.

"Twenty-eight," concluded Mandelson. "A bit short of your magic number, Miko."

"But still the best part of a company. Perhaps others are in the mountains, getting supplies, or else were lost on the way down here? The mountains are treacherous."

"They are from the Black Tree regiment of Tartax-Kul," observed Archaen, holding up a small wooden shield on which a skeletal symbol had been painted. "We were warned these were about. Ullah-Bor is much nearer than their homeland; their presence implies that com Durrel is searching for something… or someone."

"Us?" wondered Sentain. His staff again provided most of the light in the tunnel. "But he knows nothing for certain, does he? He is guessing."

"Yes—but *intelligent* guessing," suggested Archaen. "I suspect our presence is still unknown to him. Without use of the Copper Gate, I do not see how the orcs that escaped from Lissom, or from upriver of Hustem, or from the entrance to the gate, can have yet gotten news of our party back to him."

"So as you suggest, we must push on," concluded Sarok.

"But what do we do with the dead orcs?" wondered Sentain. "It doesn't seem right to just leave them here?"

"Are you going to bury them yourself?" sneered Mandelson. "Perhaps say some kind words over their graves? Weep a bit?"

"No, I mean—"

"Nature will take care of them, Irvan," said Archaen, more gently. "And in any case, it is good that they are all within the tunnel. External eyes will surely need to descend into the valley to look for them and waste more time." She tossed the shield onto the pile of corpses, which was starting to smell. "We are now on the last stretch of the passage. The tunnel is uninterrupted from here to the exit gate, perhaps twenty kilometres away. We may be at the end by late afternoon. Lead on, Irvan—our torch bearer."

A long walk; a short break by a small grotto; then another long walk. The featureless tunnel seemed like it would never end until, suddenly, it did.

"The gate!" cried Omdanan, once more at the front of the company. He darted out of the staff's light and into the darkness.

Seconds later, the others caught the reflected glint of light from copper. Omdanan was before the closed stone doors, running his hand over the cold copper bands at their join. Then he moved over to the left-hand edge, where a small stone altar sat, atop of which was a trio of copper bowls. On the surface of the altar was the expected copper script, written in Elvish.

Archaen smiled at the sight but approached no closer: instead, she slumped to the floor.

"Enabeth—are you okay?"

"Yes, Irvan, I am. But I have been walking and fighting for more than twenty hours. Outside the gate, evening must be settling over the world. It would be safest to sleep here and to take the gate at dawn."

"Fucking *A-men* to that," said Vuller, shucking off his pack.

"Eloquent as ever, Vuller," grinned Sarok. He too dropped his pack, then put his back against the stone wall and slid down onto his seat.

Soon, most of the company were splayed out across the tunnel. Two clumps of the bioluminescent moss—set in tin bowls from their packs—was placed to give additional light.

But not all of the party chose to rest. Sentain watched Reddas approach the altar and bend down to look at it. He too had some of the moss in a bowl—which had been the sole source of light for the man and his mother as they had travelled together from the entrance gate—and he set this down next to the copper receptacles. As he seemed to be having difficulty in making out the script in the dim light, Sentain struggled to his feet and walked over with his softly glowing staff.

"Does this help?"

The Leaguer glanced over his shoulder. "Ah, thanks. My eyes are not functioning well."

"Ah, were you… were they… damaged? By the ape?"

"No, Sentain. I am just tired. And pained—although I should not admit such weakness."

"But your legs are better?"

"They are good enough. The wounds no longer weep, though they ache. But enough of this. I wish to test my mother's teaching." Reddas bent down to peer more closely at the line of script, running one finger beneath the letters.

Sentain allowed the other to concentrate, though his face was unreadable, being covered in a dirty bandage. An unpleasant odour seemed to emanate from the covering, suggesting that Reddas may not have been as immune to infection and decay as his mother had asserted. "Do you understand what it says? The riddle?"

"It is brief and seems more a command than a question. *Life… a life… must…* Must what? The last symbol is not one I think my mother covered. Or is it? It looks similar to a rune. Similar sound or similar meaning?"

"A life must be *something*?" mused Sentain. "What can be done with a life? I suppose you can *save* a life. *Make* a life? *Live* a life? That doesn't make sense. Could it be *save*?"

"No. There is a negative connotation here."

"*Taken?* A life must be taken?"

Reddas nodded slowly. "Perhaps. Or *given*, or even *sacrificed*."

Sentain frowned. "That seems a bit *harsh*. I can't believe Yasmina would expect travellers to kill one of their own party just to get out. And if there was only one in the party, that would really suck. Doesn't it elaborate further? Are you sure it is *life*?"

"Yes, Doctor. I am clear on that symbol. And as you can see, the message is succinct."

"Okay. But it can't mean for us to sacrifice one of our own. Then what sort of life? Who else? An orc? No. They are not meant to be in here. Then what else is there?"

Reddas tipped the tin bowl, as though this might somehow increase the bioluminescence or perhaps reveal some other, hidden text.

Sentain watched, and then broke into a smile. "Life comes in many forms, not all of which has arms and legs or even moves."

Reddas cut off a laugh. "Very good, Sentain, *very good*!" Without thinking of the consequences of success, he scooped a small amount of moss from the bowl, looked at it, and then crushed it in his hand, at which its light began to dim. "I sacrifice this life," he muttered, and then he repeated the expression in Elvish, verbally rearranging the script and adding a personal pronoun. As the dead piece of moss fell from his hand and touched the bottom of the largest copper bowl, the doors beside the men shuddered and slowly began to open outwards.

Behind them, the rest of the company began to stir.

Miko was closest and spoke first: "What... what are you doing? Reddas?"

The bandaged Leaguer stepped back in surprise. "I seem to have been a reasonable student after all. The riddle has been solved." And then he turned to look through the doors into a twilight world. There were dim shapes that seemed to be rocks and trees. A cool breeze entered, refreshing the stale air.

As Archaen drowsily struggled to her feet, and Omdanan leapt to his, Reddas contemplated the tempting vista. After a moment's thought he took several steps, through the stone doors, and into the shadowy outside.

"Reddas—*no*!" exclaimed the woman, suddenly alert.

And as if from nowhere, a spear took the son of Enabeth Archaen in the side of the head.

The Price of Freedom Part II: Velasia

Chapter 16

"They've got one!" Yadzen strode across the throne room floor.

Lounging on his nightmarish throne, Anda com Durrel looked up sourly. Beside him stood Rostus Dettler; the nearest of the imposing orc bodyguards stood against the walls, well beyond spear-thrust range. Dettler had just been updating his downbeat master on the latest food situation.

"Got one *what*, Yadzen? A deer? A dose of the clap?"

"A prisoner. An… *elf*." Yadzen came to a halt in front of the throne, standing on the roughly woven red carpet that led from the broad, sentry-guarded doorway. As he halted, he rested one hand upon the hilt of the blade he had brought with him from Verano.

Com Durrel was suddenly alert, rising from his slouch, sitting forwards, nursing the staff of power between his arms. "Elf? Is it a… is it a woman?"

"No. I'm afraid not."

"*Fuck!* Then what's the point? I'm not into boys. *Fuck!*"

Dettler managed to catch the newcomer's eye: he frowned and gave a slight shake of the head. Then he leant in: "But this is still good news, sir. The intel from him and his captors might be useful and, ah, he might be a commodity we can exchange."

"For a woman? Are you fucking mad, Wormtongue?"

"Ah, no, I meant maybe for some food. Some luxuries. Some concessions."

Com Durrel flopped back against the iron-and-wood chair. He ground his teeth and shook his head. Then he leant forwards again and thumped the staff onto the floor as an outlet for his anger. "Very well. Not a completely fucking useless development. Fine. Where is the prisoner? Who caught him?"

"He'll be here in an hour or so," said Yadzen. "I just received a runner from the lower gate. There's a party of orcs from Krajja-Min waiting there for permission to approach. They come with a message from their king and this gift.

I took the liberty of promising safe passage and inviting them to come on. It'll take a while for the runner to collect them and return."

Com Durrel sighed and tapped his staff on the floor several more times with increasing vigour. "Okay. Fine. You'd better gather the generals. They should hear this. It'll be a chance to remind them of my power."

Yadzen bowed and turned to head from the chamber.

***

The orcs from Krajja-Min numbered an even dozen. They arranged themselves behind their prisoner, whom they made kneel on the red carpet, with half of their party to either side.

"Is your king here?" demanded com Durrel, tersely. "And who the fuck are you?"

One of the orcs, just to the left of the prisoner, took a nervous pace forwards. "I am Detfair, commander of the Red Fang Regiment, brother of King Denfair."

"So your king didn't have the guts to come personally and sent a lackey instead? Or is he too fat to travel?"

The orc was two metres tall, muscular, and wore a thick, padded leather uniform that was dyed a dark blue colour. It was currently weaponless, having been compelled to leave its spear outside the chamber like the rest of its party. Yet in spite of its objective heft, the orc somehow seemed small and uncertain. On entering the throne room, its keen eyes had lit upon the famed God-Sorcerer—but then looked away when com-Durrel turned his full attention onto it. The emissary averted its eyes, save for quick glances up to ensure that its host still bore interest. "The king never leaves his halls. It is our way. I am his mouthpiece and his spear carrier."

Com Durrel was amused. "I have been wondering about your kingdom. I think it might go nicely alongside that of Ullah-Bor in my collection. You have heard about what happened there, eh?"

"I have."

The man was silent for a moment, letting the orc sweat, allowing it time to think about the tales of what had happened at the capital of what was once the strongest orc kingdom in Velasia. Eventually, he said: "But that is perhaps a matter for later. I have other fish to catch, gut and fry first. So tell me: why are you here? You have brought me a gift?"

The orc bowed its head even lower. "I bring greetings from the king, good will, and a gift to prove our friendship. We heard that you sought live elves. This one was caught below the Cobalt Gate."

Com Durrel turned his intense gaze from the orc to consider the kneeling man. He was dark skinned, had a full black beard, and wore black leathers with a silver swan insignia on one shoulder. "What happened to his arm?"

"It is many days from Krajja-Min to Tartax-Kul. We grew hungry. He doesn't need two arms, so we took one."

The God-Sorcerer laughed, and then caught sight of Dettler, standing a few metres off to his right, near to one group of his generals. Aside from sentries at the doorway and along the walls, the only others present were Yadzen, who stood to the side of the throne, and a second, smaller group of his generals, which occupied some space over to his left. The sight of the small man, looking pale and nauseous, somehow cheered him further. "Chin up, Wormtongue. These orcs are really something, eh?" He turned back to Detfair. "Are you still hungry? Would you like a little snack? But Wormtongue would be *such* a little snack, barely an appetiser. You'd probably spend more energy consuming him than you'd get back from his digestion. Don't worry. I'll give you better fare shortly."

The orc looked up and over at the small man, seemingly confused as to whether the offer was genuine or not. "Er... thank you, God-Sorcerer."

"Right, so..." com Durrel leant forwards to better study the prisoner, who had his sole arm bound diagonally across his chest, and nothing but a padded stump where his other should have been. "Who are you and what were you doing, skulking about by the Cobalt Gate?"

The man met the other's gaze boldly. "I am Maddowu Hansa, of the High Guild of the Silver Swan. I was travelling from Narvik to the settlements of Bratha to assess their condition and see what help we might offer."

"Help? Oh, how noble. And how pointless. Do you really think you can prevent me from doing whatever I want with those dirty little towns? And now I have you. So what use are you to me?" He paused a moment to ponder, then nodded to himself. "Ah, yes. The gates. Now that would be useful. My forces need to clamber over the mountains to get at you. It's a fucking pain. If we could use your gates, that would make my conquest *so* much easier. I think you had better start talking or else I'll let Detfair have your other arm, and then perhaps your legs. What do you think? Does that sound like a fair exchange?"

Hansa did not flinch. "Your threats are meaningless. I could not help you even if I wanted to. I do not have the information you want."

Com Durrel's expression darkened. "What do you mean? You were caught outside the Cobalt Gate. How the fuck did you get through that? You opened it. And if you opened it once, you can open it again, and the other gates, too."

The man gave a slow shake of the head. "Not so. Every gate is locked with a different riddle. And there is a different riddle to open each gate in each direction. I solved the riddle to open the Cobalt Gate's western entry and eastern exit. I would need to see and solve the eastern entry riddle and then the western exit one in order to return to the Northlands. And the same is true of the Iron Gate, and of the others."

Com Durrel stared at the man, as though attempting to detect artifice. As the man seemed unphased, he turned to Dettler: "What do you think, Wormtongue? Is that your understanding, too? Did you learn anything else from... *before*?"

Dettler glanced at the prisoner and flashed a sympathetic smile. "I do not recall this matter being discussed. But it sounds plausible. I am sure he speaks the truth."

"You're sure? Well, I'm not. Perhaps a little torture might help answer the question. At least it might prove entertaining. But how—?"

"No!" Dettler responded instinctively. "Mr com Durrel... sir... this isn't right. You know it. This is a man. This is—"

"Wormtongue—you forget yourself!" com Durrel rose from his throne, suddenly enraged at the challenge. "*Choose your words more carefully!*"

"Yes, sorry, my lord. I meant, this is an *elf*. You should be careful in harming him. He is not an animal." Dettler suddenly looked at the orcs around him, which were appraising him with curiosity. "This goes beyond a game."

"No it *doesn't*. Not beyond *their* game, not at all. Haven't you learnt anything about this place, Wormtongue? This elf put himself in harm's way. It was his choice. And now he is at my mercy." Com Durrel suddenly turned to face the bearded prisoner. "Isn't that so? You know what I am, who I am, don't you?"

The man stared back, unbowed. "I have heard, yes."

"Then would you care to reveal this secret to all here present, including my generals and soldiers? Would you like to tell them?"

The man gave a wry grin and slowly shook his head. "You know what I will tell."

"Which is? Go on!"

"You are a great... *sorcerer.*"

"From where?"

"No one knows. Some say from a land far away. Some say that you emerged from the bowels of the earth. Some that you came down from the skies on a flaming meteorite."

"From the heavens?" com Durrel was enjoying himself now. "Like a god?"

This time the stern-faced man simply nodded.

Com Durrel turned back to Dettler. "You see? He remembers his lines. It's not that hard."

"But still..." Dettler turned to look towards Yadzen, who stood next to the throne, one hand resting on his sword. "Yadzen—come on, man! You cannot condone this."

"Wormtongue!" hissed com Durrel, his rage rising again. "I said—"

"No." Yadzen spoke quietly, yet his firm word carried through the chamber. His expression was troubled. He leant towards com Durrel. "Sir, you know I have protected you from excess before. This is—"

"*Before*, Yadzen!" com Durrel's wide eyes turned to his bodyguard. "That was *then*. When people thought they could fucking tell me what I could and couldn't do. When fucking *peasants* could bump into me and swear at me and I couldn't do anything except kick them out of my park. When men could steal my bitch and laugh in my face. When *he*... when *he* could belittle me and insult me and mock me! That was then. Now? Now I can do what the fuck I want. Whatever I want. You..." he turned again and raised his staff: "*Rentarum-Falasia-Termanum!*" A jet of flame surged from his staff and enveloped two of his generals, standing several metres away. As the orcs screamed and flapped at the flames, he turned and called out a slightly different spell, and the party of visiting orcs to the right of the prisoner flew through the air to smash into the nearest wall, smearing blood and gore across a wide expanse. "And now... and now..." he raised the staff so that it pointed towards the kneeling prisoner, from whom Detfair and the remains of its party had scampered back in fright.

"Sir!" Yadzen placed one gentle hand upon the outstretched arm. "Sir—you have the right. But you do not *need* to do this. This man is not *him*."

Com Durrel looked down at the hand on his arm, and took one step away, leaving the hand trailing. He slowly moved the staff and rested it on the other's mail-clad chest. In a barely controlled hiss, he declared: "Touch me again, Yadzen, and you will die. I will command you to gut yourself with your own knife in front of everyone. Understood?" But he didn't wait for an answer. Perhaps afraid of what else he might say or do, com Durrel about-faced and stalked to the rear of the room and the door that led to his personal chamber.

The two orc generals had stopped screaming and lay on the stones, gently burning. For a moment, no one in the chamber spoke. At last, Dettler, his heart still racing, cleared his throat. "I... er... think the audience is over. Take the prisoner to a cell..." he waved an arm towards two of com Durrel's orc bodyguards that had backed against one of the walls. "And do not mistreat him." Then he turned to the surviving members of the party from Krajja-Min. "The God-Sorcerer thanks you and will reward you. Stay tonight. *Ganna*..." Dettler had spotted the orc, standing with the clutch of generals near him. "See that these are well-treated and fed. Then, ah, get someone to clean up the mess in here. Yadzen—can we talk?"

***

"He's getting worse."

"I know," affirmed Yadzen. They were in a chamber a level above the throne room. There was scant furniture, so the two men stood. Light and cold air came into the room through two windows in the curved stone wall.

"I had hoped the conquest of Ullah-Bor might sate him," continued Dettler, "but since our return his mood has darkened further. It is being isolated here, I think. He has nothing to divert or interest him save wanton cruelty."

"He should have gone with the force to conquer the yeltoi towns," mused Yadzen. "It's not too late. If we set off in the next few days, we might still catch them before the first assault."

Dettler looked down and frowned. "Yes, perhaps. But he is determined not to expose himself until the Leaguers make their play. In any case, I dread to think what he might get up to against the yeltoi. They are a legitimate enemy to him, so all restraint is likely to be removed. At least here, he appreciates that the orcs are meant to be his allies and servants, and that stays his hand to *some* degree."

"But not today, eh?" Yadzen ran one hand through his short, iron-grey hair. "And maybe not tomorrow. He needs an outlet for his rage."

Dettler looked back up at the other. "There is only one way he will ever work through that, and he will never do it here, in Velasia, or on Arkon."

"Agreed. His brother is on Maloratious."

"So where does that leave us now?" Dettler's eyes narrowed and he looked at the bodyguard more intensely. "I am constantly afraid that he is going to serve me up on the menu of a banquet… but he even threatened *you* just now. Maybe your position is not so secure?"

Yadzen shrugged. "I know this. But there is nothing I can do. I cannot raise a hand against him, so do not ask me to. My conditioning will not allow it."

"Really? Nothing? And if he carried out his threat, and ordered you to… to kill yourself? Surely self-preservation would kick in? Surely no conditioning could override such fundamental instincts?"

"I would rather we not put that theory to the test. Still, I do not believe that he would do it. He has relied on my services for many years. I am not sure how he would cope without me. Or without you. He may bully and taunt you constantly, but he also needs you. I think you are safe for now."

Dettler laughed. "We should be renamed *the two crutches*! I see what you say, but we cannot assume whatever sanity he retains will remain for long. The cripple may yet discard his crutches even if it means he has to crawl on his belly ever after. And even if we are temporarily safe, what of the Leaguer, Hansa? I am not a bad man, Yadzen, at least, I have never considered myself to be. I know… I know I have arranged and mediated crimes that have led to death, and so perhaps I have some guilt by association, but I would never…" he waved an arm, unusually for him unable to find the words. "I would never… I would… I would see this man saved."

A tight smile settled on Yadzen's face. "Because it is right, or because it might be looked upon with merit by the Leaguers, with whom we must ultimately settle?"

Dettler glanced at the man, then looked away, almost shamefaced. "Is that it? Maybe you know me better than I know myself." But then his expression firmed and he looked back at his companion with greater certainty. "No. That's not it. At least, not all of it. I would see this man saved, even if there was no profit in it for me."

Yadzen's smile twitched. "If you say so. Then I am glad to hear it. As a man of war, I also have certain morals. I am a soldier, not an executioner."

"Good! Then if we cannot conspire to topple com Durrel, we can at least conspire to save a man's life."

***

"Mr Hansa, I am sorry about your arm." Dettler stood outside a small chamber that was essentially a bubble in the mountain rock sealed off from the corridor by a cross-hatched iron grate. The jail cell was not a familiar concept to orcs: punishment in their society was instant and usually brutal, so there was little need to confine a miscreant or prisoner of war, hence the cell was a recently converted larder.

For a moment, Dettler was uncertain as to whether the prisoner had heard him. An orc guard had placed a lit torch in a bracket in the wall behind him, but the light provided by this was insufficient to see to the back of the chamber: he saw the Leaguer's legs stretched out on the rough floor, and a bit of the man's torso, but nothing of his face. He cleared his throat and tried again. "And… I am sorry for your captivity and for the threats made against you. I am afraid my… *master*… has become a little unstable."

At last there were signs of life: the booted feet shifted and pulled back a little. The voice that came out of the dark was deep and clear. "Your master?" The man lapsed into silence for a moment, and then he climbed to his feet unsteadily, using his one arm to help push himself up. He stepped into the torchlight and approached the bars.

Once the man got close, Dettler was able to appraise him fully for the first time. The Leaguer towered over him, being not much shorter than the orcs that had brought him, and he was powerfully built. His beard was long, to the top of his chest, though his hair was short. Deep brown eyes looked down into his. "Yes, *master*. That is the, ah, term he prefers me to use. Of course, there are many other terms I have for him, and some I mutter to myself out of his earshot, though the worst I keep inside my head. You see, we actually have something in common, Mr Hansa, in that we are both prisoners of the God-Sorcerer."

The man contemplated this statement for a moment, then nodded. "Yes. I see. And I should thank you for your earlier intervention. It clearly took some courage to question him. So I guess I owe you my life… and health. And the other man, too."

"Yadzen? Or should I say *the Terminator*? Our great sorcerer has a sense of humour—and now complete freedom to inflict it upon the universe. He calls me Wormtongue, though my name is Rostus Dettler. Few seem to feel intimate enough to call me *Rostus*, so *Dettler* I am."

"Then I thank you, Dettler. And Yadzen? Who is he and why did he intervene? Is he also a prisoner?"

Dettler gave a wry smile, and then he quickly looked up and down the corridor. There was only one guard, and he was some distance away. "In some ways, he is even more constrained than you or I. He is *conditioned* to serve. I will not elaborate here, but in short he is compelled to obey at the deepest behavioural level. I suspect he would be as happy as either of us to strike down the sorcerer. But believe me, in spite of appearances, he is with us."

"Us?" The man frowned. "You seem to be implying some sort of mutual conspiracy."

"I guess I am. To be blunt, Mr Hansa, I am not here of my free will. I have had no part in the tragedy that is now occurring here in Velasia. And I am running out of options. Yadzen thinks I am safe because I am useful to our master, and because tormenting me is one of the few pleasures he presently has in life, but I am not so sure. Rationality is my strength. I solve problems. But rationality in my master is being overwhelmed by insanity. So what can I do? I cannot escape. I am not brave enough to sneak up on him and stab him in the dark. So maybe… maybe your appearance is something of a godsend."

The man smiled, revealing bright white teeth. "I do not feel like a godsend. But… how do I know your presence here is not part of an elaborate trick? An attempt to convince me to trust you so that I give up whatever secrets you think I have to give up?"

"A fair question. My first answer is that, as you saw earlier, the sorcerer has no compunctions in using extreme force to get his way. He would much rather use force and pain on you than stealth. My second, is that you have no secrets to give up. You stated this, and I believe you. So what need is there for subterfuge?"

The man grasped a bar with his one hand and bent down to look more closely into Dettler's eyes. Whatever he saw made him nod. "I did not truly doubt you. Your earlier efforts already convinced me of your… *goodness*? Maybe that is not the right word, but it will do for now. So what are your plans?"

"I will protect you for as long as I can, although realistically this is unlikely to be long. The only way you will be safe is if you are free. Yadzen will help. We are working on a plan."

"And if you manage to free me, what then?"

"Ah, then we will have to see. Three options occur to me, though the one we choose must depend upon circumstance and opportunity. In the first, we hide you until you can get away by yourself. In the second, you will take me with you when you go."

"That sounds like a fair exchange," said Hansa. "And what of the third option?"

Dettler looked about again, making doubly sure that they were alone and out of earshot. Even so, he leant in so that he was close to the bars and mere centimetres from the other's face. "The third is that you become a hero. You gain a reputation foremost among your people. You kill Anda com Durrel, the God-Sorcerer of Tartax-Kul."

***

The two men stood on a natural platform jutting out over the sea—which lapped and surged at the rock far below. Yadzen stood with his hands resting on an iron rail that ran across the open space from the rock to either side—providing some obstacle to a death slip—while Dettler stood with his back pressed against the rock, at an angle, half in the tunnel that led from the mountain interior, and half out on the platform.

"I don't know why we had to meet here," said Dettler, unhappily.

"The air is clear of the stench of the caverns, and the views are spectacular. I could spend all day here."

They were at the highest of the platforms of Tartax-Kul, at the end of a two-kilometre-long tunnel that sloped downwards from the courtyard before the upper gates of the fortress. Beneath them were other platforms at the end of further tunnels that cut through the mountain from the inhabited parts of the city. It was from these lower platforms that orc fishermen dropped their long lines into the surf below, which teemed with an abundance of fish. From this angle, the tops of the heads of different clusters of fishers could be seen, although their lines and hauled-in catches could not.

"There are other parts of the castle that are also private," said Dettler, "although admittedly, none so much as this. But our alibis for being absent for so long will need to be tight."

Yadzen had his back Dettler. He continued to admire the view for some seconds more, then gave a small shake of the head and turned around, resting his back against the rail. "He was taking his afternoon nap when I left. He sleeps more now. I think he appreciates unconsciousness as an antidote to his unhappiness."

"But what if he wakes early and you are not nearby?"

Yadzen shrugged. "On Maloratious, he had many servants, but here he has only two he can trust. Like you, I have other duties beyond hovering at his shoulder. He frets at my absence when he is awake, even though he knows he has more need of me when he is asleep and vulnerable, which is why he expects me to do these duties when he sleeps. I will be back before he is due to wake."

Dettler was still unhappy. He made a point of looking straight ahead rather than at the terrifying drop just beyond his right foot. "Regardless, why here? You know how I feel about heights. This is the sort of sadistic thing he would do."

"You know I am not like that, and nor is this for my own pleasure. I need you to get a sense of the escape route."

Dettler felt a prickling sensation at the nape of his neck, some instinctive animal response to fear. "*The* escape route? Singular? Definitive?"

"Yes. I have considered other options, but none seem achievable. I don't doubt Hansa's martial abilities, but there is no way he could escape his cell and get through the fortress, then the upper gate and the orc dwellings, and then past the lower gates. And even if he managed by some miracle to do this, he is incapacitated and alone: the orcs would hunt him down in the wilds in no time. But a credible story might be woven that he escaped his cell, killed a guard, and accessed this tunnel. The Leaguers are good free climbers, and com Durrel knows this, although I worry about whether he might buy Hansa being able to climb down from here with one hand. And then there is the issue of swimming long distances in the turbulent waters below."

"That is perilous to say the least."

"It is. And the harsh nature of this challenge needs to be put to Hansa before we aid his escape. Should he try, I think we can be assured that there is little risk of him being recaptured and tortured to reveal our involvement. In this plan, he will either escape or he will die falling from the rock or in the waters."

"Knowing the nature of Leaguers, I suspect he will attempt this and die. No, I cannot countenance such a suicidal plan."

Yadzen nodded sombrely. "I concur. I think he will accept this option and then die. The only way he might succeed—and the main reason I suggested we meet here—is if he has help. The *other* option."

Dettler closed his eyes. He had already worked out Yadzen's gist. "You mean I go with him."

"Yes. This tunnel is rarely used. It is too high for the fishermen's lines and no one else comes here. Long ropes, inflated skins for flotation, some food… all could be stored here and used in the escape. Com Durrel appreciates your intelligence, so it would not be far-fetched to imagine you did this alone and I would not be implicated. It would still be risky, but there is a chance for you both to get away."

Dettler's eyes were still closed. He tilted his head back and gently tapped it against the rock behind. He felt sweat on the palms of his hands, making their contact against the stone slick.

"I... *cannot*. If... if there were a choice between walking into a flame or facing the abyss, I would take the flame." He opened his eyes to look at his colleague. A tear sat in the corner of one eye. "I am sorry, Yadzen, I just... can't."

Yadzen held up one calming hand, a sympathetic look on his face. "And I am sorry, Rostus. But I had to present this to you. We talked of two options, to facilitate the escape of the Leaguer, or to facilitate the escape of you both. There was always going to be a cost, especially in allowing you to go too. I see the price is too high. I suppose we must now adopt a third option—which is to find ways to keep the Leaguer alive. I think this is feasible. We can argue that we need him to get the army through the Iron Gate when it is time to assault the lands to the west. Com Durrel will buy that."

Dettler found a weak and embarrassed smile. "I hate myself for this lack of bravery. Please don't think too badly of me. But, yes, the third option you mention makes sense."

Dettler looked down. *The third option.* He had presented a different third option to Hansa—one he dared not mention to Yadzen, knowing that he could not, would not, allow it. But the meeting had not been in vain, for he now knew the exact time when a released Hansa might strike: when com Durrel was napping and Yadzen was employed on other duties. And then he looked up sharply at the other, suddenly wondering. Was *that* the real reason for Yadzen arranging their meeting here?

The other returned Dettler's gaze, his expression inscrutable.

Chapter 17

Reddas Archaen fell before the Copper Gate.

Elian Omdanan saw the spear flash out from the Leaguer's right and make contact with his head. His sword was in his hand and he was moving before the other reached the ground—yet he was still not the first to react. A shape was suddenly next to him, and then past him. Light from Sentain's staff, from deeper in the tunnel, glinted off the silvered edge of a black blade, sparkling off the rim of a helmet...

Ignoring the shouts of dismay and confusion from behind, Omdanan followed the woman into the twilight. Archaen passed her fallen son without a pause, emitting a scream of rage, and split the skull of the surprised and now weaponless orc that stood dumbly in her path, and then she continued forwards a dozen metres, past several stunted bushes and into an area of stony ground where a camp of sorts had been set out. The orcs dotted around the area barely had chance to react. Two were dead before Omdanan joined the fray. He barrelled into one as it tried to bring its spear to bear, cutting down into its shoulder. As the creature let out a hideous scream, he left it, knowing that it posed little further threat, and looked for another target. He saw Archaen's sword sweep down, splitting a spear held crossways in an unsuccessful attempt at a parry, dissecting an albino creature's face from brow to chin. Then he caught movement to his right: an orc attempting to flee. With his own bloodlust up, Omdanan bounded after the creature and caught it in several strides, taking it from behind at the neck. He spun to see Archaen's sword arm fall once more, dispatching the orc he'd already mortally wounded. And then the scene was alight, as Sentain emerged from the tunnel with his staff held aloft, backlighting the rest of the party, which moved almost as one, holding swords and spears in front of it. But they were not needed, for the orcs were all dead.

Archaen had dropped her sword and was kneeling beside the fallen man by the time Omdanan got to her. Mandelson and Vuller moved further into the scrub before the gate, to watch and guard, while Miko, Sarok and Sentain stood over the woman and her son. Omdanan watched as Archaen discarded her helm, then reached to inspect the scene. Reddas had fallen on his face, dislodging the spear. Archaen pushed the bloodied weapon away, placed a hand upon the other's neck to feel for a pulse, gave a brief shake of the head, and then she removed her hand and ran it over her face, where it left a streak of blood that almost seemed to sparkle in the unnatural light from the staff. And then she hunched forwards and gently turned the neck of the dead man, whose face was still fully bandaged, in order to confirm what she already knew by looking into lifeless eyes.

Miko spoke softly: "Reddas—hero of the hidden valley—your name will live on." Then he touched Sarok on the arm and looked across at Omdanan. "Let us leave a mother to grieve for her son. You too, Sentain. Bring away your light: some things are best done in the dark."

***

The gate had been opened, so Miko cajoled the party to collect its gear while he stood in the doorway, asserting that it would not close while there was a human impediment. When this was done, he set a tin bowl containing some moss in his place. "I don't know if this will hold the gate open or not," he said quietly to Sentain, "but I don't wish to disturb Cousin En for advice. It is best if some are not trapped on one side of the gate, and some on the other. When Enabeth is ready, we can decide our best plan for the night."

The party were shuffling about in silence before the gate and beneath the steep mountainside—a smattering of scraggy trees and bushes forming a kind of screen between them and the lower lands to their north—when Archaen moved into their midst. She still bore a streak of her son's blood on the side of her cheek. With a faraway expression in her eyes, she announced: "My son erred. His game is over.

I will not leave him here to be discovered or picked over by beasts. I will leave him in the tunnel. Who will help me carry him?"

"I will," blurted Sentain, before looking down in embarrassment as others twisted to observe him.

A vacant smile crossed Archaen's face. "Thank you, Irvan, but we need you to light our procession."

"Miko's arm is not good," said Vuller, gruffly. "So I will."

"And I," murmured Sarok. "He's a big man, Ms Archaen. Let's carry him with dignity, eh?"

And so Vuller, Sarok and Archaen carefully lifted Reddas and carried him back through the Copper Gate, following Sentain and his illuminated staff, with Miko, Omdanan and Mandelson remaining watchful outside. Vuller and Sarok then returned to their colleagues, while Sentain provided the light for Archaen to arrange her son into a respectful pose, crossing his arms over his chest. Then, with a long knife, the woman spent some time scraping away at the wall above the corpse, carving the dead man's name into the rock as a memorial.

At last, Archaen rose. She again gave Sentain a soft smile. "There is nothing more to do here. Go. I will follow in a moment."

But it was several minutes before the woman came out from the black tunnel, and when she did, all could see that the blood on her cheek was smeared and pale, as though diluted by water.

***

"There were orcs at the southern end of the Copper Gate, and in the hidden valley, and now here," said Miko. "And by their insignia, these ones were also of the Black Tree regiment of Tartax-Kul. I think we can assume that there will be more between here and the western entrance of the Iron Gate, and there will almost certainly be another contingent lurking by the pass."

"Makes sense," grumbled Sarok. "But as we can do nothing about those awaiting us at the other gate, we should put all thoughts of them aside for now. The immediate problem is how to get there without being seen and caught. I have a nasty suspicion we are going to have to travel at night. How far is it to the Iron Gate?"

"I am not the best one to answer that. Enabeth?"

"Five days." The woman had been content to allow Miko to lead the discussion, listening distractedly. "At least, it would be five days if we were able to march rapidly in daylight. But I agree we should now travel at night, and that is likely to take a day longer, maybe two. We sacrifice time, but I think we have no choice."

"So we are here for some time," said Sarok. "A night and a day. Does that mean we should wait back in there?" he gestured with one hand at the now-closed copper-banded doors.

"Oh no, Mr Sarok," said Archaen, grimly. "We will not remain here any time at all. Twilight has all but gone. Night is upon us. We must see to our gear and decide upon our marching order. We leave *now*."

"Enabeth, *no*." Sentain was suddenly animated. "You said yourself, you've been on the move for twenty hours and that was before… before… the fight. That's crazy. You need to rest and, well, we all do. I mean, I'm exhausted. Surely, it makes more sense to rest a while now and then push on refreshed. We'll probably be able to make up time later."

Mandelson scoffed. "You want to wait here for twenty-four hours, sleeping next to a corpse? You're welcome to it. But I am not tired. I can push on."

"Corpse? Ah, sorry Enabeth, I didn't think."

"No matter, Irvan. And thank you for your concern. But we are made of sterner stuff. I would rather get away from this place as soon as possible."

"Of course."

Archaen smiled at Sentain sadly, then considered the party clustered about. "Elian, you lead off. Navigation is simple. Keep the mountains to our south. Head east, towards the Skythrust range in the distance. Use your skills to pick an easy route. We will travel single file. Ryven—take the rear and keep us in check. No one talk. And Irvan—you'll have to extinguish your staff. We must rely on moon and starlight to avoid drawing attention to ourselves. Now, no more discussion: the decision is made."

***

They walked and walked. Because the land was rocky and steep in places, Omdanan veered them further from the mountains to slightly flatter terrain, where the ground was carpeted in low, heather-like foliage. In daylight, they might have been easy to spot from any high position, but in the night it was difficult to see more than a few metres ahead under the light of Arkon's small moon and the heavenly ceiling of stars. The Meridian seemed disinclined to stop, but even when he did turn to raise the question—three hours after they started—Enabeth Archaen was there to shake her head and urge him on.

After around four hours, they paused for a rest. Sentain was asleep almost the second he dropped onto the furred ground, and he was then confused when shaken awake half-an-hour later, his limbs aching, his mind barely functioning. When they stopped for a second time, after what seemed to him like an eternity, he again fell into an instant sleep, unaware of where he was or what he was doing.

When Sentain woke naturally, he first noticed that he was lying face down in a soft, springy fuzz of red-brown vegetation. The sun was warm upon an ear and one side of his face; his helmet had tipped off of his head and was a short distance away; and he clinked as he rolled upright, being still in his chainmail surcoat. He tried to push himself up, coughed, and spat out some small leaves that he'd somehow inhaled as he slept.

"Welcome back online," said a voice from nearby. *Vuller?*

Sentain made it into a sitting position and turned to the voice. "Ah... Vuller... what time... where?"

"You're in a real state, Sentain," said Sarok, moving into view to join his bodyguard, who was sat upon a boulder, watching him with amusement. Sarok handed the other a tin bowl, containing something unseen. Food? Drink? "It's late afternoon. You've been out for the entire day."

"Yeah, we've been waiting for you," confirmed Vuller. "Miko has been keen to do his duty, but Ms Archaen said to let you sleep. Feel better?"

Sentain flexed his neck and thought about this a moment. "In truth, not so much. Where…?" He looked about their camp. They were in a slight dip in the land, with a bed of the heather-like plants in the bottom of the bowl—where he had dropped—and a couple of tallish trees rising from the lip just behind Vuller. The other direction was dominated by the mountains of the Sundering chain, rising steep, several capped with snow. He saw Mandelson over there, relaxing against the slope of the bowl with her hands behind her head and eyes closed, and further off, Miko and Archaen were conferring. The latter pair saw him; Miko turned to say a brief word to the woman, and then he led the way over.

"Dr Sentain, our white wizard— at last!"

"Uh, we're not about to leave, are we? I mean, it's still light, and I haven't eaten, and—"

"No. Don't worry. You have time. But before then, it is important that we bring some closure to the events of yesterday. Are all here? Mandelson—please." Miko turned and looked up. In a slightly louder voice he called: "Elian—if all is clear, please descend from your eyrie."

Sentain noticed one of the trees begin to tremble: this had a thick grey trunk and several rings of up-curled branches bearing red-brown leaves. He watched the upper branches start to wave and then the lower ones, and then caught sight of a dark shape. At last, Omdanan was clearly visible in the bottom skirt. The Meridian dropped the last two metres to the ground.

"All are here," declared Miko. "Good. Now we must briefly honour our fallen comrade. I will start, and Cousin Enabeth will end, and then we will lay poor Reddas to rest in our minds until we have time for a more fitting and fulsome memorial." He looked around, ensuring that he had the eyes of all present, and then he looked down, composing his thoughts. Looking back up, he began: "I knew Reddas when he was younger, but met him most recently on Ghuraj, where it was clear that he had borne his captivity with stoicism. During his escape, he thought nothing of sacrificing his foot to be rid of an explosive anklet. He did not complain about the pain, not then or during his recovery. And then he accepted the quest to pay for his indiscretions in the Confederation with good grace. Since arriving in Velasia, he was tireless and brave. He fought well in the Shadow Forest, where he was grievously injured. Again, he did not complain. He then sought not to delay us, even though the cost of separating from our fellowship might have been high. And when he did re-join us, he fought bravely in the hidden valley. In short, Reddas was a true man of his people. He was strong, and brave, and lived life fully and without compromise. In life he burned bright, if only too briefly. He will be remembered with merit. I will miss him."

Miko closed his eyes and bowed his head. Then he looked back up and around the party.

Vuller cleared his throat. "I guess I will speak next, but briefly. I met Reddas first on Ghuraj. On our journey to Arkon, I got to know him somewhat. In spite of being an outsider, he was always polite to me. He was clearly a man of opinion, but also great skill and strength. Our fellowship is less without him."

Sarok was next. "I had less to do with Reddas than my men. I never knew what he thought of me. I suspect he held my size against me, but he was respectful when we did speak. As you said, Miko, he was a brave man, and I rue his loss… and Ms Archaen's."

Mandelson shrugged when Sarok turned to look at her. "What can I say? He was strong in resolve, whereas most here are weak. We could have done with more like him. Oh, and he was a good lay."

Vuller coughed at the last pronouncement, while Sarok's eyes grew wide and Miko smiled wryly. Omdanan, who was next, was suddenly lost for words. He glanced quickly aside at Mandelson, and then cleared his throat. "Ah… I… also first met Reddas on the ship. He… tolerated me at the start. Not many people in my life have accepted me, but he did after he saw what I could do. Then he treated me like a younger brother. Now I am sad."

Sentain took over the baton reluctantly. "I haven't got a lot to say really. In truth, he didn't think much of me. But he was Enabeth's son, and to spare her the pain of his death I would have burned half of the world… uh… metaphorically." He was suddenly embarrassed and refused to look over at Archaen, whose eyes he now felt upon him. "That's it."

"Enabeth?" said Miko. "Your words?"

Archaen's eyes were still fixed on the anthropologist. "I have only this to say: he was my son. Nothing else matters." She turned and walked out of the circle.

***

For two more nights they walked on, led by Omdanan, resting up during the daylight hours. The highlands in the mountains' lee undulated gently, so the going was not especially tough. Trees were rare and clustered around water sources—the occasional stream or small pond—but mostly absent in the thin and acidic soil, which instead bore hardy grasses, heathers and tough bushes. There was little sign of animal life beyond insect-like creatures and the occasional bird in the sky. Once, they glimpsed a fire in the mid-distance away to the north-east, which raised their guard and caused them to veer back closer to the mountains, although sight of the unnatural phenomenon was soon obscured by the folding land.

Along with an absence of sights, there was also an absence of sound. The world was quiet except for their shuffling feet through the foliage and occasional pants of exertion or curses caused by misplaced steps and twisted ankles. The only exception to this was on their third night of travel from the Copper Gate: a single, sudden scream came out of the night, from off to the north, which made more than one of the party jump.

"What the fuck was that?" asked Vuller, drawing to a halt.

"Aye, that went right through me," concurred Sarok, wincing.

"Nothing to concern us, I hope," said Archaen, although she refused to elaborate.

As dawn started to brighten the horizon, they began to look for a place to stop, and found a dip in the land containing a small pond of still water, inches deep, and a cluster of thorny bushes around one side.

"This will have to do," said Archaen. "I will take first watch. The rest of you, eat, sleep." She wandered off, alone, to scout the perimeter of the bowl.

Sarok fell asleep under the shadow of one of the bushes. He woke twice during a fitful sleep, with lucid dreams. In the first, he was back on Ghuraj with Mandelson on a causeway crossing a lake of blood. In the second, he was alone by a lake, fishing, with a vague unease about what it was he was trying to catch. He eventually fell asleep, and then on his third and final waking, he remembered parts of his dreams, and spent some minutes staring up at the dried twigs above him, trying to make sense of them, but coming to no clear conclusion. At last, he decided to emerge from his bivouac. He rose to his feet on stiff knees, and then shook out his sleeping cloak, dislodging insects, soil and small leaves. His mail surcoat was nearby, with his pack resting on it. He stepped over to his pack and rummaged about, pulling out a leather water bottle. Only after drinking, did he give any attention to the camp.

The party were widely spread throughout the bowl. Sentain was still asleep, and Miko was absent—probably keeping watch on the boundary—but the others were dotted about, in various states of wakefulness. Omdanan was nearest, sitting on a boulder, toying with his bow, which he had retained despite an absence of arrows, ever hopeful of acquiring some.

After a moment's thought, Sarok ambled over to the young man. "I'm not sure there's much point carrying that around," he said tersely. "You should have taken one of the orc spears from outside the gate."

"Ah, maybe, sir." Omdanan was clearly flustered by the unexpected attention. "But their spears are mostly for cutting and badly weighted. I couldn't hunt with them, and they'd be more cumbersome than my sword in a fight."

"I suppose so," said Sarok, frowning at his choice of seating. There was another boulder near the Meridian, but it was smaller than the one on which he sat and of an awkward shape. But it was either that, or stand, or demand that the young man give up his seat. Sarok decided to accept the compromise. As he turned to sit, he noticed Vuller across the bowl smile and nod his head. He gave his bodyguard a puzzled look and returned his attention to Omdanan. "We've never really talked, have we, boy? I've maybe not taken the interest in my men I should. You're good at all this," he waved one arm in the air, "and I'm wondering how you got this way. Tell me about your home."

"Meridian?" Omdanan seemed surprised, but not unhappy at the approach. "Well, it was settled during the Environmentalist Diaspora. The population isn't high. Enbargo—my town—has just a few hundred. The people believe in living in tune with nature. You know, leaving a soft footprint. The town is half underground, and the half above is designed to blend into the environment. They see themselves as guests on the planet and do everything they can not to cause harm or disruption."

"Very noble," said Sarok, somewhat sarcastically. "So how do they eat? What do they do with their time?"

"They grow protein in vats and have a few orchards and fields. Machinery is generally frowned on, so a lot of work is labour intensive. But they also see themselves as protectors and chroniclers of the world. They collect and analyse everything—from every lifeform to every feature of geography."

"Sounds tedious. But I don't see how that made *you*." Sarok sat up straighter, flexing his back. The boulder *was* uncomfortable. "I hear Meridian has some famously vicious creatures. Com Durrel once told me he had imported some into his park. And come to think of it, aren't some of the Leaguers' hybrids based on your fauna?"

Omdanan smiled shyly. "Yes, sir. That's right. Anywhere else, the most dangerous animals would be culled or penned. On Meridian, they are allowed to roam free and do as they want."

"So, you have experience evading such creatures, but not killing them?"

"No, not killing them. In fact, they are seen as more important than humans, with a right to exist on the world that we don't have. The punishment for harming one is as great as for harming a human."

"Interesting. So, are all Meridians like you? Expert trackers and gymnasts? Is it a planet of secret superhumans?"

"No!" Omdanan's expression hardened. "No, sir, it isn't. My peers are not like me. I am unique."

Sarok caught the other's change in demeanour. "I seem to have touched a nerve. Very interesting. I suppose you must be different—after all, you were sentenced to Ghuraj. So, what makes you different? An aggressor in a world of pacifists? A wolf among sheep? A killer?"

"No. Not a killer. Not a murderer. A defender. An avenger. A… *human*."

Sarok observed the young man for a moment in silence. At last, he said: "Being human isn't necessarily such a great thing. Humans range from the weak to the strong. We are a mixed bag. In fact, the Leaguers don't seem to regard the rest of humanity highly at all, and also question whether most of us are better than animals. They appear to be seeking to become something more. You were seen as an abomination in your society for thinking too much of humans, and I for thinking too little. Maybe neither of us belong back there, in the Confederation, eh?" He frowned to himself and sat back. Had they both accidentally found their real home?

"Oh, *look*," said Vuller, from across the bowl, interrupting the conversation. "Elian, I wish you had some arrows for that bow."

Sarok looked at Vuller, then followed the other's gaze. At the lip of the sink, some ten metres away, a small creature had appeared. It was a red-brown colour—like the heather—and the size of a rabbit. It had two large eyes, four legs, long ears, and a flaccid sack at the neck. Its demeanour was wary. It observed the party, switching its attention from one member to another, and then looking towards the pond in the hollow. It edged forwards, then seemed to have second thoughts and edged back again. It did this several times, making gradual progress towards the water.

Sarok watched Omdanan put down his bow and look about. He noticed Vuller and Mandelson also following the creature. The nearest spear in range of the young man was near Enabeth Archaen, who was several metres away, staring into some unknown space, almost detached from the rest of the group.

"Uh, Ms Archaen?" said Omdanan, quietly. "Enabeth?"

At last, the woman responded. Her shoulders straightened and she turned around just as a second creature appeared over the rim of the depression close behind the first. She stiffened at the sight.

"Ms Archaen," continued Omdanan. "You are best equipped to hunt…"

Sarok noticed Mandelson reach for her own spear—a movement also caught by Archaen, who suddenly came to life: she stretched out an arm and hissed: "*No!*" The Leaguer slowly stood and took half a step back.

Sarok and Omdanan exchanged quick glances, then both followed Archaen's lead, rising cautiously. Mandelson's brow furrowed and her hand ceased its quest for the haft of her spear, while Vuller's amused smile froze as he focused more intensely on the two snuffling creatures.

"Everyone back away carefully," said Archaen, taking another step. "They just want to drink. Move away. Leave them to it. Leave your gear: we will collect it when they are gone."

"What of Sentain?" asked Sarok, matching the woman's low volume.

"He will be fine as long as he doesn't wake. Move now."

The company did as asked. As they backed away, the two creatures continued their arthritic advance. And suddenly there were two more, and then another three.

Eventually the members of the company made their way from the hollow, picking up Miko on the way, and reassembled on a flat piece of grassland a couple of hundred metres to the north.

"What the fuck was that all about?" scowled Sarok. "Have we just run away from a herd of over-sized hamsters?"

Archaen adopted a wry expression. "Sometimes, Mr Sarok, danger doesn't come from the large, but from the small."

"Don't tell me: the bunnies are venomous and multiply in size when enraged?"

"Not quite. But do you remember that scream last night?"

"Fuck yeah!" said Vuller. "It gave me the willies!"

Archaen nodded. "As it should have. We call them *screamers*. They have an interesting defence mechanism. When attacked, they inflate their neck sacks and emit a high-pitched sound of over one-hundred-and-eighty decibels. They could have permanently deafened everyone in the company."

Sarok shook his head. "Once more, Ms Archaen, I urge you not to die. Without your knowledge, we'll be well-and-truly fucked."

***

"Enabeth—care for some company?"

It was late afternoon on the fourth day since they had emerged from the Copper Gate. They were in a small cleft of land through which a stream cut, populated by a score of trees—some by the water, and others lining the lip. Unlike their previous campsites, this self-contained area provided the company a moderate amount of privacy, allowing its members to spread out rather than forcing them into close proximity. Sentain had watched Archaen wander off along the stream into the shadows and grown concerned when she didn't return. After around an hour, he sought her out and found her near the end of the depression, sitting on a rock that jutted from the slope over the stream, staring through the cleft gap towards the Skythrust Mountains on the eastern horizon.

The woman looked around, her expression unreadable. "Company? No. Not really."

"Ah, okay. Sorry to disturb you."

But as Sentain turned to go, Archaen had second thoughts. "No... Irvan... wait." She sighed deeply and cast the smooth pebble she had been holding into the shallow stream. "Perhaps I could use some company. *Different* company."

"Different?" Sentain's momentary low had been replaced with a high. He approached the woman once more, looked about, and settled on a spot just across the stream from her, putting his back against a tree and sliding down into a sitting position. "Different from what? From whom?"

"From myself mostly. I seem to have gotten into a depressing thought-loop, going round and round the same subjects in my head, the same images."

"Ah. I can guess what you're thinking about. It's only natural. I'm no psychologist, but I am here if you want to talk to me about it... if you can."

Archaen gave a short bark of laughter. "And there lies the problem. I cannot. Should not. It is not *our* way. It is something that lies in the past. Something that has happened and cannot be changed. Dwelling on it can only fill the mind, distract, slow responses, cripple. Our way makes sense, but that doesn't make it natural or easy."

Sentain nodded slowly. "You are people who live in the moment... for the present. In the face of danger. I guess you need clarity of thought. In the Confederation, we are a cautious lot, and often have long hours in which to think without pressure or immediate risk. So thinking about the past isn't taboo. We think a lot about the future, too. About what education we might need, and how that might affect our career, and what we might need to do to advance. We allow the present to slide past, almost unnoticed, as we worry about a long-distant time when we are old and can no longer work and must rely upon the state to take care of us, so that we can eventually wither and die with a degree of material comfort. We constantly sacrifice the present for the future. I guess you are more confident than that—confident in your abilities, unconcerned about growing old, and perhaps comforted by your guilds and their support."

"Perhaps so," replied the woman. "But if we are 'lucky' in our environment, it is because we have made it so. We have decided to live this way and created social structures to support our philosophy. In any case, although we tell ourselves we live for the present, that isn't entirely true. In fact, we obsess about the past as well as about how we might be seen in the future. The badges on our skins tells our personal histories. We each have keepsake boxes in which recordings of our glories and our heroic failures are kept. But my real skin also tells a story. Beneath my breast—as is the custom of our women—I have tattooed the names of my children." She paused and looked away, captured by some deep thought or memory.

After some moments, Sentain volunteered: "Your children? Your society allows you two, doesn't it? A boy and a girl? So with Reddas' name you have that of a daughter?"

Archaen looked back at the man, an expression on her face he'd not seen before—somewhere between surprise and a pained concern. "You forget, Irvan, that we have two *living* children. When one dies, we are allowed to bear a replacement. There are not two names beneath my breast..." she gently touched the area under her left breast with her right hand, "there are *seven*."

"Seven? That means... oh! I'm sorry!" Sentain covered his mouth, although he couldn't hide the shock in his widening eyes. "Of course, I didn't think. You have had other children..."

"Had... and lost. Of the seven, only my daughter, Annelie, now lives. For my people, this... *sacrifice*... is seen as something of an honour. All six died well, and with accomplishments. But, Irvan, I am so, *so* tired of burying them." She looked away, and Sentain thought he glimpsed a sparkle of light off an unexpected tear. "I have done my best for them, even for Reddas, who in truth was not the most pleasant of men. But I would have done even more... given more... for him." She looked back at Sentain, and tears were evident in the corners of both of her eyes.

"Maybe next time, it would be nice if I could bear a child somewhat less heroic. More cerebral. More empathetic." She pinched the space between her eyes, squeezing away the tears, and somehow managed to compose a soft smile. "Of course, Cousin Ryven and many of my kin would think this a perverse and not entirely noble wish, but I think I could live with their disapproval." She suddenly stood, sliding from the boulder. "But these are maudlin thoughts. Reddas died three days ago. By custom, we should not speak or think of him until we are safely home, and we have both now uttered his name."

"I don't know what to say. I am so sorry, Enabeth. If there is anything I can do… any way I can help. You can talk to me whenever you want about whatever you want." He found a pained smile of his own. "And I promise, I won't tell Ryven your words or thoughts. Your secret will be safe with me."

"Thank you, Irvan. I will not burden you any further now. But afterwards… there may be something you can do for me." And then, without further elaboration, she turned and headed back to the centre of the cleft where the rest of the party were gathered.

***

"Orcs—as expected," said Omdanan, rejoining his comrades where they waited under a small copse of trees. It was still dark, with dawn perhaps an hour away on this, their sixth night of marching since the Copper Gate. The sky above was clear of cloud and there was a chill to the air.

"How many?" asked Miko, his face in complete darkness. "One squad? Two?"

"No. More than that. Several companies at least—"

"Companies!" exclaimed Sarok. "You mean there are dozens of them?"

Omdanan shrugged, though the gesture was lost in the night. "Yes. Over a hundred. Maybe two. And their camp is well organised and seems more permanent. They even have sentries."

Miko turned to Archaen beside him. "This is something different. This isn't just a trap to snare a few elves."

"I agree. This seems like an attempt to shut the gate completely, and maybe even establish a base camp for an invading force. A couple of hundred orcs is almost an entire regiment. Elian—did you see any symbols or banners in the camp?"

Omdanan faced the woman, who stood in just the right spot for moonlight to pierce through the trees and silver the end of her nose and chin. "I saw more black tree symbols, but there were others from another regiment I've not seen before. Their armour was stained white, and they had a banner on a pole—white, with a black hook and a drop of red blood on its tip."

"The Tormentors Regiment from Tartax-Kul," said Archaen. "It is one of their fiercest regiments. I would have expected com Durrel to keep it close by. If he has sent it here, it suggests he is serious and well advanced in his invasion plans. It also suggests he may have already dealt with Ullah-Bor. I do not see how he could spare it unless that other threat has been neutralised."

"Great," muttered Sarok. "We have raced across much of Velasia, and find we are already too late. What do we do now? If we can't take the Iron Gate, what then? The mountains? Though I don't doubt that you—Ms Archaen—and maybe Omdanan the goat, might scale the peaks in good time, some of us…" he waved a shadowy arm towards the incapacitated Miko, "are less agile. From what you have told us, it is the gate or nothing."

Archaen nodded in the gloom. "True. And we do not have the time or even energy to trek north to the Cobalt Gate, which may also now be watched. Elian— how closely do they guard the gate? Might we sneak past them?"

"No. The centre of their camp is on a little knoll no more than fifty metres from the entrance. They would have to be drawn away somehow."

"How closely packed are they?" asked Miko. "Would Sentain be able to blast them with his staff—or at least get enough of them to give us a chance to fight the rest and make the gate?"

"I can't say. They are spread out around half-a-dozen well-spaced campfires. I'm not a strategist. I think someone needs to come with me to assess the site."

"But perhaps not now," said Miko. "We have walked all night. Cousin En, I think we need to retire a safe distance and establish a hidden camp. Tomorrow night, you can return with Elian to consider options. I admit, I am too tired to think. A night's sleep—or should I say, a day's sleep—may let our unconscious minds work on a solution."

"That is a sound plan," agreed the woman. "There was a rise topped by trees a couple of kilometres back. The trees might give us shelter, and the height perspective."

***

They didn't get a full day's sleep.

Sarok woke on being prodded by Mandelson's spear. When he looked up, he saw the woman standing over him with an odd expression on her face, the spiked butt of her spear hovering near his chest. Sarok's eyes widened and he scrambled back, suddenly apprehensive. But Mandelson's firm expression turned to humour, and she slowly drew back the spear and set it against the ground.

"Mandelson—what the fuck?"

"There is something going on. I thought I'd tell you first, *Boss*. Come on."

By the crest of the small hill, beneath the shade of low, gnarled trees with twisted trunks and desiccated brown foliage, Mandelson pointed off to the north. The land in that direction was generally flat, only slightly undulating, and mainly featureless and dry with very few trees. This contrasted greatly with the land behind them to the south, and to their right in the east, which rose steeply into ranks of tall mountains.

At first, Sarok saw nothing unusual, although he never for a moment doubted the woman's perception. But then he noticed a smudge in the distance, an area of indistinctness, of dust. Then light reflected from a point within the roiling cloud, and then a second time, and then several more. "Okay. Got it. It's not a stampede of creatures—unless they have glass or metal horns. Another force of orcs?"

Mandelson said nothing for a moment, then noted: "They are moving at speed. I didn't realise orcs could run so fast."

"Good point. Rouse the others—all of them. I think things are about to get interesting."

***

"Quickly!" said Enabeth Archaen. "They may need our help!"

The woman had responded with urgency on being shown the anomaly, which was closer and clearer by the time she was brought to the lookout point. She immediately demanded that all don their mail shirts and hoist their packs. Then she set off down the hill, back towards the Iron Gate—perhaps three kilometres distant—with Sentain struggling at the back, his pack flapping open as he tried to close it on the move.

Sarok jogged beside the woman, already several metres back from the easily loping Meridian. "From Narvik? On horses?"

"Yes. There is no other credible explanation."

"They will beat us to the gate."

"Yes."

"And the orcs will see them first," huffed Sarok, "unless their sentries are asleep."

"Yes."

"What are their odds?"

"That depends."

"On what?"

"On their number," responded Archaen, still breathing easily.

And then the first clang of metal on metal, and the first cries of pain, carried to them on a moderate westerly wind.

Chapter 18

The sounds of battle rose and fell on the inconstant wind as the party hurried on—the clash of metal on metal, the shouts and screams of combatants, the whinnying of horses. So desperate were the Leaguers to aid in the fight that the party began to string out, although neither Archaen nor Miko were able to outpace Omdanan.

Struggling with his pack and staff, Sentain rapidly became detached from the others—although he was not completely forgotten, as the ever-protective Vuller occasionally paused to look behind, caught between sticking to Sarok's shoulder and ensuring that the company remained coherent. Eventually, Sentain found a natural rhythm and began to catch up with the two men in front, who had themselves been dropped from the breakaway group.

Sarok looked aside at the anthropologist as he came up beside him. "Nice… to see… you… again," he gasped. "I've not… got the… legs… for this…"

Sentain could only grimace back, without the breath to respond. Ahead, he caught sight of Mandelson, spear waving about awkwardly, disappear over a rocky rise through a gap between a sparse thicket of red-brown bushes. It took the trio another thirty seconds to get to the gap in the foliage and then, suddenly, the volume of battle rose. Looking down a slope, with mountains as a backdrop, they saw chaos swirling in the largely open area below.

"Hold up!" panted Sarok.

Sentain drew to a halt. At the foot of the slope, he saw Omdanan surge into the rear of an unwary phalanx of about thirty orcs, whose spears were lowered and pointed towards a dozen skittish, spear-wielding horsemen. Archaen and Miko—right behind the Meridian—also piled into the white-armoured creatures, screaming war cries as their swords rose and fell. Mandelson was soon into action too, swinging her wickedly curved spear at unprotected legs and scything the members of the disintegrating formation as though they were stalks of tall grass. And with the phalanx broken apart, the horsemen spurred into the confused front of the orc band, now able to draw close and pick off their opponents with skilful thrusts.

"*There*," said Sarok, pointing. "More."

Sentain followed the arm of the Corvan. In an area to the left of the mêlée were scattered bodies, most of which were still, though one or two rolled or twitched, and a riderless horse—jet black, like all of those ridden by the horsemen—nuzzled at a shape on the ground. Beyond this was another zone of activity: figures on foot, some with spears, others without, running, turning, screaming, pursued and ridden down by a second clutch of horsemen.

"And over there, too," noted Vuller, indicating another knot of conflict. "To the right."

Sentain quickly shifted his gaze between the different battles. "Okay, so, what do we…"

Sarok took off his helmet, wiped his brow, and slid down onto his bottom. "Relax, boy," he said. "It's over. Or nearly so. Enjoy the rest of the show."

At that point, five horsemen broke away from the nearest fight and rode towards three orcs that had split from the phalanx and were trying to head for the mountains. They quickly closed the gap, passed through the refugees, and then wheeled around to head back to their compatriots, leaving three more unmoving shapes on the stony ground.

The sounds of battle that had upswelled when they crested the rise, now abated: from a constant din to a sporadic shout or scream, and then to a low, murmurous hum.

"That was quick," noted Sentain.

"The ends of battles often are," said Sarok. "They generally begin with lots of pushing and shoving to little effect. It's only when one side blinks and breaks formation that the slaughter takes place. Right. I've got my breath back. Let's join the party."

***

Elian Omdanan breathed heavily, though in a controlled manner, his chest rising and falling as he maintained a straight-backed pose. His sword—dripping blood—was in his right hand, its tip resting on the cracked, thin soil. Miko stood to his left in a more awkward pose, as though pulled down by his heavy sword and unable to counteract the effect with his weakened left side. Enabeth Archaen stood to his right, utterly still, like an elegant statue, showing no evidence of her previous exertions, her black blade now completely red. And though he could not see Mandelson, Omdanan sensed her presence behind him, and noticed the elongated shadow of her spear stretch across the ground in front of him.

The majority of the horsemen they had aided now dispersed across the field to ride down the remaining orcs or deliver the coup de grâce to the badly wounded. A small group remained, however, and this pulled up before the party. One of the riders handed his spear to a neighbour, then dismounted to stand before Archaen. He reached up to remove his helmet—which was of similar design to that worn by Omdanan and the Leaguers, with nose and cheek guards—revealing a rugged face above a large black beard.

"Enabeth Archaen—wielder of the Nemesis Blade—what a surprise and honour." The man towered over the woman, nearly two metres tall. He wore clinking mail over black leathers, with silver swan emblems at the shoulders. "I don't think we've met. I am Torsten Regnarson, leader of this little band."

"Torsten—son of Luka? I know your father. It is said he will lead your guild one day. I am *very* pleased to meet you. We weren't sure how we were going to access the gate with this force of orcs in front of it."

"It seems we are both in need of the passage, and your assistance also could not have come at a better time." He glanced at the others around Archaen—and then looked over their heads, spotting the remainder of the party making its way down from the higher ground to the west. "And greetings to the rest of you, although I see no symbols on your attire."

"These are my companions," said Archaen. "We started as nine, but now number seven. You may have heard of Ryven Miko…"—the man bowed his head at mention of his name—"of the Guild of the Golden Spear. The others are outlanders, who I will introduce properly when all are here and we have a better chance to talk."

"Outlanders?" Regnarson frowned with uncertainty. "And one from a lesser guild? Ah, apologies for speaking bluntly, Cousin Ryven. No offence intended."

"None taken," said Miko. "The hierarchy is there for a reason."

"Thank you. But… an odd company, Enabeth."

"Yes, it is odd. We've been given special dispensation and charged with rectifying a wrong. You are aware that the Dark Wizard is of… *external* origin? It was our company that brought him here, without suspecting he would behave as he has, and so it is our task to remove him, one way or another."

"A stiff challenge! Your need for the gate is therefore understandable, though even with your sword, Cousin, I do not know how you will achieve this feat."

Archaen gave a half smile. "We also have a wizard with us. A *white* wizard. And he may provide us with an advantage. I will explain more shortly. But—what are you doing here with your party?"

Regnarson's eyebrows had risen in surprise at mention of the wizard, and his eyes shifted from Archaen to Sentain as the staff-bearer and his small party came to a halt at Miko's side. Still appraising the newcomers, he answered: "We are the vanguard of Narvik, set to scout the route to the Iron Gate and clear it of foes. We numbered forty, though we are fewer now." He looked back at Archaen. "Fewer, yet no doubt greater than we would have been had you not showed up when you did. These Tormentors have some stubbornness to them."

"Forty?" said Archaen. "So many? And as the vanguard?"

Regnarson laughed. "Indeed! All of Narvik has been emptied. We forty were the most-ready with the fastest horses, but behind us, perhaps a week away, comes the host of Narvik, some three hundred strong. We intend to aid the men of Bratha."

"A formidable force! But, Torsten, you face an even more formidable foe. Do you move in step with the Black Lightning of Ranvik and Golden Sword of Sorvik?"

"Ah, well, as to that I cannot say. Communication across the Sundering Range has been difficult. We are not well coordinated, though by now the other guilds will have received messages about our intentions, and I trust they will respond with their own musters."

At that, a new horseman rode up—a woman, with long blonde hair cascading down her back from beneath her helm. She pulled up her horse and planted the butt of her long spear on the ground. She quickly glanced at the company, and then addressed her leader: "Torsten."

"Belias. You have something to report?"

"Yes. The last band has been routed. There is no more resistance."

"And do you have a list of casualties?"

She closed her eyes and bowed her head. "Four have played their last. A dozen have wounds, but only three are serious and will need attention."

"So we are reduced by seven? A significant loss."

"Seven?" muttered Sarok. "To kill over a hundred orcs? Fuck me!"

Regnarson caught the comment. He looked down at Sarok and smiled. "Cavalry versus infantry on open ground, my friend. And our skill at arms might surprise someone from outside our realm."

Sarok matched the other's smile. "Yet still, without my boy, who broke the phalanx here, you would have had a harder time of it."

Regnarson looked at Omdanan. "You too are an outsider?" He gave a little bow. "Then I wish to learn your name and toast it. But let us see to our camp. We have other names to glorify first."

This time Omdanan did catch his breath, his chest expanding as though it would never deflate.

***

The late afternoon bled into evening. Soon, the sun disappeared beyond the western horizon, and the sky was left to Arkon's small moon and numerous stars. Three campfires were lit: two large ones, around which most of the Narvik host assembled—save those set to guard the perimeter or picket the horses—and one smaller one, around which the Company of the Black Sword settled. The latter were initially let be, to quietly observe events at the other fires, where the members of the vanguard took it in turns to stand and speak brief words about their fallen comrades. It was only after the eulogies had finished that Torsten Regnarson came to join them, settling in between Archaen and Omdanan, and directly across from Sentain, who'd been watching events keenly.

"It is done. The fallen have been honoured. No more tears must be shed. It is time to discuss the battle and the brave deeds that were done, and to think on the playing of the game—what errors were made, and how we might perform better next time. But first, tell me your names and plans…"

They had been talking for little more than five minutes when they were interrupted. A helmeted warrior with a spear and a black, leaf-shaped shield, emblazoned with a silver swan, marched up to Regnarson.

"What is it, Mikkel?"

"We have a prisoner. A Tormentor. He was hiding under a thorn bush at the edge of the camp."

Regnarson shook his head. "Damn! So, he gave in freely?"

"After trying to slice Merrida's face off, yes. He only nicked her, but then he thought better of continuing the fight after she bust his nose with the hilt of her sword."

"Double damn!"

"You don't seem best pleased, Cousin," said Archaen. "Surely a prisoner is useful?"

Regnarson shook his head. "Not here, and not now. I have no resources to watch him. And he is of the Tormentor Regiment. Questioning him would be useless. If he were of a lesser regiment, we might be able to scare or bribe him into revealing his orders and his force's disposition, but not this one. So, I have to kill him or let him go free, neither of which option appeals to me."

Mikkel volunteered: "Merrida will take him. She is still angry."

"Take him?" said Sentain, unable to restrain himself. "You mean, execute him?"

Regnarson look at Sentain, through the flicking flames, and frowned. "No. He will be given his spear and a chance. Trial by combat. If he wins—which is highly unlikely—he will go free."

"What a waste," scowled Mandelson, who sat to Sentain's right. "We need information, and you have a prisoner who has it. Fucking stupid!"

The leader of the Narvik contingent redirected his gaze to the woman. Mandelson had a small knife in her hand, its blade attached to an iron ring that looped around one finger, which she had been using to clean her nails. "It is unfortunate, but—"

"No. It's not unfortunate. It's stupid beyond belief." She directed a hard stare at the other, who appeared disconcerted at having been challenged. "Let me have a little time with the creature. I'll get it to talk."

To Sentain's other side, beyond Vuller, Sarok barked a laugh. ""Let her go to it. Mandelson has ways of convincing others to cooperate. The orc *will* talk, and soon you will know all you need to know."

Sentain noticed Archaen frown, open her mouth to speak, and then close it. Regnarson also seemed troubled, his eyes fixed upon the small knife in the woman's hand. "That is not our way. It is ignoble. Though the orcs might not hesitate to treat us in a similar manner, we are not like them."

"Nor am I, and nor are we," said Sarok. But then he smiled grimly. "Or at least, nor are *most* of us. But my people—from Corvus—deal in reality not fantasy, in pragmatism not idealism. In *necessity*. There is more at stake here than a bruise to your honour. The entire population of yeltoi in Bratha are at risk, no? Sometimes a small evil is necessary in order to prevent a bigger one. So, sit back and relax.

Any stain from this will fall upon Mandelson for the act, and if you wish, on me for endorsing it."

Regnarson shook his head unhappily, but he was not denying permission. "We *do* need information. We've had no news from Bratha for weeks, and I fear what we will find there." He glanced at Archaen. "Enabeth?"

Archaen looked grim. "He is your prisoner, Cousin. It is your call. I hate what Mr Sarok's necessity demands, but…" She shrugged.

Sentain watched Regnarson's internal struggle play out across his face: he closed his eyes and touched his forehead and remained this way for several seconds. At last, the Leaguer opened his eyes and looked at Mandelson. "Very well," he sighed. "Much as I detest this, and though I may face condemnation for the decision, go ahead. The yeltoi of Bratha deserve every chance. But only do what you must, and no more. I will spare the orc after: he will go back with the injured to meet the main host and be released somewhere en route." He turned to the standing warrior: "Mikkel—take her to the prisoner."

Mandelson laughed, rose up, and strode after the departing warrior.

Sentain noticed that Sarok wore a humourless smile. He watched the crime lord scan the faces of the others around the fire. Most of the party looked down or away, even Archaen. Miko was the only one to meet the man's eyes and match his smile. Then Sarok glanced at him and raised an eyebrow.

"I expect you have a problem with this, eh, Sentain?" he said. "I'm surprised you didn't try to talk us out of it."

Sentain looked away and down. How did he feel? Slightly numb, but… he looked back up. "I think you have me wrong." He paused to choose his words. "Not everyone from the Confederation thinks the same way, well, not all of the time. It's true, I don't like what Mandelson is going to do, and I would speak against it if there were another option, but I don't think there is. And through my studies of other cultures—and my time with you, and here on Arkon—I have come to appreciate that dogmatic idealism can lead to, ah, greater harm than good. Wearing a perpetual mantle of virtue is, well, a glib way to avoid making difficult decisions, a smug way of avoiding responsibility. So I'll accept a share of the stain from this act too."

"Well," chortled Sarok, "you have changed your tune."

"Have I?" Sentain suddenly wondered. "Well, I admit I was less than comfortable with some of our earlier decisions, and I have always been keen to consider options that don't involve violence." He glanced at Archaen, who he noticed was studying him intensely. *Curious*. "But I never condemned Enabeth for attempting to rescue her son, even though… even though I thought he belonged where he was." He looked directly at Omdanan. "And I didn't condemn Elian for taking a knife to the ear of my colleague after the prison break, because that was what he *needed* to do. And… and I have never condemned the Leaguers for their risky behaviour and violent games—which are seen as reckless, immoral and even insane by many in the Confederation. My training leads me to observe and record, but not to judge."

"Those are fine words," muttered Miko, from across the campfire, "but I am not sure I believe them. I remember a different attitude when you learnt of the yeltoi and ganeroi. Your response caused a certain amount of consternation." Miko glanced at Archaen, then back to Sentain. "Or have I misremembered?"

"No, you haven't. But that's different. I understand your philosophy. I get your desire to challenge yourselves, and live significant lives. I understood it conceptually, and after the last few weeks, I now understand it… *viscerally*. I have experienced it. I have faced danger and been scared stiff, and yet afterwards, I have felt… *bigger*." Sentain noticed Archaen from the corner of his eye, and saw that, in spite of her efforts at disguise, she was smiling behind her hand. "So… I *get* all this. But your philosophy didn't compel you to do what you have done with the first intelligent life found beyond Earth. You could have taken another path. I don't accept that it would have been onerous for you to have informed the Confederation and the rest of humanity about them. Instead, you saw a quick chance to enhance your games and thought little of the natives of Omicra. At the time, when I learnt of this, I admit I was shocked and outraged."

The Price of Freedom Part II: Velasia

"At the time?" Miko's expression was difficult to read. Wry? Incredulous? Annoyed?

"Well, yes. *Then*. But I admit, I have become less certain over time."

"What do you mean, Irvan?" asked Archaen. "Less certain? Less outraged?"

Sentain looked down at the fire and frowned unhappily. "I guess… I guess I have seen something of the yeltoi, and though you have lied to them, and in some ways constrained them, you haven't abused them. You say they live better lives in Velasia than back on Omicra and I believe you. So although they have become pets to you, people are fond of their pets, and often treat them better than they treat fellow humans. And as for the ganeroi, I have seen their savagery. But they are victims of their evolution and their environment rather than of your treatment. Even they perhaps live better here than they do back on their ancestral home. And after all, what *would* we in the Confederation have done if we had found them first? I'm not sure I know. Perhaps we would have killed them with kindness? At the very least, we would have attempted to force our own morality onto them. So, I don't know how I feel now. Not happy, that's for sure, but…" he shrugged, glancing once more at Archaen before fully meeting Miko's eyes, "there you go. That is how I see it, truthfully, and you must ultimately judge me on this."

Miko nodded slowly. "I *do* trust your word. It also makes matters less clear from my… from *our*… perspective." Then he smiled and waved a hand. "But why are we talking here in coded terms about a future that may never happen?" He turned to Regnarson. "I'm sorry for inflicting this debate upon you. As you might imagine, allowing strangers onto Arkon has brought certain complications, and it is not something I would recommend us permitting again. But we should not be discussing these matters here: they are out of scope of this *play*. Forgive us."

Regnarson raised his hands. "In many ways, I would like to hear more, as all of this touches upon the foe we now face and his origins. But as you say, this topic is taboo here and now. I forgive you, but please try to limit your conversations while you remain with us."

Shouting and cheers erupted from those around one of the other fires, drawing the eyes of the select group. A giant of a man, possessing perhaps the longest beard of the entire Narvik party, was at the centre of this: he was standing and waving about a flagon—presumably filled with something alcoholic—and making bold toasts.

"I wish I was with them," muttered Vuller, just loud enough for all around to hear, "rather than with this depressing ensemble."

Regnarson looked at the other, and then broke into a laugh. "Of course. Let us change the subject. Our comrades have been honoured appropriately, and now we should celebrate our victory. Our quartermaster insisted on loading a couple of supply horses with casks of beer—and he was so concerned about protecting them, he was left behind in our charge and missed the fight. I will consult with him and try to claim a share." He clambered to his feet.

As Regnarson walked past him, Sentain couldn't help but mutter, in a voice not meant to be heard: "Yes, let's make some noise. At least it'll mask the screaming that's about to start."

***

By the time Mandelson returned, Omdanan was feeling much more relaxed, having drunk a couple of flagons of beer from a cask delivered by the Narvi's quartermaster.

Mandelson appeared out of the dark and slumped down beside him, occluding Sarok, who was sat to her other side. She still toyed with her small blade—the kerambit—whisking it into and out of her palm, like a magician practising a trick. Earlier, she had planted the butt of her spear in the ground to reserve her space, while the rest of her arsenal—her kris sword and long dagger—splayed from her belt upon the ground behind her. Omdanan noticed that there was a smear of blood on the leathers of her thigh, which he was sure hadn't been there before she left. He was not sure what he felt about her—on the one hand, appalled, but on the other, he was glad that they had with them someone who was unafraid to do what needed to be done.

Regnarson had been speaking, but he stopped mid-sentence at the woman's return, and like the others turned his eyes upon her. "So, you have done the deed. The orc still lives?"

Mandelson looked up, a hard expression on her face. "It does. And it is largely whole. In many ways, it's fortunate I came across a pain centre at the base of its skull. Humans don't have this. Did you know about it?"

"No, we did not."

Mandelson smiled malevolently. "Then there is a bonus finding for you. Press a blade in there and the creature starts spasming in agony. It's quite impressive. It meant I didn't have to amputate anything, so in the end, everybody won."

"You're a sick bitch," muttered Vuller, *sotto voce*.

"And you're weak and squeamish, Vuller. You all are. So do you want to hear what I found or not?"

"Go on," said Regnarson.

Mandelson looked down at her weapon, turning it one way and then another, allowing firelight to reflect off its surface, almost as if drawing memories from the blade. "There were four companies here. One of the Black Tree, and three of the Tormentors' regiment. The Tormentors only arrived three days ago, so we were unlucky… or perhaps I should say, *they* were unlucky. They came from Ullah-Bor."

"Ullah-Bor!" Regnarson looked to Enabeth Archaen at his side. "As you thought, Cousin." He looked back at Mandelson. "So… it has fallen?"

"Com Durrel has been busy. It seems he sent the Tormentors and another regiment to increase the orc presence in the Northlands and Southlands, and he has combined the rest of his forces into an army to raze all of Bratha."

"How long ago was this?" said Regnarson. "Do we have time? Or are we already too late?"

Mandelson shrugged. "Three weeks, or thereabouts. The orc didn't seem to have a clear conception of time. It has taken them that long to make their way here, taking paths over the mountains. And their main army marches slowly on foot. Make of that what you will."

Rgnerson had been leaning forwards eagerly, but now he sat back and looked up—to Omdanan, appearing as though he were seeking inspiration from the stars. At last he declared: "It will be close. But we cannot afford to wait for the main host. Taking the gate, and moving fast, we may reach the mannish towns in time to organise a defence or provide some relief. If we are too late to save Haradan, we might still be able to aid Faltis and Jinna and buy some time for our main force to arrive."

"What about com Durrel," asked Sarok. "Did he go to Ullah-Bor? And is he still there, or has he returned to his HQ?"

"I asked *nicely*. The orc said the God-Sorcerer *did* lead the army to victory—but it could not guess his plans now. He was still at Ullah-Bor when it left."

"And what force waits at the other side of the gate?" asked Archaen. "Is it of similar size to the one that was here?"

Mandelson smirked. "On this matter, the creature was a bit more cagey. It did try to resist and distract initially. I had to be *firm* with it. In the end, it revealed there is only a single company waiting outside the gate at the Bratha end, since they do not expect anyone to get through the Gap of Gelion and the force left here. But it did admit that there might be further plans for reinforcements that it didn't know about. I think it spoke the truth."

Archaen turned to Regnarson. "If you are going to continue through the gate, it makes sense for us to travel together. We should then have enough strength to push through whatever reception committee awaits. Then you can continue north to the towns of men."

"Agreed. But what of you? Once we are through to the other side, what then?"

Archaen shook her head. She glanced first at Miko and then Sarok. "That... is currently unclear to me. Around three weeks ago, com Durrel was at Ullah-Bor— if the orc is to be believed. He could still be there, or he may have returned to Tartax-Kul—"

"Or he may have gone with his army to the fight," volunteered Sarok. "That sounds like the sort of fun he wouldn't want to miss out on."

"Yes, true," said Archaen, pursing her lips. "That is a third option. So, Cousin, I can't say as yet. But it will take several days to pass under the mountains, giving us plenty of time to work out a plan."

"Good," said Regnarson. "We will leave first thing in the morning. I will send my wounded with a couple of guides to take this news to our host, and that will still leave us about thirty spears for the task. The tunnel beyond the gate is tall and wide enough to accommodate three horsemen riding abreast. We now have spare horses for you and your party. Although we will not be able to ride fast, we will make much better speed than on foot. The crossing will take three days if we are lucky."

"Then let's hope we are lucky!" said Archaen.

And Omdanan thought: A horse? I'm going to have to ride… a horse? He could just imagine the horror of his kin back home at such exploitation!

Chapter 19

"What the hell am I meant to do with *this*?" asked Sarok.

"You sit on it," said the woman called Belias, her face largely obscured by the nose and cheek guards of her helmet. "Then you tell it to go using your heels. And you tug on this—*the reins*—to tell it to stop. There's no power button, if that's what you're looking for."

"Ha-*fucking*-ha," muttered Sarok. "I get that it's not an air bike, but do you really expect me to ride such an ugly beast? I've no experience for a start."

"I understand," said the woman, speaking slowly as though to a child, "but you only gain experience by *doing*. We will not be galloping through the tunnel, though we will be moving faster than you can walk, and for longer, so if you don't mount up, you will be left behind."

Omdanan was already at his horse. He'd watched the Narvi mount up and then skilfully weave their horses into a formation, three abreast, that stretched back from the doors to the Iron Gate—the riddle to which had already been solved, with the doors now gaping wide open. The company had then waited patiently as Belias led a group of black horses—spares, and others from those killed—over to the party of outsiders. Archaen had mounted swiftly, and Miko with rather more difficulty, having only the use of his right arm. Now Omdanan followed suit, grasping the pommel of the saddle, placing one foot in a silvered stirrup, and swinging his other leg over. The horse took a couple of steadying steps forwards and gave a soft snuffle, but didn't otherwise object.

"See?" said Belias. "Your colleague had no problem. Do what he did."

"Omdanan—you're getting to be a right fucking show off! It's easier for him anyway—he's got longer legs."

The woman smirked. "I am sorry. Would you rather we got you a child's pony?"

Sarok swore under his breath and then, following Mandelson and Vuller, he too successfully mounted up, leaving just Sentain on the ground, looking between his horse and his staff and trying to calculate how to get up while encumbered.

"Vuller, give him a hand," said Sarok. "I can't steer this thing."

"Sure, Boss." Vuller managed to nudge closer to Sentain, where he held out a hand to temporarily take the other's weapon. Sentain nodded thanks, then mounted his own wary steed with minimal difficulty.

"At last!" sighed the woman. "Now follow after the baggage horses. I will stay at the back with Mikkel to ensure that you don't fall behind."

"And I will ride in your midst," said Archaen, as she confidently guided her horse in a small circle. "You'll soon get the hang of things."

"Soon?" scowled Sarok. "Since when did you take up comedy, Ms Archaen? *Go forwards, horse!*" he commanded, and a ripple of laughter spread through the ranks of watching horsemen.

***

Unlike the passage between the Copper Gates, the one between the Iron Gates was an uninterrupted tunnel, without any breaches to the outside world. For two days they travelled without seeing the sun, in a grim, enclosed tomb, suffocating and claustrophobic.

The tunnel was high enough for mounted riders—just. Sarok now had the advantage over his taller colleagues, some of whom had to crouch over their rides' necks to stop from scraping their helmets on the rock ceiling. "Make fun of my height," Sarok had muttered once, "well—who's laughing now?"

As before, there were occasional side grottos filled with natural water pools and the ubiquitous bioluminescent mosses, which added some distraction to their otherwise tedious journey. Most of these were small, but the one they came across near the end of their second day was spectacular, like the interior of a giant cathedral, with several interlinked caves full of stalagmites and stalactites.

As the party came to a halt, the horsemen spread along the tunnel to create enough space for all to dismount and access the grotto along the right wall.

Sarok groaned as he slid from his horse. "My arse feels like it has been pounded with the hammer of an ancient blacksmith."

"Mine too, Boss," agreed Vuller, dropping beside him, before leaning in to note conspiratorially, "though I bet Mandelson's hardly noticed. She's probably disappointed we've stopped."

"But it'll be a relief for her horse and its bruised back, no doubt." Sarok looked at his own mount, standing patiently, and momentarily wondered what to do next. Then he simply dropped the leather reins. "Sod it. Stay, horse. *Stay!*"

"It's not a dog, sir."

Sarok shrugged, losing interest. "So, what do we have here…" He noticed Regnarson approaching Archaen, who was several metres in front. He took a number of quick steps and reached the woman at the same time as the leader of the Narvik contingent.

"This is the Jewelled Grotto," announced Regnarson, "…which you must know well, Cousin."

"I do."

"Then you appreciate we cannot stay here long. I think we can risk half an hour to fill our bottles and stretch our legs, but then we must put good distance between here and our next camp."

"Agreed. An hour's ride should see us safe."

"Risk? Safe?" queried Sarok. "These are not comforting words." The whole right wall had opened out for perhaps fifty metres, though the cavern was clearly much longer than this. He could see a black pool further in that stretched the length of the far wall. "What is it with these grottos that cause you to be so skittish? Archaen—before you mentioned small creatures…?"

Archaen and Regnarson exchanged quick looks and frowns. "In most, yes, the creatures are small but persistent. I mentioned the cave crabs to you before, no? They are shy, and will not bother us in general, but should anyone fall asleep nearby, time brings boldness, and it is not pleasant to awake being snipped at by these creatures… to open your eyes to find yourself surrounded by a hundred shining, *hungry* ghosts with pincers. But this is a bigger cavern and—"

"And has bigger dangers? Bigger crabs?"

"No, Mr Sarok, it has the things that feast upon the crabs."

"You always know how to cheer me up, Ms Archaen. Would you like to elaborate on what we face?"

Again, Archaen looked to Regnarson, and this time the man responded. "If we are cautious, then nothing. Stick to the main cavern. I do not know what creatures inhabit this chamber now: there are several species that compete with each other for dominance in this domain. But whatever is here will not challenge so many opponents."

"How reassuring!" Sarok glanced at his bodyguard, then reached for his water bottle and handed it to the man. "Off you go, Vuller. Suddenly, the company of *Stinky* doesn't seem so bad after all. I'll rest by the horses."

***

"Er, I wouldn't go in there, Ms Mandelson. We were told to stick together."

"Told?" The woman turned to look at Omdanan. They were standing at the far edge of the main cavern, near a two metre wide hole into a second, smaller cavern. The rest of the party clustered in one spot by the black, underground pool, where some filled their water bottles, others sat propped against stalagmites, and still others stood about, stretching their legs and conversing. "You're not my mother, Omdanan. And I'm not sure what you're doing following me. Think I need your protection?"

"Ah, no. Of course not. I just thought we should stay close and I… sense something."

Mandelson was in the act of turning back when the Meridian's statement made her pause. In a lower voice, now bereft of sarcasm, she muttered. "Okay. Given your talents… wait here. I need a piss, and I'm not going in front of that lot." She crouched down slightly to peer more intently into the small cave, resting one hand on her kris sword. Then she nodded to herself and picked her way over the uneven floor between a couple of slick, limestone mounds.

Omdanan watched the woman go, then moved closer to the opening. He could see that this chamber was about ten metres wide, but of uncertain length—its furthest reaches being in total shadow, without any of the softly glowing moss that helped give dim illumination to the immediate area. The right half of the cavern held a long pool of water, which disappeared beneath a ledge that jutted from the rock wall and presumably led to another submarine chamber, or perhaps a chain of these. Mandelson kept away from the water, disappearing from view to the left of the opening, where the floor was dry.

Omdanan decided to go no further, allowing the woman her privacy. But as the seconds ticked by, the feeling of wrongness continued to grow. He found it difficult to explain these feelings, even to himself. Somehow, his subconscious was able to merge information from all of his senses, making comparisons and calculations that his limited conscious mind could not. In short, he just *knew*. And that was when he realised Mandelson might be in trouble. There was some sort of shift in the air, an extra sound to the one made by the rustling woman. He touched his sword hilt, but then shifted his hand over to the haft of his long knife and swiftly drew it. He took one deep breath and moved forwards into the chamber…

Mandelson was eight metres away, facing the wall, adjusting her clothing, her mail shirt scrunching softly. She seemed to be alone. *Seemed.*

Where is it? Where is…?

There was a stalactite hanging over the woman's head. In fact, there was a cluster of these, growing down from the cavern ceiling, but one was longer than the others, longer… and *growing?* Whatever the creature was, it was superbly camouflaged in a mottled white-grey that matched the down-jutting rock.

Omdanan took one careful step forwards, and then a second. The tip of the stalactite gradually took on a more familiar form to the Meridian—that of a serpent with a rounded, wedge-shaped head, but no eyes. The sight brought old memories flooding back…

"Mira… no!" he hissed.

But his warning was superfluous.

Mandelson moved as fast as any striking snake: she grabbed her kris and in one motion drew it and slashed upwards, slicing the descending creature through its thick body, just above the bottom of its head. She continued her turn and stepped nimbly back as the rest of the creature's substantial body unravelled from its purchase in a crack in the ceiling and dumped messily onto the cavern floor.

The woman then used her wavy-bladed weapon to hack at the corpse several times, muttering: "*fucking voyeur.*" She stopped and looked across to Omdanan. "Seems I'm not a defenceless maiden after all, eh, Omdanan? But I owe you for the warning." She re-sheathed her sword and stalked past him, back to the main chamber.

***

After a third night spent sleeping in the foetid tunnel, they came upon the eastern gate a couple of hours into the fourth morning. The Narvi spread out along the tunnel as on previous stops, dismounted, and saw to their needs and that of their horses, distributing oats from sacks carried on the backs of the half-dozen supply animals. Belias and Mikkel did the same for their own horses and those of the outland party.

Archaen and Miko headed forwards on foot to see Regnarson at the gate. For once, Sarok felt no great compunction to join them. With Vuller at his side, the pair acted as a magnet for the rest of the outlanders.

"Well, thank fuck that's over," said Sarok, stretching his back. "I can't wait to see the sun, no matter how many foes are waiting for us outside."

"And to return to your feet," mused Vuller, with a half-smile.

"That too. What anyone sees in these creatures, God knows. Omdanan, stop fondling your horse! You seem to have developed an unhealthy attachment to it."

"Er, sorry, Boss."

"And what of you, Sentain?" continued Sarok. "Where do you stand in the horse debate?"

The anthropologist jumped in surprise; he had been staring up the tunnel towards the dark, closed doorway. "Ah, what? Horses?" He shrugged. "They're useful, aren't they? Saves walking. And they give us an edge against the orcs."

"I should have known you'd be in favour of them. It all helps you fit in and identify with the objects of your studies, eh?"

"Well, since you mention it, yes, sure. But I don't believe you are as antithetical to the beasts as you are making out. Anyway, they're coming back."

The party turned to face the trio of Archaen, Regnarson and Miko. Archaen quickly threw a smile towards Sentain before addressing Sarok directly. "The riddle is straightforwards, and there seems no reason to wait. We don't want to waste the rest of the day. The Narvi will charge through the gateway once it is opened, and we will form a reserve on foot, while Mikkel will look after the pack horses as well as our own. Ready your weapons, although if the interrogated orc was right, and there is just one company outside, we shouldn't be needed."

Sarok nodded. "Good. The sooner we are in fresh air the better. Anything else?"

Mandelson stirred. "Yes. There is. Regnarson—don't get carried away. We could use some more intel. Keep one of the orcs alive."

The giant locked eyes with the woman—and nodded once.

***

"Nothing," said Mandelson, strolling up to the party as it stood around a random boulder at the edge of a copse of twisted, leafless trees. She was wiping her kerambit on a piece of cloth. "Or at least, nothing new."

"It must have said something, Mandelson," growled Sarok.

She shrugged, then slipped her knife into some hidden fold of her clothing. "The orc was from a company of the Bone Gnawers regiment from Ullah-Bor, which replaced one from the Black Sun about a week ago. It was surprised when we burst through the doors, as the orcs apparently thought this deployment was a complete waste of time, and were resentful at missing out on the attack on the men of Bratha. It seems they've little food and have been trying to scavenge small game with little luck. They are not due a supply delivery for a couple more weeks."

"So not exactly *nothing*," said Sarok, as Archaen, Miko and Regnarson allowed him to lead the interrogation, and the rest of the company looked on. "You're saying there's a company from this Black Sun regiment about a week away, which we might overhaul in a couple of days on horses. Where are *they* going? And where are the supplies coming from—and so where else might we soon encounter orcs on their way to that spot?"

"Ullah-Bor in both cases," scowled the woman. "The one place out of our equation—or am I wrong?"

Archaen spoke placatingly. "No. You are right. It is away to the south. Tartax-Kul is almost exactly due east, cutting across the Desolate Quarter, and the mannish towns are away to the north-east."

"Still, it's important to know how much time we have until we are discovered," mused Regnarson. "Two weeks is good, I think. If the riders I left behind meet the main host as planned, and they hurry on, they will arrive here before then, and they can either ride out to take the supply group or push on as they see best. I will leave a message in the passage by the door."

"And com Durrel?" continued Sarok.

"As I said, *nothing*," replied Mandelson. "Only the generals know of his plans—not lowly company commanders and their grunts. And that really is it. Trust me, the creature didn't hold anything back."

"I suppose I should thank you for doing this," said Regnarson, "although it pains me to do so. But what is the condition of the orc?"

Mandelson gave a sly smile. "Ah… at the end, my knife slipped. It's a shame, I know. Still, it wouldn't have been wise to release the creature here, so close to its home, eh?"

Regnarson looked down. "What have I done?"

"You opened a door," said Mandelson, "and invited me in."

"This will taint me," the giant man muttered. "I will be deemed a cheat—"

"*Cheat?*" sneered Mandelson. "Will Yasmina deduct some points from your score? Will you be shown a yellow card? A *red* one? If you're going to play, play to win, that's my advice. That's what I do." She turned and stalked off. After a moment, a head-shaking Regnarson headed in the opposite direction. Archaen frowned at the remaining company then followed the man from Narvik.

Sarok couldn't stop a grin developing. "Harsh but fair, I think. It's a lesson we all learn in my trade." And then he frowned. "And one in which I was once severely schooled by a competitor."

"Only once?" asked Sentain, who could not help himself.

"Oh, aye, Sentain. You're right. It's been a very long and enduring *once*. It's why I'm here now, having to ride stinking beasts, chew on barely edible food, and endure attacks by monsters from every direction. At least I am trying to learn, rather than sticking my fingers in my ears like Regnarson." As he looked about he noticed Miko, and his smile bloomed once more. "And I am not the only one. You've been very quiet lately about your precious honour."

"Don't remind me of it," said Miko, uncomfortably. "I fear I have also been tainted by too many years away from home in the presence of your kind."

"You mean tainted by the Confederation?" wondered Sentain. "How can that be? The Confederation is also rule-based, though its rules are enforced by statute and not left to the interpretation of individuals and their peers."

Miko looked askance at the anthropologist. "True, but have you ever thought on how your smug sanctimony might lead a man to rebel? I have wandered your worlds for many years and seen your law-abiding sheep obeying a thousand petty diktats—from wearing masks in minor viral outbreaks to standing at crossings by deserted roads while awaiting permission to cross from a signal, to honestly following alcohol consumption rules in bars. *Pathetic.* It makes me feel unclean. My ambivalence to Mandelson's disregard for the rules undoubtedly stems from this." He seemed to shiver in disgust. "I need to get away from you people to regain my spirituality. Excuse me—I think I will go empathise with my cousins."

As Miko stalked off, Sarok considered his three remaining companions—Sentain, Omdanan and the ever-watchful Vuller. "I thought I had that one. Still, I don't think he will stray too far from the dark side. Even Sentain is coming round to my philosophy of necessity."

Sentain held up his hands. "Whoa! Don't drag me into this. I am simply being adaptable to the situation. It's an important human trait. As is the propensity to try to cheat, or so Levanko once told me. Oh…"

Vuller recognised the other's sudden discomfort. "She was one of your colleagues from Ghuraj, wasn't she?"

"Yes… yes, she was. Someone I should have tried harder to protect."

Sarok was suddenly less glib. "Another victim of Brundt, and perhaps a point of difference between her and I."

"And between you and Mandelson?" suggested Vuller.

"Yeah, her too. Perhaps I shouldn't encourage that one so much. Perhaps I should make the difference between us clearer to our hosts? We're a varied, fucked-up race, aren't we?" He shook his head, then looked over to Sentain and softened his voice. "Don't worry, lad. Brundt has no reason to harm your friend, and every reason to ransom her, especially as the hostages can only implicate me and the League, but not she herself."

Sentain looked doubtful. "You're right—we truly are a fucked-up race."

"And there's only one solution to this, in my book," said Vuller. "And that is to find their quartermaster and ensure he doesn't keep his last barrel of beer to himself. Are you all coming?"

Sarok slapped his bodyguard on the shoulder. "Too fucking right. I have a very bitter taste in my mouth that needs cleansing. Lead on…"

***

"I have decided," said Archaen, as she returned to where the outlanders were lounging, eking out the last beer from the final cask brought from Narvik. Miko was in tow behind the woman. "We will continue with Regnarson for now."

"Well, thanks for involving me in your deliberations," muttered Sarok.

"I do value your insight, Mr Sarok, and I took your views from our previous conversations into account. But it was time to decide, and this option suddenly seemed right."

Sarok waved a dismissive hand, the beer having gentled his mood. "It is of no matter. You're a big girl. I trust you as much as anyone here."

"Thank you."

"So... tell us more. Where exactly is Regnarson headed, and how long will we stick with him?"

"We are in something of a rain shadow here. The land around—from here all the way across to Tartax-Kul, and also north and south for many kilometres—is known as the Desolate Quarter. It is not a desert, but semi-arid, with no rivers or lakes. Where the Skythrust Mountains join the Sundering Range due south," Archaen waved a hand in the relevant direction, "the land becomes more fertile, which is why we seeded the bastion of Ullah-Bor down there. The land also becomes greener and more fertile away to the north, and that is why the yeltoi live up there. Their four main settlements sit inland by a number of large lakes. If we head directly east by horse, we might be visible to watchers, but we will be uncatchable by those on foot, and in any case, there is little sense in the orcs leaving contingents in this wasteland. Also, if com Durrel has added regiments from Ullah-Bor to his army, these will undoubtedly travel to his base along the foothills beneath the Shield Range—as that is the most direct route to his capital, and the one offering the best scavenging—and so we are unlikely to encounter his main force and may avoid detection altogether."

"But from what you say, Regnarson will be heading north-east, and we need to head due east?" noted Sarok. "Won't this take us further from our goal, if we are going to Tartax-Kul?"

"It will… *if* we are going that way. But we still can't be sure com Durrel won't be travelling with his host. I hope if we get closer, we might benefit from the intel of scouts Regnarson is about to send ahead to try to catch his army and to spy on it. Then we will get a definitive answer. In any case, we are liable to make better time travelling on horseback with the others than we will on foot or by horse without support and guidance—and so even though we might travel further than otherwise, going this way might not lose us much time."

"Horseback? *Fuck*!" Sarok drained the last of his beer and tossed his borrowed flagon onto the ground in disgust. "I thought we would be done with those foul beasts. No wonder you made this decision without my counsel."

Archaen could not restrain the twitch of a smile. "I am sorry, Mr Sarok, but as sacrifices go, this is a minor one… Elian, you wanted to say something?"

"Uh, yes," the young Meridian had reacted strangely to the woman's announcement, his arm twitching up as though he were a schoolchild seeking to ask a question, his mouth opening and closing as though he wanted to say something but wasn't quite sure how to phrase it. "You said… you said *scouts*…"

Sarok was quickest on the uptake. He laughed: "Omdanan wants to play."

Archaen's smile became more fulsome. "Of course he does. And given his precocious talents, it would be remiss not to take advantage of them. Though… he is one of yours, Sarok. It would be appropriate to gain your approval for this."

Omdanan looked at Sarok, a number of emotions competing on his face—embarrassment, hope, desire. The crime lord's own expression turned serious as he appraised the other… but he couldn't keep up the play for long. He broke into a smile. "Of course, lad. Off you go. If anyone is going to uncover what the fuck is going on as quickly as possible—and get me off that fucking horse and back to civilisation—it's you. Knock yourself out."

Omdanan failed to mask his own smile and looked expectantly at Archaen.

"Very well. The scouts will be heading off shortly. Grab your gear and your horse, Elian. I will inform my cousin."

The Price of Freedom Part II: Velasia

Chapter 20

"Mr Hansa, are you there?"

It was a stupid question—for where else would the captured Leaguer be?—but the torch in the corridor behind Dettler burned fitfully, and the light did little to illuminate the back reaches of the makeshift cell.

"I am. Wait."

Dettler heard sounds of movement and then jumped a little as the man appeared from the gloom closer than anticipated. He seemed to have lessened in the few days since their last encounter—his cheeks were just a little hollow, and his warrior physique didn't fill his leather tunic quite so well. His fulsome beard was also now unkempt and somewhat matted.

"Ah, are you… well?"

Maddowu Hansa grasped a bar to the cell with his sole remaining hand. "I am hungry. They feed me rotten fish—but not a lot of it, so I suppose there is a bright side to my predicament." Somehow, the large man found a smile, his still-pristine teeth almost glowing in the dark.

"I'm glad you've retained your sense of humour. I've come to discuss your future. Do you remember, I mentioned three options when I last visited?"

"I do."

"And have you thought on your preference among these?"

Hansa's smile lessened and his mouth drew tight. "Of course. You know my preference, I suspect, even though you are an outsider."

Dettler nodded slowly. "That's good. In any case, two of the options are proving difficult to organise. It would be difficult for you—or us—to get far from here with com Durrel still alive. In the third option, you do not need to go so far, at least at first."

Hansa said nothing for a moment, his deep brown eyes exploring Dettler's face beyond the bars. "That was my estimation. But I have also been thinking about what would happen after—not just to me, but to you. You seem a cunning man. I do not believe you have overlooked this."

Dettler looked away, sighed, shook his head, looked back. "You're right, but also wrong. I have some thoughts about how to extract myself—and you too, perhaps—but they are not well formed and their success will depend upon considerable luck and my ability to bluff. But *he* has become so unstable, I fear waiting any longer."

Hansa's smile returned, but it was a wry one. "So, you realise that you also have skin in this game? If I fail, you might be suspect; if I succeed, you will need to extricate yourself from the heart of the orc domain without a protector."

"I might have one… and a second, counting you. But I can move freely in Tartax-Kul, and as I speak for the God-Sorcerer I can make an excuse that he is not to be disturbed, and that would buy us extra time. But I'll need the staff from him, too, to flourish and use as a threat once the deception is uncovered and we are hunted."

"Of course—the staff." Hansa's eyes narrowed. "I do not know how it is operated. Do you?"

Dettler shifted on his feet uncomfortably. "I've memorised the spells he's used, but I'll not be able to use the staff unless I can convince him… trick him… into relinquishing control. And I have been musing on strategies to do this. But if he's killed, then I'll not have that opportunity, as control will remain with his corpse until, I suppose, the staff's creator regains and resets it. Still, I think trying to kill our self-proclaimed god stands a better chance of success than me trying to wrest control of the staff from him, particularly as I wonder about my courage to even attempt this."

"It sounds as though you have made your decision then. And now you are here. You must have a plan, and you must mean to implement it soon—as I am weakening by the hour and my own chances of winning a fight diminish. So, what is it?"

Dettler took a deep breath and looked back down the corridor. He couldn't see the orc guarding the door to this level, so poor was the light, but he knew it was there, and he knew its eyesight was no better than his own. He reached into his rough, ill-fitting tunic and brought out a long knife of the sort carried by most orcs for close-quarters butchery. It was wrapped in a scrap of cloth. After a pause of indecision, his hand jerked forwards: the die was cast.

Hansa took the knife through the bars of the cell and placed it within his own tunic, next to his chest. He undoubtedly knew what it was by the shape. "No key?"

"No. Only the guard has the key, but he keeps it on his belt. You'll have to take the key from him. I am not a warrior. I cannot."

"This seems to leave much to chance. I need to draw the guard close and then strike hard and fast as I cannot win a wrestling match with one arm. But the key will still be outside the bars of the cell, and I will have to hope I am able to haul the creature's corpse close enough to retrieve it."

"I'm sorry. Can you do it?"

Hansa's smile turned from wry to grim. "The killing? Yes. The rest of it? We will have to see. But I will try."

"The odds…" Dettler cursed under his breath and shook his head. "Then there's nothing for it. I'll have to help. I'd hoped to give you directions to com Durrel and stay out of the way to reduce suspicion should you fail. *Deniability*. But you may need help, if only a distraction or to collect the key. Very well."

"Bravo, Dettler. I see your fear, but also your resolve. What now?"

"In two hours, you'll be fed. The jailor will bring your food and I'll accompany him. I'll be there if somehow needed. And then… the hallways will be quiet at that time, and com Durrel will be having his afternoon sleep. There are no guards on his personal level, as he does not trust the orcs. The doors are locked and only Yadzen and I have access. So, I can get you to him, and then you can strike—"

"While he sleeps?" Hansa was suddenly unsettled. "Like an assassin?"

"If you want, you can wake him first," said Dettler sternly. "Just make sure his staff is not within reach."

***

"Get back from the grate," commanded the orc guard. "You know the routine."

Hansa stood in his cell, two metres away from the orc, which held a knife in one hand and a bucket of foul-smelling fish in the other. "What are you afraid of, creature? A one-armed elf locked in a cage? Hurry with my food. I haven't retched for some time."

"I said get back, or I'll throw the food through the bars."

Dettler stood just behind the orc, his head barely coming up to the height of its chest. "He needs to come close so we can speak."

"Then speak. I don't need to be here." The orc put the bucket down by the grate and turned to head back towards its guard post.

"Oh, *fuck*!" said Dettler, and threw himself into the side of the orc, making it stumble up against the bars.

Hansa was quick—so quick, Dettler had no time to pull back. He had forgotten how fast the Leaguers moved in the games he'd been forced to watch in Arakkan and Verano, forgotten about their almost inhuman fluency. And the man's aim was precise, too: he stabbed with brutal strength, once, twice, and blood sprayed over Dettler.

The orc gurgled and sagged: the first thrust had been to its heart, the second into its throat, angling up under the chin.

Dettler fell back, his heart racing, momentarily blinded by an ejection of blood into one eye. He scrabbled on the floor, his back coming up against the opposite wall of the narrow corridor, and then he felt the orc fall across his legs, its head smacking noisily onto the ground, causing another spurt of fluid to spread across his arm and hand. He squawked and pushed the dead creature off of him, then pawed at his face and eyes, frantically wiping the blood from them.

The Price of Freedom Part II: Velasia

"Calm down, Dettler," came the deep voice of Hansa. "It is dead. You are alive. Fetch the key."

Dettler took several deep breaths. Once calm, he finished wiping his face and only then did he open his eyes. Hansa was standing serenely behind the lattice iron door, tapping his bloodied knife on the locking mechanism. Dettler smiled weakly, then scanned the tall body next to him, set in a small lake of fluid that was still expanding around it. He scrambled away from the sanguine pool and then carefully reached over to the key, set on an iron ring knotted on the orc's belt. He pulled the knot undone, plucked up the key, and stumbled to the door. With shaking hands, he managed to open the rough lock.

Hansa nudged the door open with a shoulder and stepped through, the knife still in his hand. "Well done, Dettler, though you look a mess. I think you will need to clean up to avoid having to explain yourself."

"Yes… yes, you're right. I… I will… follow me." And then Dettler stopped and tapped his head. "Stupid!" He turned to look at the corpse, then up to Hansa. "You need to take its knife and give me yours to dispose of. If anything goes wrong, it will appear as though you took the knife off the guard."

Hansa did as asked.

Now holding the incriminating weapon gingerly in one hand, Dettler concluded: "Okay. I'll lead you to the back stairwell, which is narrow and leads all the way to the top of the tower. It has doors opening onto every level, including com Durrel's private floor. Because it's unused, and was locked when Tartax-Kul fell, it's been largely forgotten, but I found the key among the possessions of the old king's chamberlain. Wait outside the door for twenty minutes, to give me time to clean up and make myself seen. I've scratched a mark in the stonework to indicate the floor. I'll wait in the throne room, several levels down from com Durrel's quarters—also marked, as you will see. There will be no guards here—they'll be in the entrance hall only. Do the deed and then bring the staff to me."

"Lead on, then," said Hansa gruffly. "As they say, destiny awaits."

Dettler led the way through the antechamber to the storage area and through another unused corridor to a battered door that gave access to the tower's back stairwell. After reminding Hansa of his instructions and asking him to delay his attack by an extra ten minutes—giving Dettler more time to dispose of his blood-splattered clothes—he then returned to the still-quiet public areas of the tower. With com Durrel at repose, and the orcs about their business—fishing, on hunting expeditions to the Splinter Forest, at their crafts, or at rest in their homes—the tower was all but deserted. There was just a quartet of guards at the portal to the entrance hall.

Dettler ascended a curving stairwell to the floor where he and Yadzen had their quarters, one level below com Durrel's. He emerged into an open space off which were four large rooms, two of which had been converted into the humans' quarters.

Exiting the stairwell, Dettler stuttered at the sight of an unexpected figure.

"Yadzen? You're here!"

"I am. You sound surprised." The other was accoutred as usual in a mail coat—which hid his Leaguer skin—with a broadsword and knife in scabbards at his waist.

"I thought you were on an errand. Com Durrel sent you to the gatehouse when he sent me to see to the supplies situation."

"Indeed. That is true. But I met Malfog in the courtyard. He was able to tell me all I needed to know, and I was able to pass on the relevant instructions." Yadzen had also been surprised, but now he noticed his companion's state and his expression firmed. "Ah, Mr Dettler, what has happened? You seem unsettled and… is that blood?"

"Blood? Where? Ah, yes, I… had an accident. I was careless. A small cut as I caught a falling knife in the kitchens. It bled a lot. I must clean myself."

But as Dettler sought to make his way around the other, Yadzen took a step to the side to block his progress. "Wounds can quickly become infected. Let me take a look."

"No. It's nothing…"

"It is not nothing. You have some on your chin… your chest… your arm… that is quite a bleed. Yet I see no wound."

"Please, Yadzen, let me pass. I can take care of it."

"*No*, Mr Dettler." Yadzen placed one hand on the hilt of his sword and shifted further to completely bar the other's progress. "Mr Dettler… *Rostus*… what have you done?"

"It's nothing. I… *nothing*."

Yadzen attempted to look into his eyes, but Dettler refused to meet the man's stare. "The prisoner?" said Yadzen. "You acted alone? You helped free Hansa without me? Why would you do that?"

Dettler switched direction, starting to move to his right, attempting to navigate past his colleague on the other side, but Yadzen matched his move and continued to block him. Dettler at last stood still and dropped his arms and his head, defeated. "I… have taken steps to solve our problem." He looked up and met the other's eyes. "Steps I know you would agree with if you were of sound and free mind, but which I suspect you'll not be able to condone in your conditioned state."

Yadzen's eyes widened. "You freed Hansa to kill com Durrel." He drew his sword with one slick motion, the blade passing close to Dettler's ear, making him shy away. "My… *master*. My master is in danger. I must…"

"No, Yadzen! You must do nothing! You must let it be!" Dettler held out his arms, but to no avail. Yadzen pushed past him as though he were made of nothing but straw, causing him to stagger and fall. He strode to the stairwell, with grim purpose in his eyes.

"Stop, Yadzen!" cried Dettler from the stone floor. "This is our salvation! It is your release!"

"I cannot!" But at the entrance to the stairwell, the bodyguard quickly looked over his shoulder, his face blank, his eyes seeming to look elsewhere, above and through Dettler. Through gritted teeth he declared: "Go quick. You must find a scapegoat in case I am in time." Then he was gone, his efforts at control having failed, vaulting up the stairs as fast as humanly possible.

A white-faced Dettler lay on one elbow. *So close!* But now all was in potential ruin. If Yadzen saved com Durrel, would he voluntarily reveal Dettler's part in the assassination attempt? He didn't think so. But com Durrel was not dumb. There would be an investigation, and blame. And then an idea occurred. Dettler scampered to his feet. He didn't even have time to change his tunic, but there was a small pool in the courtyard—he'd have to make swift use of it on passing. He rushed to the stairs, this time headed down.

***

Yadzen unlocked the iron door to the suite and quickly entered. There were several rooms on this level, all off a small central area. He paced quickly to the room in which he knew com Durrel slept, the door to which was still shut. Opening this, he peered inside—and saw the form of his master lying on the large bed in the centre of the room, his staff propped against the wall by his head. A few quick steps brought him close enough to confirm—from the other's soft breathing and the rise and fall of his chest—that the self-styled God-Sorcerer still lived.

He crept back to the door and returned to the undecorated, stone-flagged foyer area. He then looked around at the doors to the other three rooms circling this space. He recalled that there had been mention of a hidden access, a door to a narrow back stairwell, hidden behind a rough curtain. Dettler would know of this; Dettler seemed to know *everything*. Had he found the passage and the key? Had he instructed the Leaguer? And which of the rooms held the hidden doorway? He didn't know and would have to check them one at a time.

Yadzen crossed to the door opposite and tried this. It was unlocked, of course. Inside was a table and chairs and some dusty racks against the wall. It was clearly unused, and of little use to com Durrel. There was a window in the wall, but no arras or sign of a hidden door. He turned back.

As he entered the central area, he was in time to see one of the untried doors slowly open. Through this, in a crouch, came Hansa, all in black, the silver swan emblem on his shoulder glinting in the light spearing down into the space from the window above, a long knife held outstretched.

The two men saw each other at the same time, froze, then stepped into the foyer, facing each other.

Yadzen held his sword forwards and down, its tip resting on the stone; he stretched out his other hand and slowly motioned downwards.

"What is this?" murmured Hansa, speaking low. "Are you here to help or hinder?"

Matching his quiet voice, Yadzen replied: "I am here to protect my master, as is my duty. Go back the way you came, and live."

"Live?" Hansa's voice rose slightly. "For how long? There is only one route for me from here, and that is through the God-Sorcerer… and through you, too, if needs be. Dett—"

"Sssshh!" Yadzen took a step forwards. "Careful how you speak and what you say!"

Hansa smiled above his matted black beard. "You outsiders play complicated games." He took a step forwards. "I say again, step aside. This game is about to end."

"End?" A third voice sounded in the space. Yadzen had left the door to com Durrel's room ajar, and now it opened fully. Com Durrel moved into the doorway, wearing a light black tunic and trousers, but barefoot, his staff clasped in his right hand and used as a walking stick. "What end? Whose end? Yadzen, what the fuck is going on?"

As Yadzen's attention was diverted, Hansa acted: he twitched the knife in his hand and was suddenly holding it by its blade. With a fluid motion, and a strong arm, he hurled the knife at com Durrel. The point of the weapon struck the man in the chest and punched him back against the door.

Com Durrel staggered, but managed to remain upright. He cursed in pain and tore at the light tunic, revealing a patch of the burgundy skin beneath—the one he'd been given months ago by Ryven Miko and had worn almost continually since.

Hansa's eyes widened at the sight. "A skin! You brought a skin… *here*!" And in a sudden rage, he leapt forwards.

In a rage of his own, but tinged also with shock at the assault, com Durrel shrieked. "Kill him, Yadzen! Kill the fucker!"

And Yadzen did.

***

Dettler hurried along the narrow ledge, for once unconcerned about the vertiginous view behind. He'd rushed from the tower, past the gatehouse, to the path down one spur of the mountain, taking one of the narrow, open stairways. A row of orc homes were set into the rockface.

"Ganna? Are you there? It's Dett… *Wormtongue*. I'm unarmed."

"Of course you are," came a dismissive voice from the interior of the cave-like dwelling, "and even if you were, what of it?"

"Ganna! I need to see you. Quick. Open the door. No one must see me."

There was a moment's silence, and then Dettler heard the sounds of a body rising from a creaking chair and the sliding of leather on stone. Several iron bolts clunked and scraped as they were pulled back, and then the rough wooden door withdrew inwards. Dettler edged further along the sill and pulled himself through the entrance. He saw that Ganna had already limped back to his chair, unconcernedly showing his back in a sign of contempt. The orc steadied himself on a poorly built table and twisted to regain his seat. On the table was a long knife with a notched blade.

"So, what do you want? Why do you disturb me? My woman waits for me to give her more children."

Dettler glanced at the locked door in the wall behind, where he knew Ganna's wife and children hid from the perils of orcish society. "Ah, I am here to help you save your existing brood, your woman… and yourself."

Ganna frowned and reached for the knife, taking it in one muscular hand. "What do you mean? Do you threaten me?"

"No! On the contrary!" Dettler remained by the door, raising his hands to confirm he posed no threat. "There is trouble in the tower. The elf prisoner escaped and tried to kill the God-Sorcerer."

The orc's eyes widened. "Tried?"

"Tried… and failed. But the guard to his cell was one of yours. The responsibility is *yours*. The God-Sorcerer is furious. You will be blamed and there will be consequences. Your regiment… your family… will feed all of Tartax-Kul."

Ganna bared his teeth and growled, pushing himself upright. "No!" In a rage, he gripped the table and slid it violently across the rough floor into the nearest wall, where it splintered. He gripped his knife and looked about—at Dettler, at the space beyond the man, and back to the door to his inner sanctum. "I must… I must…" Then he looked back at Dettler, dropping into a crouch, holding out the knife. "Why?"

"You have looked out for me. More than any of the others. I… You deserve a chance. But you must act quickly. Fight or flee. But do it now. I must return to the throne room."

As Dettler backed to the door outside, Ganna gave one abrupt nod to the man. "My flesh belongs to me, and no one else." He turned to the door behind, and Dettler scampered from the dwelling as fast as he could.

***

By the time Dettler passed through the eastern gate and entered the courtyard before the tower, it was clear trouble was brewing. A squad of the God-Sorcerer's most trusted troops—part of a company of Mangu's Reapers, which had returned with them from Ullah-Bor—purposefully trotted across the courtyard towards the gatehouse from the barracks at the side of the tower, while Paramok, general of the Two Horns Regiment, briskly crossed from the western gate with several of his champions in tow.

Dettler reached the stairway to the entrance hall before Paramok. The two guards started to lower their spears, appearing uncertain, but they recognising him and let him pass. However, the orc general following did not gain access so easily: from behind, Dettler heard harsh words and the clang of weaponry being dropped and confiscated. Guards at the foot of the stairs to the throne room also looked at him suspiciously, though they did not challenge him, and nor did the pair at the top of the stairs.

Com Durrel paced in front of the throne, while Yadzen stood by the side of the frighteningly carved chair. A dozen orcs lay prostate on the floor, overseen by more of the red-armoured Reapers. Dettler heard com Durrel shriek a command, and one of the guards brought its curved spear down onto the head of one of the humbled orcs. Blood spurted upwards, and when the wounded creature raised a hand in limp defence, the spear descended again and sliced it off. A second bodyguard—armed with just a knife—then knelt down, applying its weapon to the screaming orc.

Dettler's pace slowed and he looked away, but com Durrel had seen him.

"Wormtongue! Come here! Come here *now*!"

"Yes... yes, my lord."

As he approached, Dettler noticed that com Durrel's pupils were dilated and his face was deathly pale, with sweat sparkling on his brow.

"Where the fuck have you been?"

"Looking into the food situation as you ordered. Talking to returning hunters. What is… what is going on?"

Com Durrel's chest heaved. "What is going on? I'll tell you… *Tarantum-Collaren-Vertobus!*" One of the orcs on the floor—now at the direct end of the pointing staff—made a peculiar sound and appeared to literally melt into the stone. Com Durrel threw his head back and roared, then he slammed the staff down on the floor, looked about, and approached the nearest of the supplicants. He repeated his spell and melted the creature's head into a puddle. Then he looked back at a trembling Dettler and shrieked: "What is going on? That fucking elf *somehow* escaped, and *somehow* found a secret passage to my chamber. He tried to kill me! What the fuck do you think of that?"

Dettler tried to calm his heart, which was no easy task faced with the volcanic wrath of the other. He glanced across at Yadzen, who looked straight ahead, a stony expression on his face, refusing to meet his eyes. "Ah, that sounds… unlikely. I mean…" he held up his hands to defer any further assault, "an unlikely set of circumstances. The elf must have been aided. Who guarded him? Where is he? What is his regiment?"

"How the fuck should I know."

"He was not a Reaper, lord!" said the bodyguard with the knife, turning to face com Durrel. He was clearly captain of the guard.

"A Rock Hammer, lord," said one of the prostrate orcs, raising its head just far enough from the ground so that its voice could be heard. "You gave the responsibility of the food and stores to the Rock Hammers and their women. The prisoner was kept in one of their larders."

Paramok of the Two Horns arrived with his retinue. Com Durrel turned his attention to the approaching party. "On your faces, you filthy scumbags! Faces, now, or I'll have them torn off! *Do not look at me!*"

Without a word, the orc champions dropped like stones onto the floor and spread their arms in supplication.

Com Durrel glowered over the heads of the newcomers, and then turned his attention back to the orcs that had spoken and to Dettler. "And who leads the Rock Hammers? Remind me."

"Ah, I know this," said Dettler, pre-empting the others. "It's Ganna. I saw him not long ago. Oh!" He raised a hand to his mouth.

"What is it, Wormtongue?"

"It's probably nothing. It's just that he seemed… distracted. I know he thinks his duties are ignoble. He wished to join the expedition into Bratha. But surely he would never—?"

And then there was commotion at the broad doorway to the room. Another orc appeared wearing the red of the Reapers. Its fellows allowed it to progress into the room, where all those standing turned to watch its approach. The creature came to the ring of supplicants and paused, wondering how to proceed.

"You come with news?" snarled com Durrel. "Stay there. Drop to your knees. That will do. Now tell me."

"Lord, there is trouble. On the eastern slope. The Rock Hammers are assembling in force."

Dettler caught com Durrel's eye. "Ganna's treachery is open now."

Com Durrel threw back his head and shrieked with rage. After bellowing curses and leasing off several destructive spells that shook the tower and maimed more of the innocent household orcs on the floor, he gave his orders: that every Rock Hammer's life was now forfeit, and that their hidden children would feed the community for weeks to come.

***

"Is anywhere truly safe?" wondered Dettler out loud.

The three humans remained in the throne room, which had been completely cleared of orcs—alive and dead—although patches of blood and melted skin mottled the floor and would need a thorough cleaning later. The broad doors to the room had been shut, and the royal bodyguards waited outside.

"No," replied Yadzen. "Nowhere in this realm."

"Not with a bodyguard like you," muttered com Durrel, though without passion. He was coming down from a huge adrenalin rush, and now appeared utterly spent. He lounged on the throne, one leg hooked over a carved chair arm, unable to find a comfortable position. "You did not stop his knife throw. Without my skin, I would have been dead."

Yadzen nodded. "That is true. But it is fortunate I was able to intercept him before he got to you in your sleep, sir."

Dettler exchanged glances with Yadzen. They'd not had a chance to talk since the encounter in their private chambers. He didn't know what Yadzen had said or how he had accounted for the stroke of fortune that had saved com Durrel, and he dare not speculate aloud. Perhaps the issue hadn't yet been raised, and Yadzen might struggle to come up with a convincing explanation? Their stories had various holes that wouldn't stand up to scrutiny.

But before Dettler could speak, com Durrel looked at the other and mused: "Yes, that was fortunate. But what were you doing in my chambers, Yadzen?"

The grey-haired man frowned and quickly looked back at Dettler. An appeal for help?

"I... I..."

"I bumped into Malfog," said Dettler, "in the courtyard. He said he'd spoken to you. Something about news from the army? He mentioned the prisoner. Were you going to question him about the threat from the elves?"

"Yes. Thank you, Mr Dettler. I wanted some interpretation from... the other side."

"And you found the guard dead," continued Dettler, "and the prisoner gone?"

"That is correct, though I didn't think the prisoner would attempt to attack Mr com Durrel." He turned to face his master. "I went to tell you, sir, that the elf was gone. I thought it was significant enough to wake you."

Com Durrel looked between the pair uncertainly. "Yes, well, it's good that you did."

Dettler rushed in to forestall any further interrogation. "And I assume Hansa must have gone through the back passage, as he wouldn't have got through the front door. We knew this existed, but didn't know where the keys were. It makes me wonder whether there might be other hidden passageways in the tower, and who might know of them. If Ganna knew, maybe others do too?" He shrugged. "Perhaps we would be safer in the open. Then no one could blindside us."

"The open?" com Durrel appeared confused and mentally drained. "Do you mean with the army?"

Dettler looked surprised. "Ah, no, sir, I didn't really mean that, but now that you mention it, maybe… maybe it's something we should think about. The army is loyal, but here? If one whole regiment is up in arms, it may take some effort to suppress it, and who knows what hidden places its troops might occupy, waiting for a chance to strike." He paced up and down, nodding to himself. "Yes, that might be for the best. You always wanted to travel with your army and take part in the assault on the yeltoi. It would be good to leave this place. And the Leaguers and their motley party with their inferior staff of power… it might be better to meet them in the open with your full force, than here, with a lesser force, and traitors all around. Yadzen—what's your professional opinion?"

The bodyguard caught Dettler's severe look and nodded understanding. "Yes, perhaps you… sir…" he turned to com Durrel, "are right. Perhaps we would be safest in the open. We could leave tomorrow and allow your loyalists time to root out your enemies here. We could take Paramok's regiment. With that and your staff, we would be invulnerable."

Once again, com Durrel looked between the two men. Did he sense that something was going on? But then he smiled. "I… like this plan. This place palls. Why should I hide away from whatever pathetic force the Leaguers are sending against me? Very well. Inform Paramok. My Reapers will come as well. We will have plenty of supplies for the troops, too, with our prisoners from the Rock Hammers. Pass on my orders."

"A wise decision!" Dettler bowed and so too, after a brief glance aside at him, did Yadzen.

***

"This is not something we discussed," whispered Yadzen, as the two men crossed the courtyard outside the tower, having refrained from speaking during their descent to the entrance chamber and the stairs outside, passing a multitude of red-armoured bodyguards on the way. "Why this strategy, and why now?"

"We must leave here," said Dettler, speaking low, "and leave here quick. There are too many loose ends, and too much incriminating evidence."

"Such as?"

"First, I never spoke to Malfog, and so that lie might quickly be uncovered. But he's of the Devil Fish regiment, and will remain here, helping to hunt down the rebels." He drew to a halt, causing Yadzen to do the same. Then he looked about to ensure that no one was close enough to hear them. "Second, com Durrel didn't ask about the slain prison guard. The problem is, if Ganna sprung the prisoner, why would he or Hansa kill the guard? But third, and most important of all, we cannot risk being here if Ganna is caught alive and tortured. He would reveal that I tipped him off—and in fact, I got him to jump when he didn't need to. I told him com Durrel held him accountable for the prisoner's release—which he didn't at that time."

Yadzen frowned. "All good points, Mr Dettler. And fourth, if we are out in the open, your chances of escape will be enhanced." He broke into a faint smile. "In any case, I should congratulate you on how you manipulated our master to do as you wanted."

Dettler blew out his cheeks and almost looked embarrassed. "Well, thank you, but it was no difficult task. Com Durrel has been torn for weeks about what to do. I simply jostled the scales."

"By presenting a scenario and then making him think that he had thought of it."

"Ah, that, yes. It's an old trick. When you are negotiating with egotists or contrarians who are difficult to persuade, the best strategy is to make them think that the option you favour is actually their own, shake your head in acknowledgement of your own inferiority, and appear to concede to their greater wisdom."

Yadzen gave a small shake of the head. "In truth, Mr Dettler, I don't know who is the most dangerous man here: com Durrel… or *you*."

Chapter 21

They travelled light, and quickly. Before leaving their comrades outside the Iron Gate, Mikkel, Belias and Omdanan had stripped themselves of all extraneous weight: gone were helmets, mail, shields, spears, and the nose guards and chest plates on their black horses. Their swords they kept—lashed to saddles—and all retained long knives, but otherwise their only weapon was Omdanan's bow, his supply of arrows replenished from the vanguard's stocks. Aside from bedding cloaks and rations, the bulk of the weight they carried was in water and some oats for the horses: while the main contingent would negotiate a planned route across the Desolate Quarter, taking in a few known sources of water and vegetation for the horses to feed upon, the scouts intended a much more direct route to the north-east, towards the yeltoi towns and the orc army they expected to be approaching these.

Omdanan cantered behind the other two scouts. On the morning of the first day, he'd initially lagged behind as he tried to come to terms with the art of horsemanship—but he was a quick learner, and by that very afternoon he had improved enough to assuage the concerns of his colleagues. Now into the third day, Omdanan was determined to completely match, and even surpass, the skills of Mikkel and Belias. Having watched them from behind, and the ways in which they shifted their balance in rhythm with their horses' movements, he had been experimenting: standing up in his stirrups to see further; hanging out from the side of the horse to pluck a random bloom from a desiccated bush; even swivelling around three hundred and sixty degrees on his saddle, with legs swinging over his mount's maned neck, to allow a complete view of the surrounds. When Belias had turned to check on him and seen him standing upright on his horse's back, having lengthened the reins to keep control, she had looked shocked and slowed involuntarily, allowing him to canter past. When she'd caught up with him again—

still behind the unaware Mikkel—she'd grinned widely and made a gesture of salute.

But what Omdanan really wanted was to master the use of his bow from horseback, yet he couldn't risk losing any arrows with wasteful practice on their journey. By the time they made camp on their third day, however—in a sunken bowl with exposed rock sides—he was ready to experiment. He noticed in the land above the bowl a dozen leathery plants with spines like cacti. Two of these were taller than the others, the height of a short person, while most of the rest resembled bloated, decapitated heads. While Belias and Mikkel settled their horses in the hollow, Omdanan deferred. He readied his bow secretly and ensured the quiver over his shoulder was well set so that he could easily reach back and pluck an arrow at need. And then—rather self-consciously—he started his horse into a walk, guiding it with his heels alone, leaving his hands free to manipulate the bow. It wasn't long before his comrades wondered at his absence and emerged to look.

Momentarily embarrassed, Omdanan avoided the amused eyes of the watchers and goaded his horse into a light trot. He then notched an arrow and loosed it at one of the taller plants. The arrow caught enough of the edge to stop its flight, though it barely lodged into the flesh and drooped down from it. He squeezed his pelvis and tapped a heel, at which his horse skipped forwards and started to turn. Omdanan plucked and loosed a second arrow, and this time it struck the plant dead centre in the midriff of the imaginary orc. At the corner of his sight he saw Belias clap, and Mikkel turn to speak to her. But he had only just started.

Around and around he rode, gaining in confidence at directing the horse with only the slightest use of the reins, drawing and firing his arrows with greater and greater speed and accuracy—first into the tall plants, and then into the smaller targets lower to the ground. He didn't always hit, and one arrow deflected to fly uncomfortably close to the spectators—who by then were sat on the lip of the hollow, calling out encouragement and hailing particularly good shots—but most did. And by the time his quiver was empty, the arrows were invariably splitting their targets right through their centres.

Omdanan was forced to dismount to collect his arrows, but now he walked with more self-assurance. The others allowed him to focus on his task without distraction, and to mount up and repeat the exercise a second and then a third time.

"Bravo, Elian!" declared Belias, at last. "But now it is so dark I can barely see you, or you the targets. Mikkel has made a fire. Join us!"

"Uh, yes, I will. After I have collected the arrows."

When Omdanan dropped down to the small fire—having tied his horse beside the others and scattered some oats for it upon the stony soil—he found Belias and Mikkel lounging on their sleeping cloaks, talking low. They turned to him, both wearing enigmatic smiles. During the previous days, they had said little to him—remaining polite, but somewhat distant.

"That was quite a show, Mr Omdanan," said Belias, who seemed to have the edge in authority in the party. She teased at her long blonde hair, which was draped over her left shoulder. "I was already surprised at your skill in the saddle for one who'd apparently never ridden a horse before. And now this? We are experienced riders, over many years, yet your skills seem barely less than ours. How is this possible?"

Omdanan failed to hide a smile of pride. "I just... I just have this way... with nature."

"With nature, or against?" mused Belias. "I hear you fought well before the Iron Gate, although I didn't see it. You seem to have a good instinct for dispatching nature's gifts, whether orcs or innocent foliage."

Mikkel barked a laugh, shaking his bearded head.

"On Meridian, we were forced to confront nature from an early age. To appreciate it. Shepherd it. Count and classify it. Education in the ways of life starts very young there. And on Meridian, there is a *lot* of life, and a lot of it is unfriendly to humans. So we learn to evade it and hide from it."

"You mean," concluded Belias, still with a smile, "run away from it?"

Omdanan's expression turned serious. "Yes."

"But you don't seem like the running type."

"*I am not.*" Omdanan felt sudden anger and had to turn from the woman to try to hide this. He felt her eyes upon him, curious, but she waited for him to say more. He looked back. "On my planet, I always ran, because I had to. But whereas my peers ran from fear of harm to themselves, I ran from fear of what I might do to whatever was chasing me. Fear of the punishment I would receive if I broke our laws and harmed the merest hair on the merest head of the most pervasive, stupid, ugly, or vicious creature. You see, to my people, humans are an aberration. We are the least of Nature's creatures, less important than an earthworm."

"An interesting perspective—and somewhat different from ours."

Omdanan nodded, and a thought occurred to him: "From sub-human to human to super-human; from Meridian to the Confederation to the League."

"Just so!" declared Belias, with delight. "Or even, from subservience, to compliance, to dominance? So have you decided where you belong?"

"I have decided that I don't like to run."

"A good answer. But... Cousin Elian... please try not to do anything stupid. We are not here to fight—which is why we have few weapons—but to observe. Yet rest assured: if we run it will not be because of cowardice."

Omdanan smiled and his tension eased. "Motivation is everything. I hear your words."

***

They came upon the orc army's wake after six days of hard riding.

"There's no doubt about it," said Belias, steadying her skittish horse at the edge of the churned, sandy soil. The area was perhaps one hundred metres wide, and of a darker colour than the surrounds, extending away in the distance north and south. Within this zone, several gorse bushes had been slashed and trampled. There were also sporadic pieces of trash.

Mikkel leant down from his horse to pluck up a piece of cloth, stained a dark red. "Something decided it no longer needed its bandage."

Omdanan caught a sparkle of sunlight from the midst of the zone and stepped his horse over to it. "And here's a fragment of bone. A big one. It's… like a human femur, only fatter."

"The orcs have been feasting on their own," laughed Belias. "It's what they do. If they had a long enough march, they'd eventually consume their entire force and save us a lot of bother."

"And deny us glory!" exclaimed Mikkel. "So what would then be the point of our presence here?"

"I was not wishing for it, Cousin," replied Belias, "merely explaining to our friend."

"I am relieved. I thought you had gone soft." Then Mikkel laughed at Belias' gurned response.

"So now we head north?" asked Omdanan.

The woman directed her mount up to his. "Yes. We need to find them. We do not need to interrogate this scene any further: it is clearly several days old. But we now need to proceed with caution. Orcs are slow creatures that do not ride horses or wagons, and they have an unsteady gait, best suited for picking their way over rough ground in the mountains and swinging from the low branches of trees. They will never win a running race against an elf, or even a man. So though these tracks may be up to a week old, we might still hope to overhaul them in a couple of days."

Mikkel drew up to the pair. "Agreed. This is our advantage. But we are not far from Haradan. Already the terrain is starting to look more lush. I see a copse of trees on the northern horizon. I fear they may have beaten us to the town, and if so, I dread what we might find."

"Then let us waste no further time." Belias turned her horse and set her heels to its flank. "Let us fly!"

***

On the second day following the broad track, in the morning, they came upon the yeltoi town of Haradan, set in a bowl of green-brown hills beside a lake. Cresting a small rise, between two clumps of trees, they saw its corpse below them.

"Damn!" Mikkel slapped his leather-clad thigh. "We are too late."

"We were always going to be too late," said Belias, sombrely. "Even if we'd reached them in time, us three could not have averted what went on here. And nor, I fear, could the vanguard."

Half of the town of one- and two-storey buildings was blackened from flames, the wooden dwellings consumed almost entirely, the stone ones like hollow skulls without crowns. Yet half remained untouched.

"*They escaped*," whispered Omdanan.

"What do you say, Elian?" asked Belias.

"I said they escaped. I feel it. I mean, *look*. The walls are mostly intact. And half of the town is untouched. Would the men have opened their gates and surrendered?"

"Not if they had any sense," growled Mikkel.

Belias stood in her stirrups for a better view. She scanned the horizon, looking around at the three other peaks, then turned her eyes again to the town. The area by the docks was largely untouched and utterly silent. "I think Elian is right. I would have expected far worse if there had been a siege. Perhaps the townsfolk took to the water and crossed the lake, and we might find traces of them on the other side. The army will have had to track around the lake…" Without waiting for the others, she spurred her horse down the slope.

Omdanan and Mikkel exchanged quick looks, then followed.

***

They entered through the main south-facing gate, which had been smashed asunder, with one of the large, wooden, iron-studded doors on the ground, and the other hanging from a single warped hinge. Belias led them down the cobbled streets, strewn with charred wood and the contents of some of the ransacked houses, the only sounds coming from the *clopping* of their horses' hooves upon the stones.

Omdanan looked about sharply, attempting to take in every detail. He saw no bodies, and no bloodstains upon the walls or cobbles. Broken pots and scattered clothing formed the main detritus. It was clear that the orcs had been unimpressed by the plunder and indeed, by the time they'd reached the dockside, there was little damage—as though the orcs had grown tired of venting their frustration and accepted that there was nothing within the remaining buildings worth eating or stealing. And by the docks, the only craft they found was a small row boat with a breached hull that lay half-sunk—only saved from complete immersion by the rope that tied its bow to an iron ring set in the stone quay.

"We will have to go around too," noted Belias. "But that is best in any case. We need to follow the orcs' tracks, and on the water we might be within view of any lingering watchers."

"Where are they heading next?" asked Omdanan. "This is one of four towns of Bratha, isn't it?"

"Yes. Ultis is the furthest south of the four, but also much further east. It is closest to Tartax-Kul and was taken months ago. Haradan is connected to Jinna by a waterway that connects the lakes on which these stand—and which stretches away from the northern end of this lake. The fourth is Faltis, which is much further north and actually lies on the coast. Faltis will be a harder nut for the Sorcerer to crack, especially without the use of his magic, and may prove the final redoubt for the men of Bratha. But I still hope we can save Jinna, where Haradan's fleeing population must have gone."

"At least they will have more spears if they choose to fight," said Mikkel.

"Yet I doubt they will be enough. The orc track is wide and their army must be large, although we don't yet know how large, or whether the Sorcerer is with them. If he is, then they have no hope."

"So towards Jinna?" confirmed Omdanan.

"Yes," said Belias. "The orcs clearly returned to the main gate from the docks, unable to progress across the water. We will follow their circumnavigation of the hills. But they are now very close. I sense this."

Omdanan stiffened. He slowly raised his bow from over his head and notched an arrow. As the others watched him with widening eyes, he muttered: "Closer than you think." Turning in the saddle he released an arrow into the shadows beneath a dock-side building, where lay an upturned and rotting fishing boat. There was a brief squawk, but nothing more.

Belias arched an eyebrow at the young Meridian. "I'm definitely taking *you* home with me after all of this."

***

They returned to the front gate and picked up the trail of the army, which had turned east towards a small hill overlooking the town. And it was soon clear that the trail was fresh. The trodden grass was a bruised green rather than a deadened brown, and they rapidly came upon the discarded remnants of a meal eaten on the march—with bones that still glistened with new blood. And then there was the smell, which rose and fell on the modest breeze, and increased as they rounded the hill—a pungent, organic smell, of sweat and exotic body odours.

They rode swiftly, but silently, cantering over flat ground and through depressions, but slowing as they ascended higher ground in case they should emerge onto a ridgeline and be easily visible to anything beyond. After a couple of hours, they came across a wider circular area of stressed terrain that had clearly been used as a campsite.

"They were here last night," said Belias. "How far will they have marched today, on their twisted legs and encumbered with gear for war?"

"A score of kilometres at most," suggested Mikkel.

Belias considered this assessment, and concurred.

And so they continued through the late afternoon, confident that that they were reeling in their quarry. Less than two hours later, with the sun of Arkon low in the sky, sitting over the Skythrust Mountains away to their west, they began to catch the first sounds of an army on the march—the clinking of metal and the low rustling of armoured bodies in movement. The smell, too, suddenly intensified and became ever-present. Belias then led the way to a knot of trees on the broad top of a low hill off to the west of the scuffed trail. At the eaves of the small wood, she dismounted and led her horse through the crunching litter of the trees. The others followed.

At the northernmost tip of the wood, Belias looped her reins around a low branch, whispered soothing words to her mount, and then crouched low and moved off. As she emerged from the trees, she fell onto her belly and wriggled the last few metres to the edge of the crest. Omdanan was soon beside her and Mikkel crawled up to the Meridian's other side.

"Damn! That is *big*," said Belias. "Where the hell did all these orcs come from?"

"Look at all their banners," said Mikkel. "There are at least a score of regiments. Probably more."

Omdanan looked down onto the rear echelons of the orc army, which marched in surprisingly good order, two regiments abreast, stretching in a thick line further than he could see. It tramped over a fringe of meadowlands, which quickly transformed into a waist-high field of a wheat-like crop that extended as far north as the eye could see. From this elevation, he could only make out eight clear groups of orcs, distinguished by different hues to their hardened leather armour, marching under different colourful banners… but the smudge ahead of these suggested a far greater number.

"We need to get a clear count of the regiments so we can estimate troop numbers accurately," said Belias. "And we need to check whether the Sorcerer is amongst them."

"And estimate their speed of march," suggested Mikkel, "so we can get an idea of how long it will take them to reach Jinna."

"Agreed," said Belias. "But how? I have never encountered anything like this before."

"We must get ahead of them," suggested Omdanan, uncertainly. "On Meridian, when we did rough field surveys of creatures, we'd get ahead of their migration route, set up a hide, and count them as they passed." He realised that the others were looking at him intently. "And… if we can set up markers, separated by a known distance, we can time how long it takes them to traverse the space."

"Very good, Elian," said Belias. "That makes sense. Come, then. We have no time to lose: every hour we delay, they get closer to Jinna. We can swing wide and find a spot further north. They'll avoid difficult high ground, so that is where we will station ourselves."

***

They raced ahead—down the slope on the far side of the hill, and then on a parallel path to the line of march to the west. Once they were a couple of kilometres ahead of the estimated front of the army, they cut back across to the flatter lands that seemed the natural route for the marching force, which comprised even more crop fields. After another couple of kilometres, they found a natural slope to the terrain, from west to east, with a small, barren hill topped by a single tree, split down the middle by lightning, yet still somehow alive and in leaf. It was not a great spot, to Omdanan's eye, but it was the best they could find for now. They picketed their horses some distance behind the hill, and Belias gave Omdanan a soft piece of cloth, showing him how to cover his horse's mouth and nose to prevent it whinnying and alerting the enemy to their presence, then they scampered back up to the tree, taking positions lying flat in the now-deep shadow. The daylight was fading rapidly.

"We haven't time to set markers," noted Mikkel.

"No," agreed Omdanan, "but if we time the passage of the front of the army between… that large rock at the field's edge and… that bare hummock to the left… we can go back afterwards and pace that distance and work out their speed that way."

"Good!" exclaimed Belias. "But now they approach. They cannot move quietly to save their lives. I suggest three tasks. Mikkel, assess the speed of the army. I will count the banners. Elian—you know what the God-Sorcerer looks like. I assume it will be obvious to all, but you know for certain and have a keen eye… so pay especial attention to his presence. Keep low now: they come on."

Omdanan saw the front of the main army trudge into view, at first no more than a hint on the horizon—a slightly darker line across the fields than to either side—and then a steadily resolving mass of armoured creatures, the spears of which forming a rippling thicket, bobbing up and down as their bearers moved across the uneven terrain, like a sea of tall grasses manipulated by the wind. And then he also noticed individual shapes before them—evenly spaced dots in front of the main body.

"They have a skirmish line," muttered Omdanan.

"I see it too," said Belias. "So they are not completely incautious. But how wide is it? Can you see the figures to the furthest sides?"

"Ah, yes," Omdanan frowned in concentration. "We may soon have company. It depends if the outrider to this side is prepared to walk up this slope."

Mikkel cursed under his breath, and Belias shifted her prone position, trying to get a better angle on the tiny figure at the far left of the skirmish line, which was strewn a couple of hundred metres ahead of the main body. At last she declared: "He is having doubts. Already he is resisting the slope and draws closer to his colleague."

Omdanan watched the scene carefully. It did seem as though the lazy orc would choose an easier route, but then the orc to its inside noticed its closing companion, gave an incoherent shout, and waved its spear. At this, the first orc shouted back, clearly in anger, but it did amend its path and once more seemed on course to take the rise and uncover them.

"Damn!" hissed Mikkel. "What now? We will be revealed." He drew his long knife.

Belias frowned, then looked at the orc, now close to the bottom of the slope. Then she looked at Omdanan uncertainly. "Ah, Elian?"

Omdanan continued to make calculations… and then he nodded curtly to himself. He could read the body language of animals, including humans, and orcs were no different. He noted the other's gait; the way it angled its body; the way it distributed its weight as it moved. He made one last estimation, and then slowly wriggled himself backwards.

Again, the woman asked: "Elian?"

"Withdraw a short distance. It won't come to the top. If we are still and cover our heads with our cloaks, it will pass ten metres away."

Belias smiled, though there was tension in her voice. "Very well. I trust your judgment. Mikkel—back up a little."

The three stayed as still as they were able, holding their breath in the deep shadow. Before long, they heard the laboured breathing of an orc, a mutter of complaint and insult, and the irritated swishing of a spear. They kept their heads down and waited. Just as it seemed the creature would pass, a voice from further down the slope came to them—an indistinct growl. The nearby orc came to a halt.

"Fuck you and all your bastard children. I am tired. You come if you want."

A further volley of insults came from down the slope. But then the orc was on the move again, ignoring the imprecations, and the sounds of its movement began to recede.

"That was a close one," sighed Belias. "Edge forwards again. Remember your roles."

Omdanan pulled himself forwards on his belly and peered from under the cloak that had covered his head. The orc army was close, and noisy. It approached the foot of the slope, but only the edge of the nearer of the two-abreast regiments lapped over it. The sight was fearsome. Formation after formation streamed past, each block of about two hundred orcs following its own banner. Beside him, he heard Belias reel off some of their names: Black Sun, Hanging Rope, Head Splitters, Blue Devils…

"They are a mix from Ullah-Bor and Tartax-Kul," the woman muttered.

And then there was a struggling party of bound orcs in the middle—*the larder*, according to Mikkel—but Omdanan saw no sign of Anda com Durrel, nor of the two men who had gone with him, nor any evidence of an exalted-yet-shrouded party within the legions. He kept watching until the rear echelon passed, and then he turned onto his back and looked thoughtfully up at the dark, over-hanging branch above.

At last, the other two also withdrew. Belias muttered something about the horses, and she descended the rear slope to reclaim their mounts, while Mikkel dropped down the front slope, to pace out the distance between the markers as had earlier been suggested by Omdanan. Several minutes later, the three reassembled on the crest of the slope, each holding the reins of their horse.

"Fifty-six regiments," Belias declared, with a sense of disbelief. "Fifty-six! That's around twelve thousand orcs! I have never heard of such an assembly before."

"There never has been such an assembly," confirmed Mikkel, shaking his head. "The largest force the orcs have ever fielded in battle before was three or four thousand, in the Southlands invasion, forty years ago. This is truly unprecedented. And what can our small forces do against them? Our main host numbers three hundred. The Lightning and Sword will not be able to field many more. Even a combined charge would be swallowed by that mass."

"And so we must deploy our forces sensibly. But these are not considerations for here and now. Elian—I saw no sign of the God-Sorcerer. Was he there?"

Omdanan shook his head ruefully. "He wasn't. So I guess that means my party will soon leave yours. I hope Enabeth knows where he is."

"You could not have a better leader or guide," declared Belias. "Now we must get this news back to our comrades. And you, Mikkel, what did you discover?"

The bearded man was still unsettled by the number of regiments they had witnessed. "Eh? Oh. At their speed, I calculate they'll be at Jinna in eight days. It will be tight."

"So true!" Belias swung herself onto her horse. "And though night is almost upon us, I suggest we waste no further time. Up! Up! We must ride as hard as we can."

Omdanan and Mikkel mounted almost as one. But then Mikkel tugged on his reins, causing his horse to step back and away.

"Mikkel?"

"You must ride with the news to the vanguard. Two messengers are enough for that. But the men need to be forewarned at Jinna, and also reassured that they are not alone. I will take this news to them and start to organise their defences. Without the staff of power, or any siege weapons, the orcs will find a resolute, fortified foe hard to budge."

Belias nodded grimly. "A good call. I hope our vanguard will arrive before eight days are up. And if we can find and instruct our main host, we may with luck be with you by a week after that. And then—if we can hold the orcs at the walls—we may buy time for the hosts of the other high guilds to come to our aid. On now, Elian."

Chapter 22

The vanguard of the Narvi, with the accompanying outland party, had to take a slightly different route to that of the scouts when crossing the Desolate Quarter.

"There are several small water sources scattered across the Quarter," said Regnarson, at the end of the first day's travel. He had several maps that were of higher scale and more detailed than the one by which Archaen had been navigating. He indicated symbols on the map now spread on the ground before the party, lit from the side by a small campfire. "The scouts are well stocked with water and can travel fast, but our supplies are not high, and the horses need forage, which they will have to graze from these sources. We will hop between these spots as best we can."

"When you say water sources," asked Sarok, "what do you mean? Like oases?"

"This area isn't formally a desert according to Old Earth definitions—it receives more precipitation than the formal limit—but if you want to call some of these places oases, no one here will argue. Most have small amounts of water, retained thanks to the geology. There are also one or two dry rivers that fill in the wetter months, but which even now may yield some water in shaded puddles or by digging into the ground a short way."

"And how much of a delay will this zig-zag route cost us?" wondered Sarok.

"Not too much," said Archaen. "We are bearing north-eastward, where these sources exist in greater number. Perhaps only an extra twenty kilometres?" She glanced at the bearded leader of the Narvi, as though inviting correction, but the man remained silent, still intent on the map. "But while we have a clear course—which the scouts have been told—they will have extra distance to travel, being unclear on the location of their objective. They will have to range this way and that until they find it, and then they will have to return to us with their intel. The sooner they return, the more time we will ultimately save in correcting our path to meet or pre-empt the army."

"*If* com Durrel is with them," corrected Sarok.

"True," said Archaen. "And if not, then that will save us even more time from following the army when we should instead be heading towards his lair in Tartax-Kul."

At this point, one of Regnarson's company—tall and black-bearded, like all of the men—emerged from the darkness beyond the firelight and leant down to speak softly to his leader. Regnarson nodded gently as the other's words, then turned to give a curt reply. As the other man turned to leave, Regnarson collected his map and climbed to his feet.

"A problem?" asked Archaen.

"No, not at all. Simply a matter of logistics to be resolved. Still, I will bid you a good night."

The outlander company watched their host disappear into the black space between their fire and a second, some metres away. There were two more fires, but these were difficult to see directly, being more distant and frequently occluded by Narvi warriors pacing about, sometimes leading horses.

"Speaking of problems," began Sarok, after a pause, "it is still unclear to me, Ms Archaen, how you intend us to handle the com Durrel situation. Perhaps the prospect is near enough that we should establish the rules of combat. What exactly do you plan to do with him?"

Archaen stroked a hand through her black hair, which had grown during their quest and now fell over her shoulder and half way down her chest. Her grey eyes looked absently at some unknown place beyond the flames. "Com Durrel?" She pursed her lips and ever-so-slightly shook her head, sighed, and directed her gaze at Sarok. "You are right. It is something I have not thought about at length. All I can say for sure, is that the staff of power must be recovered and he must be removed from Velasia."

"So you have no preference?"

"I have a preference," muttered Mandelson, propped on one elbow, twirling her kerambit in one hand. "Though I doubt he'll stay still long enough for me to detach them."

Sarok grinned as he turned to look at the woman. "And for once, our minds are probably not too far apart on this—given the trouble he has caused us all. Alas, he is not likely to let you get close enough for what you desire. Perhaps we can take him down from a distance, though? If we can get within sight of him, Sentain can blast him with his staff from afar."

"Uh, well, I'm not sure I like that idea." Sentain looked between the two Corvans, then quickly to Vuller, who was by Sarok's side, but the bodyguard's eyes were fixed on the dancing flames. "I mean, getting close may be a problem. He will have bodyguards. I might miss."

Mandelson scoffed. "Stop making excuses. We know the real reason for your reticence."

Sentain frowned. "Well, yes, I'd rather not kill him unless necessary, although I *would* if that were the only, or the best, way. But, Enabeth," he turned, "is it?"

Sarok intervened. "But what else is there? To capture him? That would be a harder task, and to what end? What would the Leaguers do with him? They have no proper justice system. Let him go on his way on his ship—with prizes he has already turned down, or with nothing? I don't see any future where that leads to a happy ending for the League, or for us."

"Maybe they'll allow him trial by combat, like orc prisoners they can't release," mused Mandelson. "My hat is in the ring for that one."

Sentain still watched Archaen, awaiting an answer. He repeated: "Enabeth?"

The woman at last looked around and her eyes focused on the anthropologist. She patted her hair against her mailed chest, then dropped her hand to her lap. "Capture will be difficult, but if there is a good chance, then it should be attempted. What his fate would be, I cannot say, as that would be an issue for the Senate. But we should assume we'll get no such opportunity, and that he won't yield as long as he has his staff and his army. So our intent should be to kill him as soon as we are able."

"To save the yeltoi," mused Sarok, with a wicked smile, "or the integrity of your game in Velasia?"

Archaen's expression did not change. "Why not both?"

"Indeed."

Sentain still appeared troubled. "But you're suggesting a kind of assassination. That's not honourable, Enabeth. You've made clear your distaste for that in the past... and you too, Miko."

Miko had been quiet throughout, and remained that way, simply nodding agreement with this claim.

"Would you rather we call him out?" asked Sarok after a pause, when it was clear that Archaen was not going to respond. "Ride up to his dark fortress and ask him to present himself, *sans* staff, for a best-of-three arm wrestle?" He threw his arms in the air in exasperation before sarcastically concluding: "A plan with absolutely no drawbacks!"

At last, the Leaguer woman stirred. Her expression was severe. "I cannot say for sure. We are playing a game of chess and making plans still several moves ahead. We do not know where all the pieces will be as we enter the endgame—or even *what* they will be. Should one piece be in a slightly different position than expected, our best laid plans may come unstuck."

"So let me summarise," said Sarok. "We catch him if we can—but expect we won't be able to. We kill him if we can—but only if we can do this politely, with maximum honour and minimum collateral damage. But we are unlikely to find ourselves in a situation where this is possible either. In other words, we are fucked."

At last, Vuller looked up. "Boss, we've been fucked ever since we signed up to this damn mission. Maybe we should have stayed on Corvus and gone down all-guns-blazing." He grinned at Sarok. "It would at least have saved us plenty of saddle sores."

The Price of Freedom Part II: Velasia

***

They made relatively serene progress for several days. The weather was hot and dry, with few clouds overhead, and with the terrain largely treeless and brown, comprising loose soil and rocks, with occasional spindly, leafless bushes. Nevertheless, the ground was firm enough to allow the company to keep up a fair pace, sometimes at a trot, other times at a walk. Once they camped on a barren, unshaded plain, but otherwise they ended their days' journeys at small oases or other notable landmarks where water could still be gleaned from shaded hollows or deep gulleys.

On their fifth day, the landscape changed.

"This is *The Sink*," declared Regnarson, bringing his horse to a halt before Archaen and Sarok—the latter having managed to supplant Sentain as the woman's immediate riding companion, to the young man's envy. "It's a giant crater from some vast cosmic impact in the past that has filled with sand. I suppose it is the closest feature to a desert in all of Velasia. There is no water here, and the going will be slow, as we need to dismount to lead the horses to distribute weight more evenly across the sand. But the Sink's breadth isn't great at this latitude, and we should be across by nightfall—or at least, by midnight."

And so the entire party dismounted, forming a long line, two horses-and-walkers abreast.

Sentain paired with Miko—behind Archaen and Sarok—their horses positioned to their outsides, forming a protective barrier from the rays of the sun and the wind, which began to whip up almost immediately their journey began, and then increased throughout the morning. After three tiring hours, they came to a halt. They ate dried rations and drank from their water bottles, leaving their horses picketed in a circle around them.

"My calves are killing me," muttered Sentain, after they had fed, with the prospect of resuming their trek drawing close. "And ankles. This sand is a royal pain to walk on." And then a strong gust of wind threw sand into his mouth and eyes; he turned away and spluttered.

"It'll get worse, Irvan," said Archaen, sitting a short distance away. She had a light black scarf draped loosely across her mouth and nose. "As the temperature rises in the Sink, it causes strange patterns of air flow. By the hottest hours, perhaps mid-afternoon, the wind may be so strong we have to hunker down and wait it out."

"Ptchah!" Sentain rubbed sand from his mouth. "Now I see why we are moving as we are. The horses provide perfect protection from the sand."

"From the sand… *yes*." Archaen leapt up and headed towards her horse.

"Enabeth?" Sentain turned to Miko. "Did she just smile? Behind her mask? I saw it in her eyes."

Miko laughed, then coughed himself as he got a mouthful of sediment. Spitting first, he declared: "Yes, I saw it too. My cousin knows more than she is telling."

Sarok looked between the two men. "More about what, Miko?"

"She doesn't tell me everything." And then he checked the long knife at his belt, easing it up and down. "Just in case."

And so they carried on. As Archaen warned, the wind did continue to rise, and it did not just throw about sand. The party soon noticed small lifeforms swirling in the air between the grains: round, ochre-coloured insects the size of beans, and small leathery creatures of similar hue, which furled and unfurled into balls. The latter seemed to be hunting the former, closing around their prey when the wind brought them close together.

Then there was something else.

Sarok noticed one of the horses on his side, three rows in front, stumble, whinny, and then tip over completely, disappearing into the orange-red haze. Suddenly, there was an explosion of activity. The horse's rider leapt after her steed, while shouts rose and fell on the wind, and the twin lines broke apart. Archaen was quickly at his side, shouting into his ear: "Follow the others…" and then she was gone, bellowing instructions at those behind.

Sarok noticed those in front draw their knives in one hand while holding their reins in the other, all turning to face into their horses' sides. Then the horses began to sink to their knees in response to downwards tugs on their reins and the shouted commands of their riders. Sarok ignored his blade, needing both hands to steady his own horse. He stood foursquare to it and began to curse: "Come on, Stinky, get *fucking* down. Come on!"

At last, the horse began to respond—though whether to Sarok's urging or taking its cue from observing the behaviour of its fellows, he couldn't tell. He glanced to his right, to the rest of the outland party, and noticed that they were struggling too, as was Miko directly behind him, consequent of having only one useable arm. "Fuck! Okay. Stay, horse, *stay!*" He stumbled across to Miko, whose horse was staggering uncertainly. Together, by pressing on the horse's back, they got it to buckle its legs. But as the men also sank to their knees, and Miko looked across to his helper to nod his thanks, Sarok noticed a shape solidify in the sand behind the Leaguer at about head height.

"Look out... oh, fuck!" Weaponless, Sarok threw himself over the horse's bent back and past his kneeling colleague. He collided with something solid that was perhaps half his height, but muscular and immovable. Instantly, he felt himself punched a number of times simultaneously, in both his chest and back... but his mail armour was strong. Now enraged, he sent a questing hand towards the knife at his side, finding it on the third attempt, and drew it. The creature had by now wrapped a limb around him, rolling him completely over the horse and onto his back. Then a peculiar, horrific face took shape centimetres above his own: an eyeless ochre head with a central ball of uncertain function, beneath which was a wide mouth. Teeth like razor blades connected the upper and lower jaws, with gaps between them through which shaved food and flesh could pass.

"Eat this!" roared Sarok, thrusting his knife at the head. It glanced off one long tooth, deflecting into the space between it and the one to its side and then into the creature's mouth. Ochre spew gushed into his face; the creature ceased struggling, dropping its full weight upon him. Sarok wriggled out from under the corpse and looked up to find Miko's outstretched hand; as he took it, he became aware of more activity from beyond the man. Amid the swirling haze, gouts of sand were erupting like silicon geysers all along the line.

"What the fuck!" he shouted, as he regained a degree of safety behind the barrier of horse flesh.

Miko yelled a response, though his words were lost in the wind, the shouts, and a sudden scream of pain. Man? Woman? Horse?

Then one of the geysers erupted close by, and Sarok was momentarily blinded, as though someone had thrown a bucket of sand directly into his face. As he raised an arm and turned his head, he sensed something rising above the back of Miko's horse.

"Oh... f—!"

But the shape was immediately impacted by another burly object from off to Sarok's side in a convergence of shadows.

He desperately rubbed the sand from his eyes with his forearm—then jolted, as a shape dropped heavily onto the startled horse, which writhed but failed to stand.

With blurry vision, Sarok saw another of the rugged creatures... this one most definitely dead, a knife deeply embedded in its head.

Miko collapsed at his side. He coughed, then cried out: *"One-all."*

The assault lasted no longer than a minute, but the party stayed in its position for over an hour until the wind began to drop and visibility improved. Several horses were injured, and one had to be put down, but apart from a couple of sliced limbs, there were no significant human casualties.

***

"They're called sand devils," said Enabeth Archaen, her nose and mouth still obscured behind her scarf. The company was forming up, ready to leave, though the outlanders currently milled about uncertainly in a rough circle, looking to their leader. "They're rare: I didn't think we would meet any during our short crossing."

Miko slapped Sarok on the shoulder with his good hand. "And there will be at least two fewer for others to worry about now. Thanks, Narovy. I am in your debt."

Sarok grinned. "And I, yours. But I'm glad that you feel you owe. A man can never have enough people watching his back." Then he turned to Archaen. "*Sand devils*, eh? Something your people engineered, Ms Archaen?"

"Actually, no. They are a unique lifeform of the planet. The Desolate Quarter is shrinking: in the distant past it was much greater and the sand devils were a dominant species—but even then, they were sparsely scattered, given the lack of sustenance in the environment. Now they are few in number and mostly reside in the Sink."

"Surely a suitable project for your manipulations, no?"

"Yes, they are." The woman didn't elaborate.

After a sufficient pause, Sarok continued: "I sense a 'but', or some other caveat."

Archaen sighed. "Not really. Our attempts have so far failed. The problem has been creating a suitable confined environment for them to live and flourish in. They are creatures of the open spaces, and of climactic turbulence. Recreating that in a relatively small, enclosed space has proven difficult. And we have so many other projects to work on, creating lifeforms that can challenge us and help us to evolve—as we help them to evolve."

Sarok nodded. "I understand what you say. But you should come to Corvus—we have plenty of vicious creatures there for you to catch and adapt. You could start by cloning Brundt—"

At this, Mandelson coughed. Sarok looked at her and grinned. "A horrific prospect, I know, and one of nightmares."

Mandelson recovered quickly and returned a tight smile. "*Your* nightmares, perhaps." She winked and walked away.

Sarok waited for the woman to remove herself from earshot, then added quietly: "And you couldn't go far wrong using Mandelson as a base subject either."

***

It was the sixth day since leaving the Iron Gate, and the company was bivouacked in a dry river bed that held several pools of stubborn water, waiting to be replenished by a turn in the seasons. Kindling for a fire had been heaped up, but not yet set alight, as sufficient sunlight remained for all to lay out their bedding and attend to their gear.

"We are nearing the end," said Archaen. "Have you considered what will happen if we succeed?"

"In truth," Sarok wrinkled his brow in thought, "not really. My previous existence seems a lifetime away. A before-time. But much will depend upon you. Matters are largely out of my hands."

Archaen nodded sombrely. "Perhaps so. But if we finish this task—one we demanded of you—well, we are not a treacherous race. I hope even Irvan will agree that treachery is not one of our many flaws. So you will be free to leave in com Durrel's ship."

"As long as I promise not to reveal anything about the yeltoi and ganeroi to the Confederation?"

"That goes without saying. Although with distance, we would be hard pressed to stop you."

Sarok gave a wry smile. "I think you can rest easy on that score. There would be little for me to gain in revealing this matter, and it would lead to many questions from authorities about how I came upon this information—questions that I would not care to answer. And who would listen anyway, eh?"

Archaen's eyes quickly flicked to Sentain, then away again. "To you? Perhaps no one."

"So I suppose I would accept the ship. But to go where, I do not know. With com Durrel gone, my only source of immediate funds would go with him. His crew must be chafing at their quarantine aboard the ship, and keen to return to the Confederation, and they too pose a problem—"

"Not really," muttered Mandelson, though Sarok chose to ignore her.

"They wouldn't follow me and might rebel and force me to take severe actions. And without them, I couldn't fly the ship, nor do I have the funds to hire new crew at whatever dock I might disembark the current lot, and nor do I have a ready explanation as to why I might be in command of a missing craft bereft of its registered owner. This wouldn't matter on Corvus, of course, but if I were to dock there under present circumstances, I would not live long," he glanced at his bodyguard, as ever close by, "even with the redoubtable Vuller by my side."

The tall man looked up and smiled. "But I wouldn't make it easy on them, Boss. A good few would join us in the afterlife."

"You are too good for me, Vuller." And Sarok was suddenly struck by the truth of this, after so many years of association and service. "I couldn't ask that of you. For fuck's sake, man, I can't even pay you."

"No worries, Boss. I know you're good for it. Besides, I knew what I was getting into when you recruited me. It's my job. It's what I do."

Sarok found he couldn't look at the man. He felt… guilt? Shame? *Affection*? To ease his discomfort, he quickly returned his attention to Archaen. "No. I didn't achieve what I achieved before my fall by making bad decisions and pointless sacrifices. So, in short, I'm not sure what I would do. I need to think about my options. About how best to play the hand I have been dealt."

No one spoke for some seconds, then Archaen cautiously volunteered: "We are a unified society, Mr Sarok. We do not welcome outsiders readily into our fold—and only very, very rarely. But you have shown metal. And some degree of honour. Abide by our beliefs and I see no reason for you to leave. You… or Theodric."

Vuller started at the mention of his given name and opened his mouth as though to speak, but no words came out.

Sarok frowned: he wasn't aware that he or Vuller had ever mentioned the man's name to the woman; indeed, he'd not heard it spoken in a long time. Years? He looked askance at his bodyguard, nodded grimly, then looked back at Archaen. "You hinted at this before—and I thought nothing of it at the time. But that might now be an offer worth considering, as long as I could return to civilisation and *never* have to ride a horse again."

Vuller now found his voice, and laughed.

Even Archaen smiled.

But in the shadows, at the edge of the group, Sentain looked troubled and Mandelson glared.

***

It was nine days since they'd left the Iron Gate, and dusk was drawing in. The landscape was now notably greener, and it had even rained a touch earlier in the day—a light shower only, but a relief to all, especially the horses.

They were mounted once more, with the Sink well behind them and the going firmer. Sarok patted his horse on the neck absently, but Archaen noticed.

"Are you growing fond of your horse, Mr Sarok? Surely not?"

"Eh? To Stinky? Gods no!"

"Just as well," the woman looked forwards once more. "There is no point getting too attached. If we have to go to Tartax-Kul, the terrain is unsuitable for horses, so we will have to euthanise them. But at least we will eat well."

"Have to… *what*? I'm not about to…" Then Sarok noticed a lift to the woman's mouth in side profile. "Ah, very funny. The ice maiden does have a sense of humour after all."

At that moment, an excited shout came from somewhere to the front of the line.

"Riders! Riders coming!"

Archaen's gentle smile broadened. "Well, Mr Sarok, we'll soon know whether Stinky's fate is sealed or not, eh?"

Chapter 23

"… and Mikkel has continued on to Jinna," concluded Belias.

Facing the returning scouts—as Omdanan hovered at the woman's shoulder—was Regnarson, Archaen, Miko and Sarok. A short distance behind these, standing in a loose group, was the rest of the outland party, while the remainder of the vanguard of Narvik spread out in a semi-circle further back, giving the new arrivals space. All stood quietly and expectantly.

Regnarson turned to Archaen. "So now we know: the Sorcerer is not with his army."

"It seems not," replied the woman. "In that case, we must leave you now. Our path is back towards Tartax-Kul. The only consolation is that most of that fortress must have been emptied to provide such a large army, although I suppose he will still have more than enough to fend off a direct assault from our small party."

"Force would never have made a difference anyway," noted Sarok. "What does it matter if he has two thousand guards or twenty thousand? We must use subtlety and artifice to get close to him… and then maybe blast him with Sentain's staff."

Regnarson nodded at this. "You will have plenty of time to plan. Though we have crossed the Desolate Quarter, it is still over a week's ride to Tartax-Kul, and maybe two to three weeks on foot. Now you have horses and some competence at riding them, I don't think your journey with us has been in vain, or too costly. For our part, we will ride immediately to Jinna."

"Yes, see to the defence of the town. But please, Cousin, don't risk all in a suicidal charge. Wait for your main host and buy time for the forces of Ranvik and Sorvik to pass beneath the mountains."

Regnarson bowed. "I will. And I will also send further scouts back towards the Iron Gate to seek our forces and update them on the plan. Don't worry, Enabeth: I want to be at the feast celebrating my feats, not under the ground. I will be careful."

Archaen gave a small bow in return. "In that case, thank you for all your help, Torsten. Good luck against the army: you will have a hard task of it."

"As will you, Black Lady." The two embraced.

Watching this, Belias then turned to the young man at her shoulder. "And good luck to you too, Elian. Kill the sorcerer and then come and find me, eh?"

Omdanan startled when the blonde-haired woman stepped close, but he was then more than happy to return the hug.

***

Sentain and Vuller rode side-by-side, far enough back from the pair in front—Archaen and Sarok—to be unable to hear their conversation. It was the day after they had split from the Narvi.

"I wouldn't worry about it," said Vuller, casting a quick glance at his companion. "I don't think he's trying to supplant you in her affections."

Sentain returned the glance. "Affections? Ah, no, it's not what you think."

"You're saying you're not envious, then?"

"Well, no, I mean, of course I enjoy her company. She is fascinating..." he sensed Vuller's wry smile even without having to see it, "it's just, well..."

Vuller laughed. "Mr Sarok's interests are in information—if that's really all you're after—and his needs are liable to be as great as yours. But he has a certain momentum that you can't match. He won't be denied. It's something he's always had."

"Always?" Sentain sensed a way to redirect the conversation. "You've known him a long time?"

"Ever since he first came to Corvus."

"*Came* to Corvus? I thought he was a native?"

Vuller continued to look ahead, the reins of his horse held loosely in one hand. "Nope. He originally came from a world settled by émigrés from Old Russia. When he first arrived, over thirty years ago, he was working for one of the syndicate's off-world partners. He'd come to see the big boss after taking over the group on his planet. He soon started recruiting, and I was among his first. Even then, it was obvious to me he was recruiting people for himself, not the syndicate. And the rest is history. He supplanted the premier within two years and has held power ever since."

"You mean, until current circumstances? Ah, I didn't mean…"

Vuller waved away the attempted apology. "Sure. It is what it is. But if anyone can rise again, it's him."

Sentain was silent for a moment, then hazarded: "But will he try? A few days ago, he seemed less certain. Do you think he might accept Enabeth's offer to stay on Arkon?"

"I honestly don't know. If you'd asked me that question any time up until then, I'd have said there was no chance. But he may have done the calculations and decided that staying might be the best option. I have never really understood his drive. I think he sees life as a series of problems to solve, and in solving them, he has ended up where he has. It's not because of some long term lust for power."

"But he has talked a lot about revenge. That seems a strong motivation."

Vuller shrugged. "I think he sees revenge as simply another tool in his armoury. In our world, unanswered sleights suggest weakness. But perhaps in Brundt's case, there is more emotion than judgment."

They rode on in silence for a short time. Sentain couldn't help but try to decipher what was going on ahead. Archaen rode stiff backed, looking forwards, but Sarok was constantly leaning across towards the woman, speaking and gesticulating. Sentain shook his head, as though to clear it of absurd thoughts. He glanced at Vuller once more.

"But what of you? Enabeth mentioned you in her potential offer too."

"I go with the boss. If he goes, I go."

"And if he stays—what then? He won't need a bodyguard here." Sentain noticed the other wriggle on his saddle; noticed him frown and raise a hand to his head to wipe a drop of sweat from his brow. He continued: "Would you go back to Corvus, your home? Don't you have friends and family there?"

"Few family and even fewer friends—especially after Brundt's clear out."

"So would you go or stay?"

"I don't know. I have been one thing, and known one life, for thirty years. Corvus would be dangerous, but what is there here for me?"

"Free beer?"

Vuller looked aside, saw Sentain smiling, and smiled back. "I'd forgotten about that. Yeah. Free beer. Free food."

"And the people are attractive. Men, women—"

"Women!" said Vuller, rapidly. "Just so we're clear!"

Sentain laughed. "I make no judgment against those of either or any persuasion. So… women. Elian seems to have had no problem. If we get through this, you might find your reputation enhanced as one of the Black Lady's party, and that might make you suddenly attractive."

Vuller laughed once more. "Stop! You're making it hard to resist. But…" he suddenly sobered. "But what of the boss?"

"What of him?" Sentain looked between Vuller and the man riding several metres in front. "Perhaps you could still serve him, but not as a bodyguard. Maybe as a friend?"

This time, Vuller was left speechless.

***

They had been riding south-east, hoping to intersect the trail of the orc army. On the second day after leaving the Narvi, they succeeded in their search.

"Well, *that's* pretty obvious," said Sarok, as they sat on their horses in a loose cluster, the bruised land before them. "So, now we just follow this path right back to its point of origin in Tartax-Kul, no?"

"That's right," said Archaen. Her eyes were on Omdanan, who'd nudged into the scuffed and trampled area. She called out: "What are you looking for, Elian?"

He swung his horse around to face her. "I'm not sure. This is similar to what we came across further north, but also somehow different."

"Different?" said Sarok. "What do you mean?"

"I need to look more..." Omdanan trailed off. He turned his mount and moved further into the trashed area. The others waited for him to enact his own magic.

Omdanan directed his horse this way and that, occasionally stooping low to peer at something on the ground, then moving on a little way and checking again. He paid special attention to a hacked-at bush in the middle of the area. Then he dismounted.

"What is it, Elian?" asked Archaen at last. "You seem unsettled."

"Ah, well, it's just that this isn't right." He paced some more, bending to look at the churned earth once again. "This is *new*. But why would you...?" He raised his head abruptly and looked to his right, further off the track. Swiftly mounting up, he goaded his horse in that direction, climbing a sandy slope and disappearing from view.

"He's clearly lost it," said Sarok. "Maybe too much sun?"

"I don't think so," said Archaen. "I have learnt not to doubt him."

Omdanan appeared again at the top of the slope, twisting his horse this way and that, a ball of barely restrained energy. "There's another trail! It's as I thought. They're not travelling in the rubbish of the army, but parallel to it."

"They?" exclaimed Sarok. "What do you mean, lad, *they*?"

"Another force. A big one, but nowhere near as big. I think it's com Durrel."

***

They moved away from the trampled land, and dismounted. Standing in a rough circle, they debated options.

"How can we be sure?" asked Sarok, carefully. "We've already spent many days in this barren wasteland. We were going to Tartax-Kul, and then detoured to ride with the Narvi until we picked up the orcs' trail. We found the army, and com Durrel wasn't with it. Then we turned south. And now… what? We turn around and head back north again?"

"You're against this?" asked Miko, standing at Archaen's side.

"Not at all. I've learnt to be flexible. In fact, I've always prided myself on an ability to change my mind in the face of new facts—a trait I rarely find so well-developed in others. I just need to be sure we are interpreting the signs right. How can we be so certain that this new force includes com Durrel? Talk me through it."

Miko and Archaen exchanged looks, sub-vocally negotiating who would answer. Archaen seemed to get the decision. "I am not sure there is much to say. It is less a case of evidence for com Durrel attempting to join his force, than a lack of evidence against. I always wondered why he would stay in his fortress rather than miss out on all the fun, so I was surprised when he was not with his main army."

"Yes, I was slightly surprised too," said Sarok. "Go on."

"There is not much more. Here is another significant force, which Elian reckons numbers several hundred. What need would his already large army have for further reinforcements? And if the new force is simply conveying a message, why so large and cumbersome? To me, it speaks of a change of mind. And com Durrel—whether for protection or simple vanity—is unlikely to travel anywhere with only a small company. Finally, there are the strange linear marks…" In one place, Omdanan had found two long, parallel indentations in the soft soil. "What are these? Not a wagon, or else they would be continuous. They suggest to me the rails of a litter. Something being carried, then set down with a change of bearers, then picked up again. What would be carried on such a vehicle, if not com Durrel himself?"

Sarok pouted and looked down in contemplation, observing his booted feet in the dust. He flexed up and down on his soles and nodded. "Why walk, when you can be carried, eh?" He looked up. "And they don't use horses, so how else would com Durrel move? That makes perfect sense. But could this be a case of twisting the evidence to fit what we want to believe? Could this be something else? A litter of supplies? But then why not similar marks in the tracks of the main host? What about a weapon of some sort—a newly developed siege weapon? A canon?"

Archaen glanced quickly at Miko. "Ah, I see what you mean. I did not think of that. But it's unlikely. There is no gunpowder in this world. I suppose com Durrel might have revealed this to the orcs, but he has been playing the game within the rules so far—given that we accept the validity of his use of the staff of power. So why up the ante when there is little need?"

"And also, why would he give anyone else another source of power that might ultimately be used against him?" Sarok hooded his eyes. "That does not sound like the megalomaniac I know." He looked down at his feet once more and spoke low. "At least we may now face him in the open." He slapped his thighs. "Good!" Looking at the Leaguers, he declared: "I'm convinced. So let's move. Let's run the fucker down!"

Archaen nodded. "If this new group does contain com Durrel, then it will be fearsome enough to tackle; but if it joins up with his main army, then it is difficult to see how any force in Velasia could contend with it. And this would also spell doom for the yeltoi of Jinna, and indeed, all of Bratha." She shook her head and turned to Omdanan: "How long, Elian?"

"Not long. Maybe three days ago. But they are travelling slowly. We can catch them soon. A day or so?"

The woman crouched down, as though that might help her think, while the rest of the party—afoot and holding the reins of their horses—waited for her to come to a decision. At last she looked up: "We will move as quick as we can—but you can move quicker, and approach more quietly. Go, Elian. Fly! Find them, and then report back to us." She stood, settled the reins in her hand, and placed a hand on her horse's shoulder. "Up all!"

The Price of Freedom Part II: Velasia

Omdanan was already mounted: he put his heels to his horse's flanks, and the beast surged away.

***

Omdanan had never felt such exhilaration. He still travelled light—his mail and other excess gear stored on the party's sole pack horse—and so he was able to significantly outpace his comrades, particularly given his skill in the saddle and the symbiosis he had formed with Matusal, the name he had secretly given his black stallion.

He galloped hard, soil and stones flicking up from Matusal's flashing hooves, only slowing to allow the horse an occasional rest. And he didn't stop for night, either, as the light of the moon of Arkon and the blaze of stars—filling the sky with glory in the absence of the interfering lights of civilisation—was sufficient to illuminate the temporary road that had been rolled into the landscape by hundreds of heavy feet. In his mind, he was back on Meridian, illicitly roaming the land alone, away from the strictures of Enbargo, but now he was armed and unconstrained. He knew he did not have to return to sour and reproving looks or castigation from his unsympathetic people in the morning; he could go on and on, wild and free and powerful.

On through the night he rode. As Arkon's star began to peer from the horizon to the east, he came across a small stream, confirming that he had truly left the Desolate Quarter behind. He allowed the horse a longer rest, and this time accepted a need for sleep. But he allowed himself three hours only, and woke naturally, according to some internal alarm clock he found he could set at will. Then he snatched a dried strip of jerky from his pack, placed it between his teeth, mounted up, and set off again, only raising a hand to tear off a chunk of the tough meat once the horse had found its stride.

As with the main orc army, he smelt this one before he saw it, and dropped Matusal to a trot. Soon after, he noticed a darker line across the northern horizon—the rear of the smaller, following force. He knew his eyesight was better than the orcs', but he didn't dare approach much closer. For an hour or so, he shadowed the party, until the landscape began to undulate more, and he recognised the hilly lands he had come across days earlier with Belias. Then he set off at a gallop, tending north-west, to navigate around this force—as he'd had done before with the scouting party—in order to find a vantage point from which to observe it.

***

"They are there," panted Omdanan, pulling hard at Matusal's reins to bring the horse to a halt. "Com Durrel, Yadzen and Dettler."

"Excellent, Elian!" said Archaen. "And what force is with them? What else did you see?"

"There are about two hundred and fifty orcs with them. Most wear brown, but his immediate guards wear red. As we suspected, he is being carried on a shaded litter by ten orcs. Yadzen stays at his side always. Dettler usually walks behind."

"How are they arranged?" asked Sarok. "If we get close, can Sentain take them down with one blast?"

Omdanan furrowed his brow in thought. "I don't know. I don't think so. They have a wide range of march. The litter is surrounded by the reds, but even they keep more than a spear's length away. The browns—apart from the litter bearers—are kept well away. It's almost as if com Durrel doesn't trust them. So I guess it depends on the range of Dr Sentain's staff."

"We may only get one shot at this," mused Sarok, "so we have to be sure. Is there any place we can force his troops together to allow an ambush? A gorge we can overlook? A forest trail?"

"The land is mostly open hills between here and Haradan."

"Haradan?" said Sarok. "I wonder…"

"Yes!" said Omdanan excitedly. "He will have to pass it. But will he stop?"

Archaen looked between the two men, then focused on the crime lord, who looked down in thought. "Mr Sarok—what do you think? You probably know com Durrel better than any of us, not just personally but psychologically?"

Sarok looked up and smiled. "You mean, from one very bad man to another? As it happens, I agree with you. In a way, I know com Durrel deeply. It's not a question of will he stop, but for how long."

"Why do you say that?" asked Miko.

"Several reasons. First, com Durrel likes comfort. He is used to the fine things in life. Do you remember how he moaned at everything and anything in Arakkan and Verano? A yeltoi town—largely whole—will offer him luxury compared to what he has had to live with in his tower and on the road. He will want a proper bed with soft sheets. A roof. A warming fire. Whatever food can be scrounged from the ruins—and I am sure there will be some. And he will be able to sleep safely away from the orcs he probably despises and distrusts."

"Makes sense," said Miko. "And second?"

"Second, he will want to bask in the destruction he has unleashed. He will want to walk through the ruins and enjoy them…" and suddenly, Sarok was back on Religon, walking through the ruins of his headquarters, imagining the satisfaction of the forces that had done that to him, their pleasure in inverse proportion to his pain… "and he will want to appraise his new possession."

"Is there a third?"

"Does there need to be?" Sarok shook his head. "No. That is enough. Com Durrel will pause in Haradan, and in those narrow streets he will give us our best chance of laying a trap. But we need to get there with time to inspect the arena and make our plans."

Archaen turned back to the Meridian. "Can we beat him to Haradan, Elian?"

Omdanan nodded enthusiastically. "We can, if we ride quick."

"Then lead on."

Chapter 24

They rode into Haradan through the main gate, the horses stepping gingerly over one fallen door and then passing a second, which was bent back and hanging precariously from a single tortured hinge.

The party travelled in silence past the burned, two-storey dwellings around the gate, following Omdanan. At Sarok's suggestion, the young Meridian led them to the town's main square, accessed via another arch that ran beneath the upper storey of a wood-and-plaster building with a single window from which an observer could watch all traffic entering or leaving the square. Noticing this, Sarok nodded to himself and looked to Archaen beside him, indicating upwards.

The square was of similar size to the one they'd encountered at Hustem, and like that one it held the main civic buildings: the mayor's palace, and a large church to Yamaga, the yeltoi god. The wanton fires set near the gate had not made it this far, although the marauding orcs had: the square was strewn with rubbish from the main buildings: clothes, smashed pots, desecrated green and blue banners from the church. Many of the doors around the square had been smashed open, and most of the lower storey windows were broken.

The party dismounted in the centre of the square and clustered together.

Archaen turned to Sarok. "It seems we are now following your lead. I am content to listen."

"Thank you. But do not mistake me as omniscient or prescient. I simply consider likelihoods. And for me, the greatest likelihood is that com Durrel will come here. He will not be content to settle into an inferior abode, so he will take the mayor's palace—which I'm pleased to see is relatively unharmed." Sarok turned to Omdanan. "How much time do we have, boy? How long until they get here?"

"Not long, sir. It is mid-morning now, so… late afternoon? Certainly they will be here before nightfall. Maybe eight hours?"

"In other words, late in the day. Good. In that case, he'll definitely stay the night, rather than camping in the wilds. To be safe, let's plan on them being here in six hours. I expect com Durrel will want to tour the town first, to measure his new domain, but he'll return here to sleep. We need to assess the state of the palace and perhaps tidy the space we want to direct him towards. Work out how he might arrange his force: what numbers he'll keep with him in the palace, and where. Consider where the rest will be barracked. Look for places where we might hide safely, and from where we might strike. We also need to remove the horses so they don't give us away. And once all this is done, we'll need to plan how to strike, and when." Sarok rasped at his beard and frowned. "In spite of what I said a few days ago, I do not think he'll stay more than the one night: that will suffice for him to leave his mark, like a dog pissing on a wall. He'll want to hurry on to Jinna."

"All good," said Archaen. "Direct us as you will."

"Fine. To start then, Ms Archaen, can I ask you to deal with the horses, as you have the best facility with them? Lead them to a spot out of town on the opposite side to the orcs' march and picket them securely there."

The woman gave a serene smile. "As you wish."

"Mandelson, sweep the square. Work out where the orcs will be bivouacked. In the square? The church?"

"Sure."

"Miko, perhaps you can check the house over the arch to the square: it is on the most direct route from the gate. I suspect we'll want to put a lookout there to watch the comings and goings of the enemy. Make sure we can get in and out and hide if needs be."

Miko smiled and bowed his head in acknowledgement.

"Omdanan—I'll need a lookout at the front gate and a tracker. You're the best. Find a place near the gate to observe our expected visitors and calculate a safe route by which you can follow them unseen and return here. Can you use the rooftops? Are they secure?"

"Yes, sir."

"And for now, Vuller and Sentain—with me. I need your tactical nous, Vuller, to work out the palace and how we might take advantage of the space. And Sentain, I need to find an ideal place for you to hide, from where you might strike if needed, when the time is right."

"Yes, Boss," said Vuller.

Sentain smiled sheepishly. "Er, right, okay."

Sarok looked around the party. "I want all back here in five hours' time to discuss what we have learnt. We'll have a brief window of opportunity to strike, so let's not fuck this up."

***

At the appointed time, with Arkon's sun half way down the sky and heading towards the Skythrust Mountains, the party reassembled in the central square of Haradan. Omdanan was last to arrive, jogging through the archway to the town's main gate.

Sarok sat on the top of the stepped rise to the entrance of the palace, while Vuller and Sentain lounged a couple of steps below him, and Archaen, Miko and Mandelson stood about on the cobbles facing these. "And now we are all here," said their temporary leader. "Any sign of them yet, boy?"

"No, sir. But I should not stay long. From this elevation, we will not see them arrive. And from the towers by the gate, we will get no more than ten minutes' warning. I measured the distance to the pass through the hills that they'll come by. And here, we are only five or six minutes' march from the gate, so it's possible they could be there by the time I return… but I think they're still be a couple of hours away."

Sarok nodded approval. "Good job. Now, what else? Ms Archaen—the horses are settled?" The woman simply nodded. "Thank you." Sarok turned: "Mandelson—you have checked the square. Your thoughts?"

The woman tapped the butt of her spear on the ground. "The church has been trashed. But it's a big space and might hold much of their force—if Omdanan is correct about their numbers. The other buildings around could only hold a few each, and they are cluttered, so I would discount them. If I were a general and thought I was safe, I would barrack most of my troops in the church and leave some to keep watch in the square—assuming com Durrel will take the palace. If so, we might have a chance."

"Why do you say that?"

"The church has a small back entrance, hidden behind drapes, and it is locked, so there is only really the one entrance you can see…" she gestured to the side of the square, where two wide wooden doors, about two metres high and of similar width, currently stood open, looking like the mouth of some giant, prostrate beast. "There is also plenty of kindling inside. It's a potential death trap. If we had a bag of incendiary grenades, we could burn the fuckers on their sleeping cloaks. Success would depend on how many sleep there, and how many they leave on duty in the square or elsewhere."

"We have no grenades, but we have the next best thing, eh, Sentain?"

The anthropologist smiled back, but he looked almost ill thinking about the prospect of what he might have to do.

"And as for com Durrel," noted Sarok, "yes, I'm convinced he'll use the palace. There's an audience chamber through the doors behind, and various rooms on the upper level. As there was little in the chamber to trash, it's generally untouched. Some of the rooms upstairs, including the mayor's bedroom, appear to have been used as toilets. But the good doctor cleaned the worst of that up."

"Yeah, thanks for getting me to do that," muttered Sentain.

"So, there's now no deterrent to com Durrel. We even found new sheets and blankets in a storeroom and stacked them nearby. It's virtually an invitation to stay."

"So, is the plan to lure him into this room, and then to strike?" asked Miko.

"Not quite. If com Durrel takes these chambers, he'll undoubtedly have the whole palace searched, and there's nowhere inside we could readily hide in silence."

"Then what's the use?" wondered Sentain. "Why did you get me to do… *that*?"

"Because, Doctor, a successful campaign depends upon knowing where your enemy is or will be. Ms Archaen made the chess analogy before. We now know—or at least suspect, with some confidence—that their *king* will be here during the nighttime hours. And from this, we can guess that Yadzen and Dettler will take the rooms next to his, and some of his red-armoured bodyguards will guard the upper storey. The rest will probably sleep in the audience chamber. With this in mind, we can now decide on where to best place our pieces."

Miko grunted assent. "And I can help with this. The upper storey bridge with the window over the arch is perfect. It gives views into the square and along the main road from the gate. It is accessed by the two buildings to either side, and they're opposite the palace…" he pointed directly across the square. "One of these must have been searched previously, but the other was ignored. I took the liberty of making both entrances unappetising. I also damaged the stairways to both—but ensured one is still usable. There is room upstairs to hold us all."

"*Nice*, Miko."

The Leaguer held up a hand to indicate that he hadn't finished. "I also broke through to the roof and stacked some chests beneath as steps. I hope it doesn't rain! But this will give us an escape route if needed. I couldn't pull myself up with one arm, but perhaps Elian could check. He might be able to travel all the way to the main gate over the rooftops."

"Excellent!"

Archaen had been quiet until now. She nodded approvingly. "I like these moves, Mr Sarok. But if com Durrel places his pieces as you suspect, and we can hide undetected across from him, what then? Do you yet have a plan?"

"A full one? No. We must see their actual numbers and dispositions. But the best time to attack is just before dawn. The orcs apparently have similar biorhythms to humans. They sleep at night, so they'll be dozy when *we* are dozy.

The Price of Freedom Part II: Velasia

From the building across the square, we are close, and may be able to break out with surprise and violence. If com Durrel is in his small room, his scope for action with his staff will be limited. There is hope we might bottle up his main force in the church, and otherwise sow confusion, then surprise him as he emerges into the audience chamber. But let's now set up in our new HQ. Omdanan—come too. See if you can use Miko's access to get to the gate and back along the roofline. The rest of us need to be battened down before the foe arrive. Let's move."

***

"Come on, come on," snarled com Durrel. "If you don't put in some effort, I'll fry you lot as well, you lazy fuckers!"

The eight orcs holding the poles of the palanquin in which com Durrel reclined—on cushions, within a rectangular wooden box with open sides—attempted to increase their speed over the gently undulating ground, but with little obvious success. Beside the palanquin, Yadzen loped along easily, in spite of being encumbered by chain mail and his heavy sword, while Dettler wheezed in exertion, in spite of being weighed down by nothing more than his dirty leather clothing. Around the palanquin, the imperial guard of Tartax-Kul—a company of Mangu's Reapers, dressed in their hardened red-leather armour and carrying spears—formed a protective square, separating their ruler from the larger force of the Two Horns regiment, which wore brown and was led by General Paramok. The bulk of the main regiment roved ahead of the litter.

Several hundred metres away, the main gate of deserted Haradan slowly drew near, its low stone walls topped by a taller wooden palisade, part of which was scorched black from fire. Two stone towers stood beside the open arch into town. Little else of Haradan could be appreciated from here, save the red tiles of roofs forming the skyline above the top of the parapet.

Com Durrel leant out to Yadzen's side for a better look. "Where's Paramok?"

"Up front. He will secure the gate."

"Secure it from what? Rats? Ghosts?"

"It's best to be sure, sir."

"Okay. This is… okay. Stop! Let me off!"

The litter bearers slowed to a panting halt. Com Durrel climbed from his transport to stand beside his trusted bodyguard. He glowered at the enervated orcs and raised his staff—momentarily tempted to castigate his bearers—but then he thumped the staff down on the firm, grass-covered earth. "You lot are lucky—*today*. Tomorrow, I might not be so lenient. Follow at the back." He turned and strode off towards the gate on his own two feet, the square of protectors around moving in synchronicity to maintain their distance and formation. Dettler rounded the palanquin and came to stride at the left of his master.

By the time they reached the gate, most of Paramok's regiment had passed through and taken position along the edge of the street that headed into the heart of the town, while some orcs had climbed up onto the parapet by the towers and looked down on the arriving party.

Standing within the open square inside the gate, com Durrel turned full circle to fully appreciate his new possession. His expression was difficult to read.

Dettler was still out of breath and had a stitch in the side. They had moved quickly over the last couple of weeks, with very little rest, urged on by com Durrel in order to put distance between them and the nascent rebellion in Tartax-Kul, and to close the gap to the main army as quickly as possible. But they were never going to catch the main force unless Haradan put up a fight and forced a siege, and even then, resistance was likely to be short. En route, they had come across a messenger with news of the fall of Haradan, and so they had known what to expect.

"Stop gasping, Wormtongue," said com Durrel. "You're like an asthmatic ancient. I can barely hear myself think." He used the end of his staff to strike Dettler on the side of the knee, causing him to squeal and collapse to the ground. Com Durrel glared at the man—then thumped him in the chest for good measure. "Stay in the dirt, man. That's where you belong." As Dettler rolled onto his front, com Durrel put one booted foot on the other's back and pressed down, leaning into him with all his weight. Around them, several of the Reapers gave amused snorts.

"What now, sir?" asked Yadzen, frowning. "The day is waning."

Com Durrel at last raised his foot and switched his attention to his bodyguard. "You too, Yadzen? Can't a god get a moment to enjoy a victory? Very well. There is always tomorrow. I don't suppose a small delay will make much difference. Let's go and find my bed for the night. Where did the ruler of this dump live? I'll have my dinner seated on his throne… on *my* throne."

Yadzen bowed. "Of course, sir. The seat of power will likely be in the centre of town."

"Then let's go. Instruct the rabble. Oh, and Wormtongue…" he turned to look back at the sprawling Dettler, whose face was smeared with dirt and ash from the cobbles, with blood trickling from a split lip. "Find me some decent food. There must be some in town—they can't have taken everything. Storehouses? Warehouses? Try the docks by the lake. Use that tiny mind of yours."

And then, just for the hell of it, com Durrel thrust his staff into the other's groin.

***

As Dettler stared morosely over Lake Haradan, he heard footsteps behind and the soft chink of iron chains sliding against each other. Only one member of his party wore chain mail; the orcs wore hardened leather armour. Without turning, he spoke softly: "So, here we are, back in civilisation of sorts."

"At least the yeltoi got out. The buildings can be rebuilt."

Dettler continued to stare at the lake. He sat on a stone jetty, his legs dangling over the water and the wreck of a rowing boat. "I suppose we should be thankful. I will never forget the carnage at Ultis." At last he turned to look up at the man standing behind him. "Carnage that we helped cause by not standing up to him."

Yadzen frowned down at his colleague. "Perhaps. But we each have our own justifications for that. And we did not take a direct part in the massacre, nor would we have of our own free will."

"Do you think that will wash with our judges? With the Leaguers, when they eventually catch up with us and put an end to com Durrel's sadistic game? Or even…" he looked up at the late afternoon sky—where clouds were beginning to pile up, suggesting rain—and lifted a hand: "Up there? I'm not a religious man—few are nowadays—but if there is some sort of creator, what will he think of us? Will our excuses be valid? Have we done enough?"

Yadzen shrugged. "For my part, I have done all I can. I was—I am—a man of war. I was damned well before Mr com Durrel took over my controls."

"And Hansa?" The men had not spoken of the incident until now. Dettler knew that Yadzen had killed the Leaguer from Narvik, but had feared speaking of the matter, feared how his colleague might respond. But now he was tired in a way he'd never been before, not just physically but mentally, perhaps too tired to even be scared.

"Yes, Hansa. I was commanded to take his life, and so I did. When my sword took off his head, I felt nothing apart from a kind of satisfaction at fulfilling an order. He is just one more name on a roll call of names I have taken."

"But surely the first in a long time? The first *human* in the many years of your service to com Durrel?"

Yadzen looked grim. "Not quite. There was one other incident in the past, when com Durrel was incautious with his commands, before he fully realised what he'd got with me. But that was covered up."

Dettler continued to evaluate the man, who glanced at him and then looked away and out over the water. At last he wondered: "Do you think there is any hope of redemption for us?"

"For you… maybe. But you will have to face your fears. For me? No. I am trapped. I will only be released when he is dead." He looked down at Dettler again, his expression taut. "*His* death is the only way. Should you dare… if you dare…

you must say nothing to me. If I hear, I will cut you down like Hansa." The grey-haired man appeared to struggle to force the words out, his teeth clenching. He finally hissed: "Please… *dare!*" And then he thumped one hand on his thigh, turned, and strode back towards the orcs who were still ransacking the buildings along the dock front.

From a rooftop nearby, a hidden observer withdrew and began to make his way back across the tiles to the centre of town.

***

Omdanan clambered down the makeshift stairs from the roof of the grand house on the main square where the rest of the party had holed up. He descended into shadow and silence.

"Boss—it's Elian," came Vuller's voice from nearby.

Omdanan's eyes took a few moments to get used to the low light, with the windows on this upper floor having been covered by blankets. He noticed the tall shape of Vuller close by, and then a shorter figure moved towards him from the other end of the room, where there was an open door that led to the enclosed bridge over the arch to the square. Other shapes closed in behind the short man, until the whole party was clustered around.

Sarok spoke low. "Welcome back, boy. It's been the best part of two hours. We're eager to hear your report. We've deliberately kept low in here, though we've heard the orcs passing beneath the tunnel. They're setting up in the square, no?"

"Yes. You're right. I followed them from the front gate. Com Durrel came straight here. He toured the square, then went into the palace. I think he's still there."

"Think?"

"Well, I waited for some time, but when he didn't come out I thought I would see what others have been up to. Most of the orcs are still in the square. As you predicted, the brown-armoured orcs have set up in the church, but they have had parties scouring the area around, bringing back plunder—mostly things to burn. But Mr Dettler was ordered to take a larger group to the docks to look for food. I followed them. After a while, Yadzen came and spoke to Mr Dettler. I followed Yadzen back to the square. When he went into the palace, I came here."

Archaen was directly behind Sarok. "So, you were right, Mr Sarok. *Impressive*."

"No, not impressive," muttered Sarok, "simply logical. But what else can you tell us, lad? The red orcs?"

"Some are in the palace, and some are guarding outside. I counted at least thirty. If they are a full company, they'll number at most thirty-six. The only others allowed in the palace are Yadzen, Mr Dettler, and one of the browns. I think he is the leader of the regiment."

"Good. Anything more? Even a small detail? Are the orcs in good shape? Are they alert? What is the relationship between the browns and reds? What is their relationship to the general? How is com Durrel and the others?"

"Ah, I didn't sense any tension. The browns are wary of the reds and clearly inferior—like the ones we've fought before. The reds are generally bigger and stronger. They seem like proper warriors, if you know what I mean."

"I do. Anything else?"

"No. Not really. Except, well, there is Mr Dettler, sir."

"What about Dettler?"

Omdanan scratched his head, wondering how to explain what he had seen. "He... does not look well. He is not treated well. Mr com Durrel humiliated him and beat him by the gate. And he shouted abuse at him in the square before sending him to look for food."

"Very interesting. Is he still at the docks?"

"He was when I left. I didn't get the impression he was keen to get back to the others."

Sarok clasped one hand over a fist. "This may be an opportunity. Who knows Dettler? Who has spoken to him?"

"I have," volunteered Archaen, "on a number of occasions. During these conversations, he made clear his distaste for his employer, or master, or whatever you wish to call him. He saw his job as to finalise the deal between us so he could escape his obligations. So—is he a devotee of com Durrel? *No*. Do I think he will help us, or at least, not betray us if we reveal ourselves to him? I cannot say. If he were one of my people, I would be sure, but Mr Dettler is one of *you*. He is clever, but is he noble? My gut feeling is that he may not be brave enough to help directly, though I doubt he'd betray us."

Sarok nodded and pursed his lips. "I rarely spoke to him, but we all saw his humiliation at com Durrel's hands in Arakkan. I never believed he joined the others of his own free will." He grinned at Archaen. "But if you're suggesting that he and I are psychologically similar and I might better divine his mentality, I hate to disappoint you. I'm from Corvus, and he's from the Confederation, albeit the fringes of their society. We're not all alike, Ms Archaen. So, I have no greater insight here than you." He paused to consider some more. "Nevertheless, I do agree with you, in that I don't think he would run off to com Durrel to squawk about seeing us. What profit would there be in this for him? To receive a pat on the head from his master, like an obedient dog? To buy enough favour for the mistreatment to stop, or reduce it? Would com Durrel really respond in this way? I suspect Durrel would likely consider him even less well, an even greater worm, and even increase his derision and harsh treatment. And if this is my conclusion, would Dettler likely come to a different one? Does anyone else have an opinion or disagree with my analysis?"

The others in the cluttered, darkened room looked at each other and Sarok. Some shrugged; others gently shook their heads.

Miko said: "Dettler is a strange and cowardly creature—but I agree with you. I don't see why he would betray us directly. But could he do so indirectly, through loose words or suspect body language? And you mentioned *profit*, and this is perhaps the key term. What are the chances of him actually helping us? To do so would clearly be a risk to him and could be terminal if we were to fail."

Sarok raised his hands. "This is the crux of the dilemma. Can we convince him that he'll benefit by helping us in some way, in *any* way? I would not expect him to stab com Durrel in the back, but he might at least provide some information, or a diversion, and this might give us the edge we need to succeed. There is risk involved with everything, but I think, on balance, approaching him is a risk worth taking. Do any disagree?"

From the shadowed figures in front of him came a couple of murmured negatives, but otherwise silence. "Very well, since there are no objections… Omdanan…" he turned to the young man, whose face was partially lit by sunlight spilling through the hole in the roof. "Can you lead me to him? Is there a chance we can intercept him before he returns to the square?"

Omdanan considered the matter for a moment. "Maybe. If we go now. He was with a party of orcs, looting the dockside warehouses. If we can attract his attention before he returns…"

"Then we two will go. Lead the way."

The Meridian stepped onto the first chest that formed the bottom step to the roof, then had a thought and turned. "Ah, sir, are you sure? We must move quietly and keep low."

Sarok unfastened the scabbard at his waist and let his sword drop to the floor. "There. I'll just take my knife. That is the quiet part dealt with. And as for the 'low', are there any here 'lower' than me?"

***

Omdanan led the way over the rooftops of Haradan. They kept to the reverse pitch of the roofs to the side facing the square, to reduce their chances of being seen from below. And once they were away from the square, the narrowness of the streets ensured that they were completely hidden from anyone walking the cobbles. They moved slowly and cautiously, as the tiles were not in great shape, and occasionally these would slip under their feet. Once, a tile was unsettled and slid across the roof to drop onto the street. The pair came to a halt, but there were no sounds from below, and after a minute or so they carried on.

Haradan was not a large town for humans. It would have taken less than ten minutes to walk from the square to the docks, but it took significantly longer than this on the rooftops, especially as they twice had to drop down into the street to cross a transverse road—and then regain the roof through the attic spaces of other houses. The third time they dropped to ground level, Omdanan bustled Sarok through a broken door at a house at the corner of two streets.

"Now I see why you were gone two hours," whispered Sarok. "I thought your travel was easier than this."

Omdanan smiled. "It was. I, er, was able to climb the walls from the outside, but maybe you…"

"Maybe I can't? Don't worry, boy. I'm a realist. But what now? Why are we here?"

"At the end of this line of houses are the warehouses and docks. If we get any closer, the orcs may see us. I am not sure about the best place to try to attract Mr Dettler's attention. Perhaps if you wait here, I can scout some more? I need to get back on the roof."

"Sure. Off you go."

Omdanan nodded once and headed back through the half-open door.

Ten minutes passed, then fifteen. Twice, Sarok heard voices from outside and withdrew into the deepest shadows, clutching his knife. But he didn't hear his third near-visitor and was startled when a shape slid through the doorway.

"Fuck, lad! Are you human, or a ghost?"

"He is coming soon. Most of the orcs have headed back, carrying sacks of food. There are five or six still near him, but they are about to come on. The problem is, they have piled up other crates and sacks to be collected, so I expect the ones that left are going to come back soon, at least once more. They are using carts they found on the docks."

"Solution?"

"Follow me."

Omdanan exited the house and turned down a road perpendicular to the main street. Sarok followed in the fading twilight as they scuttled along—keeping tight to the edge of the street. They soon came to another main street that headed towards the docks, parallel to the one they'd initially been following. Relying on the orcs sticking to their usual route, they followed this road, and before long came to the apron before the dockside, with the lake spread in front of them, small, wind-whipped ripples sparkling with reflected light from the setting sun.

Omdanan held out a hand to keep Sarok back, then peered around the corner. He stayed that way for a minute, then two. Then he ducked back and turned. "The orcs have just gone. They were speaking to Mr Dettler. There is still a pile of stuff to ferry back, so I'm guessing they'll return. Mr Dettler has gone back to sitting on the jetty. If we move quick, we can get to a warehouse doorway, and we can hail him from there if he doesn't hear us first…"

"You mean, if he doesn't hear *me*, first? Understood." Sarok gestured the other should go, and when Omdanan turned, he followed him.

Sure enough, Dettler was lost in thought, staring at the water. They got to within ten metres of the man, then ducked right, into the broad open doorway to a large, mostly empty building, with splintered crates and filthy sacks strewn across the shadowed floor. Now it was Sarok's turn to wave the other back into the dark. He looked over to his right, to where the main street opened onto the docks, about another twenty metres along. Seeing and hearing nothing, he gave a harsh whisper: "Dettler!"

The other didn't hear, so Sarok stepped further from the doorway and spoke again, slightly louder: "Dettler!"

The small man on the jetty stiffened, and his head jerked around. On seeing who had hailed him, the man's eyes grew wide, his mouth opened but emitted no sound, and he frantically looked off to his left, towards the main street.

"Come on, Dettler. Quick! Here!"

The man paused in indecision and then—as if suddenly shocked by electricity—he jumped to his feet, quickly looked to his left again, and scurried across the stone apron. He got to within three metres of the other and then halted, various emotions fighting to control his face. "I... Mr Sarok... I... I didn't do it. I had no choice! I—"

"We know. Come here. Actually, no. Don't come. Lean against the wall and face the road. Don't look at me."

"I... sure... right!" Dettler did as asked.

"It's good to see you, Dettler. I never wished you harm—"

"He made me come!" blurted the small man. "On that night, he tricked me to come to the roof of the tower. Yadzen was there too. They forced me to go with them..." and then a thought seemed to occur to the other, a need to elaborate: "But Yadzen is not bad. He's been conditioned. He follows that bastard because he must."

"So, we cannot rely on him?"

"No. No you can't. But if you are going to kill him, kill com Durrel, please spare Yadzen if you can."

Sarok was silent a moment, processing this new information. "Aye. So, you know why we are here?"

"We have been expecting you. We got news a few weeks ago—in Tartax-Kul— that you were here. And you were seen with another staff."

"Seen? Weeks ago? *Fuck!* We have been trying so hard to remain in the shadows. What do you... what does *he* know?"

"Not much. You were seen at a town on a river. I can't recall the name. A description matched that of Brutus, and someone was seen to wield a staff. I suggested it was you."

"Me? Why... well, that doesn't matter. But you don't know our full strength, or where we are, or where we are meant to be heading?"

Dettler shook his head, though Sarok couldn't see his face. "To answer your questions: no, no, and *no*. How many are you?"

"That is perhaps best known only to me at the moment. I hope you understand. I am taking a risk being here, talking to you now."

"It is no risk. I will not betray you. I'll help if I can. *Within reason*. But I am not a fighter, Mr Sarok. Do not ask me to pick up a sword."

Once more, Sarok lapsed into silence. Thinking. *Calculating*. "If we were to move against him this night, how could you help?"

"I'm not sure. He will sleep in the palace. You will somehow have to get past the orcs in the square, and his bodyguards are Reapers. You should not treat them lightly."

"How many?"

"There are thirty-two Reapers, and there are just over two hundred from the Two Horns regiment. There were more, but he lost his temper with his bearers. He loses his temper all the time now. Every day, someone, or something, dies."

"Am I right in assuming that only these Reapers will be with him in the palace?"

"That's right. He doesn't trust the orcs at all. The law is that they must keep a spear's length away at all times—unless they absolutely cannot."

"That's useful, Dettler. But there must be something more you can tell us or do for us. I believe you are innocent, but others might need more persuading. Sitting on the sidelines might not be enough. Do you understand?"

This time it was Dettler's turn to fall silent. Behind him, Sarok could sense some sort of struggle going on—the man with himself, his conscience? At last, Dettler sighed, then in a small voice said: "There may be *something*. Com Durrel's staff—"

"What is it? Tell me more!"

"His staff… it… well… you wield one, too. You know how it works. You know how it only answers to one person, using voice recognition, until a word of release is spoken."

"Go on."

"Well, I've been thinking. There may be a way. Using my skills…" and now he shook his head, and actually chuckled. "He calls me Wormtongue. He thinks I deceive... make false promises... use my voice to influence, as though using witchcraft. Wouldn't it be ironic, eh?"

"Sorry, Dettler, I don't know what the fuck you're talking about."

"There's one thing I could try. I've been thinking about it for some time. *Word association*. Maybe if I get the chance... if I can get close. Distract him. But I'm afraid, *so* afraid."

"You know, Dettler, someone pointed out to me some time ago that the expression *brave and fearless* is an oxymoron. You can't be both. You're afraid, Dettler, and I understand that. But that means you now have the chance to be brave. I don't clearly understand what you might do, but I urge you to do it. Try! You have the one necessary pre-cursor for heroism. Be a hero, Dettler."

And then both men caught the sounds of a trundling cart and distant shouts. Sarok finished: "Prepare for tonight. And remember my words."

***

They returned to their secret headquarters without incident, by which time the only evidence of the sun was a highlighting of the peaks of the Skythrust Mountains away to the west.

"It's on," declared Sarok. "I have a rough plan. We will wait for the early hours, then strike. Dettler may or may not aid us, but he certainly won't hinder us. Until then, eat, sleep, prepare. It'll soon be time to draw this play to a close."

Chapter 25

The party descended the staircase, stepping over the smashed table that had been left at its foot as a disincentive to lazy searchers, and assembled in the ground floor room, which seemed to have functioned as a formal dining area for whoever once owned this building. Though the single door in the wide entranceway had been left ajar, and the two long windows in the front wall were shattered, they were confident they could not be seen from the square beyond as there was no illumination to backlight them.

Sarok turned to the huddle in the space where the main table—now in splintered ruin—had once stood. "Just two, Omdanan? Are you sure?"

Omdanan stood nearby, his bow in his hand and his sword in a scabbard at his waist. All were fully armed and dressed in their mail shirts—and helmets when they had these, which the Meridian did not. "Two in the square by the fire and two of the Reapers by the palace entrance. But none by the church entrance."

"We need to strike both pairs at the same time, with as little noise as possible, so Sentain can cast his spell at the church. At that point, all hell will break loose, and we will have to force our way into the palace through the bodyguards. Are all clear on their roles?" Sarok looked about the party.

When none demurred, Sarok turned to Vuller and Mandelson. "Go now. You will have to keep to the right of the square, opposite to the church. Decide between yourselves on your targets. We have to rely on your discretion when to strike. As soon as you see or sense the guards in the square stumble, move fast, then hold the doors until we arrive. Kill anyone who comes out to investigate."

"Sure, Boss," said Vuller. "We're on it."

The two crept through the front door and disappeared into the night.

"Now we wait. Omdanan—you have the best internal clock. Say 'when'."

Several minutes passed in tense silence. Archaen stood beside Sentain, her face occluded by the cheek and nose guards of her helm, her hand resting on her still-sheathed black sword. Sentain shifted on his feet continuously, rustling gently in his mail, but helmet-less like Omdanan. At last he muttered: "I don't know how you lot can stay so calm."

"It's just experience," responded the woman in a soft voice. "The rest of us have faced dangers before. We have each found a way to control and channel our energy."

"I hope I don't let you all down. I couldn't sleep. I'm all over the place—"

"Just remember your spells and speak them with confidence when the time is right, then stick behind me. I will protect you."

"*Time*!" hissed Omdanan.

"Right, no fucking about. Boy, you lead: we will stay ten metres behind. Shoot well." Sarok looked back at Sentain. "Be ready with your first spell. Let's move."

The clouds that had started to accumulate in the late afternoon had formed a shroud across the heavens, blocking out the moon and most of the stars. The corners of the main square were pitch black, the only light coming from a large fire in the centre and torches ablaze above the entrance to the church and the palace. Three roads entered and left the square: the one beneath the arch behind them, which led to the main gate, and one to either side of the square, of which one led directly to the docks. The palace side of the square was uninterrupted by roads and dominated by that building, the entrance to which was accessed by a broad flight of stone steps.

The party moved slowly, unsure of the Meridian's exact location as he was quickly lost in the night. But after some moments, Sarok caught sight of the low-moving man, outlined by light from the large fire. The two orcs were clearly lit in front of the flames, resting on their spears and talking. The light from the fire petered out some metres from the blaze, and close to this fuzzy shadow line, Omdanan came to a halt: when he did so, the rest did also, lying flat on the filthy cobbles.

More time passed. And then the guards seemed to exhaust their conversation or perhaps think that they ought to continue their patrolling, turning away from each other. After a moment, Sarok noticed Omdanan pluck an arrow from the quiver on his back, notch it, and then fade away to the right, following one of the guards.

The first action of the night was marked by a low hiss, as the arrow from Omdanan's bow cut through the air. This struck one guard in the side of the head beneath its leather skullcap. The guard stumbled and pitched forwards, its spear clattering onto the ground. While the noise was not great, Sarok noticed Sentain tense up; he reached out a calming hand to rest on the other's arm. But the noise went unnoticed by the second guard, who continued to move away from the fire and the now-lifeless body of its colleague, perhaps unhearing amid the tapping of the butt of its spear on the stones.

Omdanan shifted position, moving left. At this, Sarok rose up and started a diagonal course in his direction, beckoning the others. Archaen and Miko followed, as did Sentain after a short pause. Then there was the whisper of a second arrow, accompanied by a throaty gurgle and another spear clatter—this one louder. The orc ahead was still on its feet, but staggering, the arrow having nicked its armour and deflected up into the base of its cranium, where one questing hand felt for it.

Sarok turned: "Now!"

As Miko and Archaen headed towards the orc, Sentain stumbled fully erect, swaying in indecision. But the Leaguers were unneeded: a moment later, the gasping of the injured orc was cut off by another arrow from Omdanan, which pierced its skull from behind.

The party converged by the second corpse, at the edge of the firelight. They would have been visible to the orcs in front of the palace, but the lack of alarm suggested that Vuller and Mandelson had dispatched the guards as instructed.

"Focus, Sentain," muttered Sarok. "Come!"

He led them swiftly across the square, until the central fire was at their backs and they were opposite the broad church doors, which had been wrestled on their smashed hinges to be largely closed, with just a half-metre gap between them.

Sarok darted a glance towards the palace, but there was still no noise from there: with the sharp motion of one hand, he directed the others in that direction, at the same time holding a hand against Sentain's chest. Omdanan and Miko set off at a lope, though Archaen paused to touch Sentain's arm and look into his face before heading off too.

"Your turn, wizard," said Sarok. "Boldly!"

***

Sentain looked at the doors and tried to put aside the thought that behind them were close to two hundred living beings. He raised his staff and pointed its tip forwards, chanting the three-word spell he had memorised—hesitantly, but accurately enough. A pressure wave coursed towards the church, twenty metres away. The doors slammed back and disappeared through the building's maw, and the whole edifice trembled.

"Again," shouted Sarok. "Now—fire!"

This time more confidently, Sentain chanted a different spell and was rewarded by a great gout of flame, which splashed against the church façade, instantly setting it alight. But Sarok was not content: he grabbed Sentain by the arm and pulled him another ten metres closer to the church. By now, the screams had started, and the heat became uncomfortable.

"Once more!"

"It's enough—"

"No, it's not. Quick. We must get to the palace."

Sentain could see writhing shapes within the church through the door and flaming holes in the front wall. With a cracked voice, he repeated his last spell, and a third blast of super-heated energy punched through the now-flimsy face of the church, igniting the buildings to either side, and bringing down much of the roof.

***

Dettler hadn't slept at all.

In the early evening, he'd organised the delivery of food from the dockside warehouse, and then arranged com Durrel's dinner with the help of the regimental cooks. At least this had gained grudging approval from his master: there had been some cured beef and pulses—food he would have once dismissed with rage, but which now appeared like a feast compared to the salt fish and old fruit that had been their staple over the last few months. But Dettler had been twitchy throughout, and eager to get away. He'd avoided any conversation with Yadzen and slunk off to his room just down the corridor from com Durrel's as soon as the latter retired.

But as the night deepened, the soft bed had provided no succour to him. He'd writhed as though he were trying to sleep on bare earth and stones, and eventually gave in, got up, pulled on the boots Yadzen had made him—which were coming apart from their extensive use—and sat on the bed, deep in thought. Where was Sarok? Where was his staff (for now that he thought back, he remembered the man had appeared unarmed)? And who—and how many—were with him?

Dettler had too much energy to sit, just as he'd had too much to lie down. After much pacing, he gave in...

He quietly opened his door onto the corridor, where the rough plaster had been coated in a light green paint. His room was at the rear-facing side of the palace, as were those of his human colleagues. In the centre of this level, as he turned right, the corridor led to an open area from where broad steps descended to a chamber behind the throne room, which acted as a preparatory space and junction. He knew this annex not only gave access to the throne room-cum-audience chamber to the front aspect, but that it also led to off the sides to store rooms, a kitchen, a dormitory for staff, and a small armoury.

The open foyer was empty, in line with com Durrel's standing orders regarding how near orcs should be to him when he slept, although Dettler knew that several bodyguards waited at the foot of the stairs in the annex below. Not wanting to disturb these, he entered one of the rooms opposite the corridor to the front side of the palace. This seemed to have been some sort of meeting room, with a long table in the middle and a variety of chairs, most of which were tipped over. A faecal smell pervaded the space, which was one reason why this and the other front rooms had been left unoccupied. Gagging slightly, Dettler negotiated around the long table to the front wall, where curtains hid a series of glass doors—all smashed—that led to small balconies.

He picked over broken glass and let a thick blue curtain—patterned with civic emblems of wheatsheaves and scythes—fall closed behind him. The balcony was narrow and only able to hold a single standing person. The balustrade was stone, like the entire palace—a characteristic that differentiated it from the wooden construction of the rest of the town's buildings. In spite of this, the stone didn't feel particularly solid or well made, and Dettler kept his back to the curtain through which he knew he could fall if the balcony started to give way. But even though he was only two floors up, and it was night, his acrophobia made his heart beat a little faster, and he felt his palms and armpits start to dampen.

Closing his eyes to counter a sudden giddiness, Dettler tilted his head and allowed the inconstant wind to caress his face. The smell from the room was absent here, replaced by other subtle odours from the largely deserted town that he couldn't recognise—beyond the slightly acrid tinge of old smoke. With his heart rate calmed, he opened his eyes once more and looked out over the square. There was little to see now, in the deepest, pre-dawn part of night, save the large fire in the centre of the plaza—which seemed to illuminate nothing but a wide ring of cobbles—a couple of torches set in brackets at the church, over to his right, and a glow from torches set beside the palace doors below. Letting his breathing calm further, he inched forwards until he was able to lean his elbows onto the balustrade. At one level, he knew the balcony wouldn't crumble, but he still found himself tensing up every time he moved, as his irrational mind insisted that the motion was from the ground at his feet instead. Gradually, he achieved a degree of peace, balancing a little fear with the need for solace, clean air, and a chance to think.

As he watched the two guards in the mid-distance doing their desultory patrolling—always keeping within the fire-lit circle—Dettler ruminated on his past, and on the circumstances that had brought him here. *One more deal.* Even from a young age, it had always been *just one more deal*—an insistent mantra of greed that had brought him low. It had begun on Taquent, when pushing for more had ended his career in disgrace as an employee of one of the capital's major employers. And it was the same imperative that had led him to overreach when running his first legitimate business—sourcing machinery for power stations—leading to charges of fraud and embezzlement. Although he'd sold himself well in court and avoided a prison sentence, he'd not escaped a ban from holding further company directorships. And so he'd had to slip into the murkier realms of the *unofficial*, which gradually led to the *downright illegal*, with each cycle leading him into the orbit of worse and worse people—until he'd come to com Durrel, who was surely the devil himself. Yet on every previous occasion he'd talked himself into trouble, he'd also managed to talk himself out of it. Could he do so this time, too?

Dettler felt sweat prickle his hands and forehead again, in spite of the cool weather. It seemed as though the ante forever rose, never fell. He focused on the guards below, then swiftly looked at the curtain behind him. When would the attack come? Where would it come? And where should he position himself?

For a moment, he wondered whether he might be able to drop down from the balcony. Could he somehow escape the imminent bedlam? He could hide out in the town. He needn't go far. If anyone tried to find him—from either side—it would prove difficult in the maze of buildings. And then he could return afterwards. If com Durrel triumphed, he could simply say he had hidden out of the way. Com Durrel knew of his cowardice. He'd be mocked, and maybe beaten, but nothing more. And if Sarok and his mysterious party triumphed, they would likely consider their mission accomplished and look on him as an incidental matter of little consequence. And hadn't Sarok said he believed him when he'd told him that he'd been forced to join com Durrel against his will? But Sarok had also talked of others needing convincing. Yet what was the worst that could happen? Maybe they'd just ship him off planet and dump him somewhere out of the way? But were either of these options good ones? To accept derision? Was there nothing worthwhile in the skin that encased the creature called Rostus Dettler?

And what of Yadzen, who'd shown him kindness when he hadn't needed to, and who—in a way—suffered even more than he did? Could he allow the man to murder others at com Durrel's bequest, or allow him to be slain while forced to defend that monster against his will?

Dettler felt tears well up in the corners of his eyes… and didn't know why. Were they for Yadzen? For himself? He clenched a fist and tamped it onto the balustrade. *No.* Not this time. He clenched his jaw. This time, he wasn't going to run. This time he was going to—in his own way—fight.

And then he noticed that the guards in the square were not moving, but others *were.* He saw a figure off to the side raise a staff, although he couldn't identify who it was. Then there was a blast, followed soon after by two mighty bursts of flame that enveloped the church. At first, there was no reaction in the palace, and then, after some seconds, there was a shout from somewhere beneath him.

Dettler smiled grimly to himself. He'd wait until he heard movement and voices behind, and then he would march out to join com Durrel. It would soon be time for him to show that he was a much bigger man than all the universe thought.

***

They assembled at the foot of the stairs to the palace, Sarok virtually dragging Sentain up to the others by one arm. Archaen, Miko and Omdanan were already present, while Mandelson and Vuller stood at the top level next to the closed double door, each holding a spear in their hands pointed at the portal—the woman's having a curved blade, the man's—borrowed from Archaen—a pointed one. Two orcs in red armour lay across the blood-splashed stairs.

"Any trouble?" asked Sarok.

Vuller gave a wry smile. "From her's, no. From mine, a little. But he wanted to fight, not shout out a warning."

"You're getting old, Vuller," mocked the woman. "And slow."

Sarok ignored her. "Doors locked?"

"Shut and maybe wedged," replied Vuller. "But not locked as such."

"Right, Sentain, time to—"

And then, as if on cue, the doors began to move, slowly peeling inwards, with noise and shapes evident in the growing space between them.

Mandelson didn't wait for a command, knowing her role: she slashed down through the gap and then threw herself at the space, with Vuller right behind her.

Archaen cried out "The lightning!", and was suddenly at Vuller's shoulder, with Miko behind, the party forming a flying wedge that forced the doors inwards and scattered the surprised orcs gathered there. Then Sarok was with them, and Omdanan too, finding a space, his hand a blur, reaching for arrows and releasing them—left, right, left, centre. Sentain watched the carnage in astonishment. Within a few seconds, the party was deep into the audience chamber and the orcs were screaming, falling back, or crawling away as their lifeblood spilled from them.

Sentain moved into the space more cautiously, not knowing where to look, until a hand moved near his foot, and he instinctively raised his staff and brought it down on the bald and mottled head of a grievously wounded orc, stunning it motionless.

"On! On!" yelled Sarok. "Don't let them settle!"

The party were experienced in the ways of war, the ways of death, and knew the importance of momentum. The company of the Black Lady chased the orcs back into the room, causing their formation to fragment. But after the initial surge, progress began to slow. The red-armoured orcs were large and they were true warriors themselves. They began to flail their spears about, to keep the intruders distant and out of sword-thrust range, although their own attacks were skilfully parried.

From the rear of the pack, Sentain noticed a door at the back of the room to one side of the raised throne, open. More orcs emerged. "Look out! To the right! By the throne!"

Omdanan raised his bow and shot arrow after arrow—but the orcs were prepared and had shields. The Meridian's arrows sank into wooden shields or glanced off stiffened leather armour or skull caps. One orc took an arrow in the cheek, another in an exposed arm, a couple in the legs. Several fell, forming obstacles to those coming from behind. With his final arrow, the Omdanan shot one of the downed orcs through the eye, then he cast aside the bow, drew his blade, and with a battle cry of his own, charged into the pack. But then a particularly large orc pushed through from the door behind, jostling its comrades out of the way, and advanced to meet the man with a snarl…

Sentain scanned the room, now strewn with the corpses of orcs, with individual fights taking place between his colleagues and the initial party of the enemy. "Miko! To Elian!"

Miko savagely hacked down his last opponent, turned to glance at Sentain, then followed the direction of his pointing staff to where Omdanan was facing a scrum of orcs.

As Miko started to move, Sentain watched Omdanan throw himself on the huge orc, his blade moving at astonishing speed, the orc initially succeeding in deflecting the blows with its spear, and then widening its eyes in shock at the fury of its opponent.

Omdanan broke the other's spear and sank his sword deep into its shoulder—but then he wheeled away, spraying blood in a great arc across the throne nearby, for one of the orcs beside the giant had struck a blow, its spear slicing through the young man's forehead, dissecting the skin and leaving one end to flap low over his eyes, blinding him.

"No!" Miko was beside the fallen man in an instant, defending him against the two remaining orcs. He dispatched one, but as he did so, he received a spear cut into his already useless arm. But he remained firm, allowing the Meridian to scrabble away in the direction of the front door, and laughed through the pain: "Wrong arm, you stupid fucker...." He slew the orc that had severed his arm.

But there was another door to the *other* side of the throne, and this now opened. Through it piled the last of the Reapers—eight in total—unopposed by spears or bows, with their own spears down and levelled. And behind these, there were others…

Anda com Durrel emerged behind the orcs, his face red with fury. Next to him came Yadzen, in chain mail with his sword drawn, and Rostus Dettler, nervously crouched at his other side. He strode into the centre of the room to stand in front of the throne, his bodyguards ensuring none got close. Off to one side, Mandelson and Vuller continued to fight several remaining orcs from the initial party, though Sarok, Archaen and Sentain now formed a close formation in the centre of the room, surrounded by bodies.

Over the sounds of clashing steel from the group to his left, com Durrel addressed those in the centre. "So… here you are. The useless henchman, the woman who wanted to steal from me, and her pet… with a staff!" He stared at Sentain, who stared back—neither man making a move. But com Durrel recovered from his trance first, started to raise his own staff, but then paused, perhaps appreciating the difficulty of leasing off a spell in the confined space, with Yadzen and his bodyguards in front of him. Still, he clearly knew where the threat lay: "Yadzen—kill Sentain. Kill the one with the staff! Kill him now!"

At this instruction, Yadzen came to life: "Sir!" He ghosted forwards with remarkable fluidity, passing through the perimeter of orcs, and slipping between Archaen and Sarok, evading a blow from the woman and shrugging Sarok aside. Then he swung his sword high and down, directly at Sentain, who only just managed to raise his staff in time to intercept the blow. The staff sparked, and bent, revealing its core of metal-encased machinery…

"And the rest of you," screamed com Durrel to the orcs, "kill the rest! Kill them all!"

As the orcs rushed towards Yadzen and the trio of elves, Vuller dispatched his last foe, turned, and threw his spear into the side of an onrushing orc with such force it pierced its armour and drove it into the others, providing his colleagues a moment to recover. Then Vuller drew his sword and was at the foe, while from beyond the assailed group, Miko—now spurting blood from his amputated limb—crashed into the other side. Sarok had time to recover his sword and surge into the mêlée, leaving Yadzen, Archaen and Sentain to his rear.

Yadzen's next swing would have cleaved Sentain, who had been driven onto his back by the first strike, but a black sword intercepted the blade and deflected it sufficiently to save him *this* time.

***

And then Dettler moved.

He knew he could not fight com Durrel physically; he knew he was weak.

But with words, he was strong.

As the battle continued, Dettler drew up in front of com Durrel. "I'm dirty!" he cried. "Dirty!" He began to caper about, waving his arms, obscuring com Durrel's view of the action. "*Dirty dirty dirty…*"

"What the fuck, Wormtongue? What the…"

"*Dirty dirty dirty*! I'm dirty! You're dirty! YOU ARE dirty. *Dirty dirty dirty…*"

"What… Dettler… you fucking moron…"

"Dirty…"

"I'm not dirty… what… I'm clean."

And as soon as he spoke, com Durrel clearly recognised his error. Something about the staff… *changed*. The subtle hum and fizz of static electricity ceased.

Dettler stepped forwards quickly, placed one hand lightly on the staff, and cried: "Mine!"

"Dettler—what have you done? What have you *fucking* done!" Com Durrel swung the staff as a club, which was all it was good for now. The blow struck Dettler on the head and he crumpled to the ground.

***

Meanwhile, the eight orcs had been reduced to four, and then three, as Mandelson—having struck down the last of those that had originally been in the chamber—slid in beside Vuller and brought her kriss into the face of an orc there. But three further metres away, Yadzen continued to rain blow after blow on Sentain, each of which was parried by Enabeth Archaen, who had no time to do more than keep the grey-haired man's blade from completing its killing arc, becoming weaker and weaker each time.

Yet there was one more player in the scene. Further off to the right, on his hands and knees, shielded from the fight by Miko, Omdanan grasped an orcish spear that he found on the stone floor next to a corpse. He pulled himself up onto one leg and one knee to give himself stability. He could not see what was going on, as his eyes were covered by a flap of skin from his forehead, and his face was awash with blood, but he could still picture events in his mind's eye. Dettler had taken control of the staff from com Durrel… *over there*. Though the long spear was meant for thrusting, not throwing, it was in the hands of a strong, skilled man. He could see where com Durrel was, even without eyes—able to ignore the extraneous sounds of battle and arrow-in on the enemy's voice. He pulled back his arm, and threw.

***

Com Durrel had already turned to run. Without the staff, he was powerless. But he had only taken two steps when the spear, dipping at the last second, took him in the back of the thigh. With a shriek, he pitched forwards and the Staff of Power skittered from his grasp. Although he still wore his illicit skin beneath his leather clothing, the blow numbed his leg. He crawled towards the staff, but then sensed someone behind him. He turned, propping up on one elbow, and found Sarok—who had dealt with the last orc to his front—looming over him.

The God-Sorcerer raised a hand. "Hold! Stop! You are my man! I own you!"

"Own me?" Sarok panted from the exertion of the fight. With his free hand, he ripped the helmet from his head and cast it aside. "*Own* me? You know, com Durrel, you're just too high maintenance. You can keep your fucking money. Contract null and void." And he swung his blade down, severing the fingers of the intervening hand, burying it into the other's head.

A groggy Dettler caught this coup de grâce and turned to shout: "Yadzen! He is dead! You are released!"

A few metres away, Yadzen paused, his sword lifted high above him. Beneath, Archaen held up one numb arm, her black blade having been shivered from her hand. With her bare flesh she still attempted to shield Sentain—who was on his back, propped up on both elbows, his shattered staff laying useless on the stone. The sword wavered a moment, and then Yadzen said: "I… *know*."

He slowly lowered his weapon and took one pace back.

"I am sorry, Ms Archaen. I hope you are all right."

Chapter 26

The party assembled in the chamber behind the throne room, which was clear of bodies. Vuller and Mandelson then went to explore the corridors and rooms to either side to ensure there were no more enemies present. In the meantime, after using a tourniquet to stop the bleeding from the stump of Miko's arm, dissected at the elbow, Enabeth Archaen turned her attention to Omdanan, using a needle and thread from her pack to stitch up the Meridian's forehead—after washing it with water delivered by Yadzen from a barrel in the nearby kitchen.

"Would you like me to do that, Ms Archaen," said the grey-haired man, his sword now sheathed. "I am well trained in field medicine from my previous existence."

Sentain hovered beside the kneeling woman, white-faced from the trials and still shocked at the ferocity of the earlier attack. He viewed the man nervously. "Maybe you should let him, Enabeth. I mean, I'd rather see him occupied than standing above you with his sword to hand."

"He might have a point," noted Sarok, trying with little success to wipe the blood from his hands and forearms. "Perhaps you should step away. I am the only fighter here able to take him on at the moment. What if he goes psycho again?"

"He won't," said Dettler, whose own ashen pallor matched that of Sentain. "The spell is broken. He has no master now but himself."

"Still, I wonder if we might take his sword in the meantime… and that staff of yours, Dettler. I don't want you getting any ideas." Dettler had collected the staff from the throne room floor, and was now using it as a walking stick.

"You may have my sword if you wish," said Yadzen. "I understand your concerns."

"There is no need," interjected Archaen, without looking up, still focused on her sewing. "I do not think we could stop him if he turned." She paused to flex her sewing arm, which still tingled from the effort of holding off the man's earlier assault. "Now keep still, Elian! I am sorry for the pain, but there is no fast-working anaesthetic in Velasia. *Still!*"

Yadzen gave a small bow and retired a safe distance, to stand guard beside the nearest of the two doors to the throne room.

Dettler watched his compatriot retreat, then looked at the staff. "And I will hand this over to you, if you wish, Mr Sarok. It was not my intention to do anything but strip possession from *him*. I have no desire to wield it." He took a step towards Sarok, holding out the weapon.

The crime lord looked at the offering and frowned. "I cannot use it and need my hands free. Give it to Sentain."

"No!" Sentain raised his hands and leant away. "Not me. Certainly not after what I had to do at the church. Once is enough."

"You don't need to use it, Sentain. In fact, you can't."

"I know. But it's the association. The *reminder*."

Sarok shook his head. "Fine. Then keep it, Dettler. But don't get cute."

Vuller entered from a side door and strode up to the cluster, carrying a bottle of transparent fluid and an armful of cloth. "This side's clear too, Boss. Mandelson found another entrance and has gone outside to take a look at the church. She won't be long. I found this. There's a small medical room—or at least, that's what I think it is. It's got a couple of beds, stacks of bandages, some surgical instruments, and this—alcohol."

Archaen looked up at the man. "Good. Thank you, Theodric. I'll take that."

"I would fight you for that bottle, Cousin," said Miko, through teeth clenched in pain. "But if there is one bottle, there is likely to be more. Mr Vuller, come show me."

The two men left.

Archaen continued with her ministrations, using the alcohol to thoroughly swab Omdanan's head, before wrapping it tight in white bandaging. Then, after a moment's thought, she found a small strip of black fabric in her pack, which she used as a final layer. "A more suitable colour for you, I think, Elian."

Vuller and Miko duly returned, with Miko clasping a green bottle to his chest with his one remaining hand. Soon after, Mandelson completed the party.

"Fire's still going, but not strong. The buildings to either side of the church have collapsed. There was some rain while we've been in here, and it's still ongoing, but light."

"And the orcs in the church?" asked Sarok.

Mandelson grinned a reply. "They'll not bother us further. Our wizard did a good job in the end. It would have taken me an age to kill so many."

Sentain blanched. "All dead?"

"Many. Perhaps most. I found a few burnt and wounded and put them down. There was a small group of survivors, but they fled when they saw me. They didn't look in any shape to put up a fight. They won't be back."

"So we are safe here for the rest of the night?" asked Sarok.

"I expect so. Having a guard would make sense though."

"I have a suggestion," said Dettler. "The rooms upstairs have proper beds and bedding. We can sleep there. We'll probably only need a single guard at the top of these stairs." He indicated the broad stairway in the centre of the room. "I could do with some rest. I didn't sleep last night after I met Mr Sarok by the docks. Too... *tense*."

"That sounds like a good idea," seconded Sentain hastily.

"Just want to take advantage of all the cleaning you did yesterday, eh, Sentain?" grinned Sarok. "Well, it makes sense to me. Ms Archaen?" When the woman nodded agreement, Sarok concluded: "Lead on then, Dettler. I won't deny, I too am fucking shagged."

***

The next morning, after only four hours' sleep, Archaen roused the party, which had spread through several rooms. While the others took a light breakfast, she checked and rebandaged the wounds of Miko and Omdanan. Then—resuming command, without dissent from Sarok—she led the group out of the palace, past the smouldering ruins of the church, and through the light rain to the gate from town. From here, she guided the company a short distance along the lake, to a small copse of trees, where she had picketed the horses the previous day.

Archaen was the first to mount up, then she turned to observe the others. "Com Durrel is dead," she began, "and so your quest is over. But the army he assembled still exists. Maybe it will disband on the news, but maybe it will not. It is the largest force ever brought together in Velasia. It is hungry from a long march. It sees a soft target. I do not believe it will crumble. So what do we do now? For my part, I will not leave the men of Bratha or my kin to die. My sword is largely unbloodied. I will not allow that to continue. There is further honour to gain. So, I will ride to Jinna, although I do not expect any here to follow. From here, you may begin to find your way back to the elven ports. Still, I will ask: are there any here who will come with me?"

Miko wore a severe expression. "Although I am a cripple, I share your concerns and desires. I will be at your side."

Archaen bowed to the man. "Of course, Cousin Miko. I knew this would be your answer."

"And I will come, too," declared Omdanan. "They are *my* kin now. I will fight for them."

"Well said, Elian!"

Sarok looked between the Meridian and the woman and grew a dangerous smile. "And why not? I have spent many years fighting for myself, or for ignoble causes. Now, I have done something different. Whatever killing com Durrel was, I do not think it was *bad* or *selfish*—and that is a start. So why not go on? Fuck it. Stinky and I are in." And then he turned to look at his bodyguard by his side. "And what of you, Vuller? This time it's your choice. No more commands."

"Well, Boss, put that way… I'm not just a mercenary. It will be an honour to ride at your side."

Mandelson barked a laugh, drawing the attention of all. "Such nobility. Still, I'll come. Not for any cause, but because I will not run. And because these fuckers have it coming to them."

Archaen raised an eyebrow at this but chose not to comment. Instead, she turned to face the cluster that hadn't yet spoken. "That leaves you, Irvan, and you two, Mr Dettler and Yadzen. What are your thoughts?"

Sentain beamed at the woman. "My staff is now bust, and I doubt I will be of much use, but you do not get rid of me that easily. I'll do whatever I can to help."

"And I owe your people a debt for taking the life of one of your kin," said Yadzen grimly. "I will repay that debt ten-fold, a hundred-fold."

Archaen's eyes lingered on the anthropologist for a moment, then she turned to look down at the final member of their party. "And you, Mr Dettler?"

"I am not a brave man. I am not a warrior. I do not want to go." He looked down unhappily, and for a moment was silent. No one else spoke. But then he raised his head, his expression firm. "But I *will* come. Dr Sentain's staff may be of no use, but I have one that *does* work, and I have some knowledge in how to use it. You may need me against such a significant enemy."

Archaen's smile broadened and she leant down to place a hand on the small man's shoulder. "I didn't want to raise this matter, but you are right. Thank you, Mr Dettler. Welcome—you and Yadzen—to our company. And so we are back up to nine—an auspicious number for such a fellowship. Mount up, then. The path ahead is clear."

***

It took five days of riding to reach Jinna, following the trampled course of the giant orc army. Omdanan alerted the party of their proximity to town, riding back from a scouting expedition. As he drew up in front of the others, he was barely able to contain his excitement: "Ahead—about three kilometres. The town still holds out."

"That is perhaps of no surprise," mused Sarok, travelling beside Archaen, "given Dettler's intel." In debriefings since the death of com Durrel, Dettler had revealed that messengers had been sent ahead by the God-Sorcerer to stall his army's assault until he arrived. "But how does the town look?"

"It's been attacked. There are repairs to the walls, and a tower is burnt out."

"An initial assault before the message arrived," wondered Sarok, "or part of an ongoing attempt to soften up the defences?"

"I can't say," replied Omdanan. "But there's more. Away to the north-west, there are horsemen. *Hundreds*."

Archaen smiled. "It seems my kin have arrived. What banners do they carry?"

"*All* of them. The Silver Swan, the Golden Sword, *and* the Black Lightning. It is… *glorious*."

Now Archaen's smile was more genuine. "Excellent news, Elian!"

"But why haven't they attacked?" asked Sentain, who rode to the other side of the woman.

"Maybe they have been waiting for all to assemble," she replied. "Or maybe they have just arrived and are considering the best plan of attack. Your thoughts, Elian?"

"I can't really say. This is all new to me. Perhaps you or Mr Sarok can read the situation better. I will take you to a rise to the south-west of the town. The orcs are closer than the horsemen, and we will have to circle them widely before we can approach the elven host. Come!" And with that, he turned his steed and set off at a trot, slowing to look behind, then beckoning the others to follow.

"If he gets any more excited," mused Sarok, wryly, "I fear his head will explode. We should perhaps indulge the young man."

Archaen returned the smile but didn't speak. She goaded her horse forwards and the rest were forced to do the same, breaking into a canter to keep up.

They came to the top of the small hill noted by Omdanan and pulled up beside him, a line of eight horses ranging along the crest, with Yadzen and Dettler having taken the spare supply horse together—the diminutive Dettler being seated before his grey-haired comrade like a child before an adult.

"The orcs appear to have used the time waiting for their god wisely," noted Sarok, peering down at the sea of orcs with their innumerable banners. "It seems they have prepared pits and stakes to fend off horsemen. On top of their sheer numbers, you will not break this force with a charge, Ms Archaen, even with the three combined hosts of the elven ports. Perhaps this explains why your kin have yet to attack."

"I agree," said Archaen.

The wheat fields below had been trampled flat, and a ring of sharpened wooden stakes projected outwards in a semi-circle, with the town wall as its base. Most of the orcs remained within this protected area, with regimental banners evenly spaced around the perimeter, and a clot of several regiments facing the town gate, looking as though they might be planning some sort of action. "Our cavalry won't overwhelm this force without intervention." She looked over at Dettler, sitting in front of Yadzen, nursing the black Staff of Power within his arms.

Sentain saw the direction of the woman's look and stirred uncomfortably. "But with this staff, Mr Dettler could stand at a distance and destroy them all, bit by bit, regiment by regiment. It would be a massacre. That's hardly playing the game."

"Yes, Irvan, that's true. You know us well by now. This poses a dilemma."

"While I've come to appreciate your ethos to some degree," said Sarok, "it seems to me that the creed of necessity requires the staff's use. Either you use it and save your kin and the people in the town, or you don't, and the orcs win—with great and preventable slaughter."

"Er, well, perhaps I can help," volunteered Sentain. "Mr Dettler—do you know the spell for creating a great wind?"

"No. But I know several others that are far more effective… in a gruesome manner. I could incinerate or melt the orcs from a distance, but I don't know how to blow them over."

"Ah, then assuming the words of power are the same across all staffs, perhaps I can teach you a new trick? It would level the playing field somewhat—literally as well as metaphorically."

"Excellent!" said Archaen. "Thank you, Irvan. If Mr Dettler can use his power to cause a breach in the besiegers' defences, that would help us greatly without undermining our ethos, as Mr Sarok puts it."

"And don't forget the psychological blow, too," mused Sarok. "When Dettler appears on the hill behind them rather than com Durrel, and he aims his staff at them instead of their enemy, that is likely to cause a degree of *consternation*."

Miko laughed at this. "Nicely put, Narovy."

Archaen pulled back on the reins of her suddenly skittish horse. "I like this plan. Let's go to the combined host of the high guilds and discuss matters with them. But I still do not see them from here. Elian—after you."

***

They were intercepted before they came into view of the assembled host by a pair of riders dressed in red leathers with mail of sparkling gold and helmets of a similar design to their own, though gilded. The two riders held long spears but kept them raised as they cantered up to the party, presumably it being clear to them that horse riders could not be enemies.

Archaen nudged to the front of the pack and raised a hand in greeting. "Kin from Ranvik!"

The riders pulled up, and one—with red hair—replied loudly: "The Black Lady! Cousin Enabeth—I missed you when you were at Ranvik. I am Forverd, son of Bastian. Have you also come to join our little gathering?"

"Little? Our scout suggests that most of the elves of Velasia must be here. I am pleased to see you, Forverd. Can you take us to your father?"

"Of course. Patryc is with him, as well as Lothar of the Narvi, and, well, you shall see." He wheeled his horse and set off, with his colleague falling in beside him.

It was only a short distance to the camp of the elven host—over one low hill and around another. As they got near, they passed other riders, alone, in pairs, or in small groups, who shouted greetings and raised their spears at the sight of them.

There were no significant defences to the camp, and soon they were among colourful tents that dotted the field and clustered around large pyramids of sticks that would be lit for warmth and light once darkness drew in. The tents of the Ranvi tended to be red, while those of the Sorvi were dark blue or mauve, and those of the Narvi were dark brown or black. Forverd led them around the camp to one particular point, where he slowed and dismounted, gesturing for the others to do the same.

"Stallos will take your horses and see them fed and watered. Pass him your reins."

The party did as instructed. The man called Stallos shouted at a pair of strollers nearby, who came to his aid, and the three then took control of the party's mounts, including that of Forverd. The latter then led them through the tents, towards a particularly large pavilion in the centre of the camp, which was made of a dyed crimson fabric and had a banner planted outside its opened door flaps, depicting a long golden sword on a red background. But before they could enter, a large man dressed in tan leather emerged through the doorway. He stuttered to a halt at the sight of them.

"Patryc!" cried Archaen, moving forwards to embrace him.

The man's handsome face lit up. "Enabeth!" He returned the embrace.

A little behind, a smirking Miko leant in to a frowning Sentain and whispered: "Don't worry, he is her cousin, *for real*. Son of her uncle."

The two Leaguers momentarily moved to the side, speaking quietly, the man at least a head taller than the woman. Forverd politely waited for them to exchange a few words; the pair then turned back towards them. Patryc appraised the party from under thick black eyebrows, his hair very short at the sides and only slightly longer on the top.

"So, this is the Company of the Black Lady, slayer of the God-Sorcerer?"

Forverd's eyes grew wide at this, and he turned to look at the others with new respect, speaking low: "He is dead?"

"It seems so, Forverd," said Patryc. "Go spread the news. I will look after these from now on."

"Of course!" The armoured man grasped one hand around the hilt of his sheathed sword and strode away, towards the main cluster of red tents to one side. They soon heard his voice calling out the news excitedly.

"I was about to see to my own," continued Patryc, "but Bastian and Lothar are still within. Come!"

The party followed the man into a wide, circular space, partially lit by sunlight from the entrance, and partially by a couple of small lamps set on the floor. Two men stood over a rough-drawn map on a camp table. They looked up at the commotion. The blond-haired Bastian was present: his face broke into a broad smile at the sight of Archaen, while his black-bearded compatriot initially showed surprise, before he too began to grin.

"Enabeth! Thank all and any gods you live—and most of your party too."

"She not only lives," interjected Patryc, "but she brings astonishing news."

"Bastian… Lothar…" Archaen nodded to the men. "It is true. The God-Sorcerer is dead." She turned to gesture towards Sarok, "slain by my off-world colleague, Narovy Sarok."

The crime lord grinned and almost looked sheepish. "Aye, but with a lot of help from the lady and her crew."

Bastian had moved close to Archaen and grasped her forearms. Now he looked about those clustered in the space and spilling around the margins of the tent's interior. "I commend you all. Ryven, you seem to have picked up a little scratch. And Reddas, where is he?"

Archaen's arms fell, tugging Bastian's hands downwards, and bringing his attention back to her. She avoided the other's eyes, and in a distant voice confirmed: "He fell outside the Iron Gate."

"Ah. I am sorry, Cousin. But he fell from an exalted height, I am sure. We will honour him properly once all this is over."

Archaen's smile had faded, and her eyes dimmed. But then she shrugged, and with effort found another smile, even though it was strained. "He… made me proud. But as you say, now is not the time to discuss this matter. We need to turn to Jinna. To its people. We must think of them now."

"Of course."

Lothar approached, his own smile having slipped after the news of Reddas' death. "My condolences, too, Enabeth. And you are right about the focus of our attention. I am overjoyed at the death of the God-Sorcerer. If he had arrived, with his staff, we would have been sorely tested. But it occurs to me that not all is now resolved. Jinna is encircled by a well-prepared force far bigger than anything ever assembled in Velasia. How to break the siege is a conundrum that has taxed us for the last three days, ever since the Sorvi host arrived with Patryc."

"What have you concluded?" asked Archaen, clearly glad to change the topic.

"A full charge is out," said Bastian, "no matter how much we might wish it."

"We have been arguing about a continuous harrying campaign," said Lothar. "To attack the orcs in small numbers, firing arrows, disturbing their nights, drawing them out to chase us away, whittling them down. But Patryc is against this, fearing it will take too long, with an assault clearly being prepared as we speak—although their delay has puzzled us."

"I suspect it was to wait for the Sorcerer," said Patryc, "increasing the need to attack immediately in force. Now, we may not need to move with such alacrity, but we *do* still need to move. The orcs have battering rams made of tree trunks, and strong shields, and will attack soon regardless. The town will not hold out long when they attack in earnest."

"We can help here," said Archaen. She turned to gesture towards Dettler and Sentain, who stood beside each other, with Sentain the taller by a head. "The Staff of Power. The God-Sorcerer's servant—brought to Velasia against his will—now controls the staff."

The leaders of the three contingents exchanged glances and their expressions turned troubled. Bastian spoke their collective mind: "That would not be fair. You know our distaste for the staff. I would not endorse its use, even under current circumstances."

"I share your reservations and disquiet," said Archaen. "Therefore what we are proposing is something far more limited. Not to use it to kill, but rather to open a door. To give us a chance where currently there is none."

"Perhaps we should speak of this amongst the generals," said Lothar, eyeing the wider party. "Us four. And I mean this with no disrespect to your worthy colleagues."

Sarok took the hint. "He is probably right, Ms Archaen. It is lunchtime for me, at least, and I'd like to see whether they've got something decent to eat." He nodded at the three leaders and turned for the open tent flap. Without a word, the rest filed after.

***

Archaen found them an hour or so later, sat in a circle surrounded by red tents, eating, drinking, and relating the story of their journey to Forverd.

"A plan has been made," the woman said, drawing to a halt, "which we all agreed on, to a greater or lesser extent. The staff will be used as we discussed. We don't dare delay further, so the attack will begin in two hours. We have chosen a position for Mr Dettler. At the designated time, he will approach the orc perimeter and use the wind spell as often as necessary to blow down their thicket of stakes and unsettle the enemy. Our entire force will then charge through the gap, into the disarray. For my part, I will ride with my guild." She looked about the seated party. "Ryven—you have earned your place in our ranks. Will you come?"

The Leaguer gave a rueful smile. "A kind invite, Cousin. But with one arm I will just get in the way, and I am likely fall in the heat of battle, to be trampled to death ignominiously. I will keep Dettler company. Take Elian instead."

"Of course. That was always my intent." She looked down at Omdanan, whose forehead was bandaged with a black piece of cloth. "Cousin Elian—are you fit to ride?"

"Am I!" The *Leaguer*, no longer a Meridian, jumped to his feet.

"And the rest of you—apart from Mr Dettler, who is needed for this other task? You have certainly proven your worth. Will you join us?"

Sarok lounged back and raised a mug of ale. "Like Miko, I would just fall off. And besides, Stinky deserves a rest. It's my turn now to act the bodyguard. I will accompany and protect our new sorcerer."

"And I will protect the protector," grinned Vuller.

"Mr Dettler is now my charge," said Yadzen. "I will stay with him."

"And I can't be arsed with all this *horseplay*," said Mandelson. "I'll watch the show and save my energies."

Then Sentain looked up at Archaen wistfully, and with some concern. "I think my best place is out of the way, instructing Mr Dettler. But what if they do break? I remember outside the Iron Gate and the way the Narvi rode down the company of orcs there. If they turn and run, it could be a massacre."

Mandelson barked a laugh, drawing a severe look from Archaen, who then returned her grey eyes to the anthropologist. "Don't worry, Irvan. Remember who we are, and why we are here. We have not come to slaughter. We are here to save the men of Bratha, and prove our worth, and create a great story. Once the orcs break and flee the field, we will cease our assault and allow them to return to their homes."

"Ah… good. That's a relief."

"Now—let's start our preparations. A guide will soon come to lead you to your position. You will have a small escort, bringing war horns, who will announce your presence to the foe. Once Mr Dettler marches into view and casts his first spell, we will charge. Are there any questions?" Archaen waited a short time, but no one spoke. "In which case, Elian—come! And the rest of you, good luck!"

***

It wasn't much of a hill, but it was the best terrain available for their purpose: a hump of land that possessed just enough gradient and height to excuse it from the agricultural use of the now-flattened cropland around. It had once possessed a score of trees, but these had been chopped down, perhaps to be shaped into the battering rams that the orcs were preparing in the shadow of Jinna's walls. The hump rose sufficiently to allow a view of the lake that abutted the north-east segment of the town, and the low hills further east, behind which the elven host had assembled. Away to the north-west, little more than a kilometre distant, a dark line marked the edge of the orcs' perimeter, with the occasional tall banner competing with Jinna's sole remaining tower as the highest feature from this angle and elevation.

"I'm surprised the orcs don't have a lookout point here," said Sarok to Forverd, who had volunteered at the last minute to accompany the party along with half-a-dozen of his kin from Ranvik.

"They did," replied the man, whose red hair spilled beneath his helm. "But we chased them away when we arrived, and they have been content ever since to sit behind their makeshift wall of spines, daring us to close on them, knowing we haven't the numbers to do so."

"So it's a stalemate?"

"Here, yes," confirmed Forverd. "They can't catch us on horseback and know it's fatal to try. It has been a frustrating few days."

Sarok rubbed his hands. "Never mind. Things are about to get lively. And they're about to get the shock of their lives. Ready, Dettler?"

Sentain and Dettler had been colluding ever since the final plan had been announced, with Sentain having led the small man to some vacant area behind a hill where he'd been able to relate the requisite spell and allow the other to practice without blowing away half the camp. Dettler looked over to Sarok, grimaced, and reluctantly held up a thumb. Sentain patted him on the shoulder, then disengaged and sauntered over to Sarok—the rest of the party having settled a little further away, on the backslope of the knoll.

"That didn't look like much of a game face, Sentain," said Sarok to the approaching man. "Is he good, or are we in the shit?"

"No—he's good. Well, not happy. And very nervous. But he's also determined."

Sarok looked deep into the other's eyes, and when Sentain didn't blink, he nodded. "It's on, then. Forverd—what now?"

"We'll move up in a line and make a show. We need to attract the orcs' attention. Who knows, maybe they'll send a party close to investigate. We are surely too far away here to have an effect?"

"We are," replied Sentain. "Or at least, we are for my old staff. I don't know the relative power of this one."

"We'll soon find out," concluded Sarok. "Let's not delay."

Forverd retrieved the rest of the party. All then mounted up, save Dettler—who worried how a horse might react to his spell casting—and formed a semicircle behind their wizard. Then Forverd held high his spear—on which he had affixed a Golden Sword banner—at which signal, the six other riders from Ranvik put horns to their lips and blew. The sound that emerged was deep and loud. Several of the party winced—or in Mandelson's case, cursed.

"Start forwards, wizard!" shouted Forverd. "And hold your staff high. We will be right behind you."

Dettler's legs at first seemed unwilling to move. He shuffled forwards one pace, then a second, and this seemed to free him up: timid steps then turned into confident strides. He descended from the hump onto flatter ground and raised his staff with both hands. As he moved, his lips moved softly, presumably sub-vocalising the spells that Sentain had taught him.

As they advanced, the horn blowers continued their warning. From his horse, looking left, Sarok was pleased to note a hint of movement between the two nearest low hills, and the landscape seem to come alive as though crawling with ants. The elven host spilled out and moved towards them, ensuring they didn't get ahead of the little group to avoid being caught in collateral damage from the spell that was about to be cast. And then ahead he noticed frantic movement: orcs scurrying about, raising their spears, and moving to the perimeter. They had travelled one hundred metres, then two hundred. As they got closer, Sarok expected some sort of charge, but nothing came—perhaps because the orcs were wary of the mass of horsemen off to their side, numbering the best part of nine hundred.

At perhaps six hundred metres from the barrier, Dettler came to a halt, causing the rest of the party to pull up.

"What now, Dettler?" called Sarok.

"This might be enough."

"Enough to blow off their helmets? We need more."

"Mr Dettler," said Sentain, "I think we need to be closer. This would be too far for my old staff. Please keep going. If the orcs charge, you will still have plenty of time to cast."

"Very well." Dettler started forwards again—another hundred metres. Then another fifty. By this time, the shouts of the orcs were loud enough that individual words of insult could be made out amid the barrage. The foreground bristled with levelled spears, and in front of these was a thicket of stakes, set at about forty-five degrees to the horizontal. And they knew from their previous observations that there was a shallow ditch set before these—another impediment to the horsemen.

"Now?" wondered Dettler, his eyes still fixed forwards.

"Sentain?" asked Sarok.

The anthropologist shrugged. "For mine... still a bit far, I think. But maybe it's worth a try. This is the great Staff of Power after all. None of us has seen its full power at work except..." he turned. "Yadzen?"

The grey-haired man looked calm—with a hint of amusement? "Perhaps. But he liked to use it up close for maximum effect, so I cannot tell its range." Then he nudged his horse forwards a couple of paces. "Mr Dettler, please ensure you have that thing pointed in the right direction. Then think of our ex-master—assume he is in front of you—and do your worst."

Dettler at first bowed his head. Then he raised the staff high, still in both hands, and brought it down so that it pointed directly forwards. "*Bellazor-tritarium-farax!*"

A great gust of wind punched through the gap between them and the orcs, blasting the nearest soldiers, knocking them to the ground, catching the fabric of their regimental banners and ripping them from hands and into the air like a flock of scrawny birds. Several of the stakes bent backwards and then succumbed to the pressure, cartwheeling behind and knocking over staggering orcs unfortunate enough to be in their way.

"Fuck!" laughed Sarok, who recalled the first time Sentain had used the spell back in Lissom: it had been nothing like this!

"Well fuck me too!" said Sentain, uncharacteristically. "It's a good job we practised on the lower spell setting."

"Forwards!" shouted Sarok, recovering quickly. "Forwards! Another fifty metres, Dettler, then hit them again!"

The orcs were already confounded. They had been waiting for their master... and now *this*. The taunts and insults ceased, and now in the babble the word *Wormtongue* could be discerned. As the party began to move again, at the pace of Dettler's short legs, the orc lines started to re-form, but with great uncertainty. Sarok looked left and noted the nearest horsemen—wearing light clothing with black lightning slashes on their sleeves—trotting closer, taking a slight diagonal, getting ready to line up with the breach that the spell craft was creating.

Dettler didn't stop at fifty metres, or even a hundred. His pace picked up. At just two hundred metres from the perimeter he raised his voice and shouted, loudly, angrily, exorcising months' of pent-up rage: "*Bellazor-tritarium-farax!*"

And this time the effect was devastating. The whole array of stakes yanked upwards, and then—once loose from the soil—flipped backwards, cartwheeling like a forest of giant spears caught in a turbine. None of the nearest orcs were able to withstand the wind or the bludgeoning timbers it carried: for a hundred metres from the perimeter, every creature afoot was smashed over, rolling away like tumbleweeds and skittling others behind. And the sound that came from the orc host was no longer haughty, but full of panicked shrieking and howls of disbelief and terror. The orcs knew what the staff could do, and also appreciated that it could do far worse things.

The rest of the host took to their horns, creating a terrible noise, like the voice of some hellish monster. But as they were on flat ground, Sarok could only see the very nearest of the riders from the Black Lightning—yet he was certain that the one out front wore a black cloth around his head, and not far behind was a warrior woman who had eschewed a spear and held aloft a great black sword.

***

Elian Omdanan, once a Meridian, now of the Jade Guild, a companion of the Black Lady, felt *alive*. As he and Enabeth Archaen cantered up to the front line of the mass of riders of the High Guild of Black Lightning, the whole host raised a loud cheer accompanied by a shaking of spears. Omdanan knew that the acclamation was largely meant for Enabeth, but he noticed that many of the tall men and women in glinting mail looked at him, too, shouting greetings and praise. In the short time since their arrival at the camp, the story of the slaying of the God-

Sorcerer, and the Company's other feats, had passed through the assembled elves of Velasia—and his role had not been downplayed.

They drew their horses around to ride beside Patryc Archaen, and the host moved off. They were to form the right flank of the army, with the Golden Sword taking the centre and the Silver Swan forming the left flank, although they only saw the other companies once they'd walked their horses from their separate camp through a low gap between two hills. Here, they settled into the space between the party of the new sorcerer—arranged in a knot on a low hummock to their right—and the riders in red and gold to their left, who were arrayed behind the Golden Sword banner held aloft by a warrior at Bastian's side. Once the three guild companies had dressed their lines, the war horns of the riders attached to the sorcerer's party announced the advance.

As they started their slow procession towards the orcs' line, Omdanan had time to think. His mind ranged over recent events… and others more distant. Less than a year ago, he had been a loner, an outlier, feared for what he might do and certainly not respected. No one had cheered him then, indeed, his feats of agility and bravery had been discouraged and condemned. He'd been surrounded by elders and peers who were negative, scornful, timid. He'd been viewed as merely one of a maligned species known as *human*, of less value than insects or serpents, a pariah species meant to forever crawl on its belly, with heads bowed in perpetual shame. He looked about now, and shook his head: what other species had been able to raise such a glorious spectacle? And more, now that his own worth had been accepted, he found he was somehow able to appreciate Nature and its bountiful children better. Whereas before, he'd scorned the creatures around him, feeling a need to push back, to prove he was greater than they, he suddenly felt able to acknowledge the power and guile of them, from the sashai and the deadly apes of the Shadow Forest right up to the ganeroi, whose horrid behaviours were merely a manifestation of their own strategies to survive a perilous world, and as such, no better or worse than humans' or any others'…

And then the first spell was cast, and excitement rippled through the ranks. Omdanan found himself grinning. He moved a little forwards of the group, just half a length, to get a clearer view of his old companions off to one side. Ahead, the orcs were now discernible as individual creatures… and an image of the Infusi popped into his mind. But whereas before that image had been accompanied by feelings of disgust and hatred, he now felt something else. Like the orcs, the Infusi were simply creatures—indeed, they were actually human—that had found a niche in the universe, and used every talent they possessed to retain it. He still did not regret the fact that some had died in his encounter with them by the river near Enbargo, just as he didn't regret the deaths of the orcs he had slain in fair battle, but now he found a sliver of respect for them—and that was an odd thought.

The second spell swept away the orcs' perimeter defences. Omdanan heard a command from behind, and suddenly the air was full of the ululating blasts of the war horns. His heart pounded so hard in response it seemed as though it might punch through his chest. He swiftly drew his sword and put his heels to the flanks of his horse, surging forwards. Just behind him, he felt the rest of the host, like a comfortable blanket about his shoulders. *His* shoulders. He was the first to leap the narrow ditch and gallop into the midst of the enemy.

***

The orcs were in disarray. Omdanan rode past them all, headed for the cluster of regiments before the front gate. He used his sword, but at first only the flat of the blade, to tap the helmets of fleeing orcs—to tag them, to tell them: if matters were otherwise, you would be dead. He only used the edge of the blade when orcs decided to stand and fight. He had ridden perhaps two hundred metres into the besiegers before he found a fair fight—a cluster of orcs around a banner showing a severed head that had decided to contest the field. He rode among these, batting away spear-thrusts, then dipping inwards to inflict a wound here and there, and then making a more determined advance to force apart their formation. Then,

Enabeth Archaen swept up, and a groan came from the orcs, *the black sword!*, and these too cast down their spears and fled.

At the woman's shoulder, Omdanan ploughed into a phalanx surrounding a pair of battering rams. These also chose to fight, but largely because they had been hemmed into the space by their fleeing comrades and the wedge of riders. At this point, more horns sounded from ahead, and Omdanan saw the front gate of Jinna open, and more horsemen surge out—the vanguard of the Narvi. The two groups formed a pincer between which the orcs were crushed, and suddenly, in front of him, was a woman, whose fair features were hidden behind the face guard of her helm, but whose long blonde hair was unmistakable.

"Belias!"

"You took your time, Elian!"

"I had a God-Sorcerer to help kill."

The woman drew up, her excited mount tugging left and right. "He is dead? That explains much. But don't think all is done. Come!"

Omdanan rode beside the woman, ranging across the field until it was clear that the enemy was completely broken, and the day was theirs.

***

With the fighting over, Archaen found Omdanan and drew him away from the blonde woman of the Narvi. The pair cantered through the trash and destruction of the orc encampment, past knots of riders from the different high guilds, returning to the original knoll from which the assault had started. The rest of their party had returned here after doing their duty—alone, as Forverd and his riders had joined the assault once it had become clear their protective services were no longer needed.

"Did you have fun?" asked Sarok, who lounged against a downslope.

"I felt the blood coursing through my veins, and for a while appreciated that there is more to living than simply existing," said Archaen sardonically. "If you want to call that fun, then yes, I did."

"And so did the boy, judging from the size of his pupils. You still wired, young Elian?"

Omdanan looked down at Sarok and realised he was grinning broadly. He glanced away in embarrassment.

"Don't worry, lad. It's nothing to be ashamed of. We've all felt it before—even our two sorcerers."

Sentain found his way to the side of Archaen's horse, holding the bridle as the woman dismounted. He was too tongue-tied to speak, but lay a hand on the woman's arm, almost as if to reassure himself that she was present and unharmed.

Sarok looked on in amusement, then—as Omdanan also dismounted—he scrambled to his feet so that all were now on a level. "The doctor has been tense, Ms Archaen. At least he'll stop brooding now. Anyway, what next? The orcs are dispersed and com Durrel is dead."

"Now? I suppose my kin will remain here for some days, to aid the men of Haradan and Jinna, and perhaps escort the former back to their homes. Some will also remain to help in the rebuilding."

"I meant for *us*, Ms Archaen. What now for us?"

"You have fulfilled the task set you. I suppose your futures are now in your own hands. We can talk more of this in town this evening. Ah, what's this?"

Two horsemen rode up, halting a short distance away. After a brief discussion, one—a woman—walked their horse over to the party.

"Elian—we are following the orcs. They can't be trusted. So, we're going to harry them all the way to Tartax-Kul to make sure they don't re-form or get up to any other mischief. Are you coming?"

"Uh, Belias, I… don't know if I can." Omdanan to turned to look at Archaen, the query etched on his face.

Archaen looked severe. "I'm glad you ask, Elian. There are two matters to resolve. Perhaps we can do so now. The first…" she turned to Sarok. "*Narovy*. He is still bound to you. Before he or we can do anything, his obligations to you must be clarified."

Sarok's eyes glinted dangerously. He looked between Archaen and Omdanan. "Yes. This is true. He is still one of mine." He looked down and closed his eyes, as if deep in thought. He managed to retain everyone's attention for several seconds. But then his frown twitched and transformed, and he chuckled to himself. Looking up at Omdanan, he said at last: "I can tease you no longer, young Elian. In truth, I am in your debt as much as you are in mine. I have no proper call on your services. You are a free man…" and then he raised a warning finger, "under one condition."

"Uh, yes, sir. What is it? Anything!"

Sarok stepped over to his horse, which stood nearby, and patted it on its neck. "This bloody horse. When I leave, he'll stay here. Look out for him, eh? Oh, and give him a proper name. I never knew what his former owner called him, though I think he deserves something better than… than what I have been calling him. Deal?"

"Deal!" Omdanan smiled broadly, but then the smile faltered. He turned back to Archaen. "Uh, and… the second thing, Ms Archaen?"

The woman's expression was still severe. "There are two parts to this. The first is, I am *Enabeth*. Or even *En*. And you may call me *Cousin*. But *not* Ms Archaen. You have earned the right to be a little less formal."

"Of course, *Enabeth*."

"And the second is your status." She paused to tease the end of her ponytail, which rested over her shoulder and came down to her breast. "You have already been accepted into one guild. The Jade Guild. But that is not one of the higher guilds, and only those from one of the three can roam at will in Velasia."

"Oh. Right." Omdanan looked crestfallen.

The woman exchanged a sly glance with Sarok, who was still grinning. "So, I will have to do something about this." She let go of her hair, and reached for her sheathed sword, drawing it in one elegant movement. "Kneel then."

Omdanan looked up sharply, and his eyes widened. Without a word he dropped to both knees.

"The different guilds use different forms of initiation. *We* believe in the old ways." She lifted the blade and placed it on the man's left shoulder. "As Master of the High Guild of the Black Lightning, I now declare you one of us, owned by the guild, owner of the guild. Now get up, Elian of the Black Lightning, and do not disgrace us."

"I won't. *Ever.* I promise!" as he sprang to his feet, the party's eyes were upon him—broad with delight, save for the diffident Mandelson, with even Yadzen's expression relaying a quiet pleasure. He reached for his horse's reins and swept around and up into the saddle. He nodded his thanks and farewell, then reared his horse onto its hind legs. Laughing deeply as its hooves came down, he spurred his mount past the blonde-haired woman and the waiting Mikkel.

Belias tipped a salute to Archaen, then swivelled her horse to race after the young man.

Chapter 27

The rules were clear: *once in, all in.*

"So, what's the best way out?" asked Sarok, as they met at a tavern in Jinna. The siege hadn't lasted long enough to deplete the food stocks of the town, though long enough to sour the last of its ale, meaning they were forced to celebrate with nothing more than water.

"That's difficult to say," said Archaen, examining the stained, dog-eared map they'd been given weeks earlier by Bastian. "I see four options, none of which are great. First, we head to Faltis and try to find a ship big and hardy enough to carry us all the way to Narvik. Unlikely. The men there only have a small fishing fleet, with nothing suitable for ocean voyages—something we have deliberately discouraged via rumours about terrors of the deep. Second, we ride to the Cobalt Gate and on through to the Northlands and thence to Narvik. But then we would need to pass close to the orc city of Krajja-Min, which was never conquered by com Durrel, and the Northlands has difficult riding terrain—sharp and rocky in places, and thick with swamps in others. Third, we return through the Iron Gate and back the way we came, via the Copper Gate. But we have no boats to take the Tessellac, so we would have to ride down the west side of the river, which is semi-forested and pathless. And fourth, we take the Iron Gate to the Stone Gate, further west of the Copper Gate, and then go overland to Ranvik. The country between is the best for riding in Velasia, and now that all have some competence in the saddle, we might hope to make better time than we did on our outwards journey on boats from Sorvik. That might be the easiest route though it's not necessarily the quickest."

Sarok grimaced. "None of these options seem especially palatable. It appears it will be weeks before we regain civilisation."

"I'm afraid so."

Sarok took a swig from his tankard and frowned even more deeply. Then he turned to Vuller: "We deserve better than this, my faithful companion."

"That we do, Boss."

With a sigh, Sarok concluded: "We are in your hands, Ms Archaen. But I am willing to dare some peril to speed our return to a comfortable bed, proper food, and sufficient alcohol to get out of my skull and stay out for a week."

"Amen to that," muttered Sentain, before turning a wry grin upon their leader and host.

Archaen returned the young man's smile. "I will see what can be done."

***

In the end, they chose the route to Ranvik—the port of the High Guild of the Black Lightning. But they didn't travel alone: Patryc Archaen supplied a dozen riders as escort, and several spare horses laden with the best supplies that could be had in Jinna. And with their greater confidence in the saddle, the party made rapid progress. They made it to the Iron Gate unopposed and passed through this without issue.

Emerging from the Iron Gate, they retraced their earlier route through the Gap of Gelion, but then carried on westward past the Copper Gate. Hugging the Sundering Mountains, they duly found the Stone Gate, easily deciphered its riddle, and negotiated the sub-mountain passage in a couple of days. Back in the Southlands, they cantered through hilly country and soon came upon small towns of men. In these, they received reports of roving bands of orcs, which were still proving a menace, though the party saw none and were never challenged—perhaps unsurprisingly, given their nature and numbers.

Within a couple more weeks, they rode into a largely deserted Ranvik, which had been all but emptied by the emergency in Bratha. There was no need to linger, or any desire to do so: they arrived midday, and within an hour were aboard a boat, using sails and oars to attain the artificial island opposite the port from which they could take leave of Velasia. Yasmina must have been watching from her control room, for they didn't even need to hoist the signal flag: a shuttle was waiting, hovering very low to the water, beneath the eye-line of any ashore.

They clambered aboard the lowered ramp, slouching into seats and scattering their gear upon the transporter's floor.

"Back to reality!" cried Sarok, once Yadzen had helped Dettler aboard. "And make it fucking quick!"

***

The shuttle touched down on the central landing pad in Verano, at the centre of the three towers. Archaen led the party from the craft over the suspended walkway to the Gamma tower. Yasmina—in her white skin, her long, dark hair billowing in the modest breeze—awaited them.

"Welcome back, Cousin, and welcome all. You have certainly written a major new chapter in the volume on Velasia."

Archaen met and embraced the woman—gently, for she still wore her chainmail armour—then stepped back. "It's good to see you. I hope in the end we haven't undermined your charge."

"On the surface, you haven't. But there is much we don't know, having no cameras in the palace of Haradan. You left nothing incriminating behind? The Sorcerer's skin?"

"We have that," said Archaen. "It was stripped from com Durrel's corpse and hidden away. Ryven has it in his pack. And Irvan still carries his broken staff."

Yasmina nodded at this, then turned to face Dettler—in his torn and dirty leathers—who was standing nearby, as far from the vertiginous edge of the platform as possible. "You have something of ours I am keen to reclaim."

"And I am equally glad to be rid of it. Here you go…"

Yasmina held up her hands: "First—the release."

"Of course. *Clean!*"

"Mine!" The woman took the black, rune-inset Staff of Power, and smiled. Then she waved it about experimentally. "I feel it thrumming in my hands. Ah, well, it is a toy too far... for now."

Archaen looked surprised. "Yasmina—you're not suggesting...?"

"No. Not now. Not with its present level of power. But the game that has been played has been so... *thrilling*... it would not surprise me if the other Masters of the High Guilds don't come to me before long, their minds subtly changed, and ask for some new storyline to be written. But we shall see. In the meantime, I must get this back to the Hall. But first I must rescind this gift myself. *Clean*!"

Sarok had watched the exchange with some amusement. He happened to be standing next to Dettler, the only one of the party over whom he had a height advantage. He nudged the small man with an elbow, and noted: "Take care, Dettler. Since the staff is an unfair tool for them to use, they'll need a stooge in any future game—a part for which you have already auditioned. Lock your door tonight, or you might be kidnapped again and dumped in some grim part of Velasia to be hunted down once more."

Dettler's eyes widened and he turned white. "Let me be clear—I am *never* going back there ever again!"

A number of the party laughed at this, and Yasmina smiled broadly. "I hadn't thought of that... but no. You played your part—better than any might have imagined. In any case, talking of locks and doors, I have taken the liberty of reserving rooms for you in the Alpha tower, on the fifth floor. Your clothes and possessions have been transferred there. The information pads on the doors will indicate who has been settled where."

"Excellent, Yasmina," said Archaen. "Thank you." The woman in mail then turned to address the party crowded around. "I suggest you go find your rooms. Change. Rest. If you want to eat or drink, or indulge in any other entertainment, you know where to do so—in the basement level. I now need to contact the Senate and arrange to discuss matters with them. Perhaps we can meet for dinner at six?"

The others murmured assent, but Sentain—standing behind Sarok—had another question. "When you say *talk to the Senate*, you mean about what will happen to us, don't you?"

Archaen's expression was neutral. "Yes."

"But we did all that was required of us, didn't we? We helped you reclaim the Staff of Power and, ah, *remove* com Durrel from the game."

"You did. And you will all gain from this. But there are still matters to resolve. For example," she waved a hand at the two men standing off to one side of Sarok, "there is the matter of what is to become of Mr Dettler and Yadzen. And there are some matters about which I have hinted at solutions but that need to be verified, while there are others where the precise outcome is still unclear."

"You mean me?" continued Sentain.

"Yes, but not only you. And Ryven, you should accompany me."

The tall Leaguer nodded solemnly. "I suppose I have functioned with one arm for some time. I can delay my visit to the regeneration ward for a little longer."

Sentain frowned. Miko had always been ambivalent towards him. "Why Miko? Is he to help you judge our characters?"

Miko smiled at the other's discomfort. "Are you afraid of what I might recommend, Doctor?" Then he laughed. "I guess my opinion will be asked, but there are other matters, too. What I have not mentioned until now, as this might have been redundant had matters gone otherwise, is that I made something of a blunder on your arrival in Arakkan. When I made you all skins, I should have made them in white. By making them in my guild's burgundy, I inadvertently endorsed you. I guess the resolution of this faux pas will also form a part of our discussions—eh, Enabeth?"

The woman simply nodded.

"I seem to always be in trouble," sighed Miko. "Bad habits picked up from my time in the Confederation, I guess. I suppose my successor as Grand Master of the Golden Spear will also want to interrogate me, though given he is my son," he winked, "I hope he will go easy on his old man."

Even Archaen found some humour in Miko's observation. "Certainly, a piece of luck! But let's move off this windy tower—I can see that Mr Dettler is disturbed by the environment, and we are more humane than his ex-master. So, at six." She took Miko's sole arm and headed for the elevator that descended through the Gamma tower. Yasmina nodded to the others and followed after, the Staff of Power in her hands.

"Let's do as the lady asks," declared Sarok, taking command of the rest. He led the way back along the walkway to the central pad, then onto the bridge to the Alpha tower.

***

"Vuller—you've beaten me to it."

Sarok's bodyguard—now dressed like Sarok himself in a burgundy skin—raised a glass of golden liquid to the newly arrived man. "Of course, Boss. I had to make sure the beer was safe."

"Conclusion?" Sarok took a seat opposite. On the table was a second glass.

"It is, and I got one for you, too."

"So I see. Well—cheers!" Sarok took a long pull. When he paused for breath and lowered the glass, a drop of liquid sat at the corner of his now-significant black beard. He replaced the glass on the table and looked about. They were in the basement area of the Alpha tower, which served as a cross between a bar, restaurant, meeting area, and even club. To one corner of the wide space, there was a stage; along one wall, there was a long, self-service bar; and along another, there were many enclosed booths that provided more private entertainments, including access to Arkon's information network and the real-time viewing of ongoing games. He'd last been here during an evening: now, one wall was folded out, allowing late afternoon sunshine to bathe a sunken terrace outside, and—through use of well-placed mirrors—flood the underground interior. At the moment, the place was deserted, save for a couple of small groups of Leaguers who were holding raucous meetings in separate corners some distance from them.

"An improvement on Corvus, eh, Boss?"

Sarok shrugged. "We know how to have fun back home, too. There's more life in Yalta and Hennas than here, though I'm sure this place will be rocking later."

"Yeah, but I meant, I dunno, more relaxed. Safer."

"You mean, no orcs?" Sarok gave a mischievous smile.

"Well, fewer *human* orcs. It's nice not to have to watch our backs. Last time I was in a bar in Yalta, someone stuck a blade into one of my men. It was done so well, he bled out in seconds and couldn't be saved. It was around the start of Brundt's coup."

Sarok's expression hardened. "That bitch must own Yalta by now."

"Probably Hennas, too. I don't think we'll be celebrating there any time soon, or maybe anywhere else on Corvus beyond our Gamma Five base in the mountains, assuming Mr Cape has managed to hold on."

"I never did like skiing," muttered Sarok. He turned to observe the sunlit area some metres away, then frowned and looked back to Vuller. "It looks nice out. Why…?"

"Old habits, sir. Got a wall behind me, and I can see the elevators from here. But we can move if you want."

"It would be good, for once, to leave the shadows and sit in the sun." But he didn't move immediately, and his expression became somewhat distant as his mind drifted. Vuller knew from long years of service not to disturb his thoughts.

***

By the time the others started to emerge from the upper level, Sarok and Vuller had resettled outside and replenished their drinks twice. Vuller managed to find a spot from where he could keep an eye on the elevators inside. "Here's Yadzen," he noted.

Sarok shifted his chair so he could also watch events within. "Now, there's an odd sight. I'm not sure I've ever seen him by himself. He seems confused."

The grey-haired man, dressed as they were, looked about uncertainly before heading to the long bar, where he programmed himself a drink. Once this was delivered, he made a more-thorough sweep of the place with his eyes, caught sight of them, and after a moment's hesitation, strode over.

"No blade, Yadzen?" said Sarok, his eyes glinting with mischief.

"No need, sir. I have no one to defend."

"Why not take a seat. We've never really spoken, have we? *Before* you seemed nothing more than com Durrel's spare arm. And since? A ghost at the fireside of our encampments."

Yadzen pulled a chair across from a vacant table and sat, stiff-backed, a small glass of amber liquid nursed in his lap.

As Yadzen didn't respond immediately, Sarok continued: "We're all in unfamiliar territory, eh? Perhaps even more so now. Have you thought about the future?"

"I have."

"And?"

The man's expression remained neutral. "And I have come to no firm conclusion. My employer is dead, so in a way, I have failed in my purpose. Yet on Maloratious, I will be tarnished by my association with him. Occasionally, I had to intercede in disputes with his relatives and with some of the other main families. I will not be popular on return, and cannot expect continued employment." His face twitched into a smile. "But Maloratious is a law-abiding world in the Confederation, and I have done nothing wrong, so I have nothing to fear—unlike you, sir."

"Too fucking right," muttered Sarok. "The consequences of my past misdeeds will undoubtedly follow me from Corvus to the Confederation and even beyond. There's no hiding place for me. In this respect, unemployment seems a minor inconvenience."

"True. In any case, I suspect my talents will find a use somewhere. But all depends upon what Ms Archaen negotiates. I could be held to account for the killing of Hansa—a Leaguer who tried to kill Mr com Durrel in his fortress. Still, I have sensed no great antipathy over this, and even some sympathy. I suspect I will be expelled aboard the *Fantasia*."

Sarok nodded. "I suspect you are right. But what—"

"And here's Dettler," said Vuller.

The others turned to face the bank of elevators, a hundred metres away in shadow. Dettler walked into a brighter area, but seemed almost pained by the light. Unlike them, he wore a Confederation jacket and trousers. He also stood uncertainly for a moment before taking the natural route to the bar. There, he ordered something. When a small tumbler emerged from a delivery slot, he plucked it up and threw its contents down his throat, then ordered again. He repeated the process. When a third glass arrived, Dettler resisted drinking, set his back against the bar, leant his head back, and closed his eyes. He seemed uninterested in the occupants of the space around, and certainly unaware of them.

"Now that is a man truly in need of a drink." declared Vuller.

"More than us even," nodded Sarok. "What the fuck did you do to him, Yadzen? He refused to speak of his experiences on the return from Jinna."

"I did nothing. At least, nothing bad, I hope. It was neglect rather than abuse. I could not have done much more."

"Really?"

Now Yadzen did bring his drink to his lips, and like the small man he drained his glass in one go. Then he stood and looked down at Sarok: "No. That is not true. I could have done more. I was never ordered *not* to aid him. I need a refill."

Yadzen stalked over to the bar. Sarok watched him approach Dettler, who startled at the other's approach. They talked, heads down low. Then Yadzen got himself another drink, touched the other on his arm, and directed him to a table within a booth by the wall.

"Seems our company is not as desirable as I thought," chuckled Sarok.

"I suspect it's less a wish to avoid us, than a need to clear matters between themselves."

Sarok pursed his lips and nodded.

Soon after, Sentain emerged from the elevator. As all before, he purposefully headed to the bar to order a drink. It was clear from the direction of his glance that he'd seen Dettler and Yadzen, but he made no effort to approach them. And when he turned, he saw Sarok and Vuller, too—but he didn't come over. Instead, he raised his glass in salute, then headed to the far side of the vast room, about as far from everyone else as he could get.

They didn't see Mandelson until six o'clock, arriving in an elevator with Archaen at the stipulated time for their dinner engagement. By then, Sarok and Vuller had drunk so much, they had to prop each other up as they staggered to the bar, where they were able to order alcohol flushes. They disappeared to the bathroom to allow the drug to do its work, and emerged five minutes later, considerably more sober and steadier on their feet.

***

Irvan Sentain was still nursing his first drink when the elevator opened and Archaen walked out with Mandelson. He'd needed time and space to think since returning to Verano, and though he'd now gotten both these things, he found thinking *hard*. His mind refused to settle on one matter: instead, a multitude of images and memories flooded his mental space, competing for his limited attention...

He thought of his mentor, Gerar Matrosier, and the day in his office when he'd revealed the news of the task force. He recalled arriving on the *Seneschal* and first meeting Jessica Warsteiner. Then there were snippets of memories from the trip to Ghuraj, and Ghuraj itself. He thought of Levanko, and Wu-Lagarde, the shocking revelation about Jessica, and the treacherous Hubert Baum laying on the ground with a bloodied face. He almost *felt* the torrential rain that had battered him during their forced march to the kidnappers' shuttle. Then there was the fight, and the shuttle flight, and the hold on the *Ceres*. He recalled vivid images of the brutal demonstration of the kidnappers' intent, as Elian had been compelled to slice off his colleague's ear—which would have been *his* ear, without Enabeth's intervention. Then there was *the offer* and the journey to Arkon, and his excitement at arriving on the planet. And there were a multitude of more recent memories from Arakkan and Verano, including revelations about the natives of Omicra. And then, of course, there was the quest—the river, the yeltoi towns, the orcs, the deaths of Brutus and Reddas, the meeting with the Narvi, the horses, and the confrontation with com Durrel, followed by the battle and their return from Jinna.

But one memory returned, again and again, seemingly more powerful than any of the others: when Enabeth had come to him in the hold of the *Ceres* and offered him salvation and his heart's desire. Or *almost* his heart's desire, for now his heart had a new desire.

He jumped to his feet, spilling a little of his barely touched drink, and hurried over to the women. On the way, he saw the men from Corvus groggily making their way over from outside—the tall Vuller supporting his shorter boss. Then he noticed Yadzen and Dettler emerge from their booth, although they moved slowly, so he was first to reach the newcomers.

"*Enabeth.*"

"Irvan." Archaen wore her black skin, her hair in its customary ponytail sweeping over her left shoulder and down to her breast. Her usually firm expression was soft now, and almost amused. "You must have spilt most of your drink on your rush over."

"Ah, well, I can get another." He noticed Mandelson at the other's shoulder, observing him forensically and shaking her head in disapproval. "Have you…," he began, "are we…?"

Archaen's smile actually broadened. "Yes. No. Maybe. Shall we take a table and eat? Ah—Yadzen." She turned: "And Mr Dettler. Are you feeling better, now that you are back in more civilised surrounds?"

And for Sentain, that was largely it.

Archaen led them to a table, where they were shortly joined by the sobered-up Sarok and Vuller, but not Miko, who was in the medical centre, setting in motion the process of growing a replacement arm in a vat. Though Sentain managed to snare a seat beside Archaen, the conversation over their grand meal, ordered through the automated galley, was largely dominated by Sarok, until Dettler found his voice, and even Vuller spoke up, and then it became a four-way exchange that was surprisingly light and full of humour. Sentain found himself little more than an observer, like Yadzen and the grim-faced Mandelson, never quite able to take the initiative and draw the conversation his way. At times, he found himself staring down at his plate, remembering uncomfortable past formal dinners, when he'd shyly sat between vociferous senior colleagues, feeling inferior and out-of-place.

He declined dessert, but gladly helped himself to wine instead. Then the food was gone—they tipped their empty plates into an end slot in the table, where machinery would sort, clean, and recycle it—and Archaen suddenly stood.

"I fear I may have eaten too much rich food too quickly, and I dare not risk more. I still have one or two things to resolve with my peers, so I'll leave you now. Enjoy the rest of the evening. But please come over to the Gamma tower for ten o'clock tomorrow. I'll send a message to your rooms about where we will meet. Then I will be able to reveal our minds, and we will bring this play to a close."

As several of the party called out their own valedictions, Archaen placed a hand on Sentain's shoulder and leant down to whisper. "Irvan, please come with me. We have things to discuss."

Sentain almost knocked his chair over in his alacrity to get up, much to the amusement of Sarok. "Steady on, Doctor. I think she's going to wait for you." He looked at Archaen: "He's been morose all evening, Ms Archaen, like a sickly puppy. I am not a cruel man. Please sort him out."

Archaen gave a small nod of the head, but said nothing, and turned to lead Sentain from the room.

They left the tower through the opened wall, crossing the terrace outside. There, they found a broad set of stone steps that led up to ground level. Twilight had ceded the world to night, its dark contested by strings of coloured lights that picked out the top of the hedge marking the boundary of the parkland that lay to that side of the tower. As Sentain fell into step with Archaen, the woman turned to smile at him, though she remained silent and walked with purpose. They entered the park through an arch in the hedge, then Archaen's pace slowed.

Still in silence, the woman led them along a softly crunching path of small stones between trees whose branches trembled and swayed in a fitful breeze. They came to a small area completely circled by trees, which held four small, curved stone benches that formed a staccato ring around a stone table. The lights from the hedge top were hidden from here, and aside from soft blue patches emanating from the three towers of Verano, the only illumination came from the stars above—the Milky Way forming a gently glowing slash across the sky.

Archaen passed through the space between two of the benches and turned, seating herself on the circular table, legs outstretched, leaning back onto her hands. Sentain paused, then moved to sit on one of the facing benches, his head lower than hers. He waited for her to speak.

"Thank you for coming, Irvan. I have some news that need not be kept until tomorrow."

"I have been waiting for this. I'm glad you're going to tell me in private. I'd rather the others not watch my disappointment." He volunteered his fear, rather than his hope, although in truth he had no idea what the League had decided to do with him.

Archaen's expression twitched—but whether it was fighting an upwards or a downwards curve was unclear to him. "Disappointment? Well, I hope our offer doesn't disappoint, but I guess that depends upon your expectations."

"At the start of the quest, my expectations were low," said Sentain. "But maybe not too low, if you get what I mean. I know Miko has been against me, and I know my attitude to… certain matters… is a concern to you all. But you are an honourable people. I guess the outcome I feared most was that I wouldn't be trusted, and would be compelled to take part in a succession of dangerous quests, never quite proving myself enough to be released, waiting for my martial incompetence to lead to the, er, *removal* of your problem."

Archaen nodded. "Yes. That could have been the outcome." She paused. "But *it isn't*. Your part in the quest to redeem the Staff of Power was watched by the whole of Arkon. Even without my testimony, or Ryven's, the Senate were clear that you performed well. In the end, you have done no wrong by us, and you have always behaved honourably. More than that, you are yourself a victim of the events that *I* set in motion to regain my son. If anything, we owe you."

"Ah, well, I was hardly forced to come to Arkon. I would have given almost anything to get here."

Archaen's expression turned into a gentle smile, just visible in the dim starlight. "True. But I chose not to highlight this to the Senate."

"Ah, thank you." Sentain felt a breeze caress the back of his neck, which chilled him. The time had come to ask the question he feared to ask: "Then… what *is* the decision?"

"The decision is that you may leave on the *Fantasia* and return to the Confederation."

"Oh!" Return? *Leave?* "But… but what of the risk? Don't you fear I might speak of the yeltoi and the ganeroi? Reveal your secret? It could imperil your whole society."

She paused once more, and he sensed she was running her eyes over his face, although he couldn't tell for sure, as the upper part of her face was in shadow. At last, she said: "If you tell, then so be it, and we must face the consequences. To hold you any longer would simply be wrong, according to our beliefs. But having said that, we still hope you might choose to be diplomatic. I told the Senate I thought you would be if I asked you."

For a moment, Sentain found it hard to speak. At last he murmured: "Are you asking me?"

"We are not a perfect people, Irvan, but we are not bad. We simply want to live our lives as we wish. As we have no interest in forcing our views on your Confederation, we expect a degree of reciprocity. And you know our views on the natives of Omicra: we do use them, but we do not abuse them. So, yes, Irvan, I am asking—for us, for *me*—please keep our secret."

Sentain bowed his head. "For you? Of course."

"You don't sound happy. I am sorry for the imposition."

"No, it's not that. It's… well…" He continued to look down. "It's… I never really… it was never really my desire to return. I mean, I guess I miss Ustaria. My home. A little. But…" he looked up: "Is there any other option?"

In spite of the shadows, Irvan glimpsed the woman's cheek and mouth, starlit, as she shifted her position. He could tell she was smiling, even as she leant forwards and touched his knee. "There is… *if* you want one."

"Yes! Well, er, *maybe*. What… what do you mean? Can I stay?"

Archaen pulled back, but only to laugh. "Of course, Irvan. I suspected that was your desire, but I was not sure, and I didn't want to seem as though I were offering a bribe for your silence."

Sentain broke into a smile himself. "Of course that's what I want! I mean, it's not that I want to join your League. Not exactly. I still have reservations. But I'd love to continue to study your people, the yeltoi, the ganeroi, and… and…" And he couldn't say what else he wanted. Not yet.

Archaen responded: "And so that is what we offer—*Irvan the bard*. You have skills and interests that we don't. Though your readership might be limited to the worlds of the League, we are happy for you to write our story and the story of our guests from Omicra. The only stipulation is that you must replace that skin of yours with a white one. While Ryven's opinion of you has tempered, he still does not see you as having the right stuff to wear his guild's colours."

Sentain was on his feet, the energy that now coursed through him needing some sort of physical release. He moved a half step closer to the woman, and before he knew it, he had placed his hands on her arms… but she didn't flinch or object. And from this height and angle he could see into her eyes, and her pupils were wide. "Yes. *Anything*. I'd happily spend my days wearing a clown costume or… or… an ancient pair of golfer's plus-fours… or even a loin cloth and bone through my nose… anything for this honour."

Archaen laughed again, a light but genuine laugh. "Okay—enough! A white skin will do. Though now you mention these other options…"

"I take it back! Especially the plus-fours. I'd rather not encourage the thought of me as a golfer."

The woman laughed once more. "I think in your next game against zombies, we will have to ensure you have a more potent weapon than a golf club." Then she unexpectedly reached up and touched him on the cheek. The gesture caused Sentain to freeze, and his mouth to go dry. "You make me smile, Irvan," she continued. "You always have."

"I… I always want to. For now. Forever."

They stayed in that position for some time, unmoving, unspeaking. At last, Archaen leant forwards, softly kissed him on the cheek, passed her hand between his side and his arm to grasp his bicep, and gently led him away from the glade, back towards the nearest tower.

Chapter 28

Rostus Dettler missed breakfast. He'd eaten so much the previous evening, he wasn't sure he'd ever need to eat again; then he'd slept as well as he had ever slept. Now, he hummed to himself as he prepared to meet his fate. He pulled on his jacket, which fit well—with his considerable paunch having been lost somewhere in the wilds of Velasia—and considered himself in the mirror. He looked *sharp*, thanks to the automated grooming salon he'd found on the first floor, where dextrous machines had given him the closest shave he'd ever experienced and sorted out the mess of his hair. Now he just needed to shoe-up. He grinned at himself in the mirror: he was about to ruin the stylistic effect, but he didn't care. Returning to his king-sized bed he sat down, pushed aside his well-shined shoes, and drew close a pair of leather boots, which the small manufactory by his bed—a remarkable piece of machinery that even the wealthiest in the Confederation wouldn't have possessed—had re-stitched, reshod, and buffed overnight. They looked almost new. With a chuckle, he pulled these on, tucking in expensive trousers that did not deserve to be treated this way, stood, experimentally bounced on the balls of his feet, then strode to the door.

Yadzen was waiting outside.

"Ready to go, sir?"

"Of course, Yadzen. And ready to arrive at least five minutes before the others. Some think it's a mistake to arrive too early, but that's for parties. For meetings, I like to be first: it gives me the chance to size up the arrivals. You never know when there is a chance to frame the mood and context of a subsequent discussion through a careful word to the right person."

"I suspected you would have a more professional attitude to the affair than Mr com Durrel—who was always late. He refused to wait for anyone. Shall we go?"

The two men took the elevator down, then crossed to the Gamma tower through the plaza that lay beneath the suspended shuttle pad. They next took an elevator up to the sixteenth floor, where their meeting was due. As anticipated, they were the first to the designated room, and took seats around the conference table, with backs to the floor-to-ceiling window, facing the door.

Enabeth Archaen and Irvan Sentain arrived next—together.

"Doctor Sentain—you look different. *Whiter.*"

Dettler was amused at the young anthropologist's discomfort at his unexpected presence, and at the blush that ensued.

"Ah… Mr Dettler… yes. I have been demoted."

"Demoted, but not executed, which is certainly a win of sorts. Can I take it that your fate has already been decided and revealed to you? Is this favouritism, Ms Archaen?"

The woman, in her customary black skin, covered in badges and symbols, gave an enigmatic smile in return. "You mean, have I bestowed my favours upon Irvan? Now, that would be telling."

Sentain smiled weakly and shuffled around the table to sit beside Yadzen, his face still red.

Miko arrived, dressed in his burgundy skin. He also looked between the young man and the woman, but chose not to speak. Instead he smiled wryly, slapped Sentain on the shoulder, and settled in beside him.

Archaen stood until the final trio turned up: Sarok and Vuller were together, Mandelson a few steps behind. These sat to Dettler's other side. Only once they were seated did Archaen take her place at the nominal head of the table.

"Welcome, all," she began. "I hope this will be brief and relatively painless. I have concluded my discussion with the Senate and appropriate others." She glanced quickly at Miko. "As Mr Dettler has already discovered, Irvan has been cleared to leave… or to remain. He has chosen to stay and become our cultural historian."

"So that's the reason for the new skin?" muttered Sarok, seeming to notice it for the first time.

"Yes. Before you arrived, Irvan suggested it was a demotion, but that is a simplification. I suspect Yasmina—who has avoided committing to a guild so that she can continue to run the gaming in Velasia—would be the first to take issue with this." She smiled at Sentain, who grinned sheepishly while trying to avoid her eyes. Then she turned to face Dettler. "Your solution, Mr Dettler, is simpler. The Senate have been watching the game, and expressed sympathy towards how you were treated. They hold you blameless for anything that happened. Later today, a shuttle will take you back to the spaceport at Villarus, where you may take the *Fantasia's* shuttle back to its mothership and then return to the Confederation."

"So—no skin for me, then?" Dettler's smile was broad and teasing.

"Would you want one?"

"God, no! Although I have enjoyed the last day or so, and the room service here is spectacular, I am not a man of this world. My talents are not the same as your talents, as well you know."

"That is true," said the woman, looking thoughtful, "and in fact, that is why we wish to retain your services. After all—as you once told me—you have really been in our employ all along, working through Trevis Mallory. You were never actually com Durrel's man in the first place. So, if you can resolve the status of the *Fantasia* somehow, I think we can make it worth your while to work for us more directly. There are still loose ends to tie up. For a start, I wonder about the hostages from Ghuraj, and would like to resolve that situation if possible."

Dettler frowned at this. *Just one more deal?* Hadn't he decided to live a simpler life on his return to civilisation? *But maybe just one more...?* Suddenly, he laughed. "Who am I kidding?" he said aloud. "Just one more deal, Ms Archaen? Well, let's see, shall we. You mentioned the *Fantasia*, and that is a conundrum. The crew are employed by com Durrel, who is dead, and it is registered to him, presumably on Maloratious. But..." he looked down in thought, then up at the ceiling. "I know a place in the Olduvai Imperium where ships can be made to disappear and reappear as something else. Perhaps the reduced crew might be persuaded—with suitable remuneration—to look the other way?"

"I'm sure if anyone can talk them into this, then it is you. But Yadzen might have a say in the matter, I suppose." Archaen looked to the grey-haired man. "I assume they will look to you to command on hearing of their master's death?"

"Perhaps," replied Yadzen, "though the ship's captain will have a louder voice."

"In any case, this brings me to you, Yadzen." Archaen turned slightly in her seat, to focus on the man. "Now that we are aware of your condition… your *conditioning*… we are satisfied that you are also blameless. The death of Hansa of the Narvi was unfortunate, but it was a fair fight. You may also take the shuttle with Mr Dettler…" she paused and fixed the man opposite with her eyes, "…although we note that you are now a free agent, without a master. Should you wish to remain, we might consider this. You are a skilful man who has also behaved with honour—within bounds—and might find a place here."

Yadzen held the woman's stare a moment, then broke into a wistful smile. "Thank you, Ms Archaen, but your facts are not entirely correct. You see, as of last night, I do have a new master. I will accompany him to the *Fantasia*, and then wherever he wishes to go."

Sarok barked a laugh. "A new master? Dettler?"

"Yes."

"That is a surprise," said Archaen. "It is your business, and yours alone, but do you mind if I ask why?"

"Not at all. You see, Ms Archaen, I am a man who fights for others. I always have been. Perhaps it is in my DNA. Maybe I have served so long that I no longer know what it means to be independent, or desire this. Maybe I am comfortable in having a clear purpose." He looked across to Sarok. "Last night, you suggested I had treated Mr Dettler badly. In a way, I did. I owe him. And I know he will be a better master than my last one. Although he is not perfect, he has—in his own way—a certain integrity. That is perhaps the best I can ask for."

Dettler smiled and patted his new protector on the arm. "And I am honoured to accept his services. For not only is he a bodyguard supreme, but he also makes an excellent pair of boots."

***

"This meeting is already full of surprises," noted Sarok, shaking his head gently. "What else do you have up your sleeves, Ms Archaen?"

"I am not guilty of the last surprise," she smiled. "And I think what comes next will not be unexpected, as I have made some hints in the past, although I perhaps overstepped in doing so."

"Overstepped?"

Archaen managed to regain a neutral expression. "Yes. But first, I should say that you and your colleagues are also now free to leave on the *Fantasia*. You were held partly accountable for com Durrel and his actions, whether fairly or unfairly, but you redeemed yourselves in Velasia. But for you and Theodric…" she did not mention the woman sitting next to Sarok's bodyguard, "we offer an alternative. You have both demonstrated characteristics that we treasure in the League. The Senate has therefore decided that you may stay and join our society if a guild will offer to induct you."

"*If*, Ms Archaen? That is one of the most dangerous words in our language."

"Indeed. The problem is, I cannot offer you place in my guild, because the Black Lightning is one of the three high guilds. We may only induct those who have already been taken into the fold of a lower guild. This is why I was able to accept Elian. But I can't take you."

"So, assuming Vuller and I have any interest in staying, we have a problem, no?"

The edge of Archaen's mouth twitched upwards; she looked off to her side.

"Happily… *no*," said Miko, taking his cue. "I have spoken to the Grand Master of the Golden Spear. I was prepared to remind him of a host of embarrassing incidents from his past, but my son has been following the game with the same interest as everyone on Arkon. He graciously allowed that I might make amends for a previous blunder and formally endorse you now. If you wish—Narovy and

Theodric—you may join us. Frankly, it would be a coup for the guild, as your pristine burgundy skins would very shortly be adorned with honours from the quest against the God-Sorcerer—once suitable designs are approved—and that would gain us kudos in the eyes of all of our peers. So, please, say *yes*."

Sarok raised one eyebrow and looked between the two Leaguers. "Trophies? You see us as… *trophies*?" Then he threw back his head and laughed. "There is another who sees me in a similar way, though rather than dressing me up, she'd rather just remove my head and mount it on a shield. Between the two options, it's clear which is better for me. But…" he turned sober. "But matters aren't as simple as that. We have unfinished business back on Corvus. We—"

"Do we?" Vuller spoke unexpectedly. "Do we really, Boss?"

Sarok found his mouth opening and closing. He looked at the man to his side, whom he couldn't recall having interrupted him before in his many years of service. But whereas he'd normally feel anger, this time he didn't. "There's *Brundt*, Vuller. Can we really let her get away with what she has done to me? To the organisation? To all of us?"

"Yes, Boss. Why not? You played a good game and lost. It happens. Ever since I joined you, I knew I had chosen the right man to follow. Other Premiers gambled recklessly, or sacrificed their people carelessly, but you always weighed the odds. You always looked after the troops. Don't feel bad about being betrayed. Corvus is full of worthless, soulless men and women: the mark of shame lies on the traitors' heads, not yours. Leave them to it. Martinus, Whiting, Killonen, Agahi… all of them… they'll soon be dead. They'll overreach. They'll misstep. And Brundt will kill them and move on. And eventually, Brundt will make a mistake, too, and she'll die. That is the nature of Corvus. You survived for many years—more than most. You have done your time. Proven your point."

"Vuller—you make an eloquent case. But I belong on Corvus. I am a violent man. But you… maybe this is the time for you to…"

"No, sir! No! If you return, I will go with you. And you are wrong. You are *not* a violent man. You are a man *capable* of violence, when needed. You don't look for it, or revel in it. And that is not the same. In many ways, I think you have more in common with the game players of Arkon than the criminals of Corvus. I think you should consider the offer from Mr Miko… and accept."

Sarok sat back in his seat, drawing away from his animated bodyguard—not in shock, or anger, but merely to look at the man better. He raised both hands to calm Vuller and signal him to stop. Then he looked around the room. All watched him keenly, with emotions ranging from surprise to expectation to—in Mandelson's case—a hint of anger. He placed his hands upon the table, and suddenly recalled a previous occasion where he had done something similar, his hands spread upon the expensive mahogany table of the *Fantasia*, after arguing with com Durrel in his attempt to get him to redirect the ship to follow the traitors. It had been Vuller then who had attempted to calm matters, and had most probably saved his life, whether from Yadzen at the time, or from Brundt's henchmen soon after.

"You are a man worth listening to, Vuller." He looked at his bodyguard once more, his face unnaturally white, perhaps shocked at his own outburst. And then a smile slowly spread across Sarok's face. He turned to look across the table, at Miko and Archaen. "*If* I joined your guild, what commitments would I need to make?"

Miko smiled back. "Commitments? None—save to represent the guild well."

"So, if I decided to, say, go on a fishing expedition for, I don't know, a month? That would be fine, would it?"

"Absolutely. I might even join you."

"As a kid, on Okana, I fished alone. On Corvus, others joined me because they had to." He turned one last time to look at his bodyguard: "Vuller, *my friend*, what about it? Fancy going fishing?"

All tension left the tall man: "Boss—I'll even bring the beer."

***

For Mandelson, there was nothing. Archaen cautiously noted that she had done good service, and though she fought like a Leaguer, her ethos did not fit well with the Senate. She was therefore invited to return to the Confederation with Dettler and Yadzen, to negotiate her passage and destination with them. Mandelson received this news in stony silence.

As the party rose to depart, Archaen made one last plea: "Yasmina reminded me that you still have weapons and gear from Velasia, and she wishes you to return these to the Hall of Weapons before you leave. If you could do this now, before the shuttle departs, I would be grateful."

***

"So, you're going to stay?"

Sarok had entered the Hall of Weapons alone, carrying his sword and knife, intending to return them to the Velasia section, when he was addressed from off to his left. He slowed and turned. Mandelson was there, emerging from between two rows of cases containing medieval weapons, her curved Indonesian spear in one hand, used like a walking pole.

"It seems that way, yeah." He allowed the woman to approach, noticing that she still wore her burgundy skin, as did he, although hers had been rescinded. "But don't worry about it. I release you from all commitments. You're a big girl. I'm sure, back in reality, you'll soon find a new employer. I'll even write a reference if you like: Beth Mandelson is a dangerous woman, capable of efficiently killing—"

"Don't bother. I don't need a reference. In any case, I already have another master."

The woman's words sent a sudden chill through Sarok. He tensed and adjusted his hold on the weapons he carried together in the crook of his arms. "What do you mean? There's no way Dettler would offer you employment."

Mandelson looked him up and down, noting his awkward posture, a wicked smile stealing across her face. "And I thought you were bright. No wonder she took you down so easily. *Try harder.*"

Sarok felt his breath leave him. As he spoke, he sent his eyes roving around his surroundings, looking for help, an exit. "*Brundt?* But that's not possible."

"Why not? Almost everyone else in your team was turned. Why not me?"

"Because you could have killed me almost any time over the last few months… killed me and had a good chance of getting away. On Corvus at the spaceport. At Gamma Five. On the *Claw*. At any time since we landed on Arkon."

"Yes, I could have. But not killing you has yielded so much more. You are the gift that keeps on giving." She started tamping the spiked butt of her spear on the floor, near to her, then close to Sarok, flicking out to tap the floor near to his left leg, then his right, watching him flinch and tense as the point darted close and then away.

"You mean the money for the prison break?"

"Oh, not just that. *She* wanted to know where your secret HQ was. You kindly took me there. That might have been it for you, but then there was news of this huge contract, so your end was deferred. I'm sure she would like me to thank you for the money—you did all the work, and she just had to collect it at the end. Who do you think sabotaged the door mechanism on the *Fantasia* to allow Martinus and the others to get away with your fee?"

"You *bitch*…" Sarok felt a surge of anger. He tensed towards the woman, but then the haft of her spear caressed his calf, warning him to stay back. Still she smiled.

"Thank you."

"And here? I suppose the plan was to allow me to protect com Durrel, and then steal the fee for that, too?"

"Naturally. The Goose that Lays the Golden Eggs. But now your paymaster is dead, and you have no plans to return to Corvus. You cease to be of use. And that leaves me in a quandary. She would like you dead, no doubt. While you're alive, you could still return to cause trouble. But if I kill you now, our hosts won't like it. You're a made man. I would probably be held and challenged to countless duels. Eventually, someone might best me. So it's better, I think, to leave you cowering here, knowing that you have been defeated." With her spear, she suddenly slapped him slightly harder across the thigh, which made Sarok's knee momentarily buckle. And then she turned away, laughing, and started back towards the area from where she had come.

Sarok watched in growing fury. He dropped the long knife to the floor and swiftly drew his sword—the one he'd used to slay Anda com Durrel. As the knife and sheath clattered to the ground, Mandelson paused... and slowly turned.

"Really, Sarok? Do you really want to do this? If you attack me, I will need to defend myself. And the Leaguers would be far too honourable to punish me for cutting you down as an act of self-defence."

Sarok found himself breathing hard, the sword in his right hand, its tip resting on the floor. "You know, Mandelson, I think not. What are you? A servant. A minion. Nothing more. Vuller was right earlier. Go back to Corvus, to the others. You'll soon say or do the wrong thing. And while you're burning in that hellhole, I'll be kicking back here. I'll even raise a glass to your memory."

Mandelson's smile disappeared; her eyes burned. "A servant? Oh, I think you misjudge me. I'm much more than that."

Sarok scoffed. "What, you're Brundt herself? I've shagged her. I think I'd know."

"No. Not Brundt herself. Not the *first* Brundt." Her smile returned, and it held devilment.

"What are you talking about?"

"We are... *family*. *Close* family. In fact, as close as you can get."

"Close? You don't mean a clone? But you look nothing like her."

Mandelson smirked. "Clones can be altered in embryo. Genes can be switched on and off. I am one of several, born in one batch over thirty years ago, edited so we'd not look identical—though in spite of outwards appearances, our genetic differences are minute. You see, my… mother? Other self? She's a strategic thinker. She was already succession planning at the time—thinking about the future; thinking about who she would leave the organisation to when she's gone. She's been collecting *essences* from her many conquests just in case someone proves worthy enough to one day give her a child, but as a fall back, she has *us*." She laughed, but without humour. "She even has a little vial of Narovy Sarok stored somewhere, though I suppose she'll now flush that away with the rest of the excrement—"

Brundt!

That one nerve was still raw, and always would be: his competitor and one-time lover was the source of all his humiliations. But it wasn't only her unusual presence here that roused Sarok's fury, but also this… this mockery… this disparagement of his very essence.

In spite of his iron will, Mandelson's revelation was too much, for even iron melts…

Sarok roared and surged forwards, swinging his sword towards the woman's face. Caught mid-sentence, Mandelson was initially surprised, though she easily deflected the blow with her spear. Still Sarok came on, driven by a rage he had rarely felt, the sword now a familiar weapon in his hand. The woman parried the first two blows, but the third caught her spear perpendicularly with force, and the haft broke, although she managed to leap back out of range of the sword tip. For a moment, Mandelson was weaponless… but only a moment, for she was surrounded by an endless variety of options. She darted around a display and pulled a sabre from its mounting.

Sarok followed the woman around the open cabinet. His next blow was caught by the other's blade and deflected to sink into the edge of the nearest wooden panel, where it caught. But Sarok's momentum allowed him to follow through and his shoulder thumped into his adversary's sternum, knocking her over. He yanked out his sword, and with a roar, swept a backhand at the falling woman. But again, the sabre intervened, parrying the sword upwards, creating an opening. Now on her back, Mandelson slashed to her left—and made contact with Sarok's thigh.

The bearded man grunted and spun away. Though the blow was strong, and would have severed an unprotected leg, his skin absorbed the force, leaving him with the feeling of having been firmly punched in the thigh. As he recovered his poise, Mandelson scrambled to her feet, putting some space between them. And then they were facing each other, both breathing hard, Sarok's initial assault spent.

"Mistake!" hissed the woman. "You had to kill me quick. You failed. Now you will see the difference between the sludge in your unedited cells and the mercury in mine." She leapt into an attack, her sabre slashing with speed and precision.

This time it was Sarok who was forced back, one step at a time. The sabre flicked in and out. He felt a tag on the thigh, then on the bicep, then shoulder. The skin saved him, but it didn't protect all of him. As he retreated, Sarok focused on keeping his sword up to protect his head, accepting stinging blows elsewhere. But the problem was, his adversary was protected in the same way that he was, and so his own target was similarly reduced.

Sarok managed to gain a fraction of a second as he sidestepped around the end of another display panel. His free hand grasped a wicked-looking morning star, ripping it from its holdings just as the woman slashed towards his unprotected hand. He continued to back up, aware that the entrance to the Hall was perhaps ten metres behind him.

"Where are you going, Sarok?" Mandelson taunted. Her next slash evaded the other's blade and came down full on his shoulder, barely missing his ear. This blow hurt, sending a wave of pain across his shoulder and into his neck and jaw, causing his sword arm to droop. The sabre swung horizontally, but Sarok managed to turn into it, catching the blade in the nest of spikes in the mace and almost wrenching it from her grasp.

Sarok straightened as the woman regained a fighting stance, flexing her arm as though to get blood back into it.

"Tiring yet, Sarok?"

And then there was another sound—the whisk of doors sliding open. Sarok watched the woman's eyes twitch, focusing beyond him, and he heard a shout. *Vuller?* Sarok used the distraction: he stabbed his sword at Mandelson's face, and though the woman parried, he was ready with a follow-up blow from the morning star, which caught her on her exposed elbow.

The woman fell back with a squawk of pain.

"Boss!"

It *was* Vuller; Sarok heard his running steps and knew the odds had changed… and Mandelson knew, too. She staggered away to his right, her arm now numb, the sword hanging loosely from her fingers. But Sarok gave her no chance: he leapt into her, knocking them both to the ground. But he was up first, and had Mandelson on her back, one knee on her stomach. He raised the morning star and stared into the woman's face: "You're not Brundt. You're a shadow of her…" and he brought the mace down twice.

Vuller reached the scene just as Sarok pushed himself to his feet. The bodyguard had a sword in his hand—the one he'd been about to return to its rightful place in the Hall of Weapons.

"What… *Boss?*"

Sarok tossed the mace aside. Beneath him, Mandelson writhed in pain, the two blows onto her collar bones having crippled her, in spite of her skin. "Do you know what, Vuller? Maybe you're right about *that* too. Maybe I'm not a violent man after all. But let's leave quick, eh, in case she gets back up…"

***

The remnants of the Company of the Black Lady gathered on the landing pad between the three towers of Verano. The shuttle was ready to depart, with Miko in the pilot seat, able to fly the highly automated machine even with one arm.

Standing by the lowered ramp to the interior, Rostus Dettler and Yadzen waited as two white-skinned Leaguers carried a stretcher past them and up the ramp. On this lay a dazed and drugged Mandelson, wearing a loose costume that had been recently manufactured to take the place of her confiscated skin, her arms and shoulders in casts to protect her broken collar bones.

Facing the shuttle were Enabeth Archaen, Irvan Sentain, Narovy Sarok and Theodric Vuller.

"It would probably be good form to ask you to look after Mandelson," noted Sarok, wistfully, "but frankly, it would be best for us all if there were a tragic accident en route to the spaceport and she fell out of the craft from ten thousand metres."

"If you wanted her gone that badly, Cousin Narovy," noted Archaen, with a faint smile, "you could have done the job yourself in the Hall."

"I recently killed one archvillain. It wouldn't be fair to kill another so soon after."

"*Fairness* trumping *necessity*, Narovy? You truly are becoming one of us."

"Don't worry. You'll soon learn how unreconstructed I am, when Vuller and I go on a massive, week-long bender, eh, Vuller?"

"Too right, Boss!"

Archaen's smile broadened. "That is not as atypical as you think. After all, our whole ethos is to play hard. But now she is loaded, so… Mr Dettler, I wish you farewell and good luck. And you too, Yadzen. When you are able, contact Mallory. We will have a commission for you, should you want it."

Dettler gave a small bow. "I will. And then I'll consider your request and tear it up. And shortly after that, I will almost certainly find myself scrabbling in the waste compactor to retrieve the pieces and stick them back together again." He sighed. "I know what I am, Ms Archaen. *Alas!* While some of you have been changed by this adventure, I have merely come to realise with greater clarity who and what I am—and that truly does suck. Still, not all has been bad: I now have a bodyguard and lieutenant who can kick anyone's arse. I'll not be cowed by the likes of com Durrel again." He turned to head into the craft. Yadzen nodded his own farewell and joined his new master.

As the ramp started to ascend, Sarok looked over at Sentain. "You've been quiet, Sentain. I've hardly heard a word out of you all day. On the one hand, this has been something of a relief, but on the other, I am beginning to worry about your health."

Sentain looked back at the man, a gentle smile on his face. "I have come to realise, Mr Sarok, that sometimes there is a time for words, and sometimes… for silence." He winked, then turned to Enabeth Archaen, twitched his head towards the exit walkway, and started back to the tower.

THE END

The Price of Freedom Part II: Velasia

Milton Keynes UK
Ingram Content Group UK Ltd.
UKHW030946261124
451585UK00001B/176